DEAD BODY ROAD™

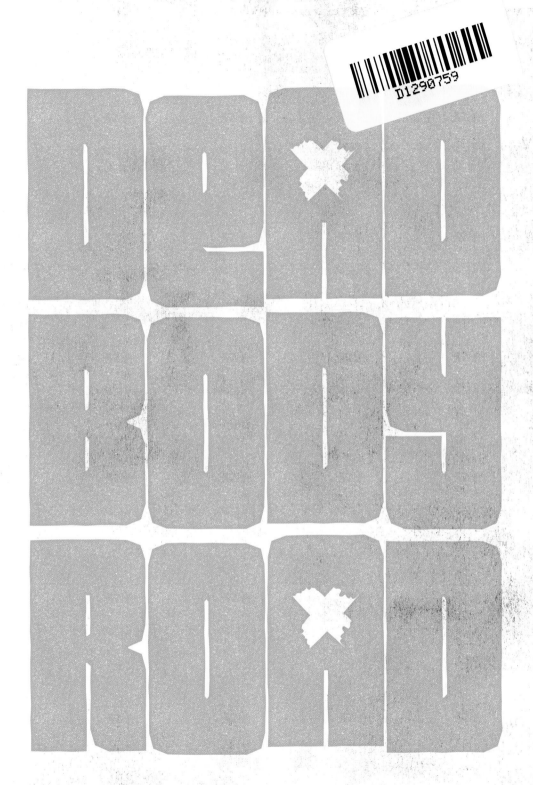

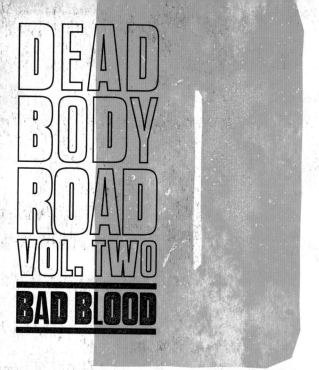

DEAD BODY ROAD
VOL. TWO
BAD BLOOD

JUSTIN JORDAN
WRITER

BENJAMIN TIESMA
ARTIST

MAT LOPES
COLORIST

PAT BROSSEAU
LETTERER

MATTEO SCALERA AND MORENO DINISIO
COVER

JON MOISAN
EDITOR

ANDRES JUAREZ
PRODUCTION DESIGN

CARINA TAYLOR
PRODUCTION

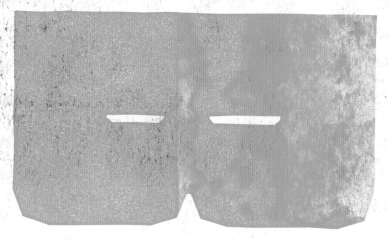

FOR SKYBOUND ENTERTAINMENT
ROBERT KIRKMAN CHAIRMAN | DAVID ALPERT CEO | SEAN MACKIEWICZ SVP, EDITOR-IN-CHIEF SHAWN KIRKHAM SVP, BUSINESS DEVELOPMENT BRIAN HUNTINGTON VP, ONLINE CONTENT | SHAUNA WYNNE PUBLICITY DIRECTOR | ANDRES JUAREZ ART DIRECTOR | ALEX ANTONE SENIOR EDITOR JON MOISAN EDITOR | ARIELLE BASICH ASSOCIATE EDITOR | CARINA TAYLOR GRAPHIC DESIGNER | PAUL SHIN BUSINESS DEVELOPMENT MANAGER JOHNNY O'DELL SOCIAL MEDIA MANAGER | DAN PETERSEN SR. DIRECTOR OF OPERATIONS & EVENTS
FOREIGN RIGHTS & LICENSING INQUIRIES: CONTACT@SKYBOUND.COM
SKYBOUND.COM

IMAGE COMICS, INC.
TODD McFARLANE PRESIDENT | JIM VALENTINO VICE PRESIDENT | MARC SILVESTRI CHIEF EXECUTIVE OFFICER | ERIK LARSEN CHIEF FINANCIAL OFFICER | ROBERT KIRKMAN CHIEF OPERATING OFFICER | ERIC STEPHENSON PUBLISHER / CHIEF CREATIVE OFFICER SHANNA MATUSZAK EDITORIAL COORDINATOR | MARLA EIZIK TALENT LIAISON | NICOLE LAPALME CONTROLLER | LEANNA CAUNTER ACCOUNTING ANALYST | SUE KORPELA ACCOUNTING & HR MANAGER | JEFF BOISON DIRECTOR OF SALES & PUBLISHING PLANNING DIRK WOOD DIRECTOR OF INTERNATIONAL SALES & LICENSING | ALEX COX DIRECTOR OF DIRECT MARKET & SPECIALITY SALES | CHLOE RAMOS-PETERSON BOOK MARKET & LIBRARY SALES MANAGER | EMILIO BAUTISTA DIGITAL SALES COORDINATOR | KAT SALAZAR DIRECTOR OF PR & MARKETING | DREW FITZGERALD MARKETING CONTENT ASSOCIATE | HEATHER DOORNINK PRODUCTION DIRECTOR | DREW GILL ART DIRECTOR | HILARY DILORETO PRINT MANAGER | TRICIA RAMOS TRAFFIC MANAGER | ERIKA SCHNATZ SENIOR PRODUCTION ARTIST | RYAN BREWER PRODUCTION ARTIST | DEANNA PHELPS PRODUCTION ARTIST
IMAGECOMICS.COM

DEAD BODY ROAD VOLUME 2: BAD BLOOD. FIRST PRINTING. JANUARY 2021.
PUBLISHED BY IMAGE COMICS, INC. OFFICE OF PUBLICATION: 2701 NW VAUGHN ST., STE. 780, PORTLAND, OR 97210. COPYRIGHT © 2021 SKYBOUND, LLC. ORIGINALLY PUBLISHED IN SINGLE MAGAZINE FORM AS DEAD BODY ROAD: BAD BLOOD™ #1-6. DEAD BODY ROAD™ (INCLUDING ALL PROMINENT CHARACTERS FEATURED HEREIN), ITS LOGO AND ALL CHARACTER LIKENESSES ARE TRADEMARKS OF SKYBOUND, LLC, UNLESS OTHERWISE NOTED. IMAGE COMICS® AND ITS LOGOS ARE REGISTERED TRADEMARKS AND COPYRIGHTS OF IMAGE COMICS, INC. ALL RIGHTS RESERVED. NO PART OF THIS PUBLICATION MAY BE REPRODUCED OR TRANSMITTED IN ANY FORM OR BY ANY MEANS (EXCEPT FOR SHORT EXCERPTS FOR REVIEW PURPOSES) WITHOUT THE EXPRESS WRITTEN PERMISSION OF IMAGE COMICS, INC. ALL NAMES, CHARACTERS, EVENTS AND LOCALES IN THIS PUBLICATION ARE ENTIRELY FICTIONAL. ANY RESEMBLANCE TO ACTUAL PERSONS (LIVING OR DEAD), EVENTS OR PLACES, WITHOUT SATIRIC INTENT, IS COINCIDENTAL. PRINTED IN THE U.S.A. ISBN: 978-1-5343-1721-5

DO YOU KNOW WHY THEY CALL ME MONK?

THIS WAS BEFORE YOUR TIME, SO I FIGURE YOU MIGHT NOT.

IT WAS MEANT TO BE AN INSULT. I DIDN'T DRINK, I DIDN'T GET FUCK-HYPED-UP ON BATHROOM METH, I DIDN'T GET A GIRL PREGNANT. ONE OF THE CLEVER ONES SAID I WAS DAMN NEAR A MONK.

BUT THE THING WAS, WHAT I LIKED WAS CONTROL. AND WHILE MY ASSHOLE CONTEMPORARIES FUCKED AND SNORTED THEM- SELVES TO GOD- DAMN OBLIVION, I EXTENDED THAT CONTROL.

I NEVER DID LET REVENGE OR RAGE CONTROL ME. AND THAT'S WHY I'M STILL STANDING.

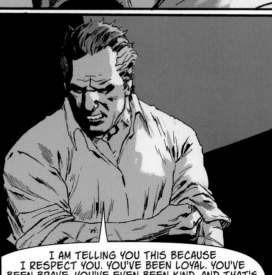

I AM TELLING YOU THIS BECAUSE I RESPECT YOU. YOU'VE BEEN LOYAL. YOU'VE BEEN BRAVE. YOU'VE EVEN BEEN KIND, AND THAT'S HARD TO COME BY IN OUR WORLD. THAT'S WHY I ASKED YOU TO PROTECT THEM. AND YOU DIDN'T.

I CAN'T LET THAT GO. I WISH TO HELL I COULD.

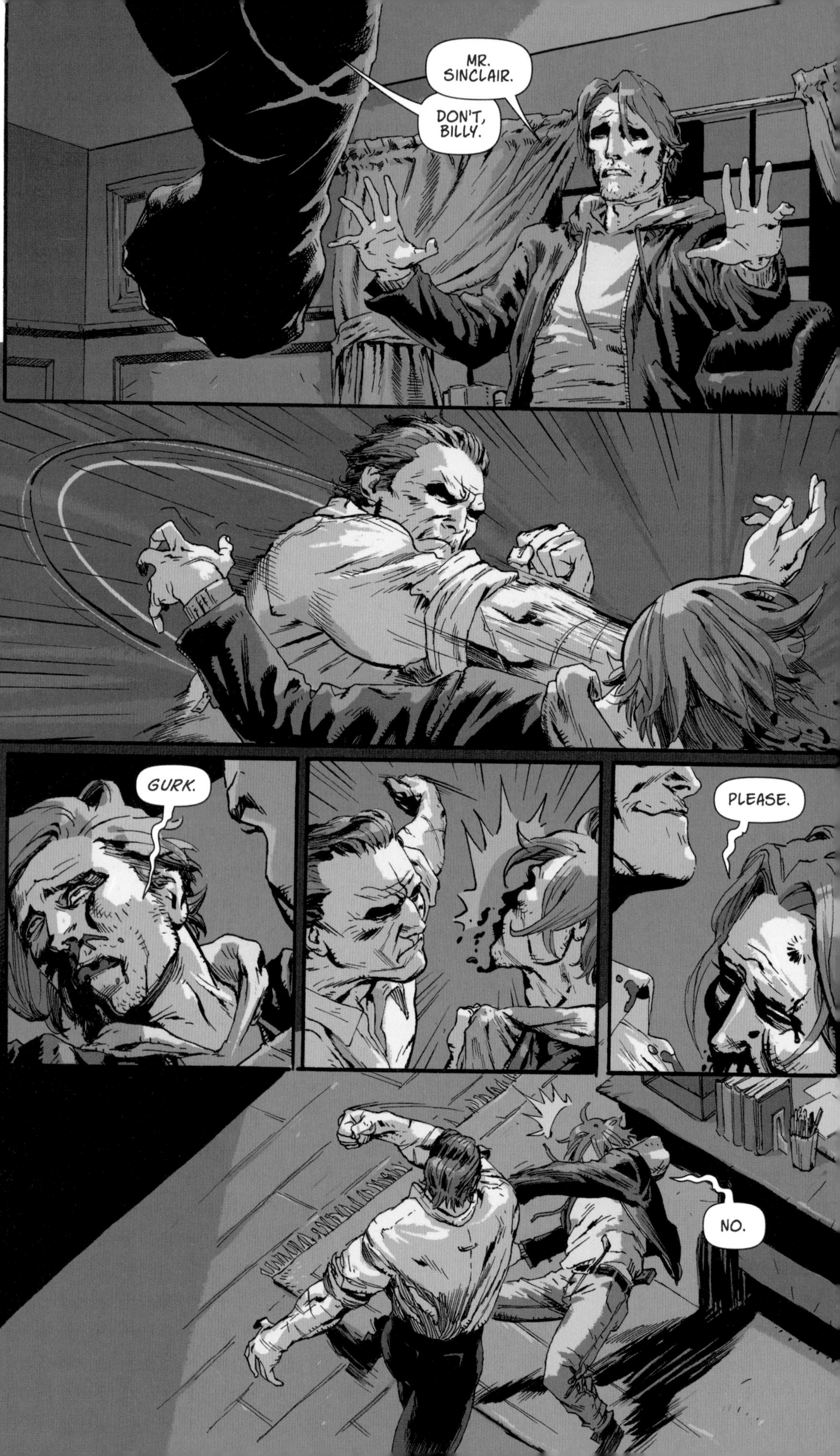
MR. SINCLAIR.
DON'T, BILLY.
GURK.
PLEASE.
NO.

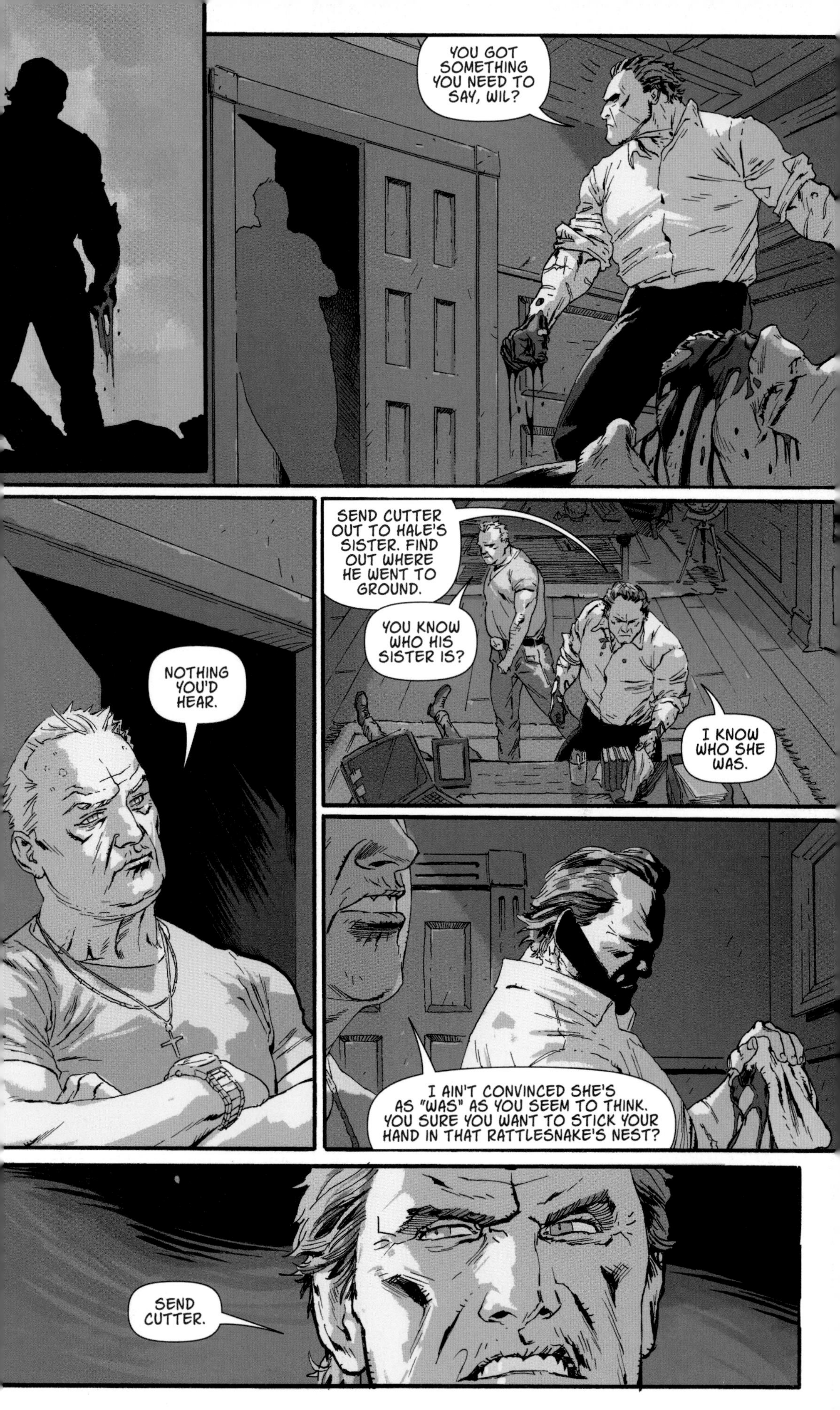
YOU GOT SOMETHING YOU NEED TO SAY, WIL?
NOTHING YOU'D HEAR.
SEND CUTTER OUT TO HALE'S SISTER. FIND OUT WHERE HE WENT TO GROUND.
YOU KNOW WHO HIS SISTER IS?
I KNOW WHO SHE WAS.
I AIN'T CONVINCED SHE'S AS "WAS" AS YOU SEEM TO THINK. YOU SURE YOU WANT TO STICK YOUR HAND IN THAT RATTLESNAKE'S NEST?
SEND CUTTER.

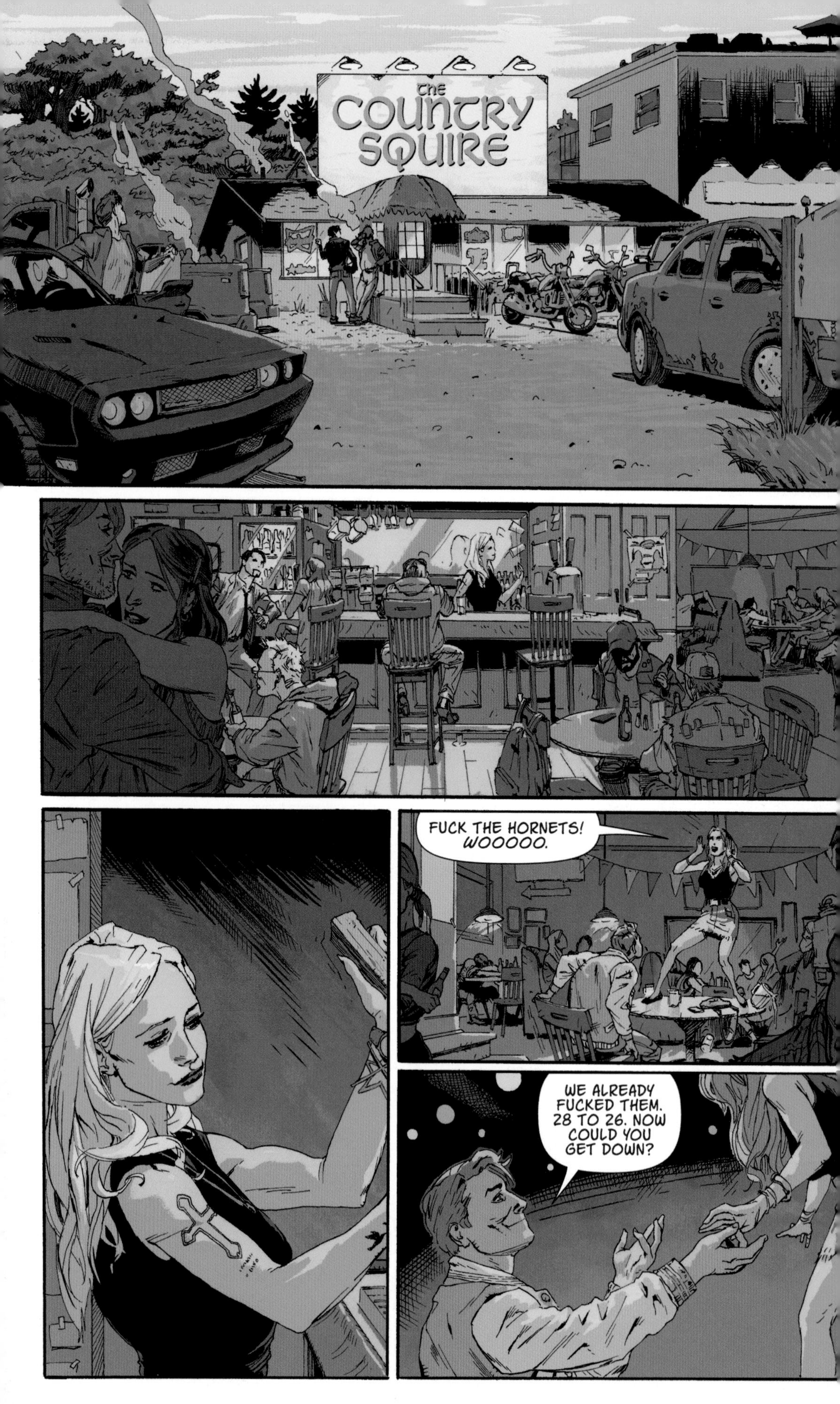
The Country Squire
FUCK THE HORNETS! WOOOOO.
WE ALREADY FUCKED THEM. 28 TO 26. NOW COULD YOU GET DOWN?

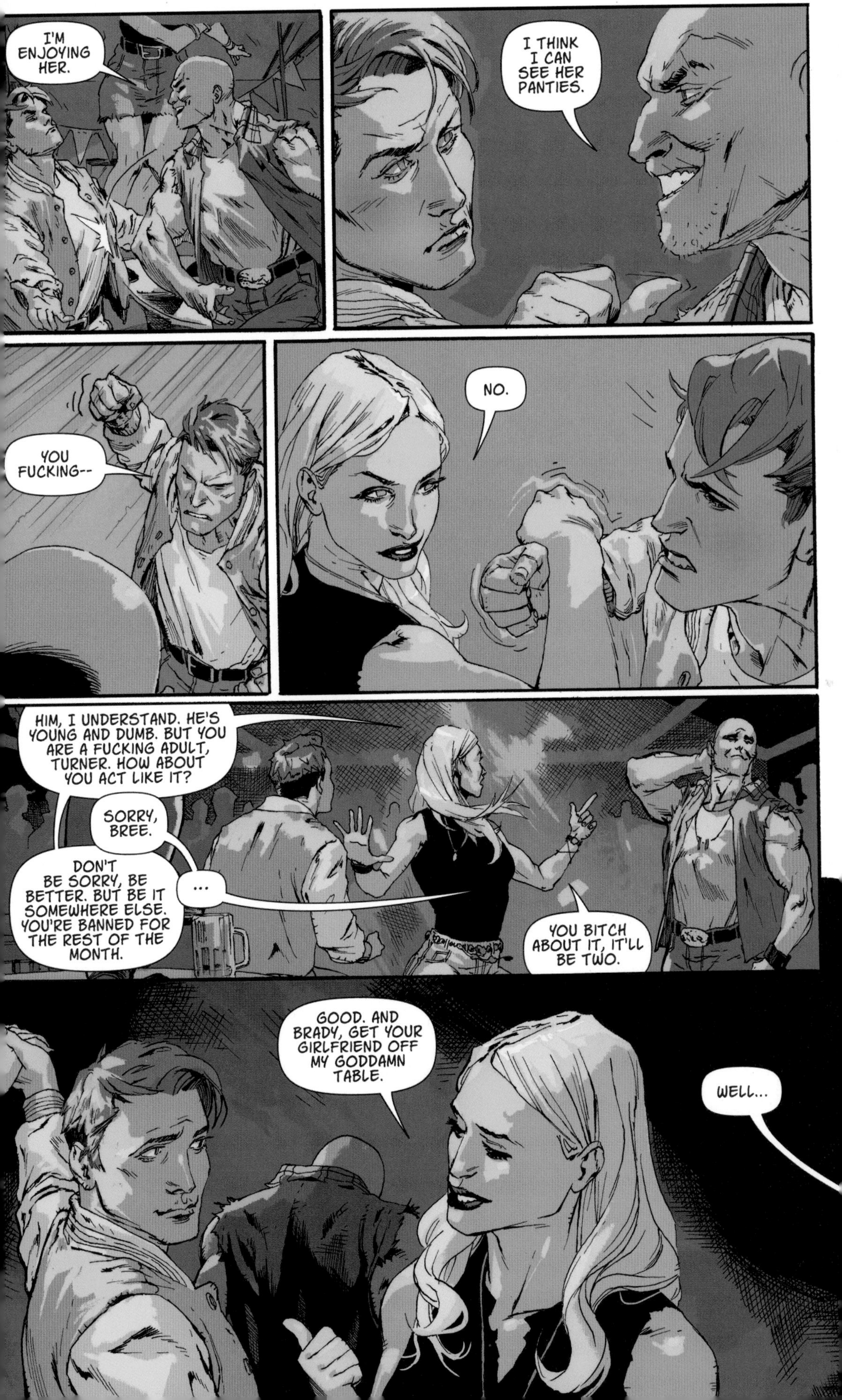
I'M ENJOYING HER.
I THINK I CAN SEE HER PANTIES.
YOU FUCKING--
NO.
HIM, I UNDERSTAND. HE'S YOUNG AND DUMB. BUT YOU ARE A FUCKING ADULT, TURNER. HOW ABOUT YOU ACT LIKE IT?
SORRY, BREE.
DON'T BE SORRY, BE BETTER. BUT BE IT SOMEWHERE ELSE. YOU'RE BANNED FOR THE REST OF THE MONTH.
...
YOU BITCH ABOUT IT, IT'LL BE TWO.
GOOD. AND BRADY, GET YOUR GIRLFRIEND OFF MY GODDAMN TABLE.
WELL...

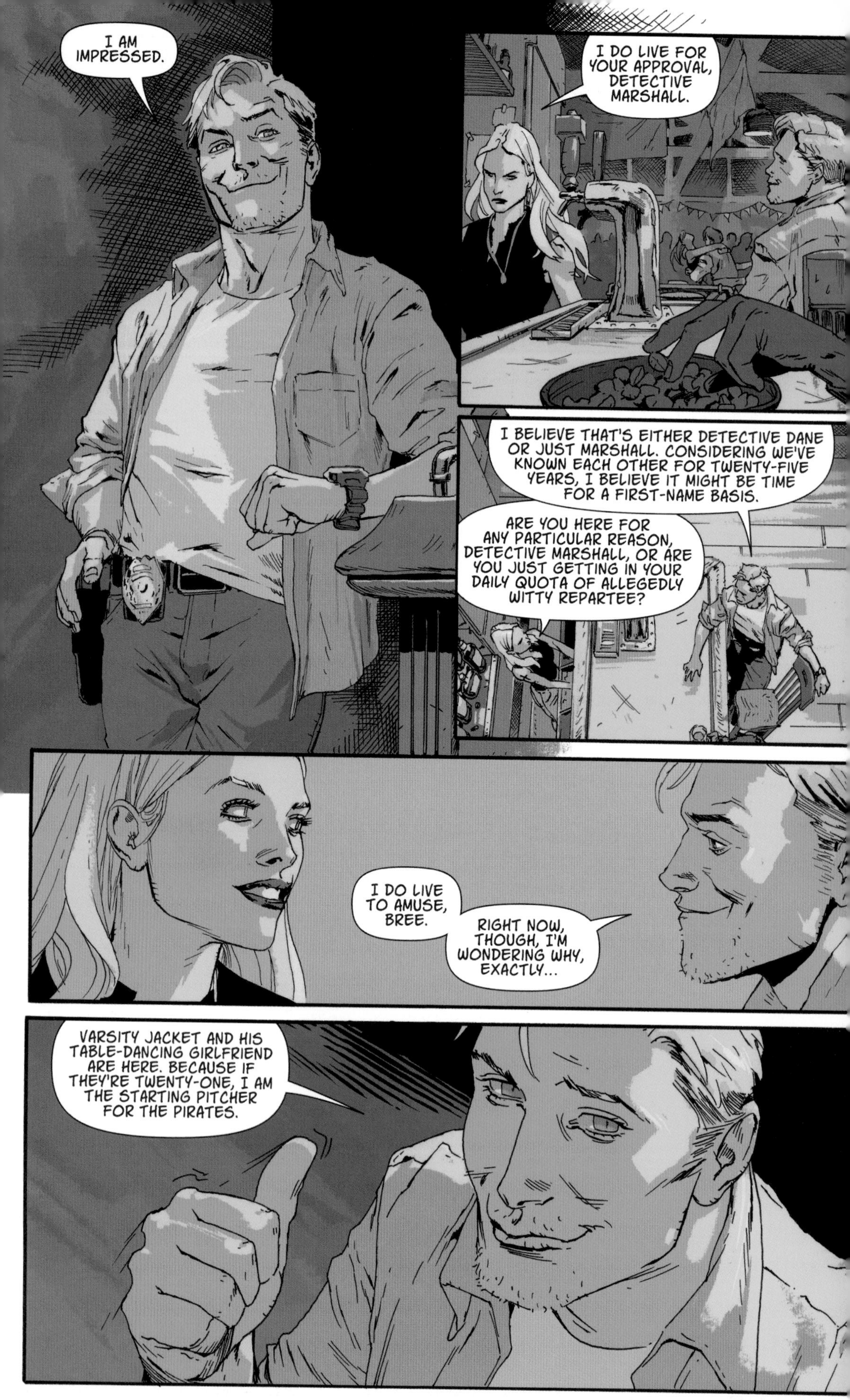
I AM IMPRESSED.
I DO LIVE FOR YOUR APPROVAL, DETECTIVE MARSHALL.
I BELIEVE THAT'S EITHER DETECTIVE DANE OR JUST MARSHALL. CONSIDERING WE'VE KNOWN EACH OTHER FOR TWENTY-FIVE YEARS, I BELIEVE IT MIGHT BE TIME FOR A FIRST-NAME BASIS.
ARE YOU HERE FOR ANY PARTICULAR REASON, DETECTIVE MARSHALL, OR ARE YOU JUST GETTING IN YOUR DAILY QUOTA OF ALLEGEDLY WITTY REPARTEE?
I DO LIVE TO AMUSE, BREE.
RIGHT NOW, THOUGH, I'M WONDERING WHY, EXACTLY...
VARSITY JACKET AND HIS TABLE-DANCING GIRLFRIEND ARE HERE. BECAUSE IF THEY'RE TWENTY-ONE, I AM THE STARTING PITCHER FOR THE PIRATES.

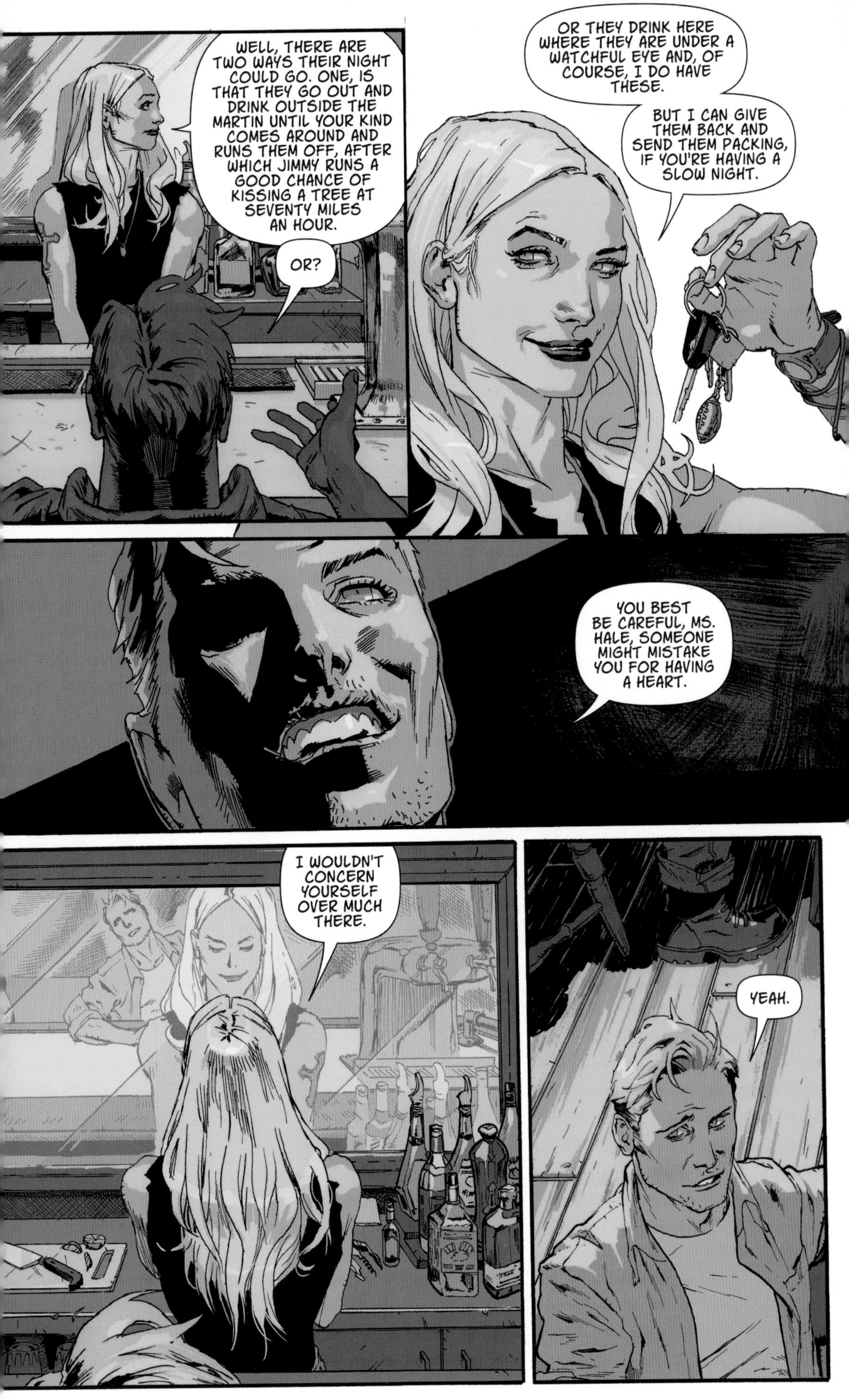
WELL, THERE ARE TWO WAYS THEIR NIGHT COULD GO. ONE, IS THAT THEY GO OUT AND DRINK OUTSIDE THE MARTIN UNTIL YOUR KIND COMES AROUND AND RUNS THEM OFF, AFTER WHICH JIMMY RUNS A GOOD CHANCE OF KISSING A TREE AT SEVENTY MILES AN HOUR.
OR?
OR THEY DRINK HERE WHERE THEY ARE UNDER A WATCHFUL EYE AND, OF COURSE, I DO HAVE THESE.
BUT I CAN GIVE THEM BACK AND SEND THEM PACKING, IF YOU'RE HAVING A SLOW NIGHT.
YOU BEST BE CAREFUL, MS. HALE, SOMEONE MIGHT MISTAKE YOU FOR HAVING A HEART.
I WOULDN'T CONCERN YOURSELF OVER MUCH THERE.
YEAH.

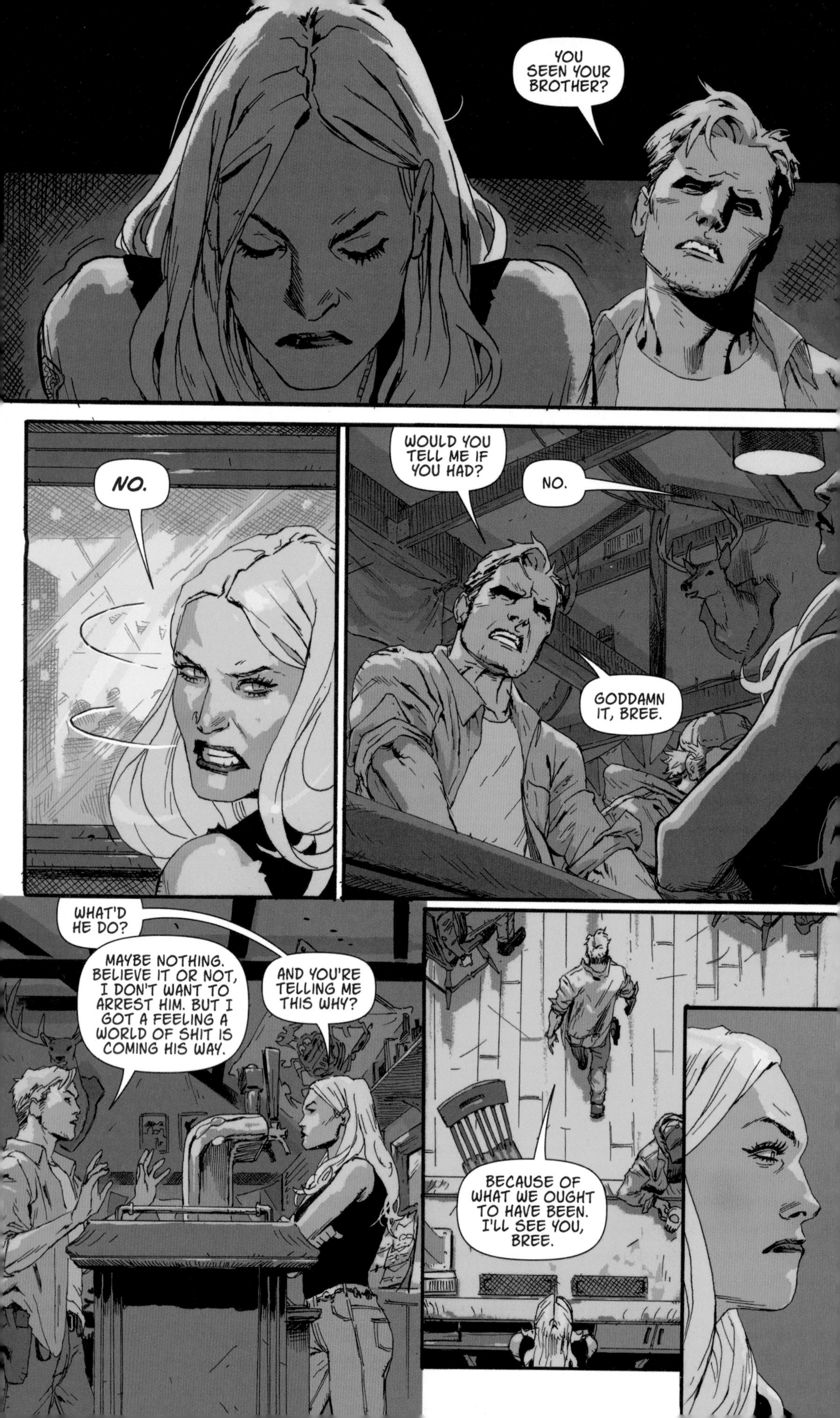
YOU SEEN YOUR BROTHER?
NO.
WOULD YOU TELL ME IF YOU HAD?
NO.
GODDAMN IT, BREE.
WHAT'D HE DO?
MAYBE NOTHING. BELIEVE IT OR NOT, I DON'T WANT TO ARREST HIM. BUT I GOT A FEELING A WORLD OF SHIT IS COMING HIS WAY.
AND YOU'RE TELLING ME THIS WHY?
BECAUSE OF WHAT WE OUGHT TO HAVE BEEN. I'LL SEE YOU, BREE.

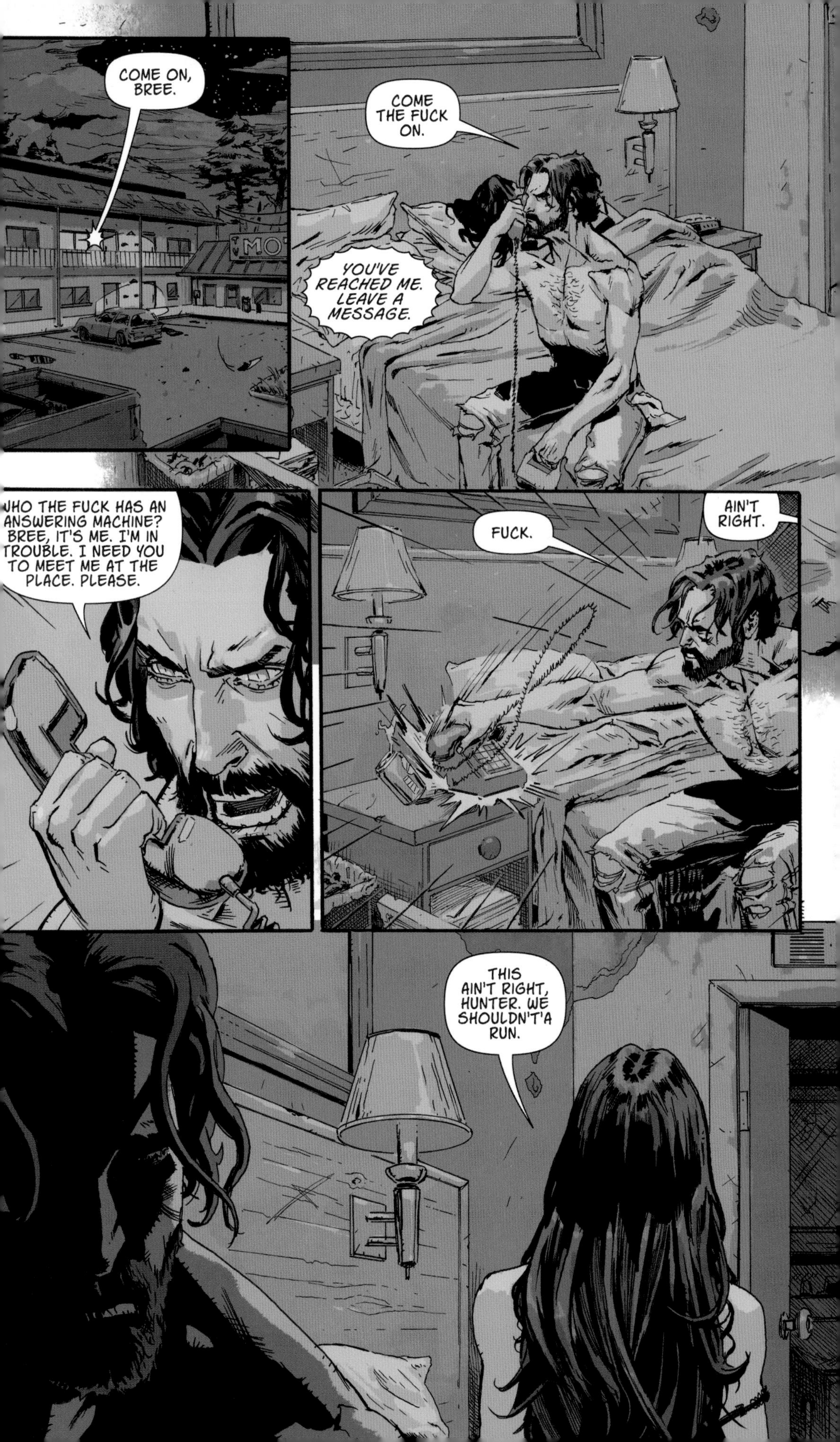
COME ON, BREE.
COME THE FUCK ON.
YOU'VE REACHED ME. LEAVE A MESSAGE.
WHO THE FUCK HAS AN ANSWERING MACHINE? BREE, IT'S ME. I'M IN TROUBLE. I NEED YOU TO MEET ME AT THE PLACE. PLEASE.
FUCK.
AIN'T RIGHT.
THIS AIN'T RIGHT, HUNTER. WE SHOULDN'T'A RUN.

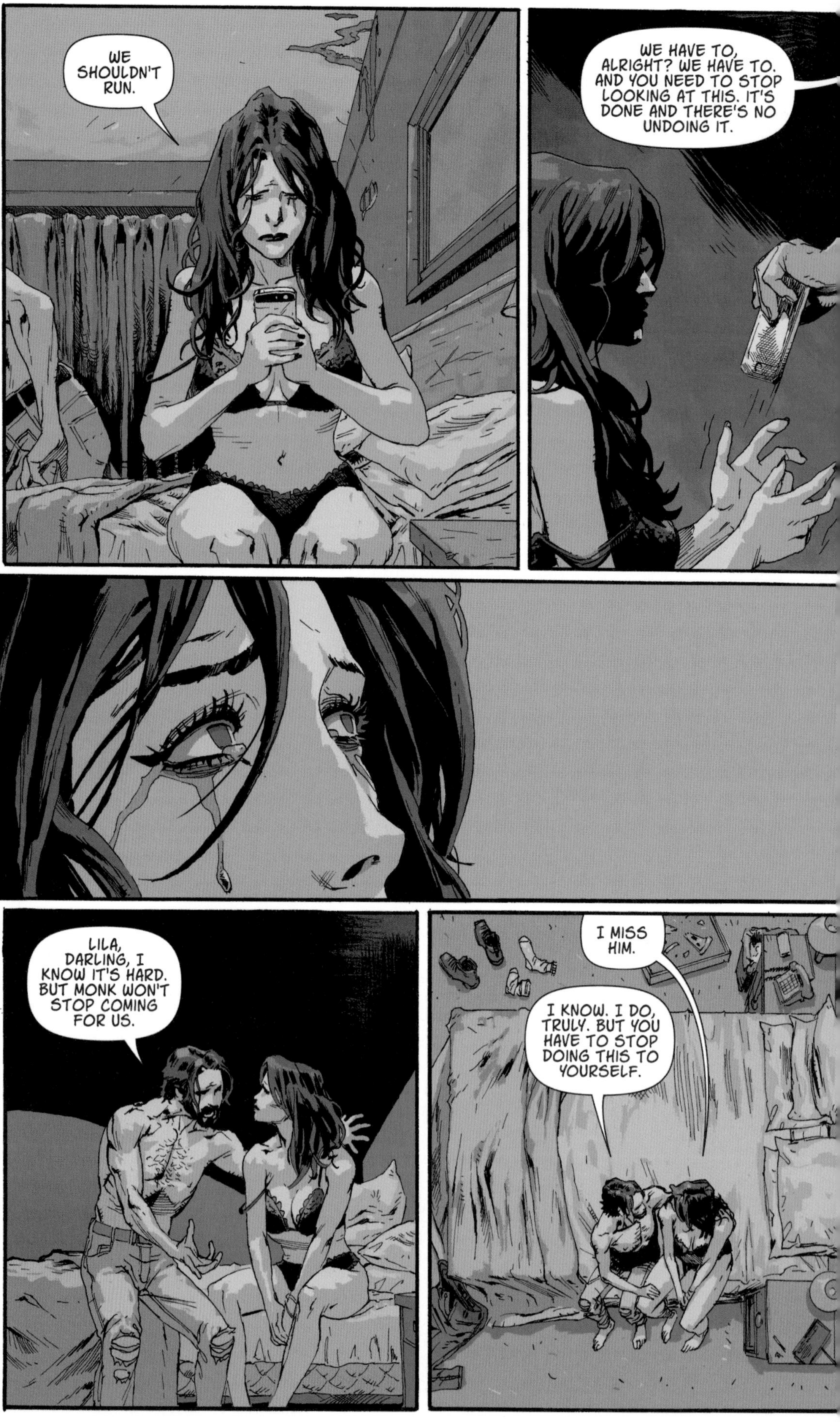
WE SHOULDN'T RUN.
WE HAVE TO, ALRIGHT? WE HAVE TO. AND YOU NEED TO STOP LOOKING AT THIS. IT'S DONE AND THERE'S NO UNDOING IT.
LILA, DARLING, I KNOW IT'S HARD. BUT MONK WON'T STOP COMING FOR US.
I MISS HIM.
I KNOW. I DO, TRULY. BUT YOU HAVE TO STOP DOING THIS TO YOURSELF.

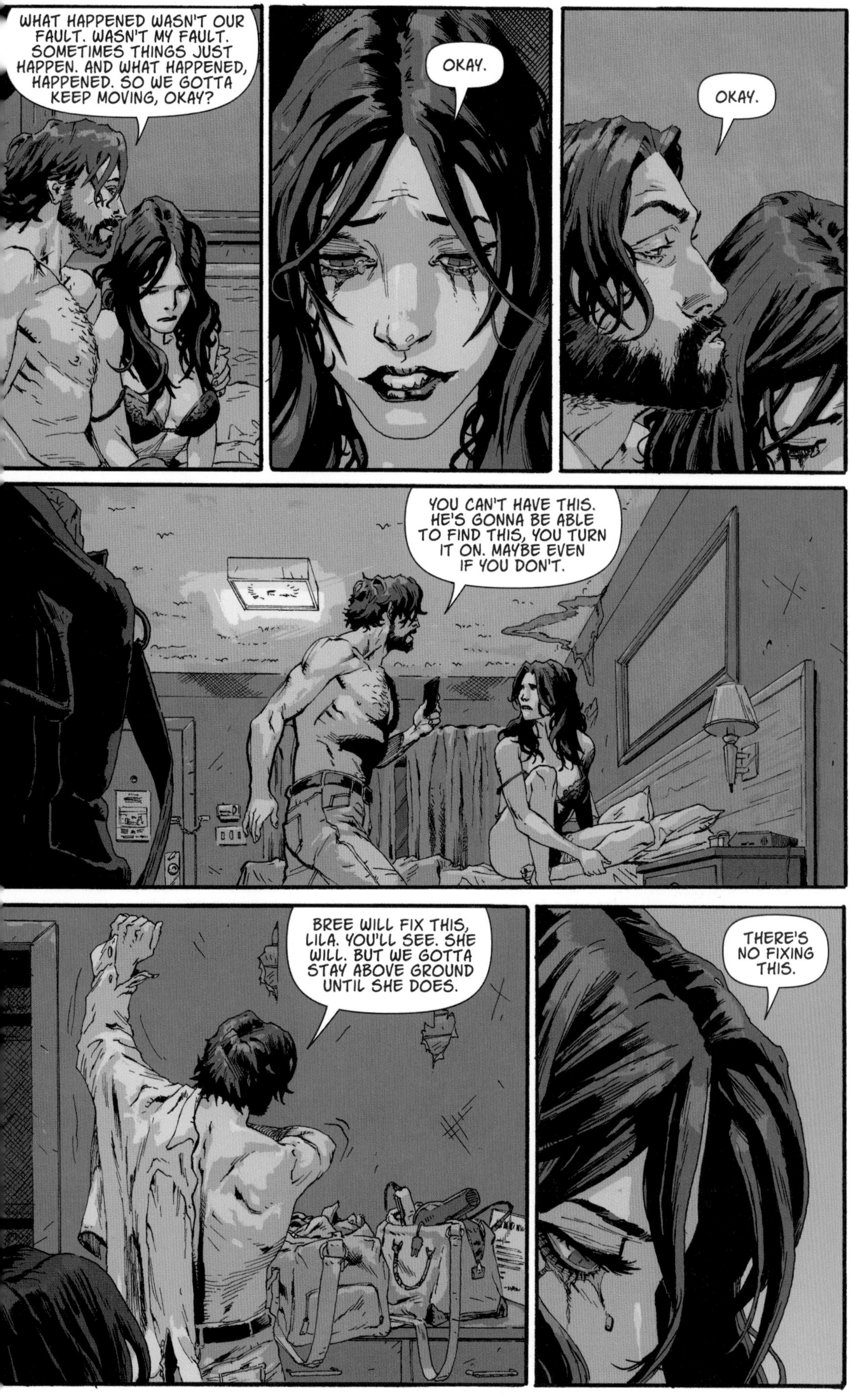
WHAT HAPPENED WASN'T OUR FAULT. WASN'T MY FAULT. SOMETIMES THINGS JUST HAPPEN. AND WHAT HAPPENED, HAPPENED. SO WE GOTTA KEEP MOVING, OKAY?
OKAY.
OKAY.
YOU CAN'T HAVE THIS. HE'S GONNA BE ABLE TO FIND THIS, YOU TURN IT ON. MAYBE EVEN IF YOU DON'T.
BREE WILL FIX THIS, LILA. YOU'LL SEE. SHE WILL. BUT WE GOTTA STAY ABOVE GROUND UNTIL SHE DOES.
THERE'S NO FIXING THIS.

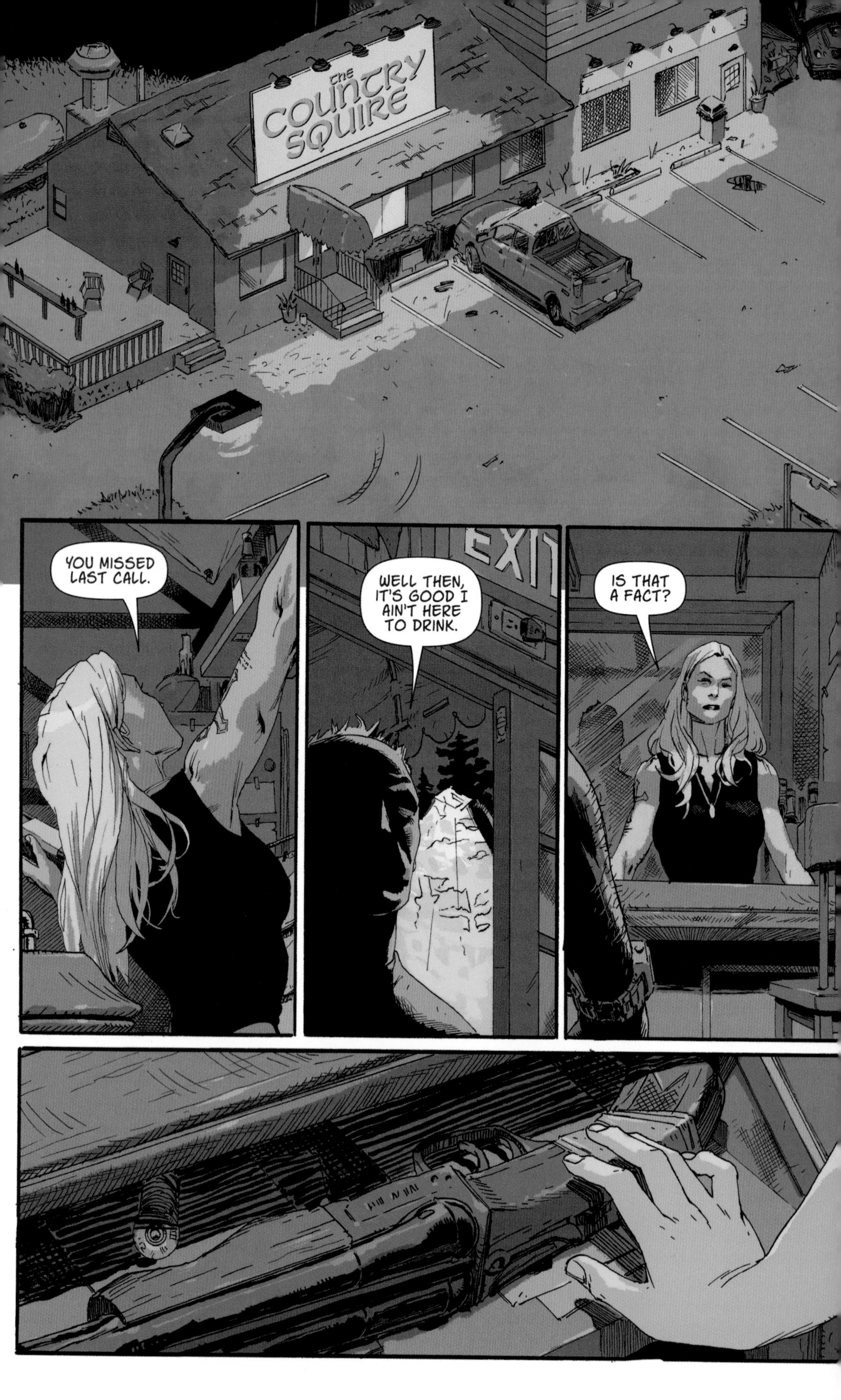
The Country Squire
YOU MISSED LAST CALL.
WELL THEN, IT'S GOOD I AIN'T HERE TO DRINK.
EXIT
IS THAT A FACT?

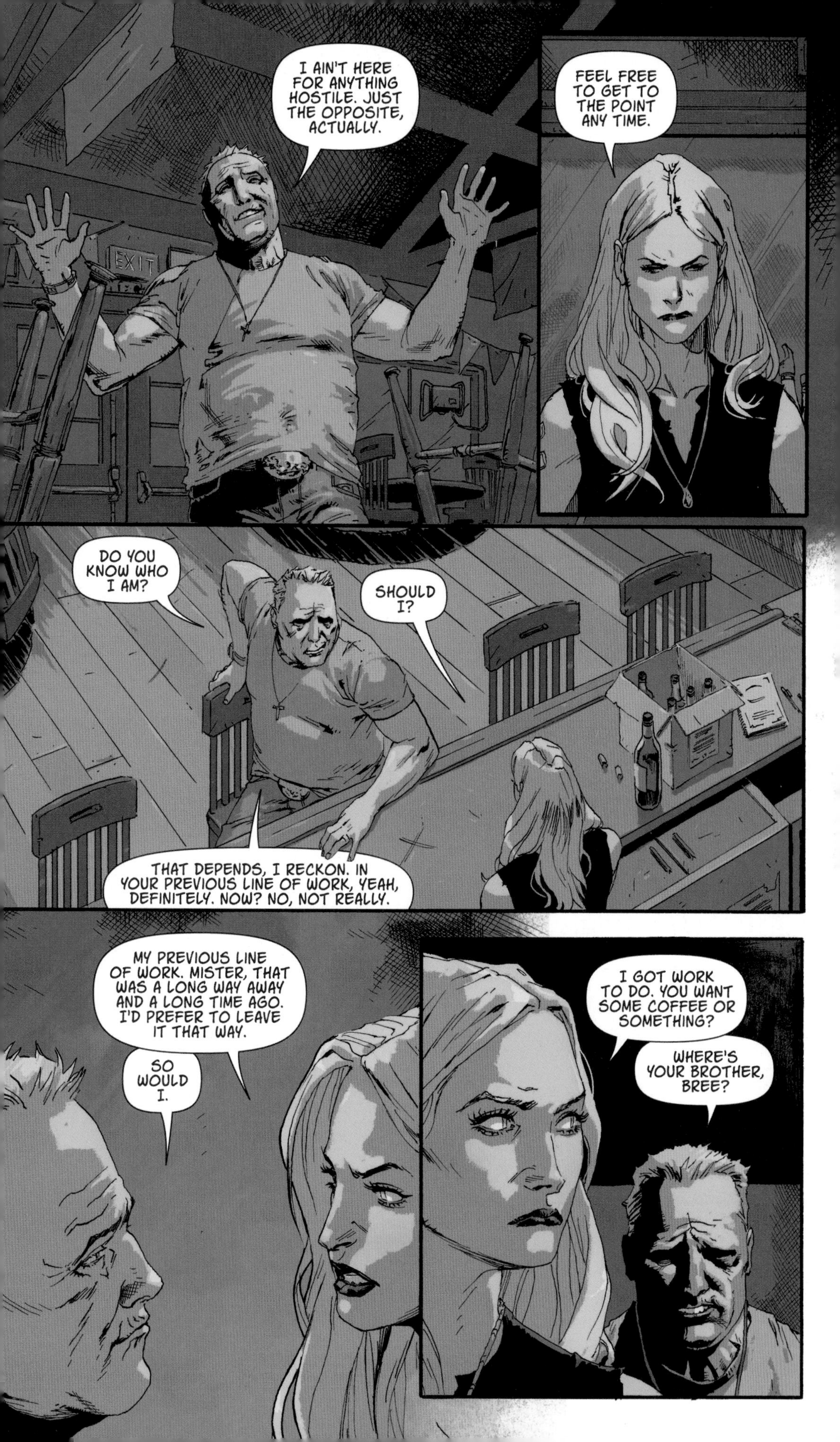

I AIN'T HERE FOR ANYTHING HOSTILE. JUST THE OPPOSITE, ACTUALLY.
FEEL FREE TO GET TO THE POINT ANY TIME.
DO YOU KNOW WHO I AM?
SHOULD I?
THAT DEPENDS, I RECKON. IN YOUR PREVIOUS LINE OF WORK, YEAH, DEFINITELY. NOW? NO, NOT REALLY.
MY PREVIOUS LINE OF WORK. MISTER, THAT WAS A LONG WAY AWAY AND A LONG TIME AGO. I'D PREFER TO LEAVE IT THAT WAY.
SO WOULD I.
I GOT WORK TO DO. YOU WANT SOME COFFEE OR SOMETHING?
WHERE'S YOUR BROTHER, BREE?

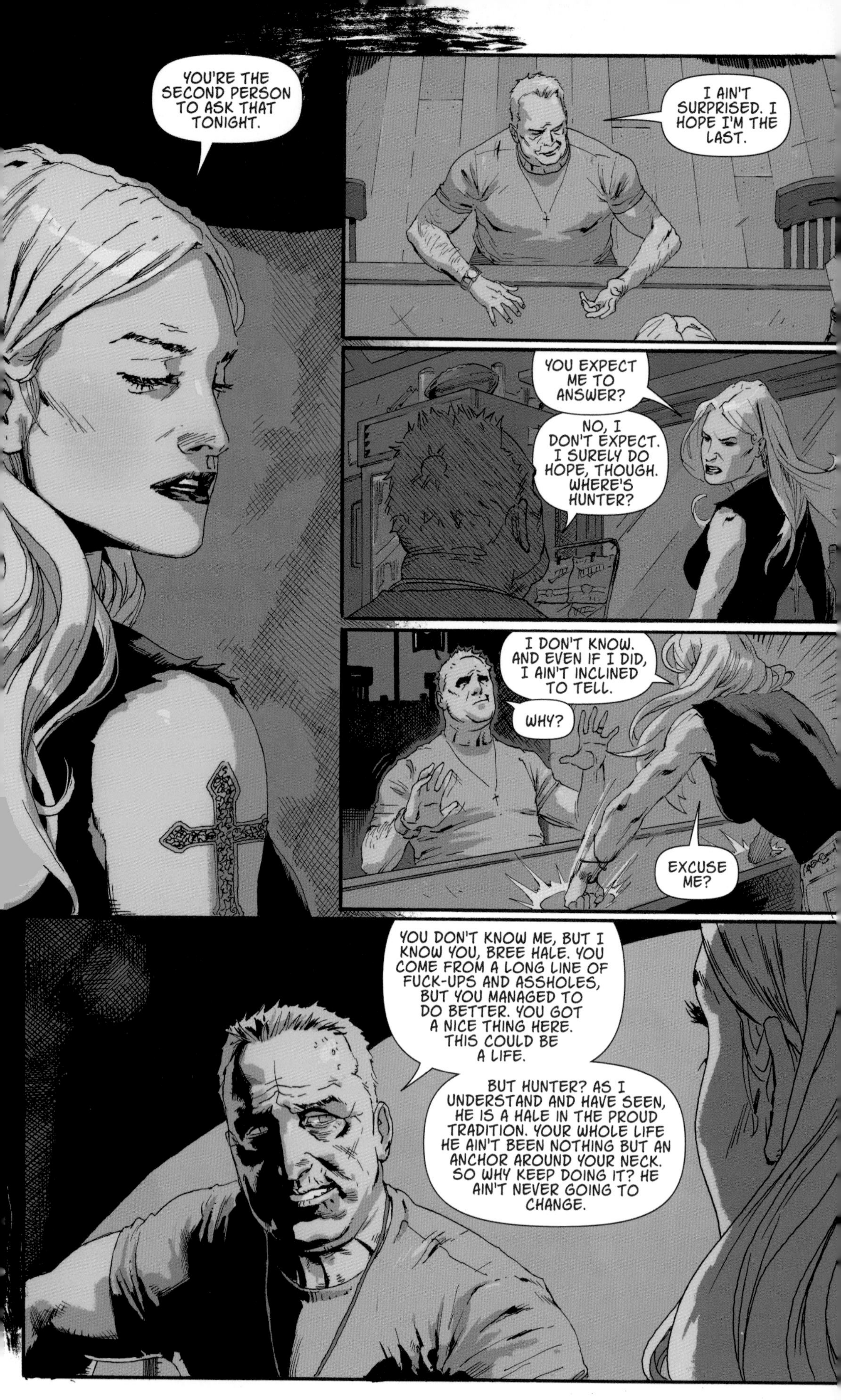
YOU'RE THE SECOND PERSON TO ASK THAT TONIGHT.
I AIN'T SURPRISED. I HOPE I'M THE LAST.
YOU EXPECT ME TO ANSWER?
NO, I DON'T EXPECT. I SURELY DO HOPE, THOUGH. WHERE'S HUNTER?
I DON'T KNOW. AND EVEN IF I DID, I AIN'T INCLINED TO TELL.
WHY?
EXCUSE ME?
YOU DON'T KNOW ME, BUT I KNOW YOU, BREE HALE. YOU COME FROM A LONG LINE OF FUCK-UPS AND ASSHOLES, BUT YOU MANAGED TO DO BETTER. YOU GOT A NICE THING HERE. THIS COULD BE A LIFE.
BUT HUNTER? AS I UNDERSTAND AND HAVE SEEN, HE IS A HALE IN THE PROUD TRADITION. YOUR WHOLE LIFE HE AIN'T BEEN NOTHING BUT AN ANCHOR AROUND YOUR NECK. SO WHY KEEP DOING IT? HE AIN'T NEVER GOING TO CHANGE.

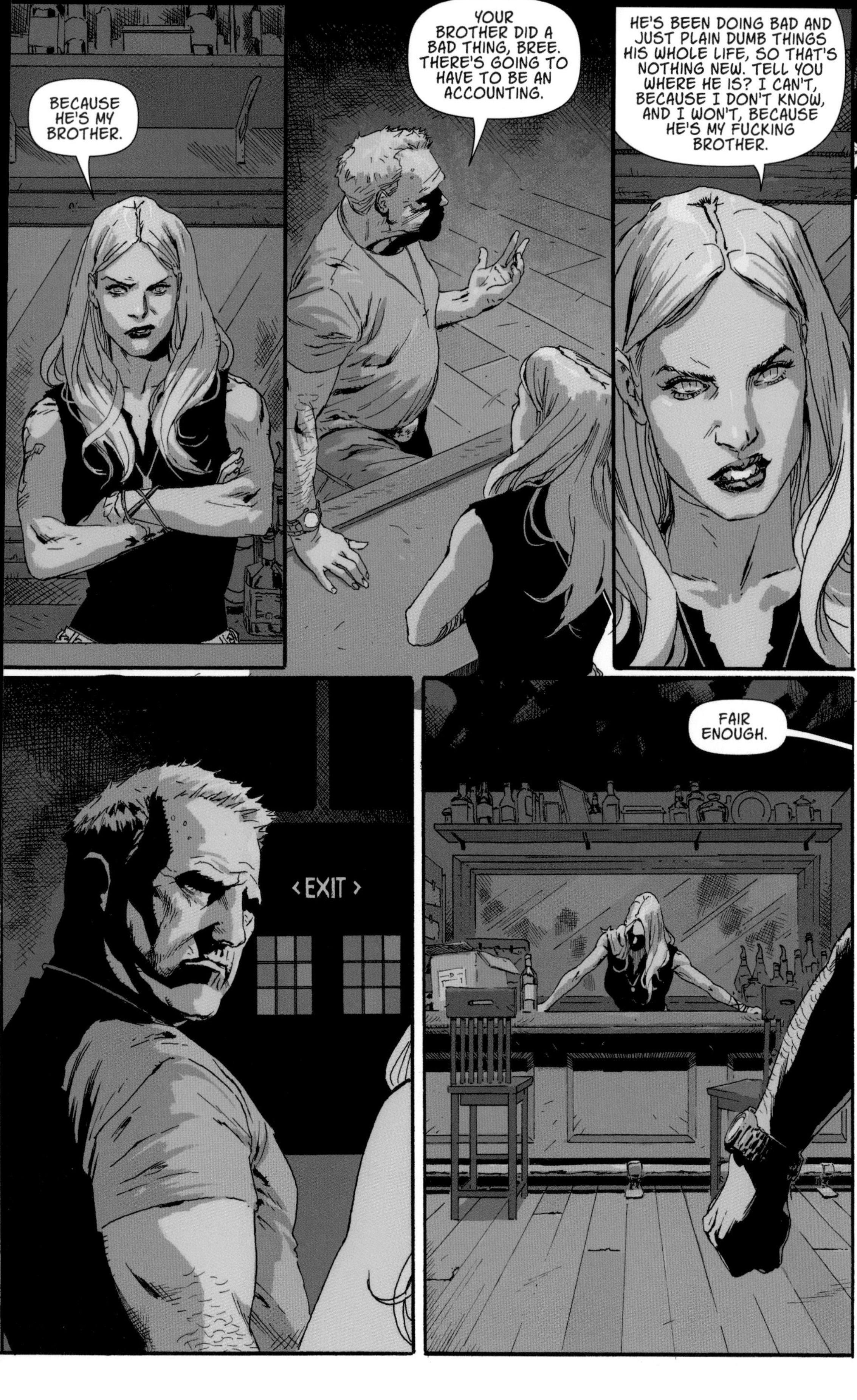

BECAUSE HE'S MY BROTHER.
YOUR BROTHER DID A BAD THING, BREE. THERE'S GOING TO HAVE TO BE AN ACCOUNTING.
HE'S BEEN DOING BAD AND JUST PLAIN DUMB THINGS HIS WHOLE LIFE, SO THAT'S NOTHING NEW. TELL YOU WHERE HE IS? I CAN'T, BECAUSE I DON'T KNOW, AND I WON'T, BECAUSE HE'S MY FUCKING BROTHER.
EXIT
FAIR ENOUGH.

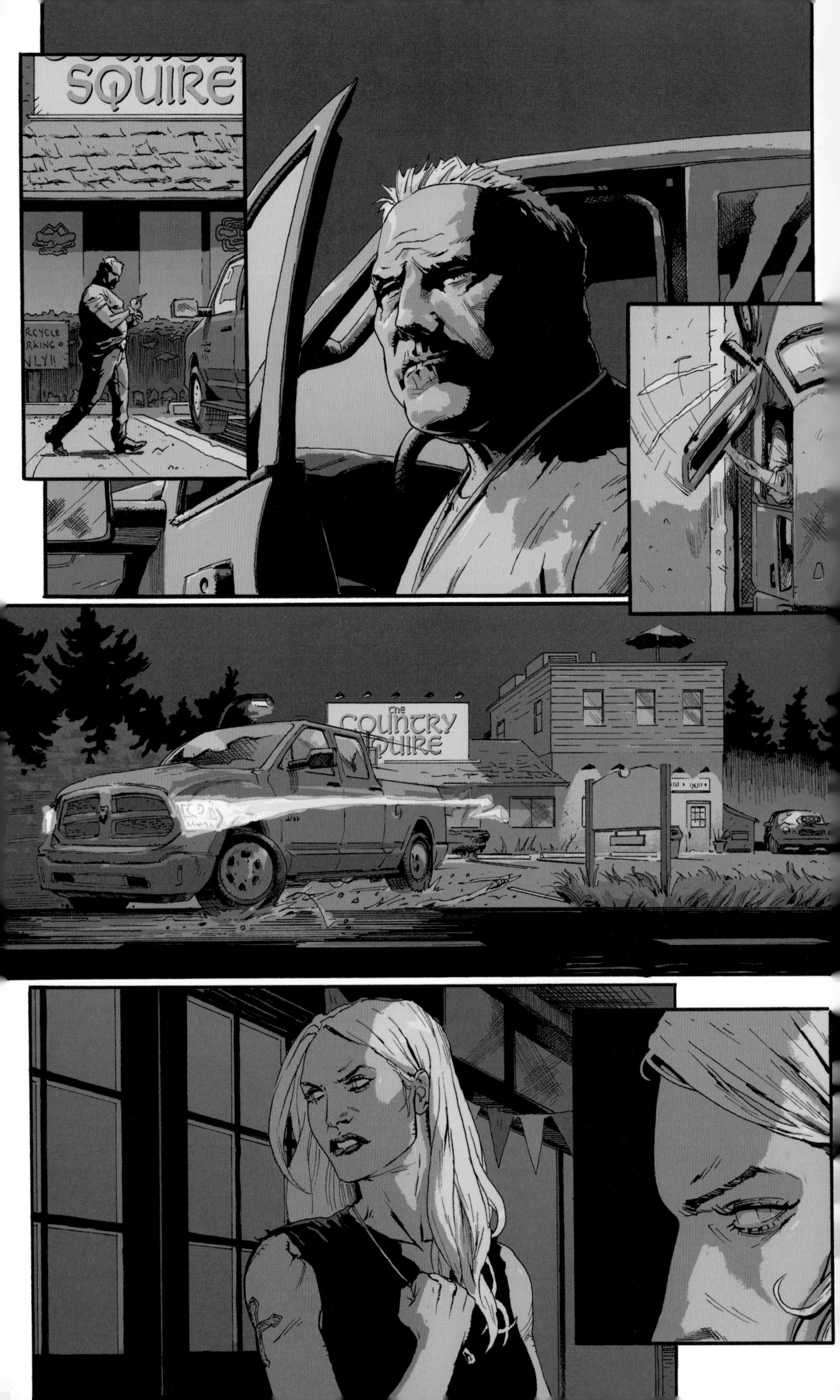

SQUIRE
THE COUNTRY

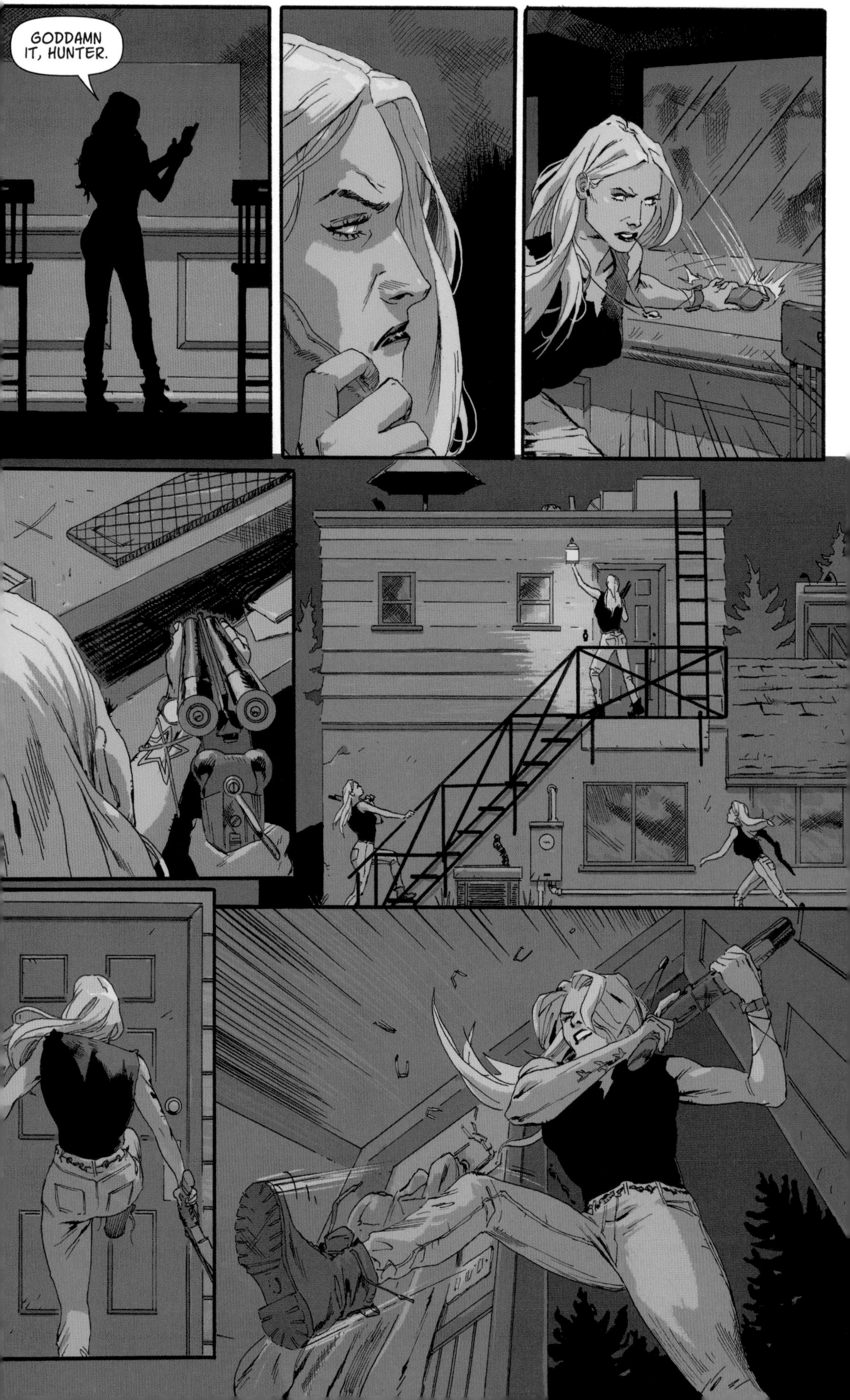
GODDAMN IT, HUNTER.

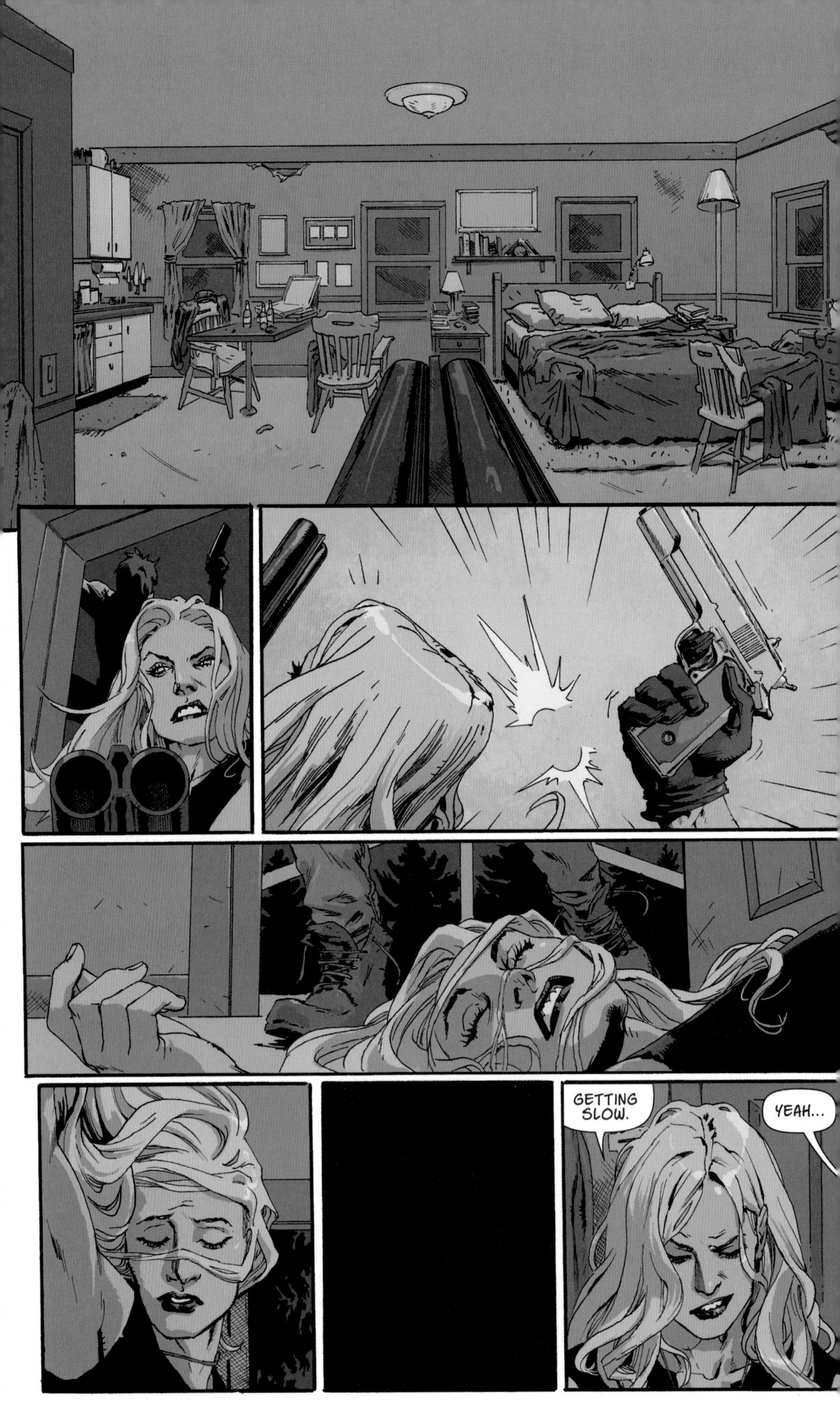
GETTING SLOW.
YEAH...

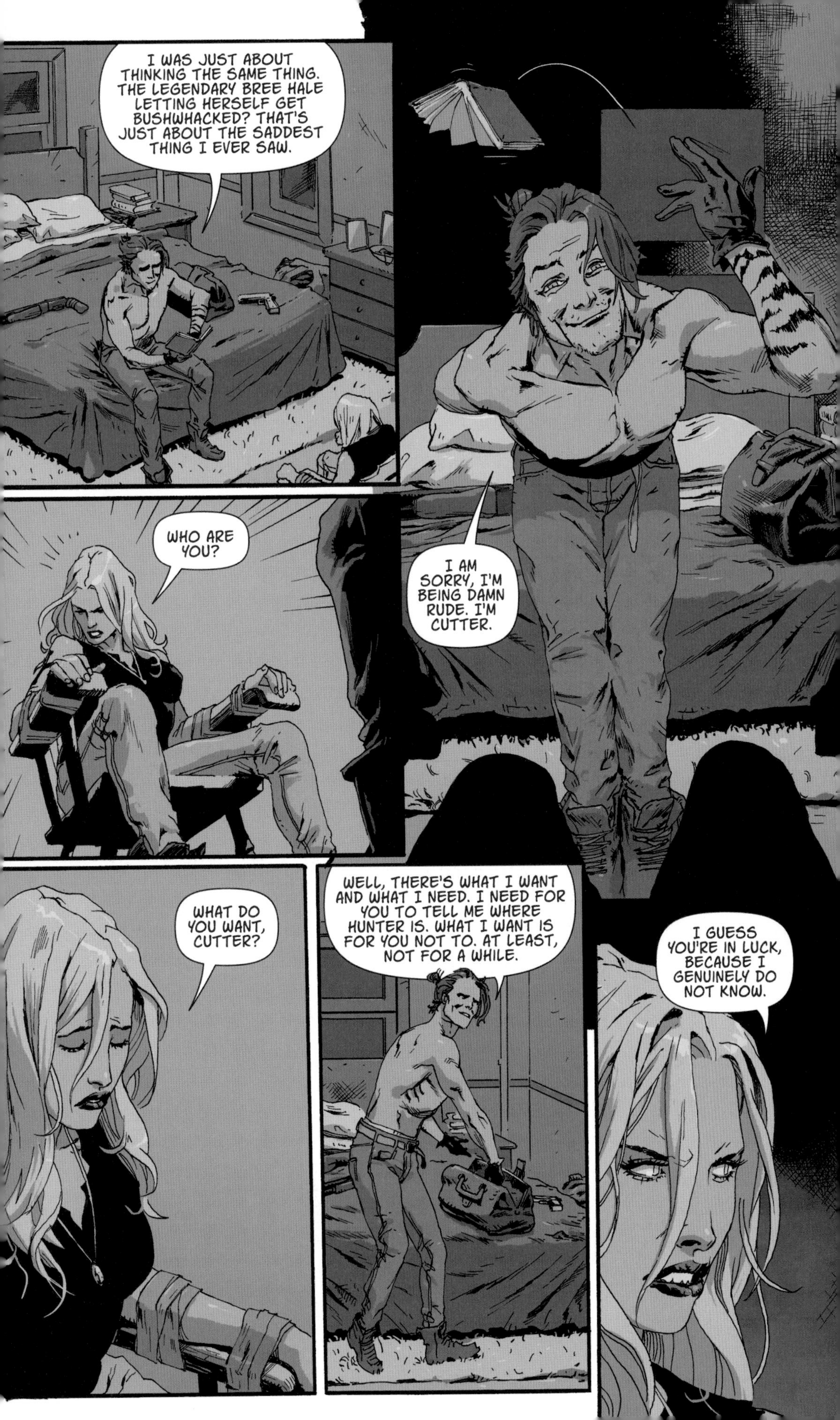
I WAS JUST ABOUT THINKING THE SAME THING. THE LEGENDARY BREE HALE LETTING HERSELF GET BUSHWHACKED? THAT'S JUST ABOUT THE SADDEST THING I EVER SAW.
WHO ARE YOU?
I AM SORRY, I'M BEING DAMN RUDE. I'M CUTTER.
WHAT DO YOU WANT, CUTTER?
WELL, THERE'S WHAT I WANT AND WHAT I NEED. I NEED FOR YOU TO TELL ME WHERE HUNTER IS. WHAT I WANT IS FOR YOU NOT TO. AT LEAST, NOT FOR A WHILE.
I GUESS YOU'RE IN LUCK, BECAUSE I GENUINELY DO NOT KNOW.

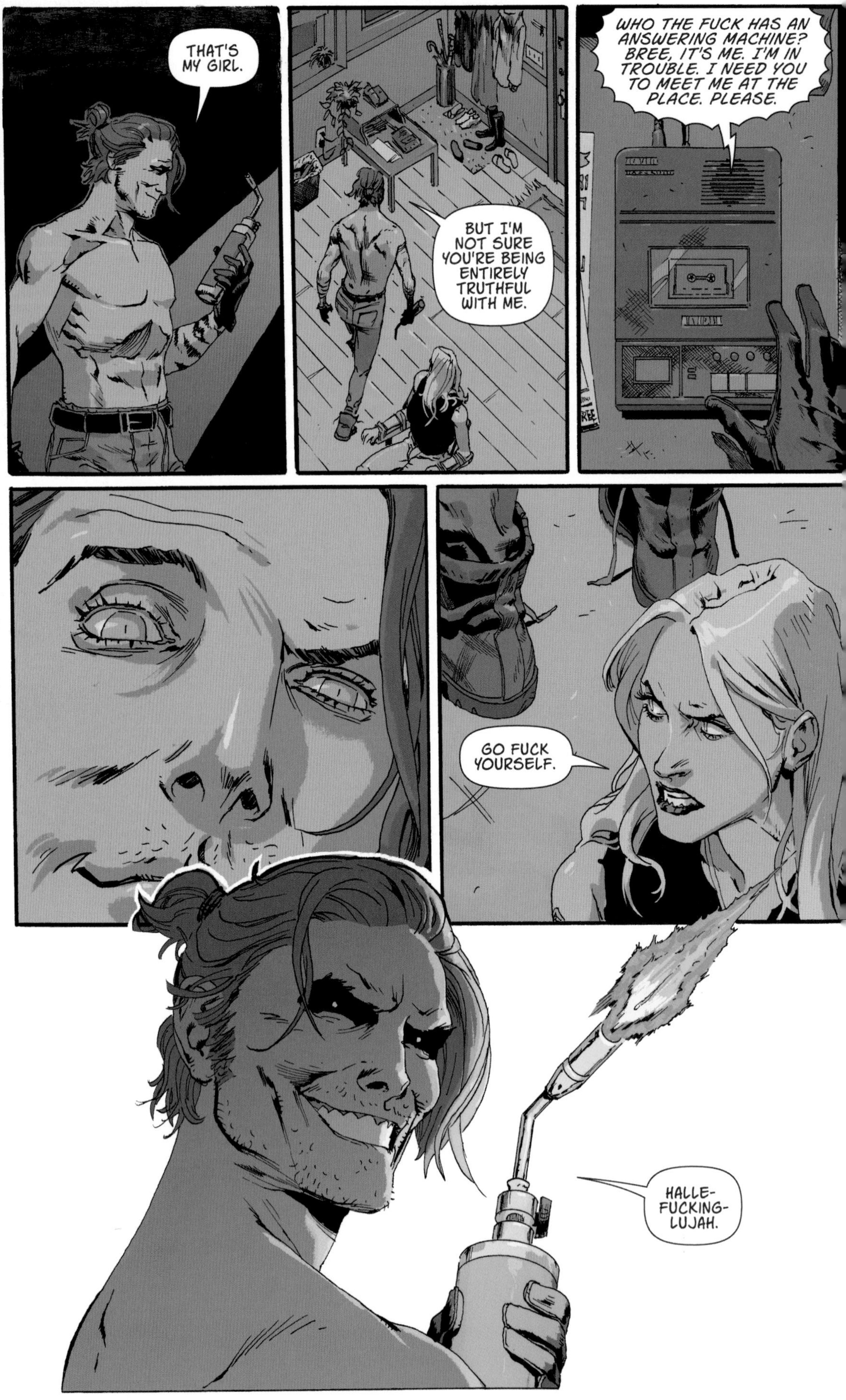
THAT'S MY GIRL.
BUT I'M NOT SURE YOU'RE BEING ENTIRELY TRUTHFUL WITH ME.
WHO THE FUCK HAS AN ANSWERING MACHINE? BREE, IT'S ME. I'M IN TROUBLE. I NEED YOU TO MEET ME AT THE PLACE. PLEASE.
GO FUCK YOURSELF.
HALLE-FUCKING-LUJAH.

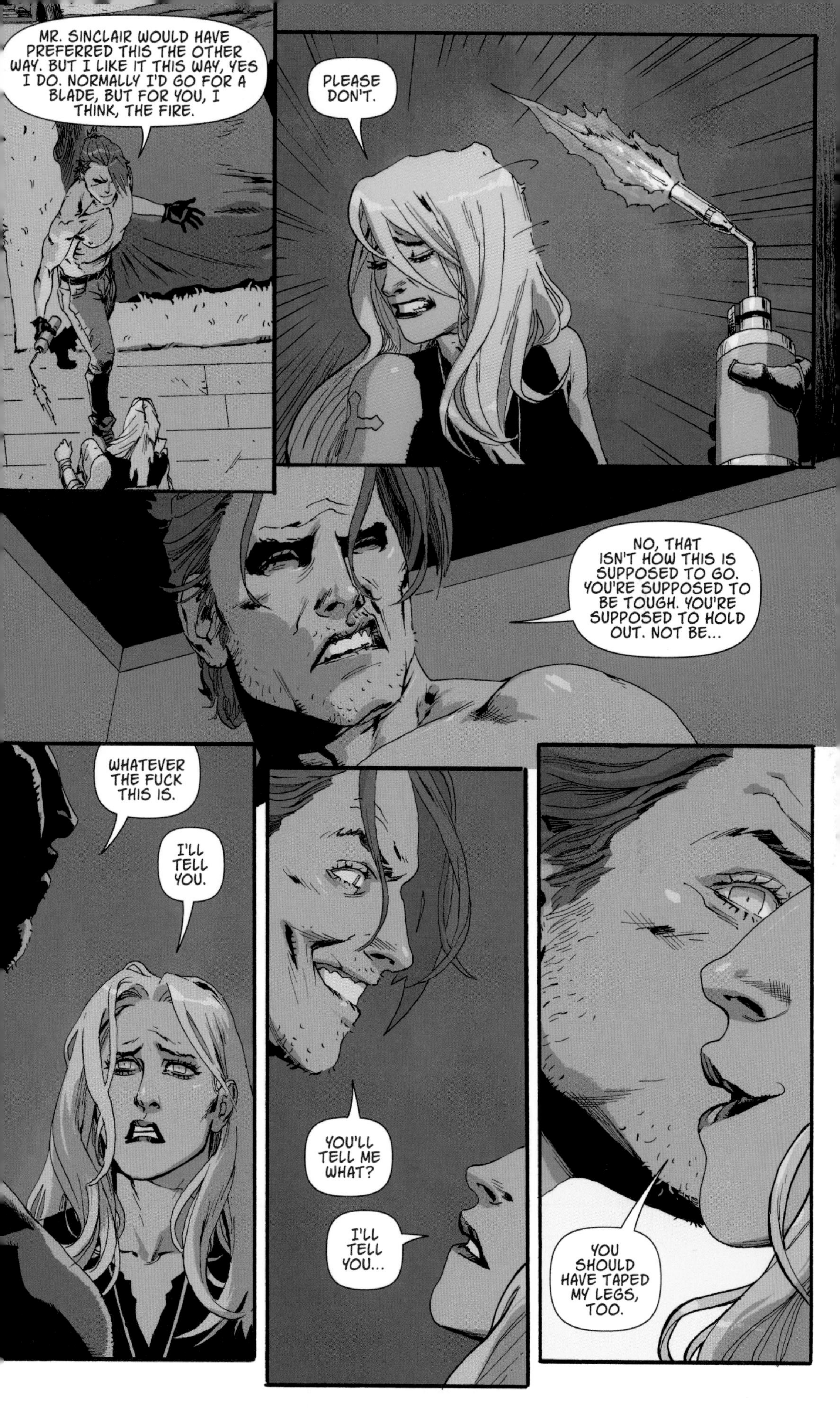
MR. SINCLAIR WOULD HAVE PREFERRED THIS THE OTHER WAY. BUT I LIKE IT THIS WAY, YES I DO. NORMALLY I'D GO FOR A BLADE, BUT FOR YOU, I THINK, THE FIRE.
PLEASE DON'T.
NO, THAT ISN'T HOW THIS IS SUPPOSED TO GO. YOU'RE SUPPOSED TO BE TOUGH. YOU'RE SUPPOSED TO HOLD OUT. NOT BE...
WHATEVER THE FUCK THIS IS.
I'LL TELL YOU.
YOU'LL TELL ME WHAT?
I'LL TELL YOU...
YOU SHOULD HAVE TAPED MY LEGS, TOO.

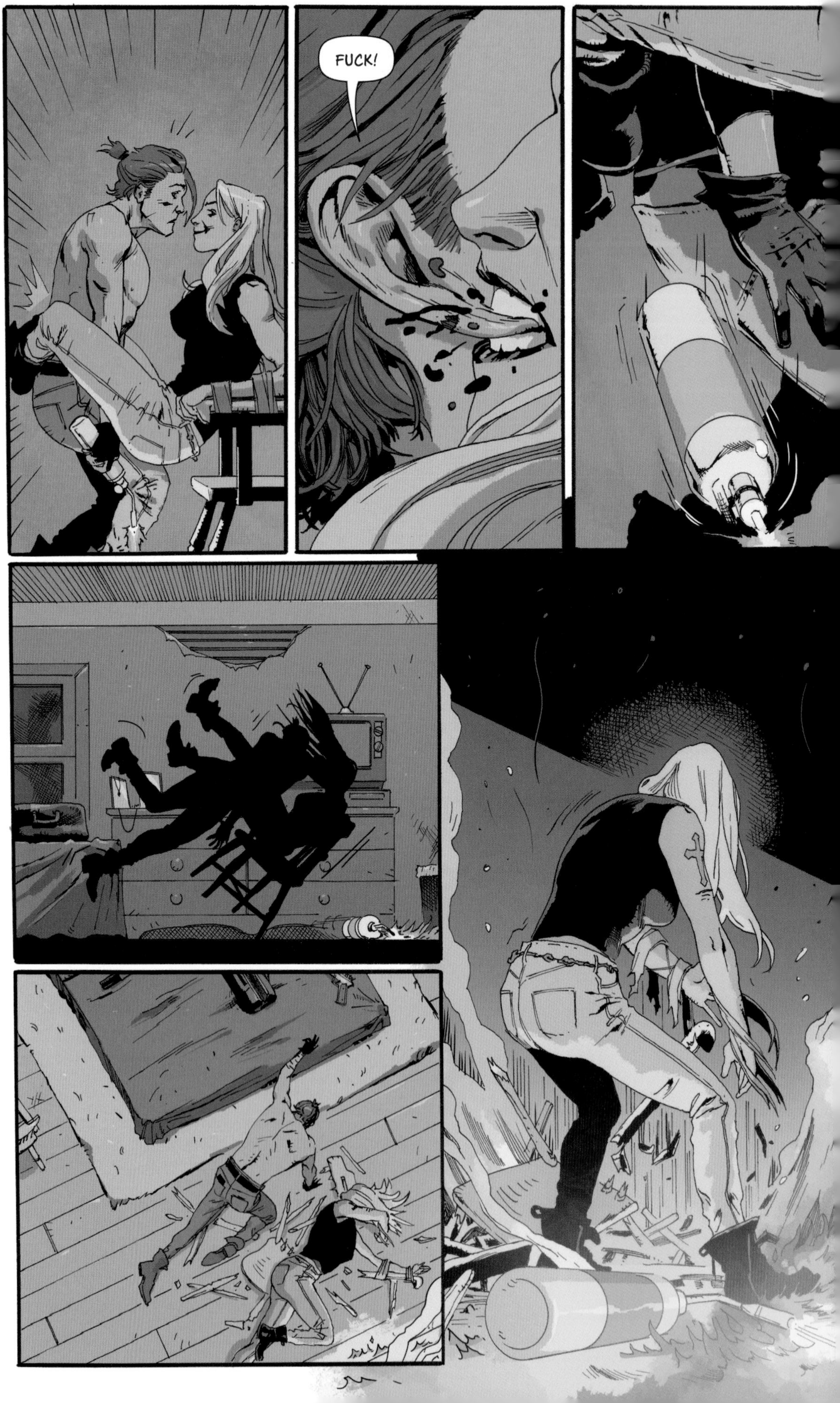
FUCK!

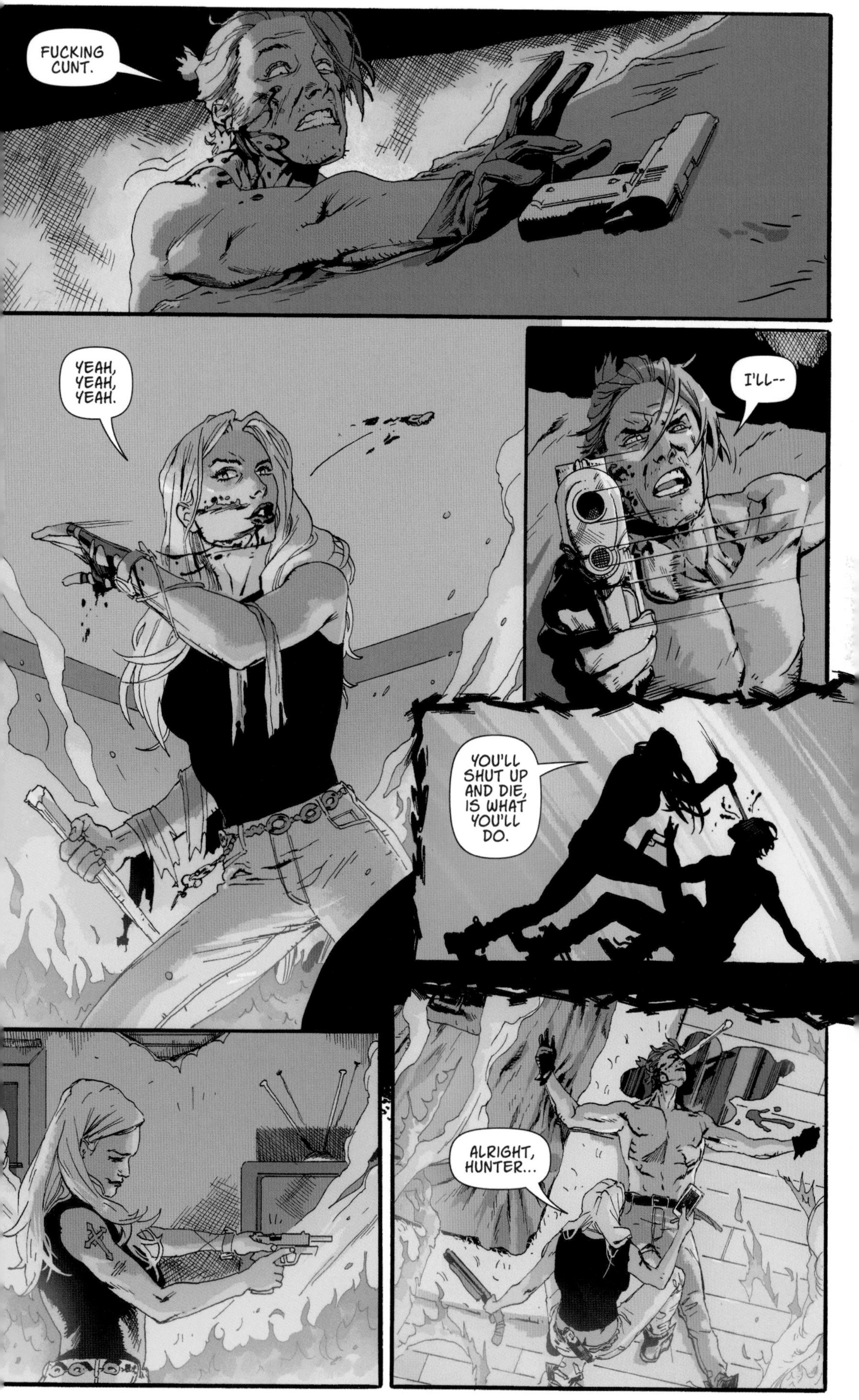
FUCKING CUNT.
YEAH, YEAH, YEAH.
I'LL--
YOU'LL SHUT UP AND DIE, IS WHAT YOU'LL DO.
ALRIGHT, HUNTER...

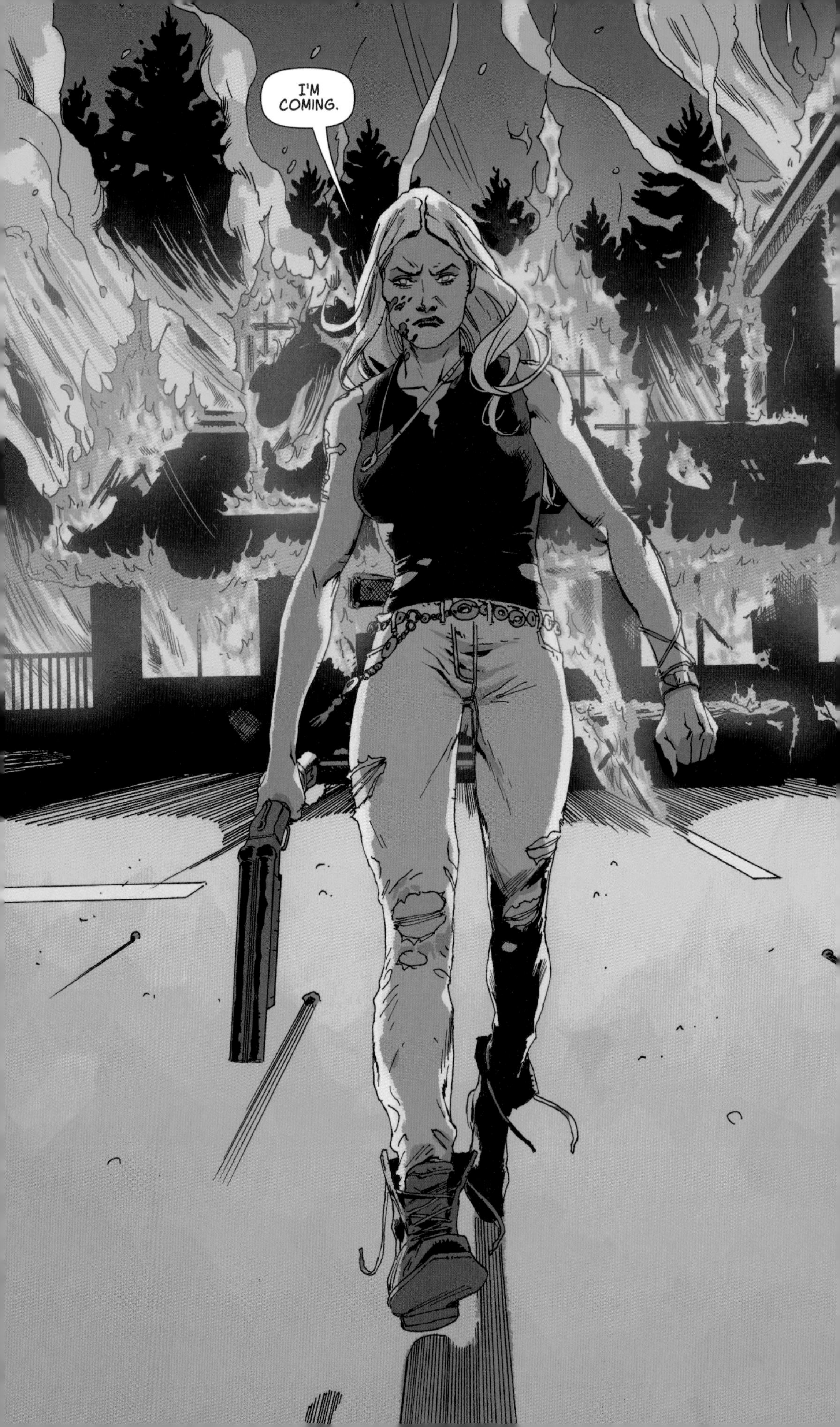
I'M COMING.

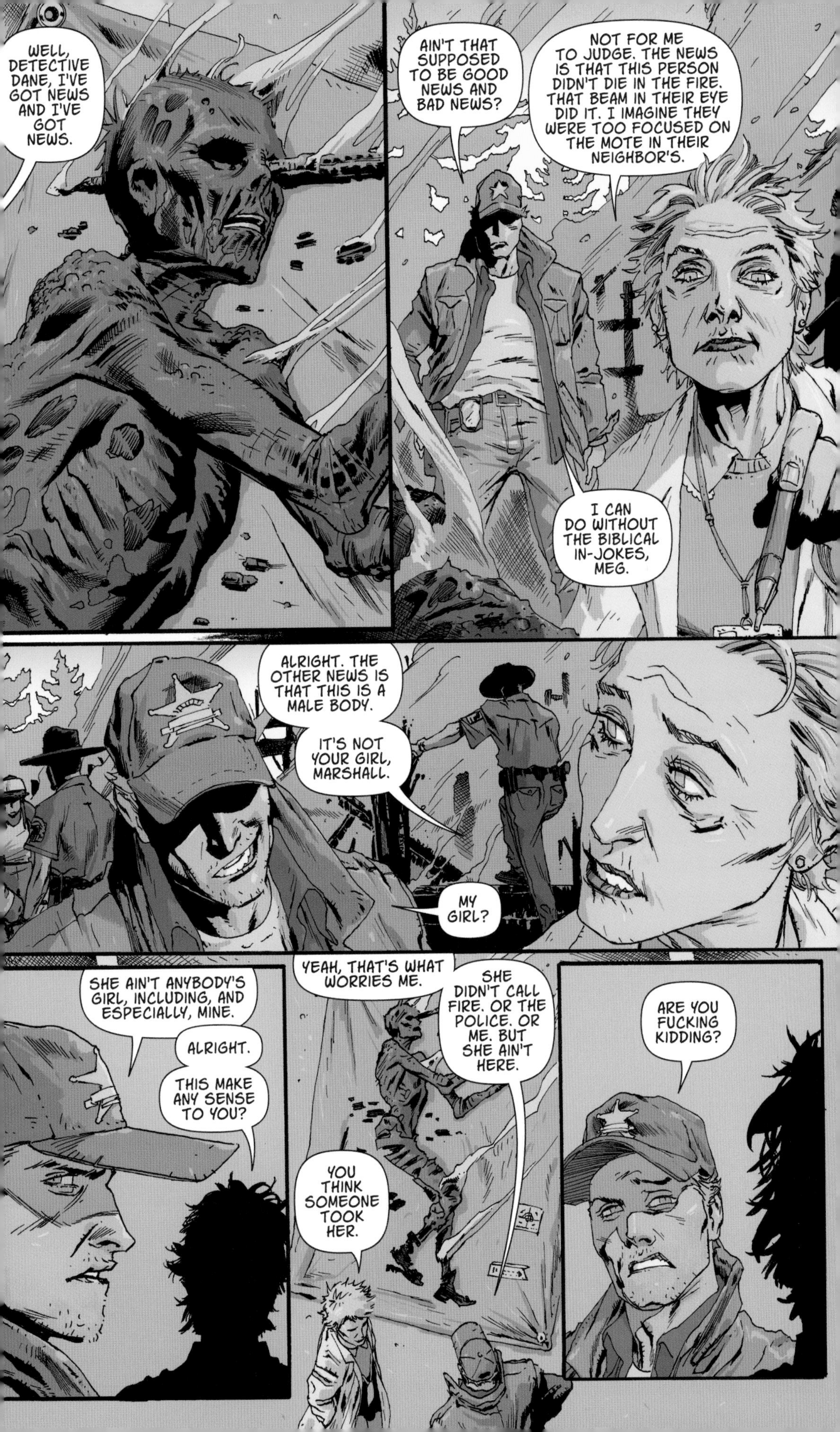

WELL, DETECTIVE DANE, I'VE GOT NEWS AND I'VE GOT NEWS.
AIN'T THAT SUPPOSED TO BE GOOD NEWS AND BAD NEWS?
NOT FOR ME TO JUDGE. THE NEWS IS THAT THIS PERSON DIDN'T DIE IN THE FIRE. THAT BEAM IN THEIR EYE DID IT. I IMAGINE THEY WERE TOO FOCUSED ON THE MOTE IN THEIR NEIGHBOR'S.
I CAN DO WITHOUT THE BIBLICAL IN-JOKES, MEG.
ALRIGHT. THE OTHER NEWS IS THAT THIS IS A MALE BODY.
IT'S NOT YOUR GIRL, MARSHALL.
MY GIRL?
SHE AIN'T ANYBODY'S GIRL, INCLUDING, AND ESPECIALLY, MINE.
ALRIGHT.
THIS MAKE ANY SENSE TO YOU?
YEAH, THAT'S WHAT WORRIES ME.
SHE DIDN'T CALL FIRE. OR THE POLICE. OR ME. BUT SHE AIN'T HERE.
YOU THINK SOMEONE TOOK HER.
ARE YOU FUCKING KIDDING?

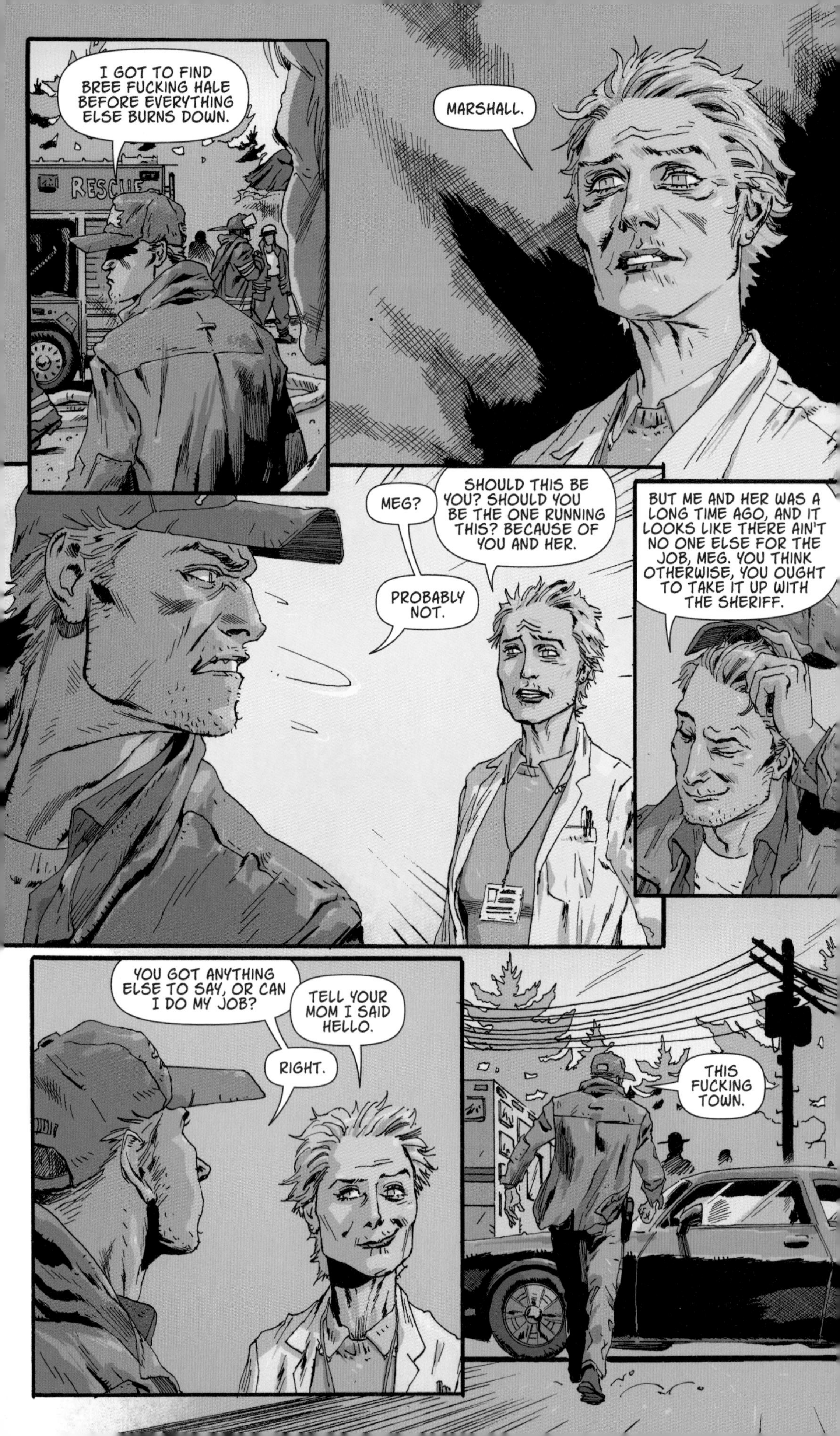
I GOT TO FIND BREE FUCKING HALE BEFORE EVERYTHING ELSE BURNS DOWN.
RESCUE
MARSHALL.
MEG?
PROBABLY NOT.
SHOULD THIS BE YOU? SHOULD YOU BE THE ONE RUNNING THIS? BECAUSE OF YOU AND HER.
BUT ME AND HER WAS A LONG TIME AGO, AND IT LOOKS LIKE THERE AIN'T NO ONE ELSE FOR THE JOB, MEG. YOU THINK OTHERWISE, YOU OUGHT TO TAKE IT UP WITH THE SHERIFF.
YOU GOT ANYTHING ELSE TO SAY, OR CAN I DO MY JOB?
RIGHT.
TELL YOUR MOM I SAID HELLO.
THIS FUCKING TOWN.

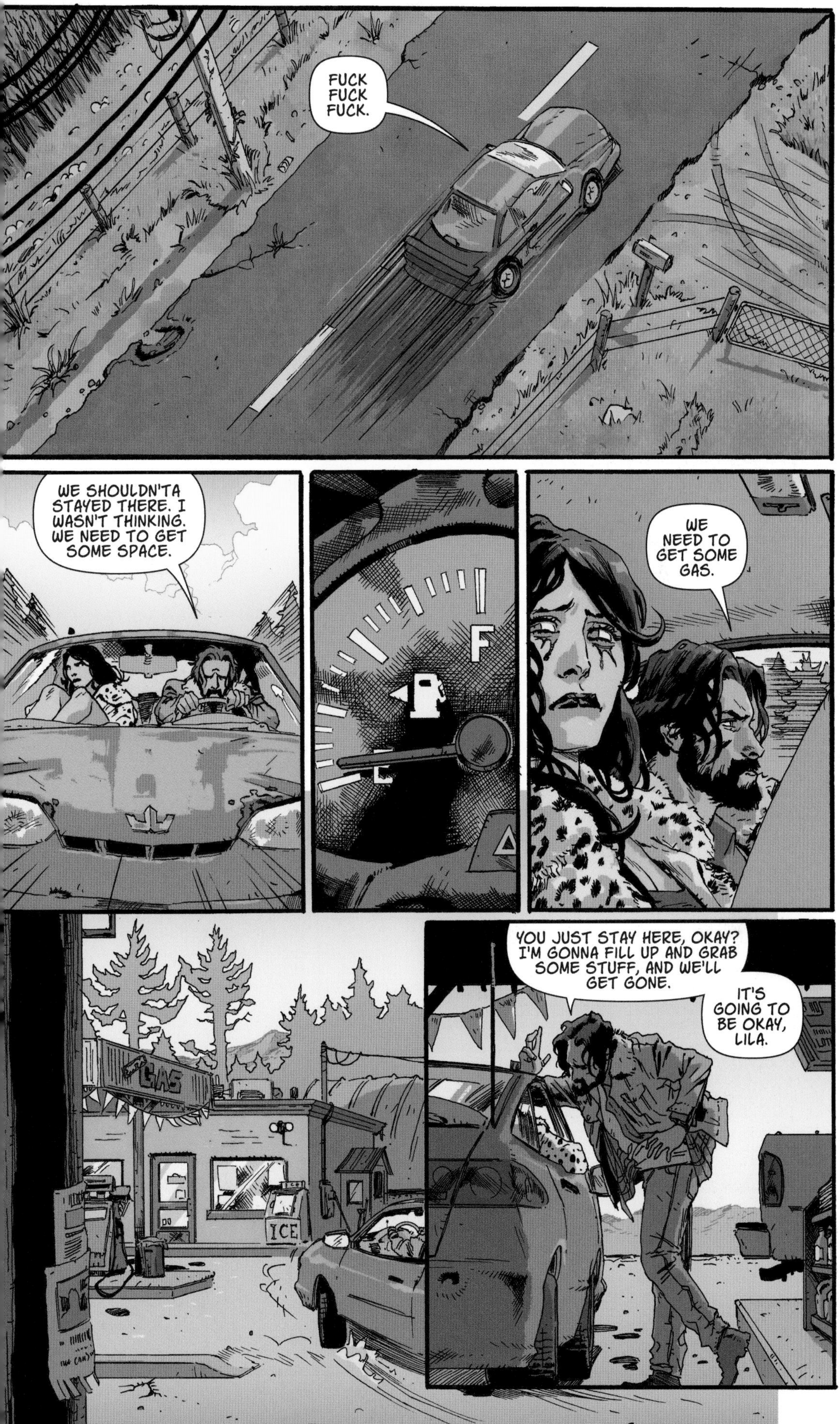
FUCK FUCK FUCK.
WE SHOULDN'TA STAYED THERE. I WASN'T THINKING. WE NEED TO GET SOME SPACE.
F
WE NEED TO GET SOME GAS.
GAS
ICE
YOU JUST STAY HERE, OKAY? I'M GONNA FILL UP AND GRAB SOME STUFF, AND WE'LL GET GONE.
IT'S GOING TO BE OKAY, LILA.

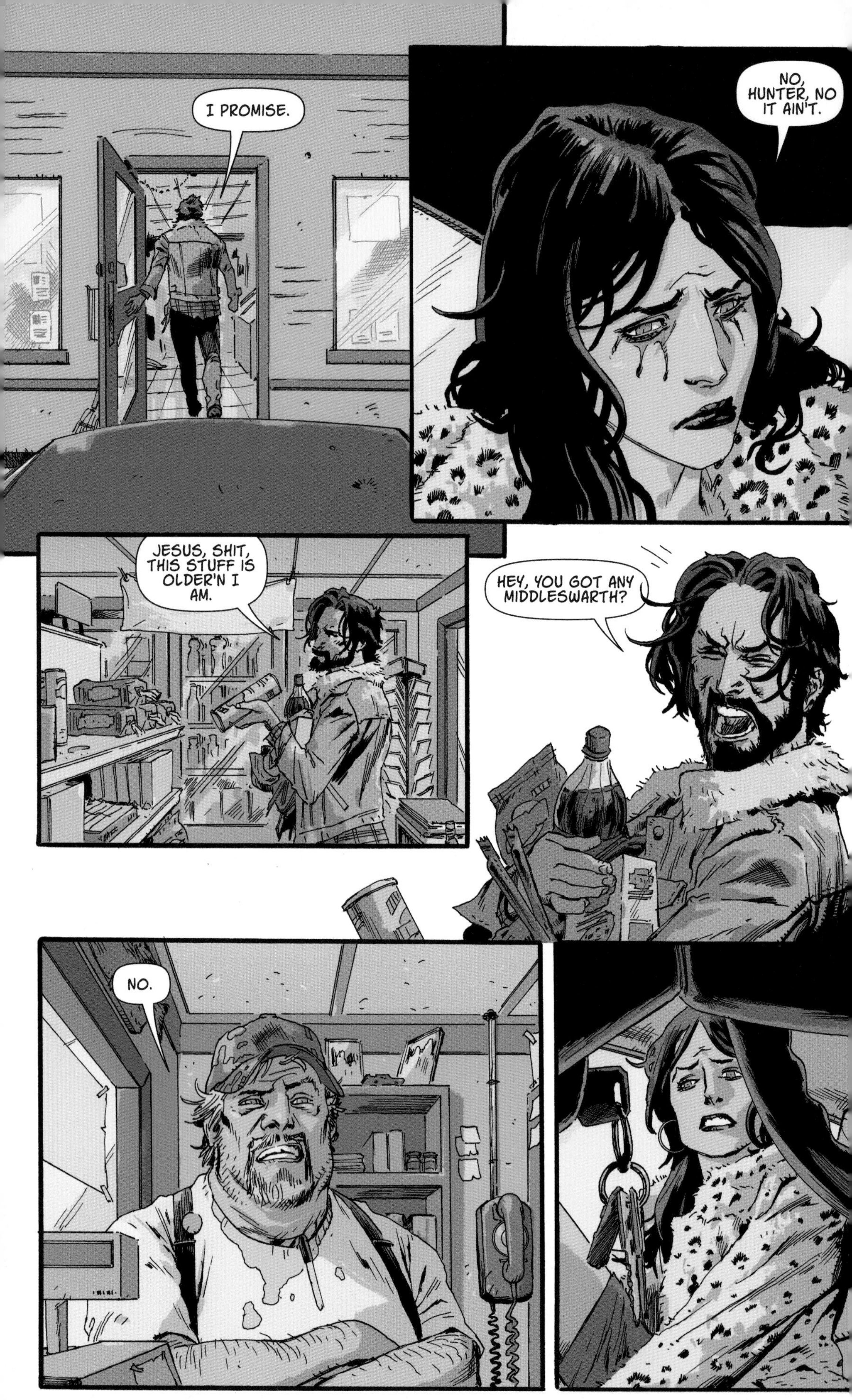
I PROMISE.
NO, HUNTER, NO IT AIN'T.
JESUS, SHIT, THIS STUFF IS OLDER'N I AM.
HEY, YOU GOT ANY MIDDLESWARTH?
NO.

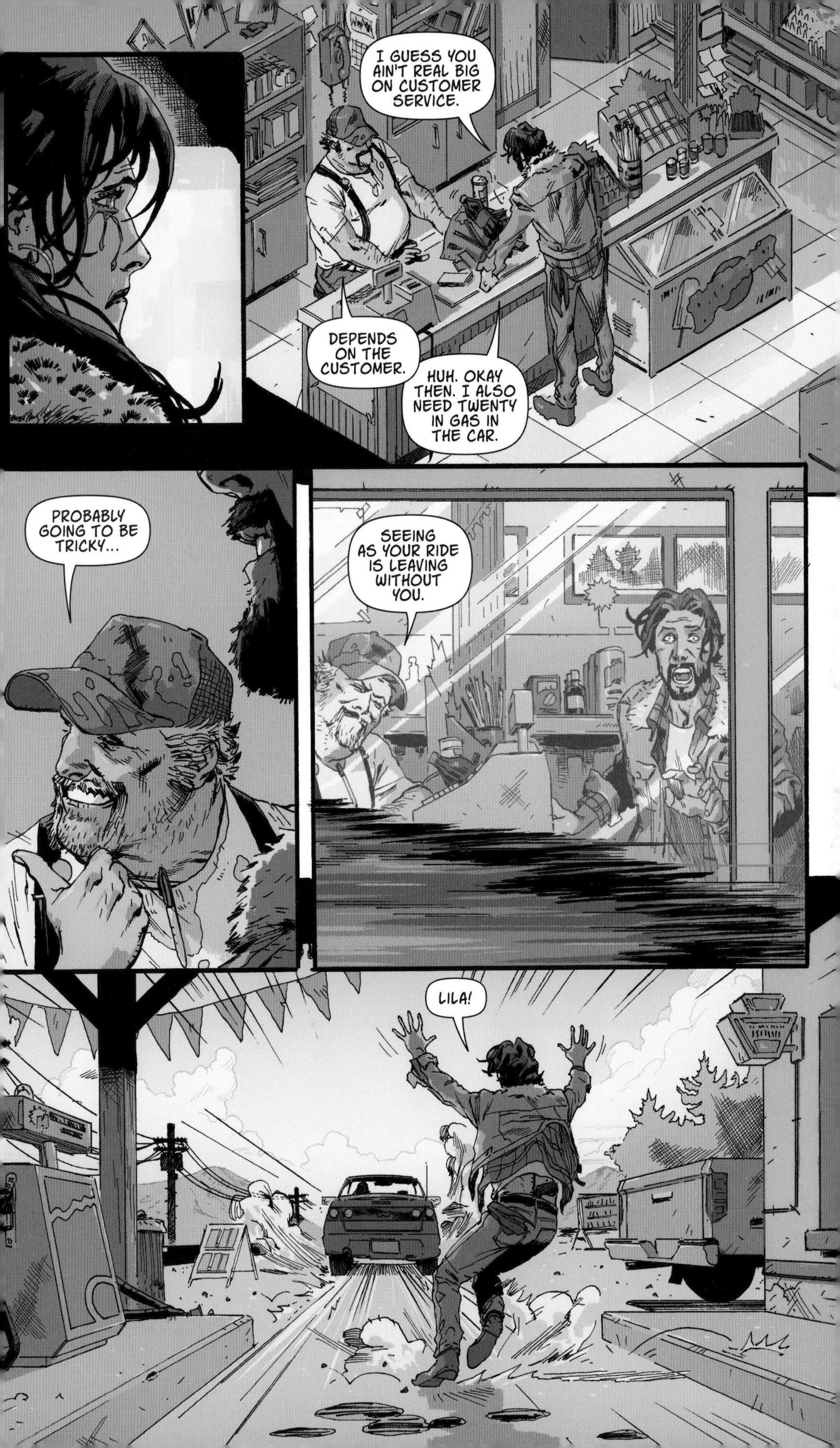
I GUESS YOU AIN'T REAL BIG ON CUSTOMER SERVICE.
DEPENDS ON THE CUSTOMER.
HUH. OKAY THEN. I ALSO NEED TWENTY IN GAS IN THE CAR.
PROBABLY GOING TO BE TRICKY...
SEEING AS YOUR RIDE IS LEAVING WITHOUT YOU.
LILA!

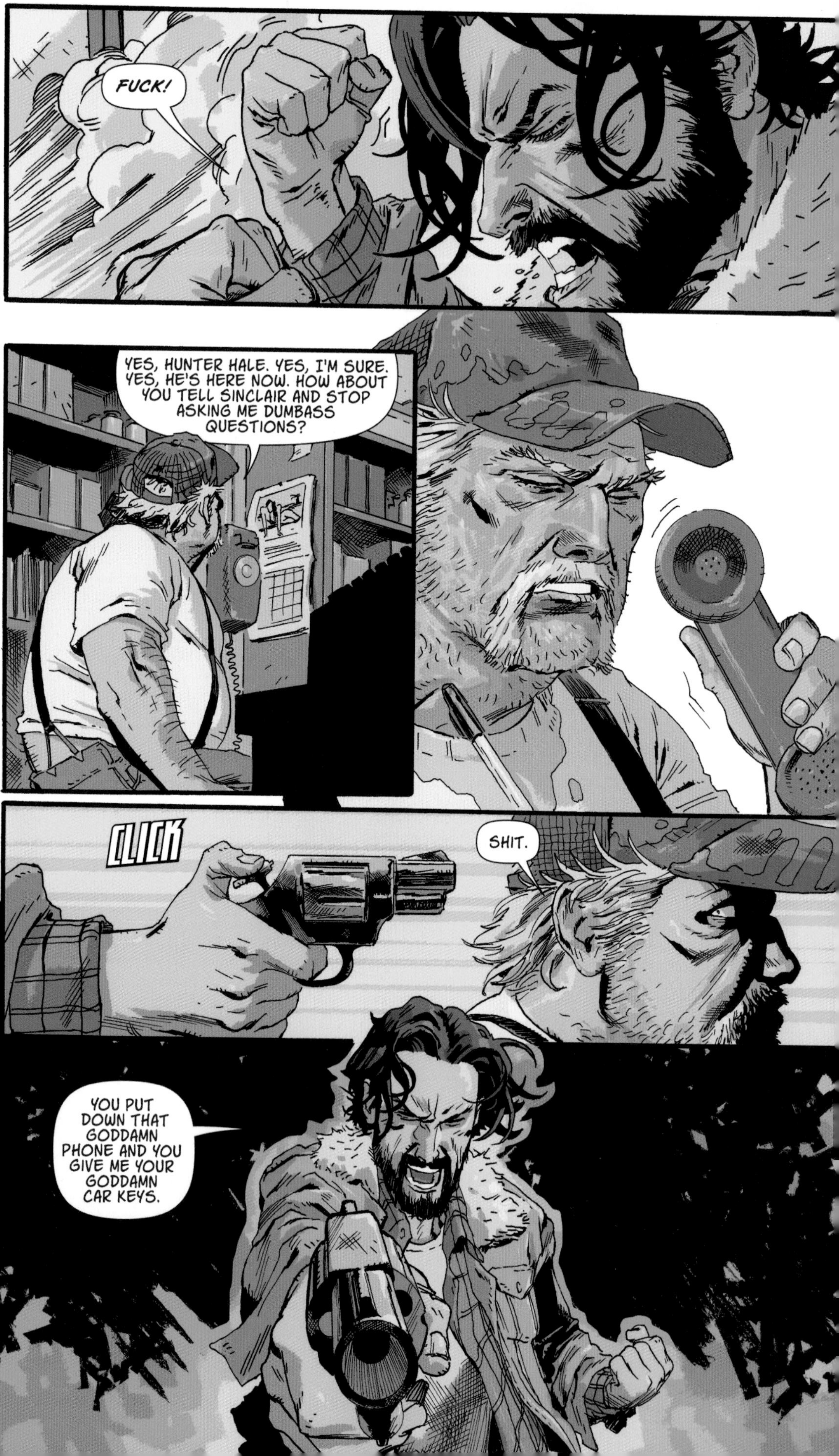
FUCK!
YES, HUNTER HALE. YES, I'M SURE. YES, HE'S HERE NOW. HOW ABOUT YOU TELL SINCLAIR AND STOP ASKING ME DUMBASS QUESTIONS?
CLICK
SHIT.
YOU PUT DOWN THAT GODDAMN PHONE AND YOU GIVE ME YOUR GODDAMN CAR KEYS.

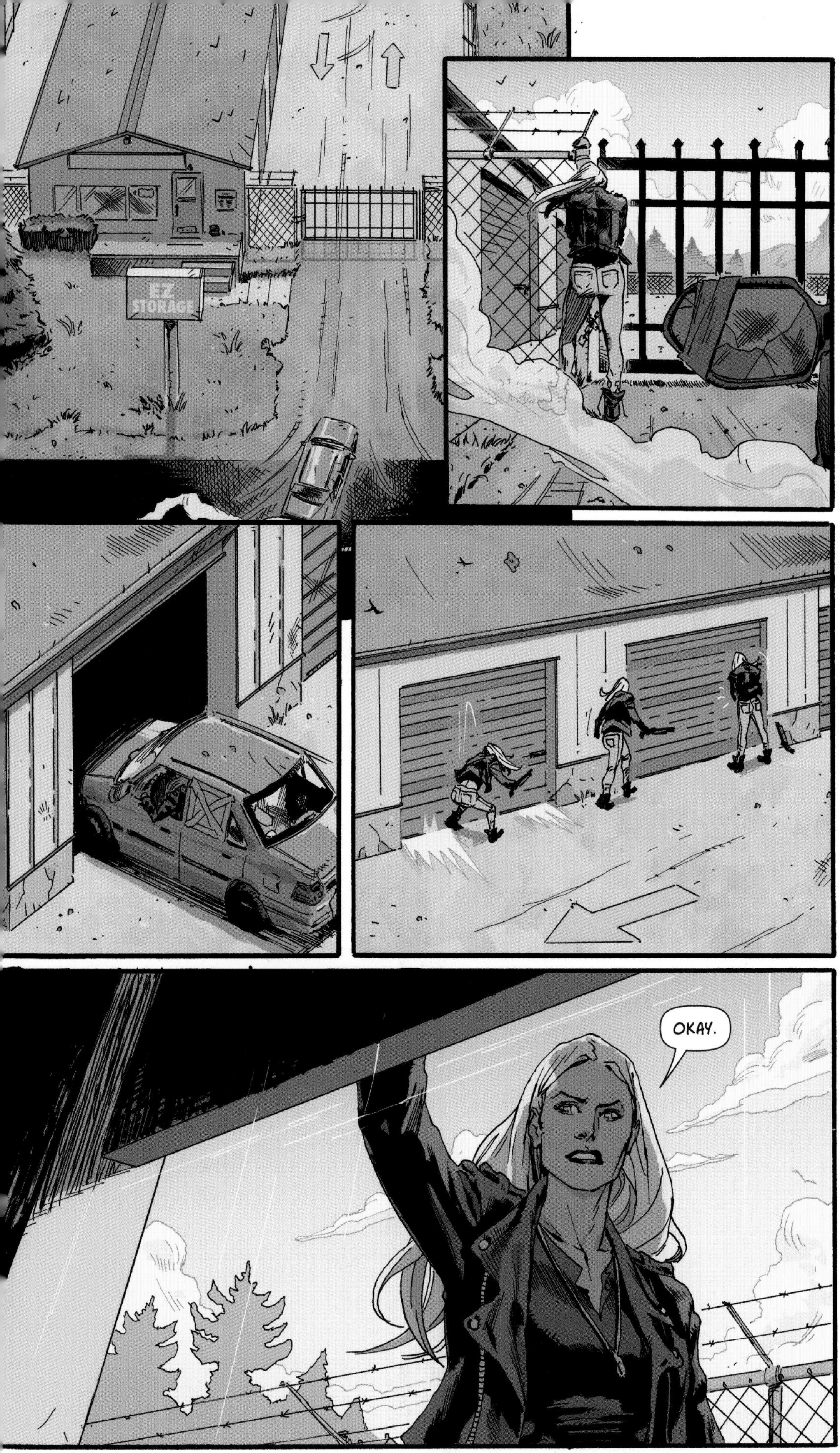
EZ STORAGE
OKAY.

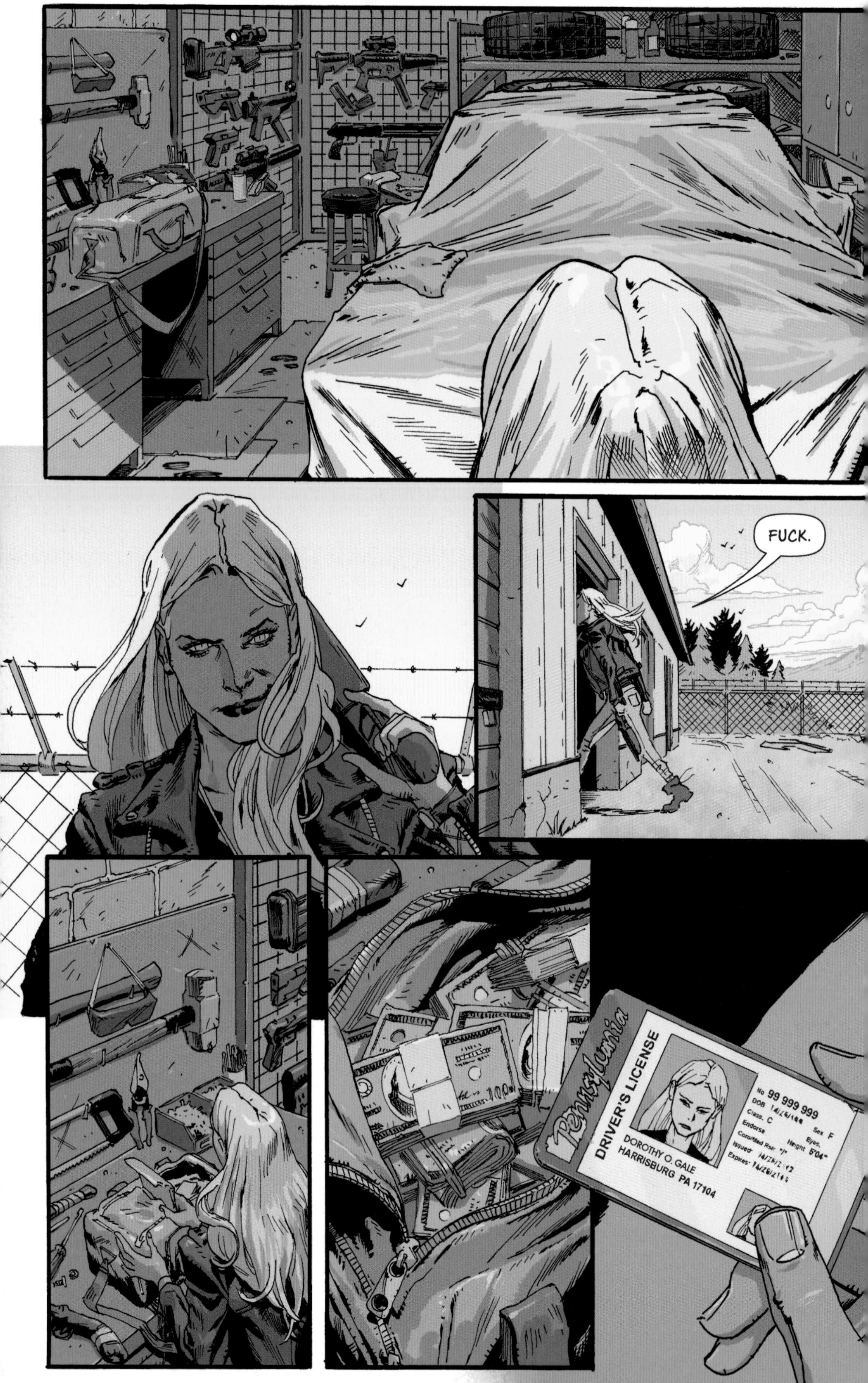
FUCK.
Pennsylvania
DRIVER'S LICENSE
No 99 999 999
Sex F
Height 5'04"
DOROTHY O. GALE
HARRISBURG PA 17104

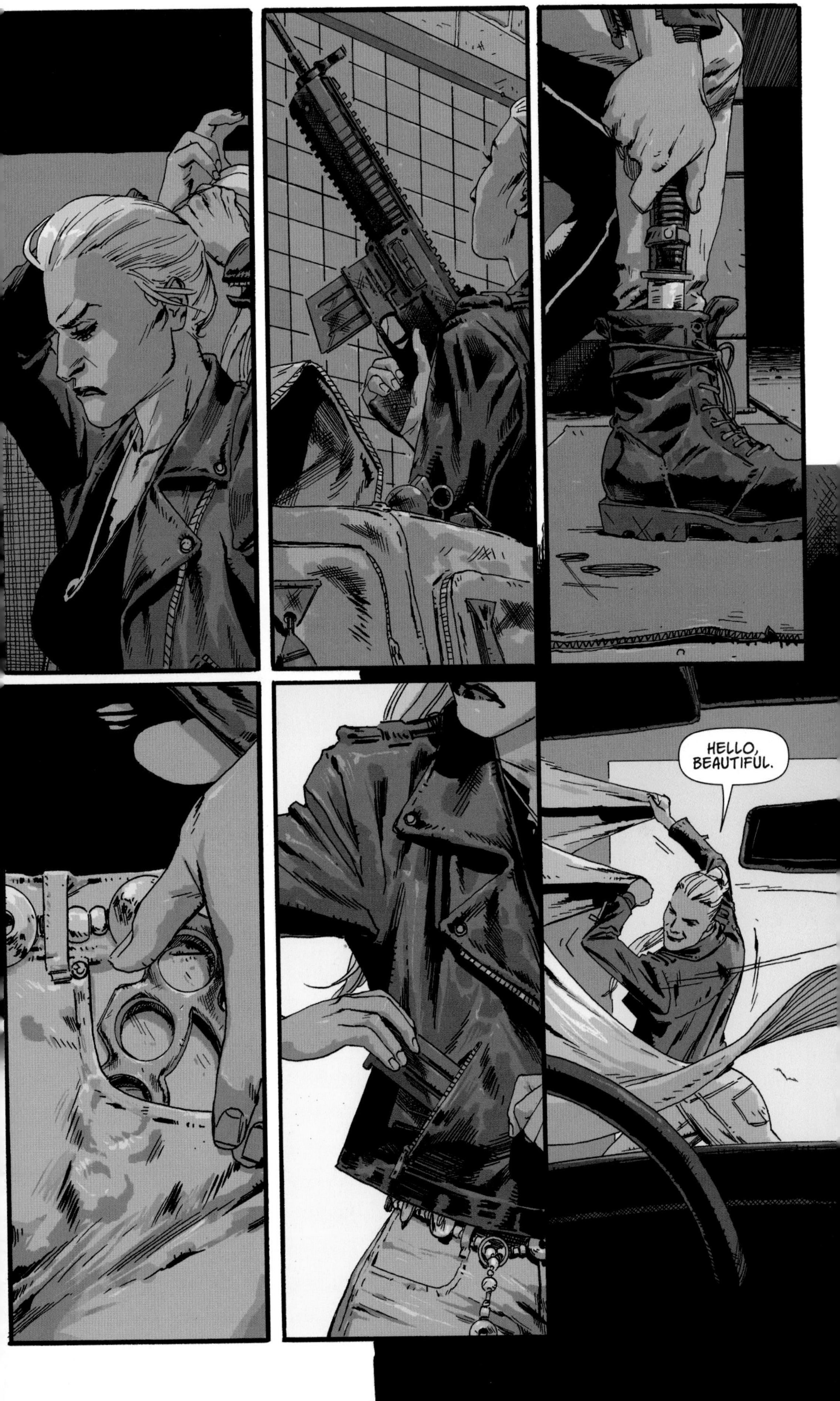
HELLO, BEAUTIFUL.

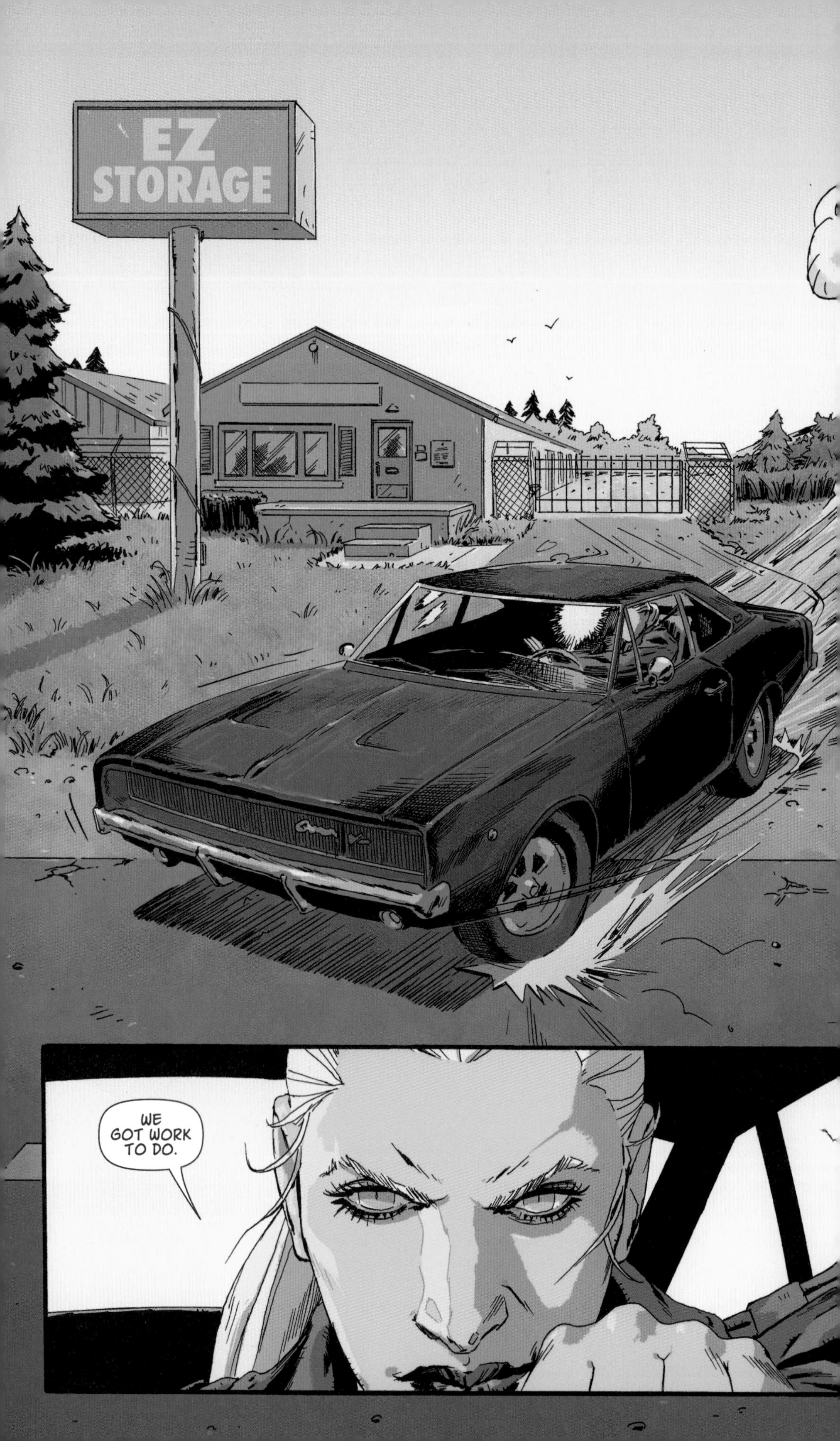
EZ STORAGE
WE GOT WORK TO DO.

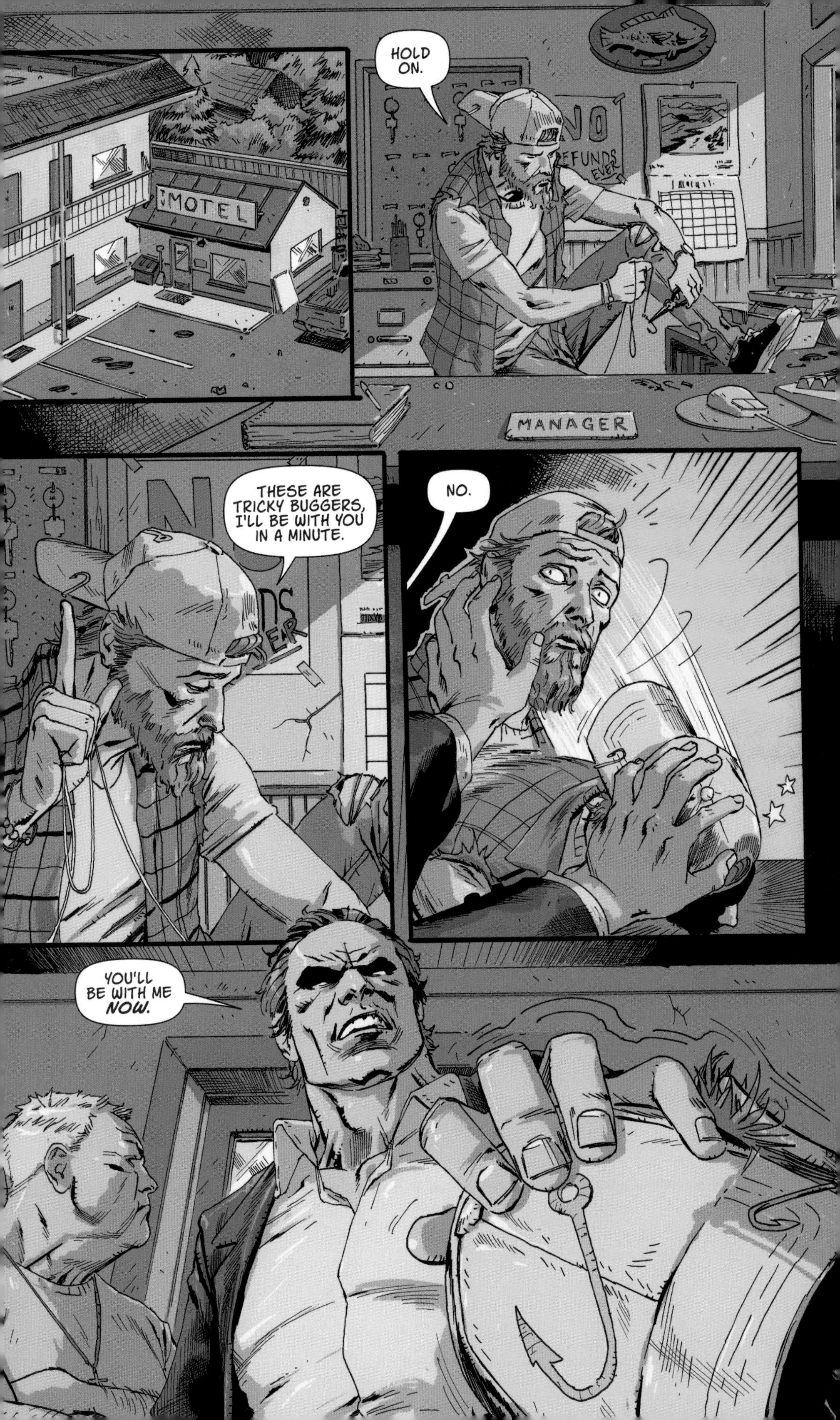
MOTEL
HOLD ON.
NO REFUNDS EVER
MANAGER
THESE ARE TRICKY BUGGERS, I'LL BE WITH YOU IN A MINUTE.
NO.
YOU'LL BE WITH ME *NOW*.

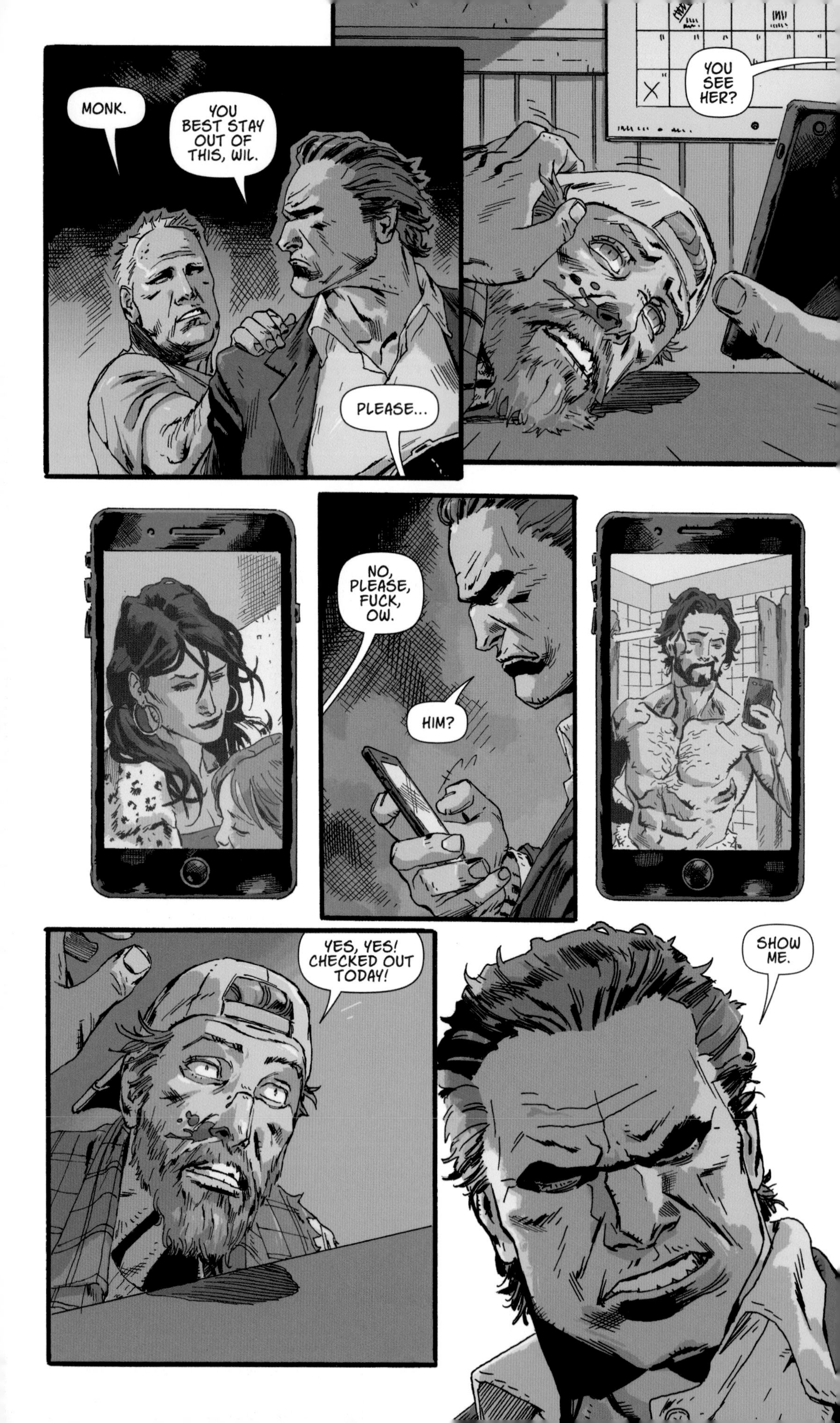
MONK.
YOU BEST STAY OUT OF THIS, WIL.
PLEASE...
YOU SEE HER?
NO, PLEASE, FUCK, OW.
HIM?
YES, YES! CHECKED OUT TODAY!
SHOW ME.

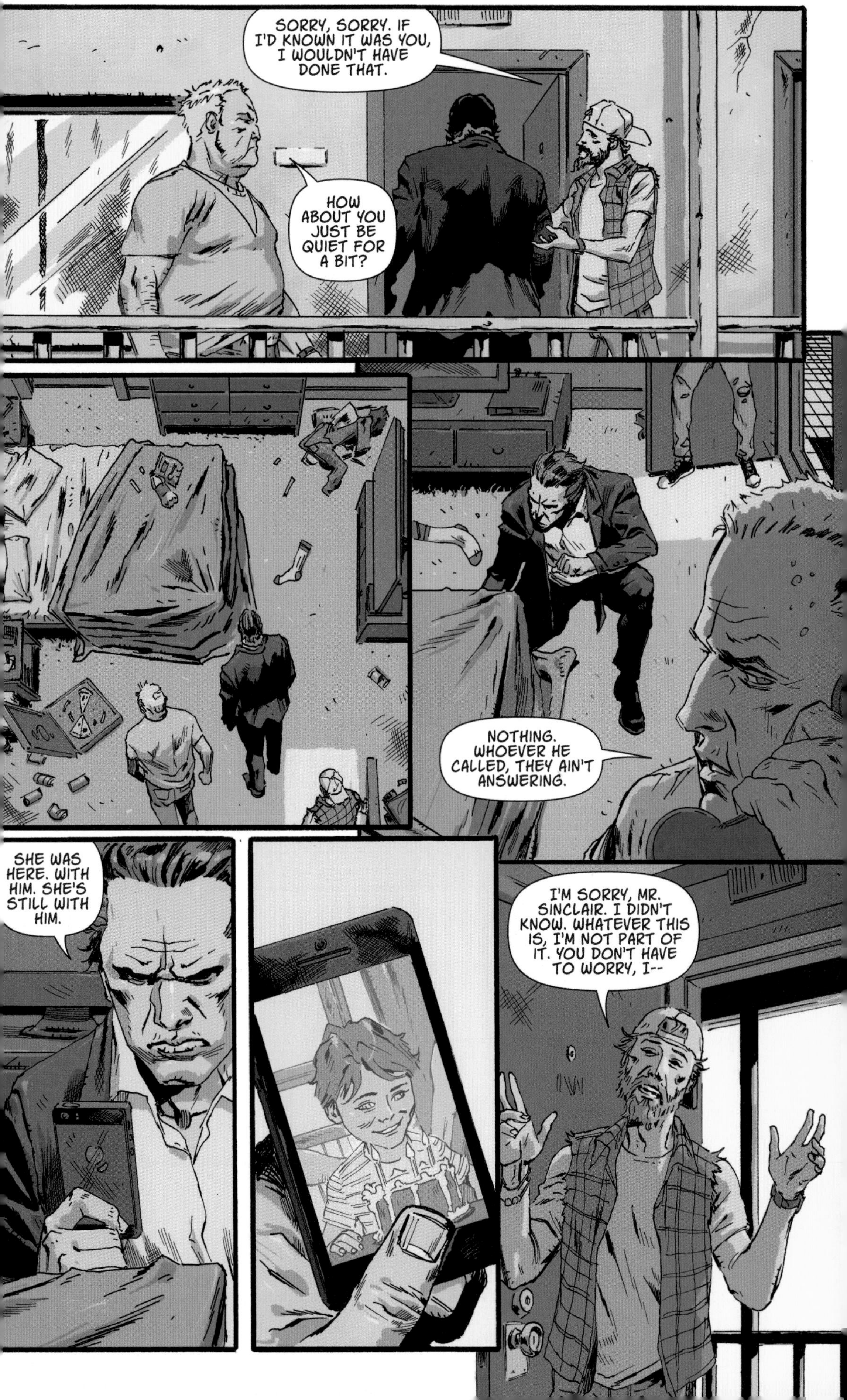
SORRY, SORRY. IF I'D KNOWN IT WAS YOU, I WOULDN'T HAVE DONE THAT.
HOW ABOUT YOU JUST BE QUIET FOR A BIT?
NOTHING. WHOEVER HE CALLED, THEY AIN'T ANSWERING.
SHE WAS HERE. WITH HIM. SHE'S STILL WITH HIM.
I'M SORRY, MR. SINCLAIR. I DIDN'T KNOW. WHATEVER THIS IS, I'M NOT PART OF IT. YOU DON'T HAVE TO WORRY, I--

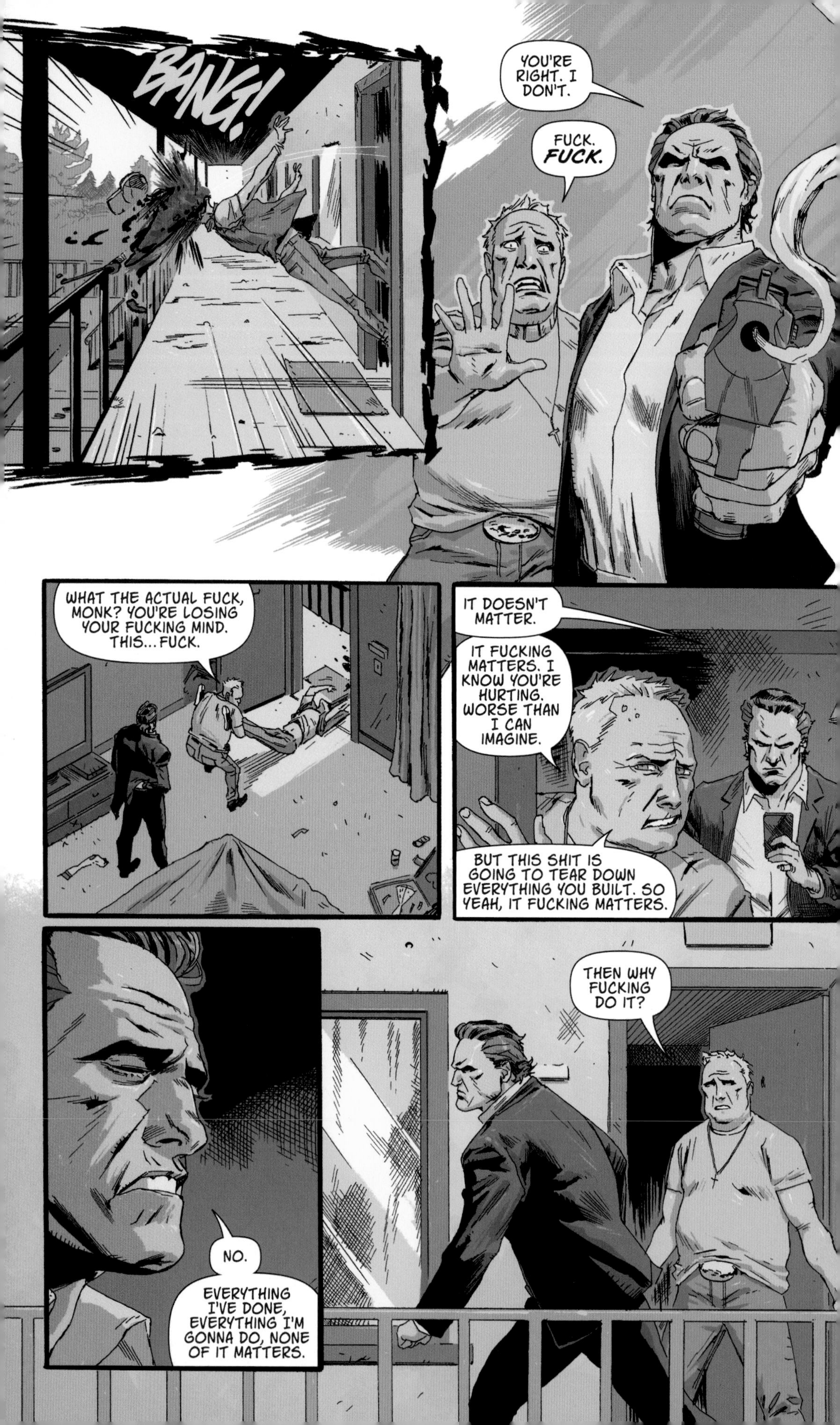
BANG!
YOU'RE RIGHT. I DON'T.
FUCK. FUCK.
WHAT THE ACTUAL FUCK, MONK? YOU'RE LOSING YOUR FUCKING MIND. THIS... FUCK.
IT DOESN'T MATTER.
IT FUCKING MATTERS. I KNOW YOU'RE HURTING. WORSE THAN I CAN IMAGINE.
BUT THIS SHIT IS GOING TO TEAR DOWN EVERYTHING YOU BUILT. SO YEAH, IT FUCKING MATTERS.
THEN WHY FUCKING DO IT?
NO.
EVERYTHING I'VE DONE, EVERYTHING I'M GONNA DO, NONE OF IT MATTERS.

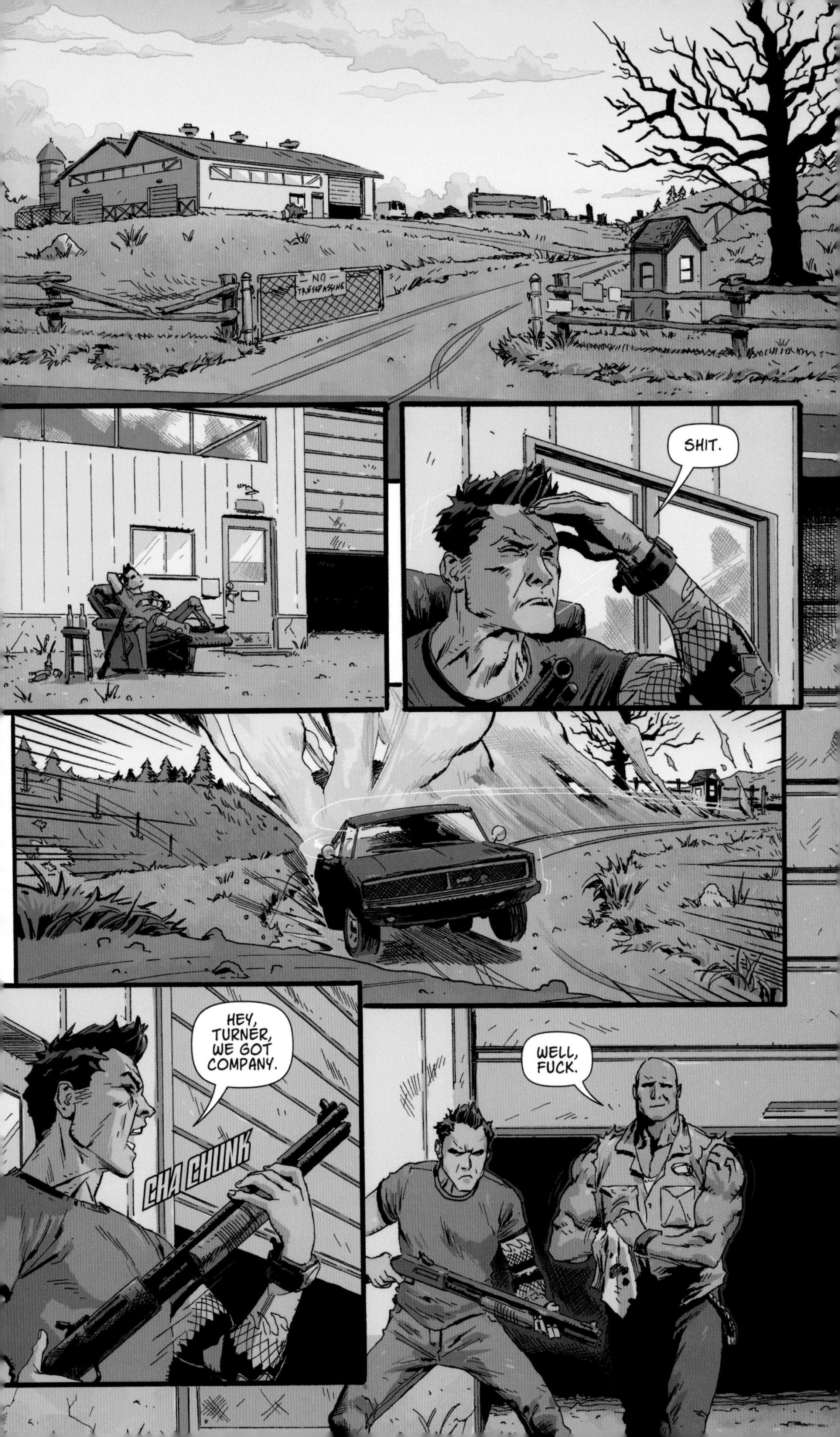
NO TRESSPASSING
SHIT.
HEY, TURNER, WE GOT COMPANY.
CHA CHUNK
WELL, FUCK.

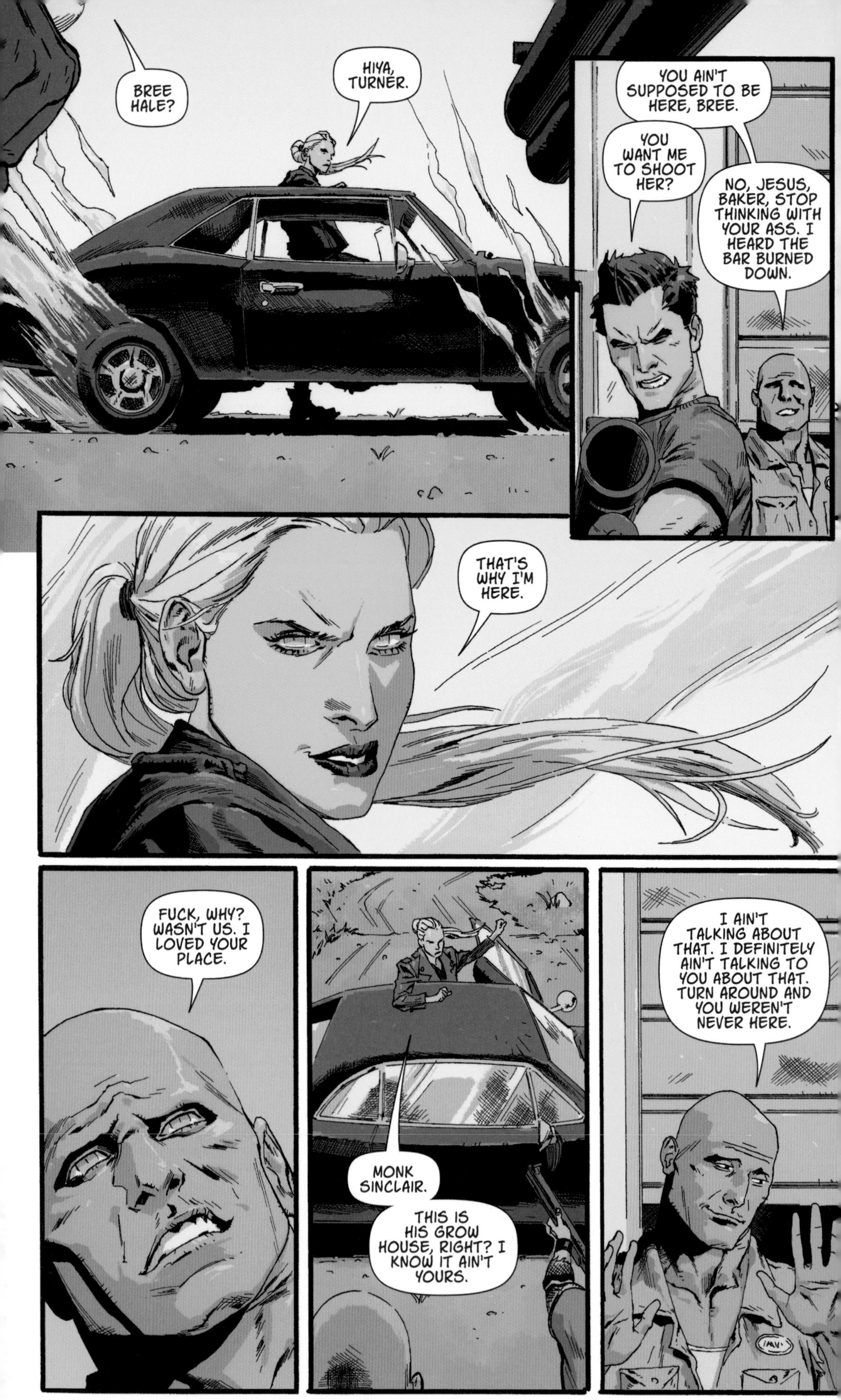
BREE HALE?
HIYA, TURNER.
YOU AIN'T SUPPOSED TO BE HERE, BREE.
YOU WANT ME TO SHOOT HER?
NO, JESUS, BAKER, STOP THINKING WITH YOUR ASS. I HEARD THE BAR BURNED DOWN.
THAT'S WHY I'M HERE.
FUCK, WHY? WASN'T US. I LOVED YOUR PLACE.
MONK SINCLAIR.
THIS IS HIS GROW HOUSE, RIGHT? I KNOW IT AIN'T YOURS.
I AIN'T TALKING ABOUT THAT. I DEFINITELY AIN'T TALKING TO YOU ABOUT THAT. TURN AROUND AND YOU WEREN'T NEVER HERE.

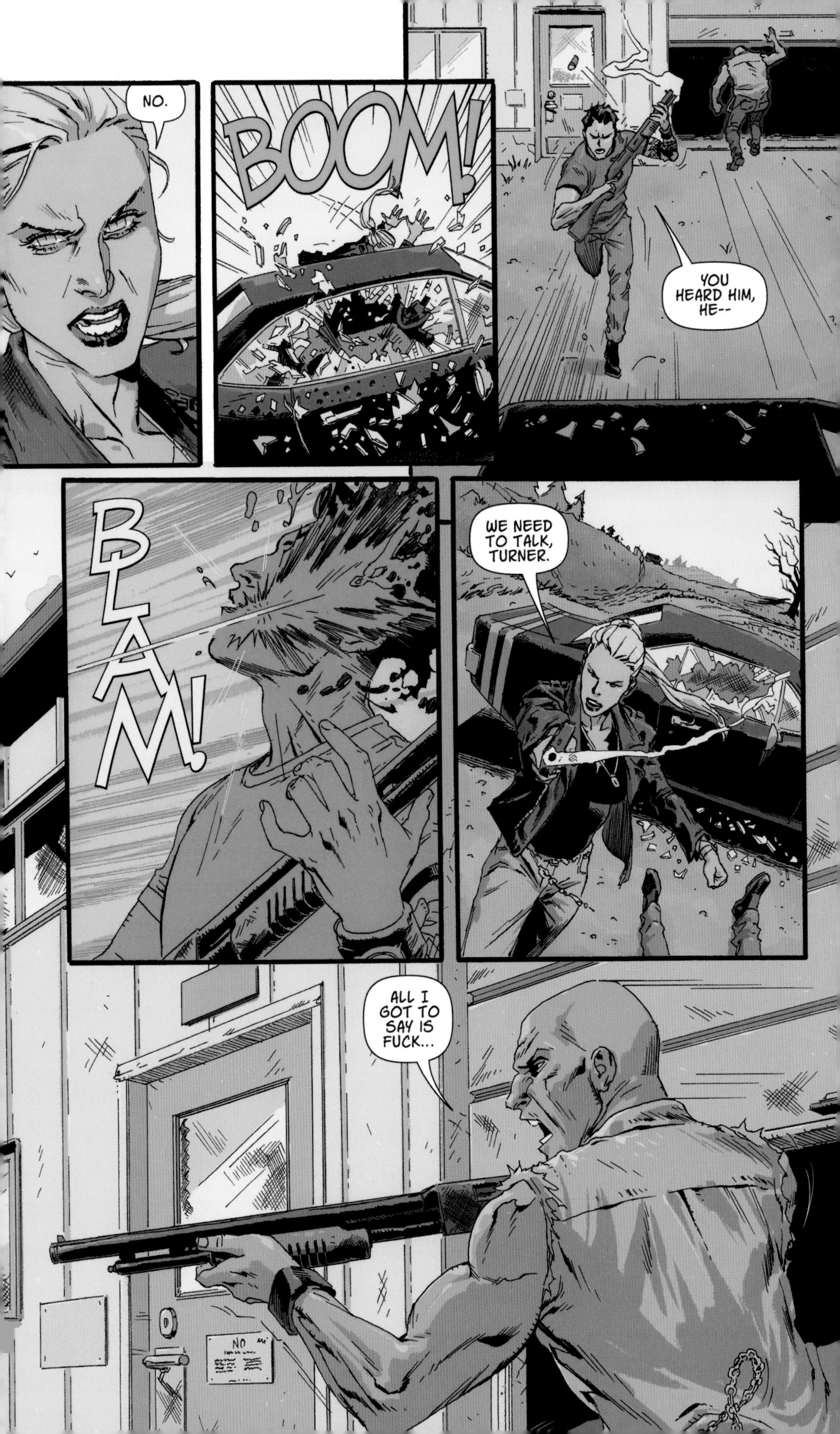
NO.
BOOM!
YOU HEARD HIM, HE--
BLAM!
WE NEED TO TALK, TURNER.
ALL I GOT TO SAY IS FUCK...
NO

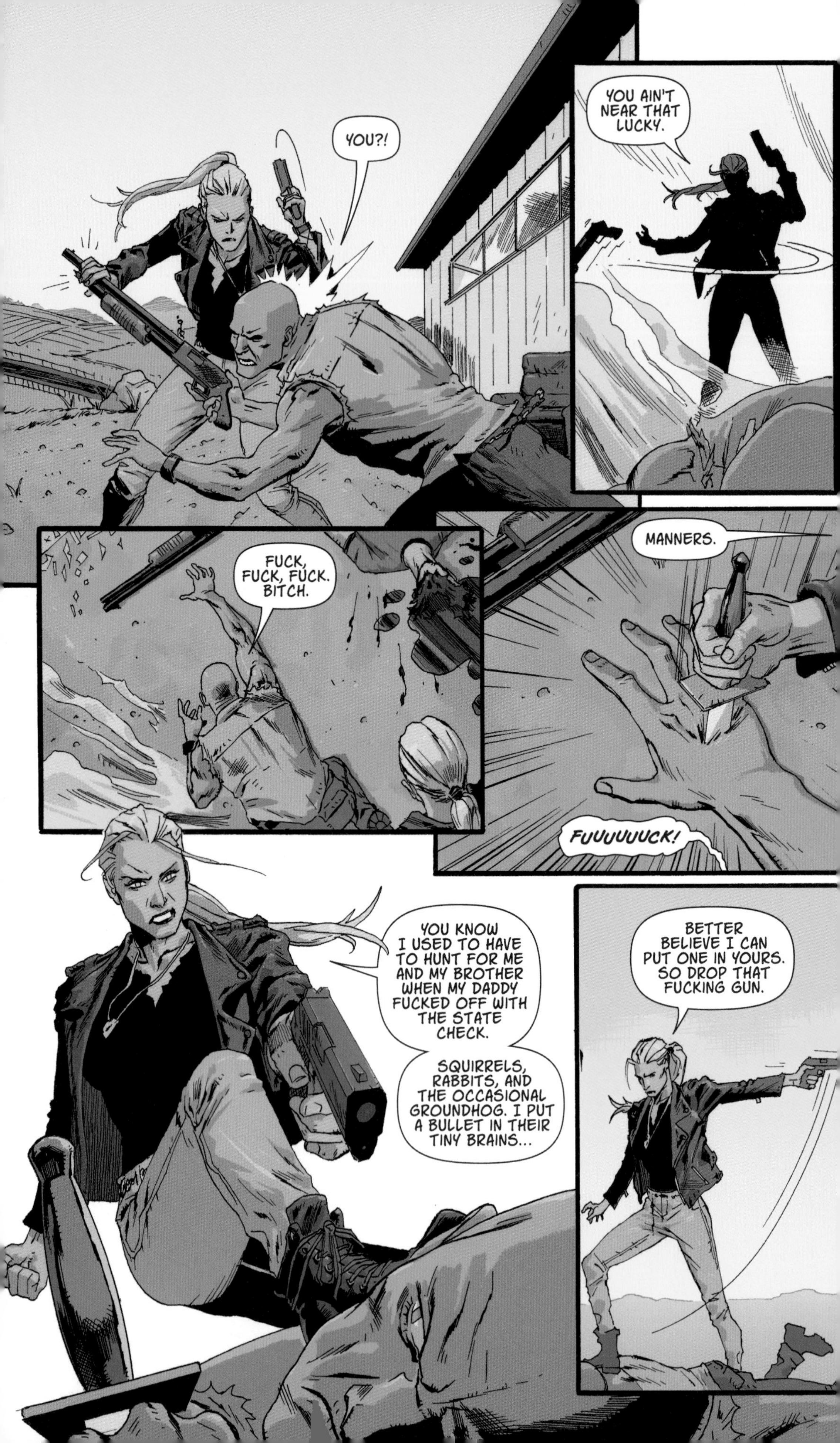
YOU?!
YOU AIN'T NEAR THAT LUCKY.
FUCK, FUCK, FUCK. BITCH.
MANNERS.
FUUUUUUCK!
YOU KNOW I USED TO HAVE TO HUNT FOR ME AND MY BROTHER WHEN MY DADDY FUCKED OFF WITH THE STATE CHECK.
SQUIRRELS, RABBITS, AND THE OCCASIONAL GROUNDHOG. I PUT A BULLET IN THEIR TINY BRAINS...
BETTER BELIEVE I CAN PUT ONE IN YOURS. SO DROP THAT FUCKING GUN.

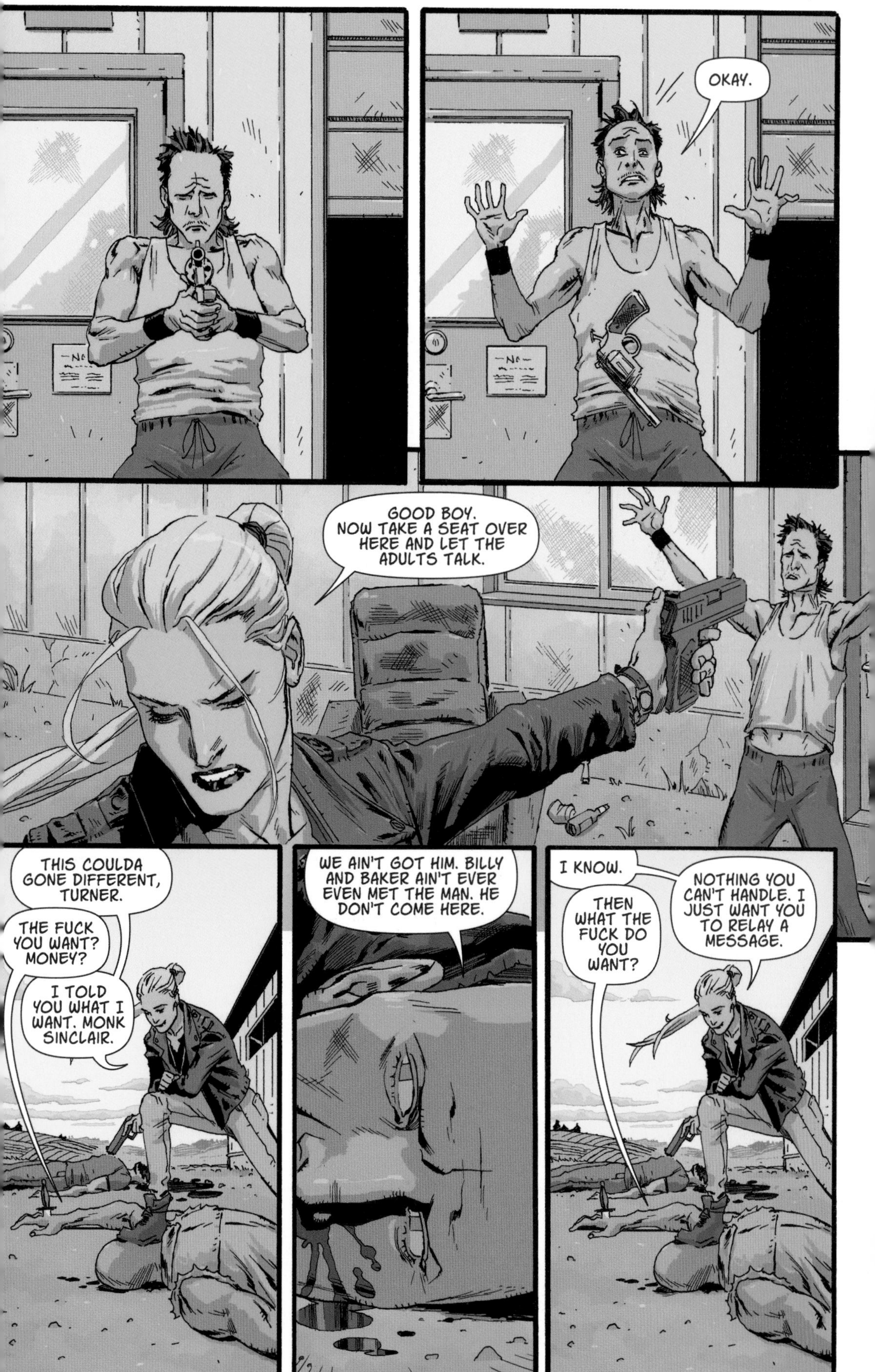
OKAY.
GOOD BOY. NOW TAKE A SEAT OVER HERE AND LET THE ADULTS TALK.
THIS COULDA GONE DIFFERENT, TURNER.
THE FUCK YOU WANT? MONEY?
I TOLD YOU WHAT I WANT. MONK SINCLAIR.
WE AIN'T GOT HIM. BILLY AND BAKER AIN'T EVER EVEN MET THE MAN. HE DON'T COME HERE.
I KNOW.
THEN WHAT THE FUCK DO YOU WANT?
NOTHING YOU CAN'T HANDLE. I JUST WANT YOU TO RELAY A MESSAGE.

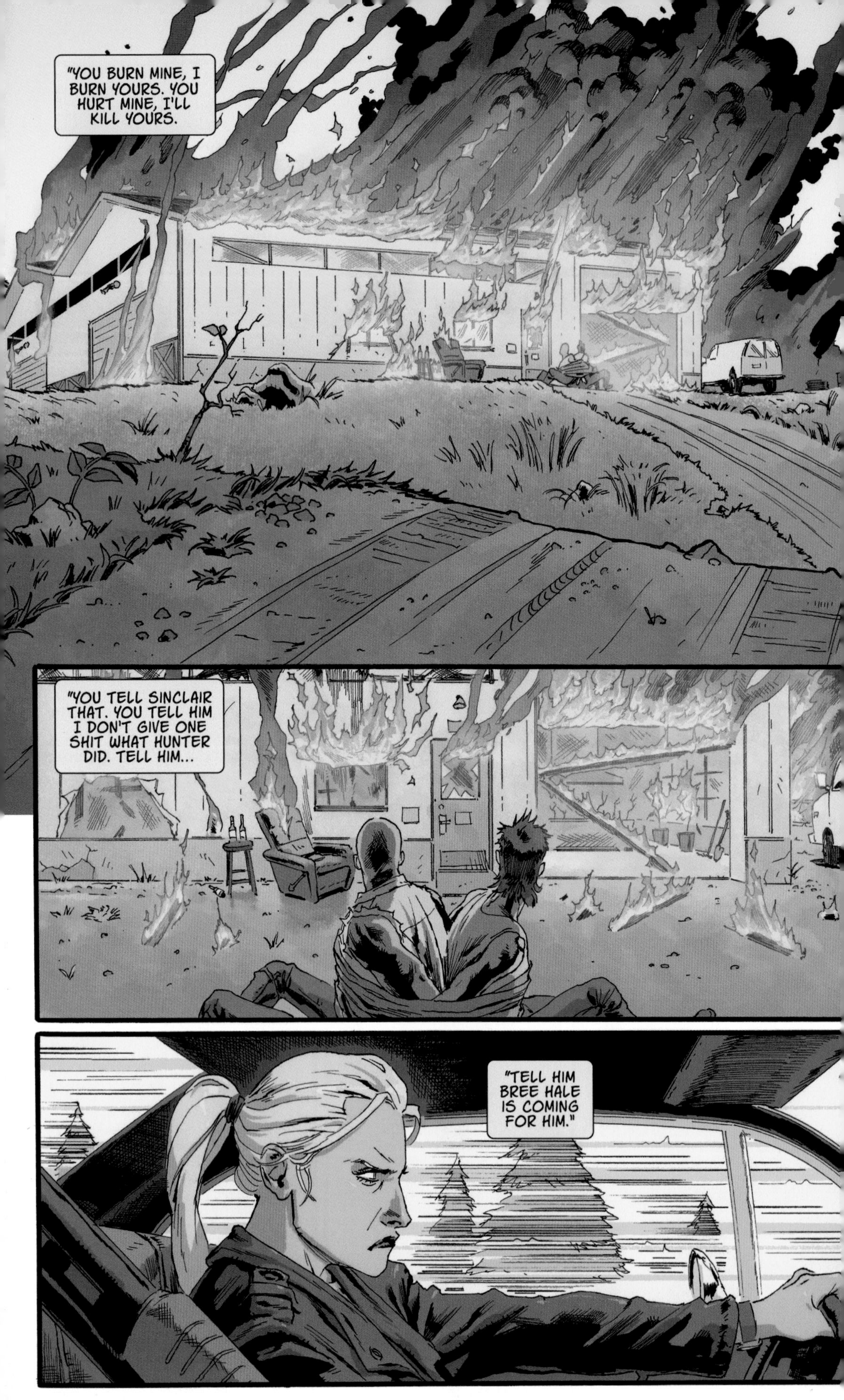
"YOU BURN MINE, I BURN YOURS. YOU HURT MINE, I'LL KILL YOURS.
"YOU TELL SINCLAIR THAT. YOU TELL HIM I DON'T GIVE ONE SHIT WHAT HUNTER DID. TELL HIM...
"TELL HIM BREE HALE IS COMING FOR HIM."

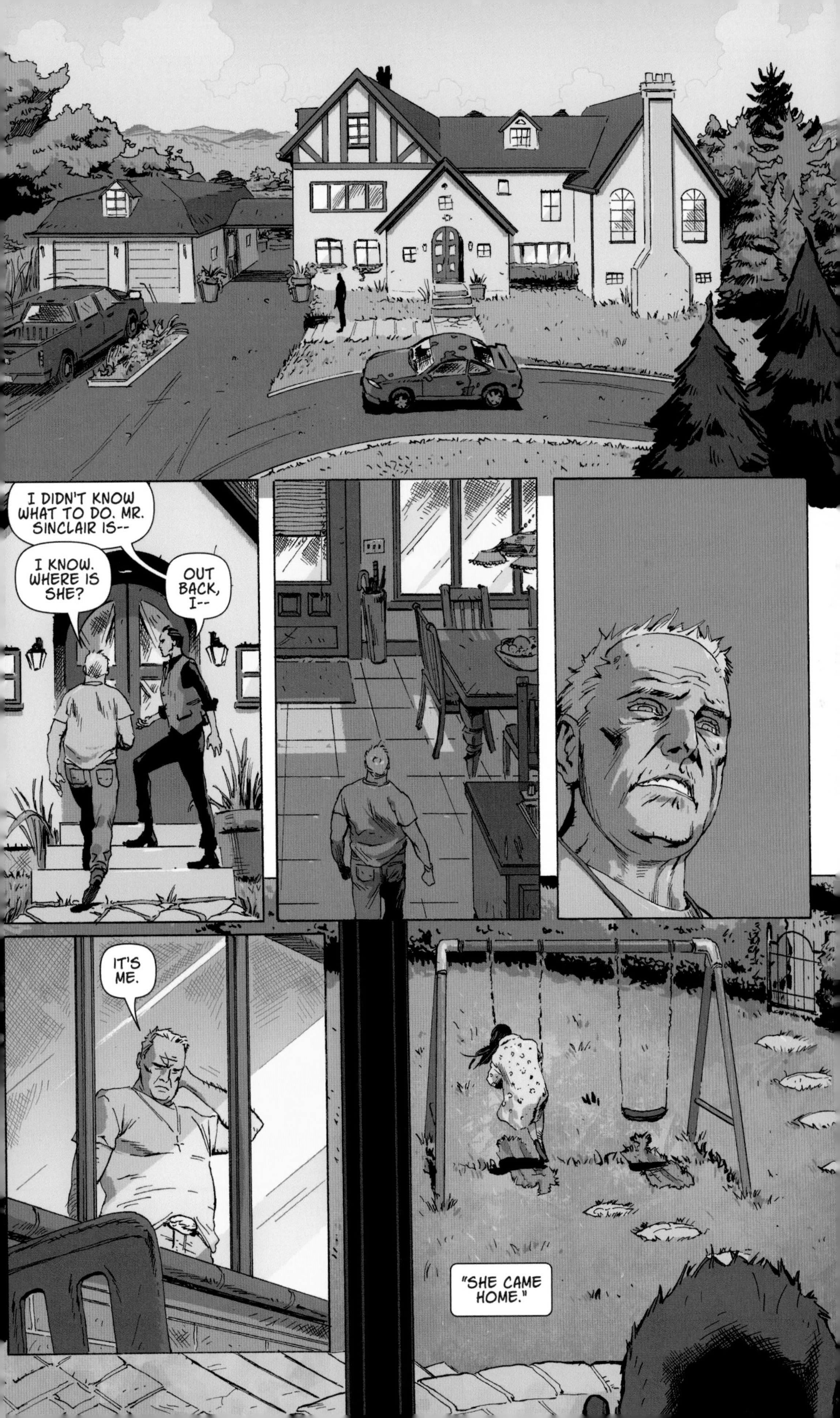
I DIDN'T KNOW WHAT TO DO. MR. SINCLAIR IS--
I KNOW. WHERE IS SHE?
OUT BACK, I--
IT'S ME.
"SHE CAME HOME."

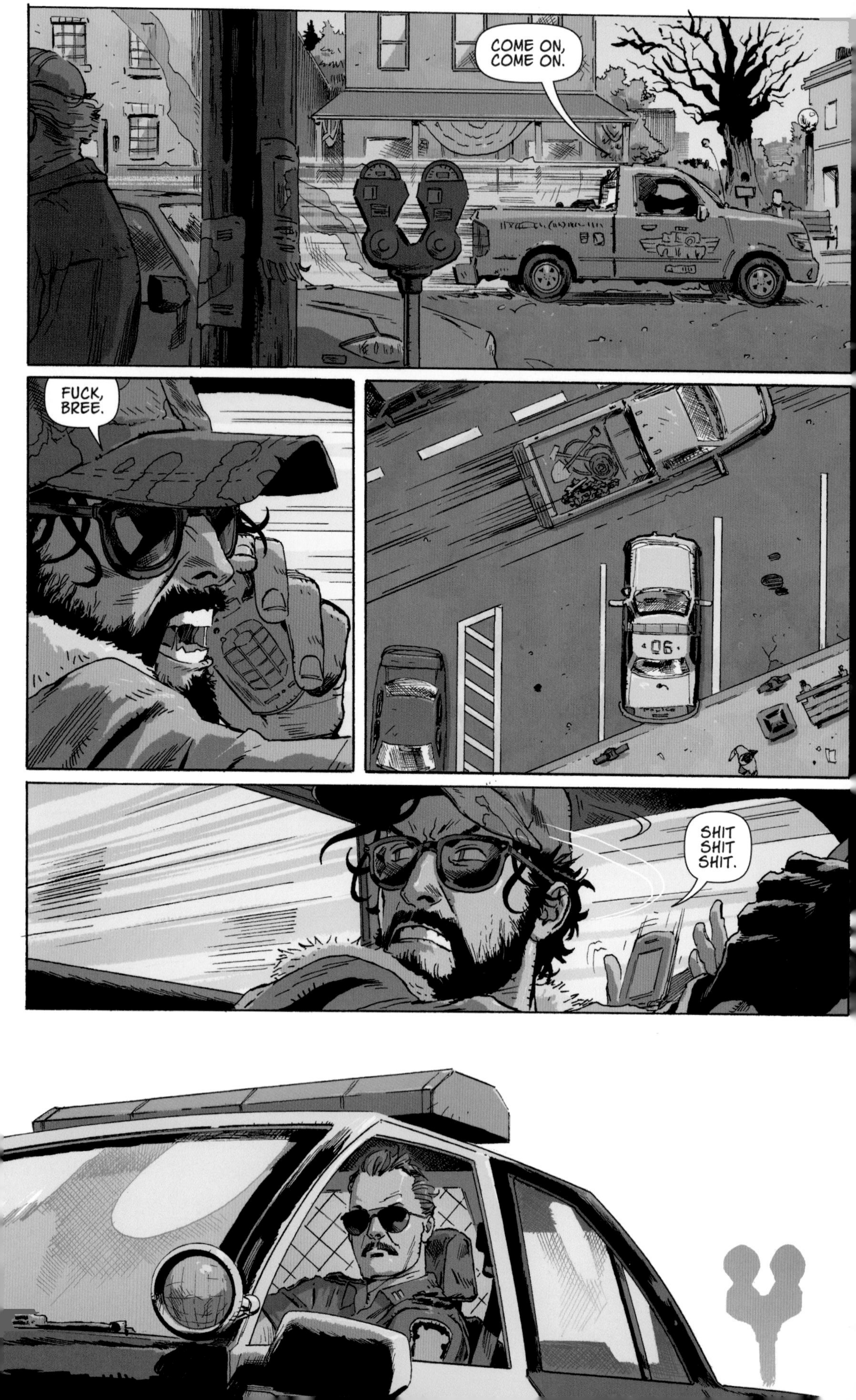
COME ON, COME ON.
FUCK, BREE.
SHIT SHIT SHIT.

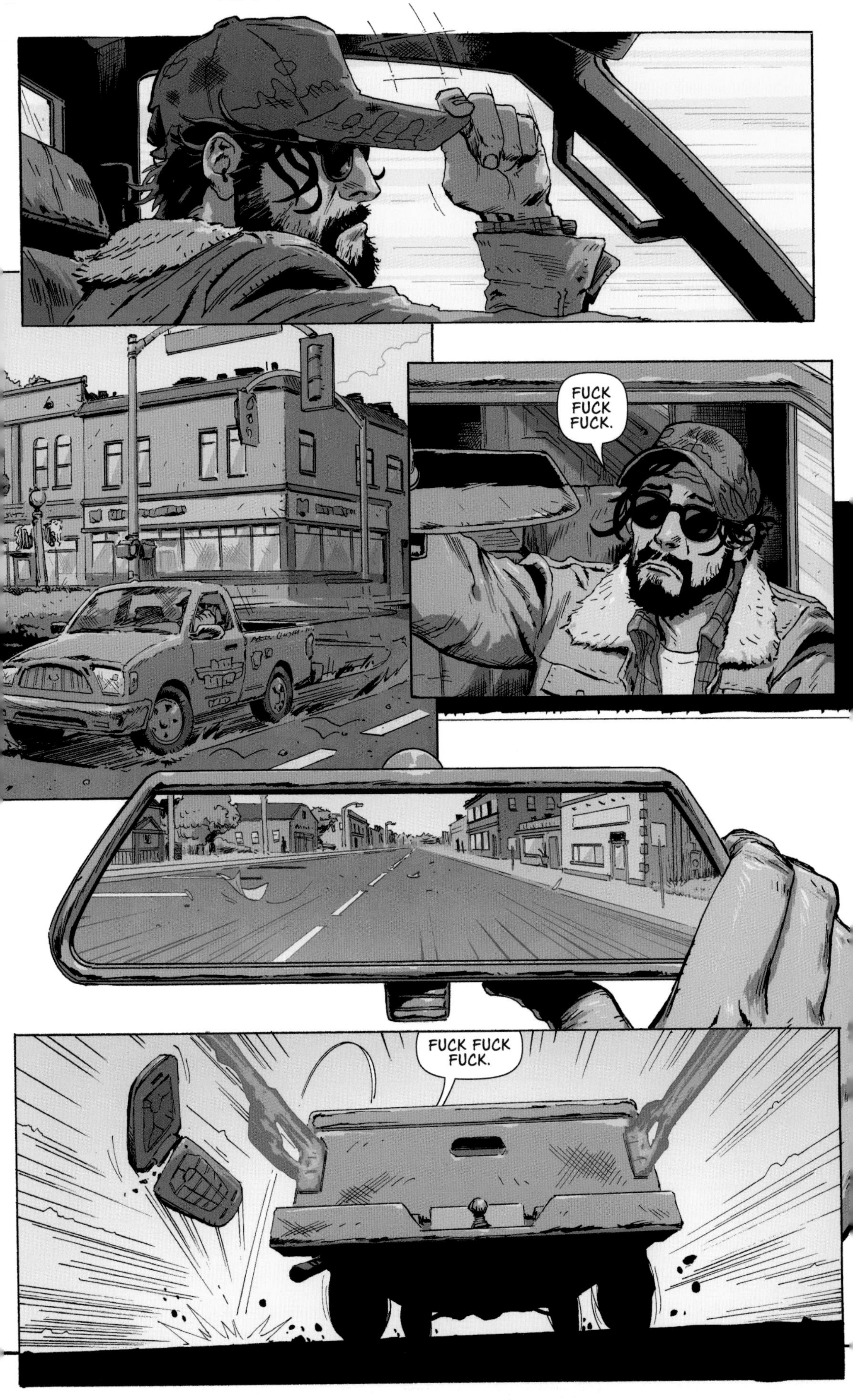
FUCK
FUCK
FUCK.
FUCK FUCK
FUCK.

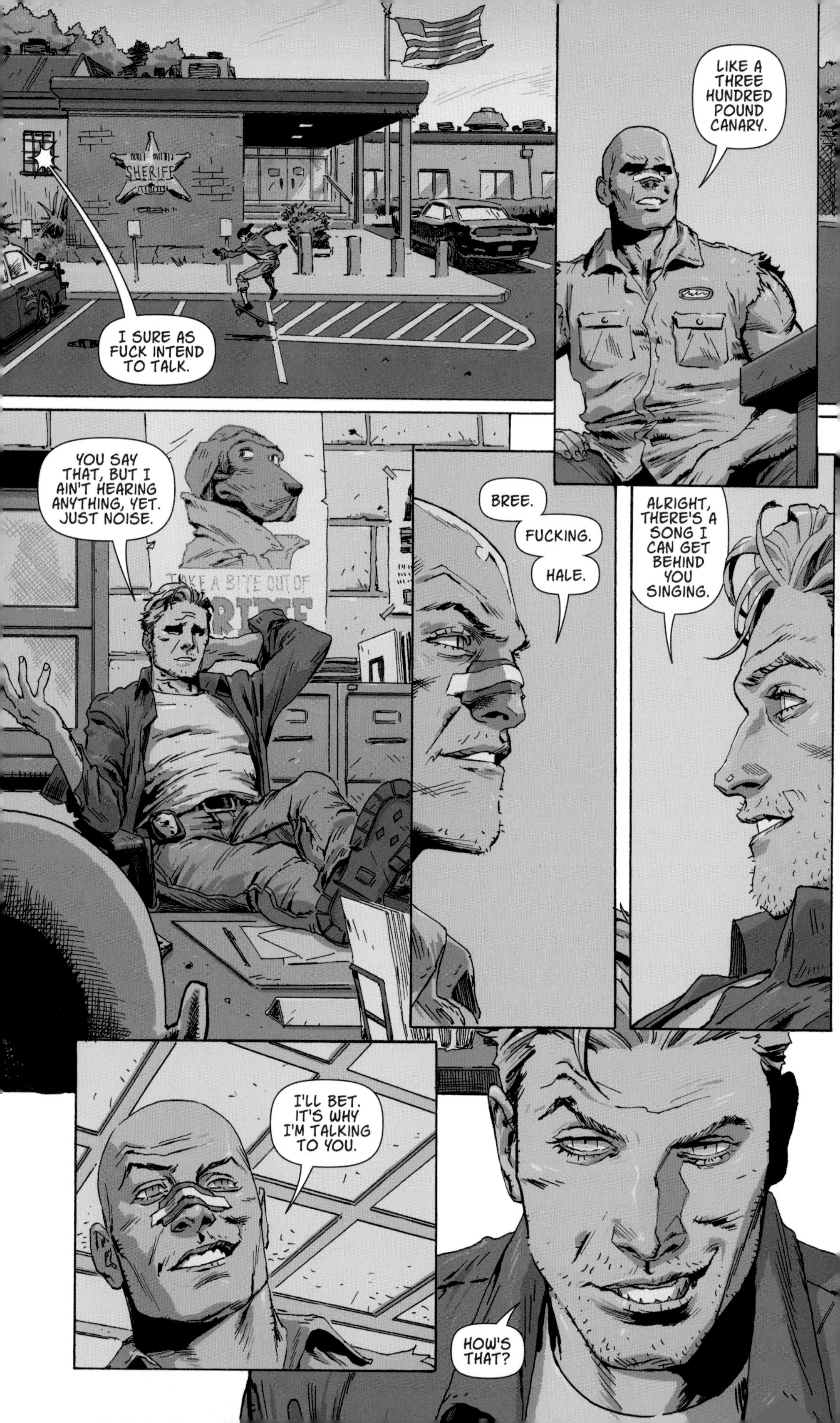
I SURE AS FUCK INTEND TO TALK.
LIKE A THREE HUNDRED POUND CANARY.
YOU SAY THAT, BUT I AIN'T HEARING ANYTHING, YET. JUST NOISE.
SHERIFF
TAKE A BITE OUT OF
BREE.
FUCKING.
HALE.
ALRIGHT, THERE'S A SONG I CAN GET BEHIND YOU SINGING.
I'LL BET. IT'S WHY I'M TALKING TO YOU.
HOW'S THAT?

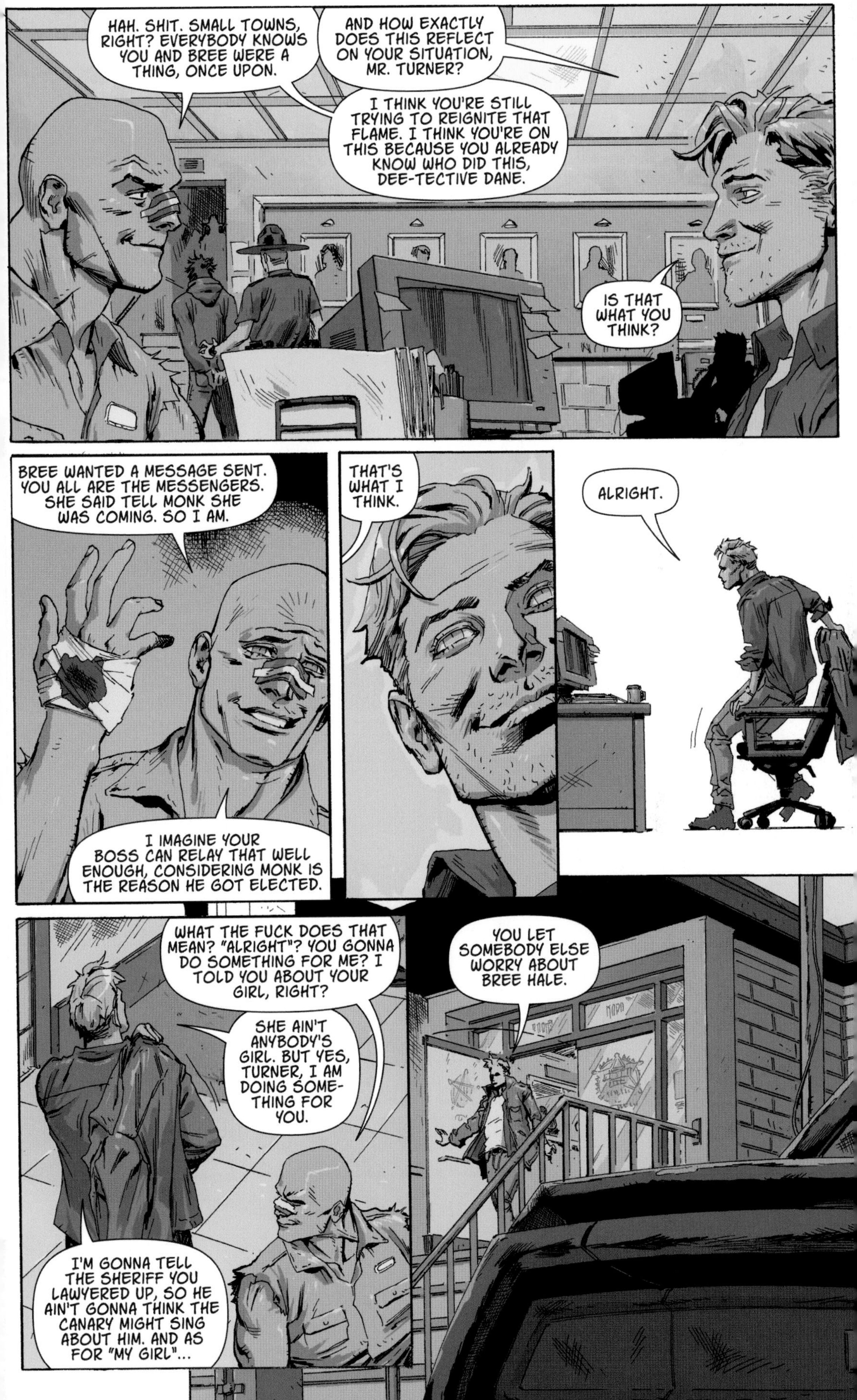
HAH. SHIT. SMALL TOWNS, RIGHT? EVERYBODY KNOWS YOU AND BREE WERE A THING, ONCE UPON.
AND HOW EXACTLY DOES THIS REFLECT ON YOUR SITUATION, MR. TURNER?
I THINK YOU'RE STILL TRYING TO REIGNITE THAT FLAME. I THINK YOU'RE ON THIS BECAUSE YOU ALREADY KNOW WHO DID THIS, DEE-TECTIVE DANE.
IS THAT WHAT YOU THINK?
BREE WANTED A MESSAGE SENT. YOU ALL ARE THE MESSENGERS. SHE SAID TELL MONK SHE WAS COMING. SO I AM.
I IMAGINE YOUR BOSS CAN RELAY THAT WELL ENOUGH, CONSIDERING MONK IS THE REASON HE GOT ELECTED.
THAT'S WHAT I THINK.
ALRIGHT.
WHAT THE FUCK DOES THAT MEAN? "ALRIGHT"? YOU GONNA DO SOMETHING FOR ME? I TOLD YOU ABOUT YOUR GIRL, RIGHT?
SHE AIN'T ANYBODY'S GIRL. BUT YES, TURNER, I AM DOING SOME-THING FOR YOU.
I'M GONNA TELL THE SHERIFF YOU LAWYERED UP, SO HE AIN'T GONNA THINK THE CANARY MIGHT SING ABOUT HIM. AND AS FOR "MY GIRL"...
YOU LET SOMEBODY ELSE WORRY ABOUT BREE HALE.

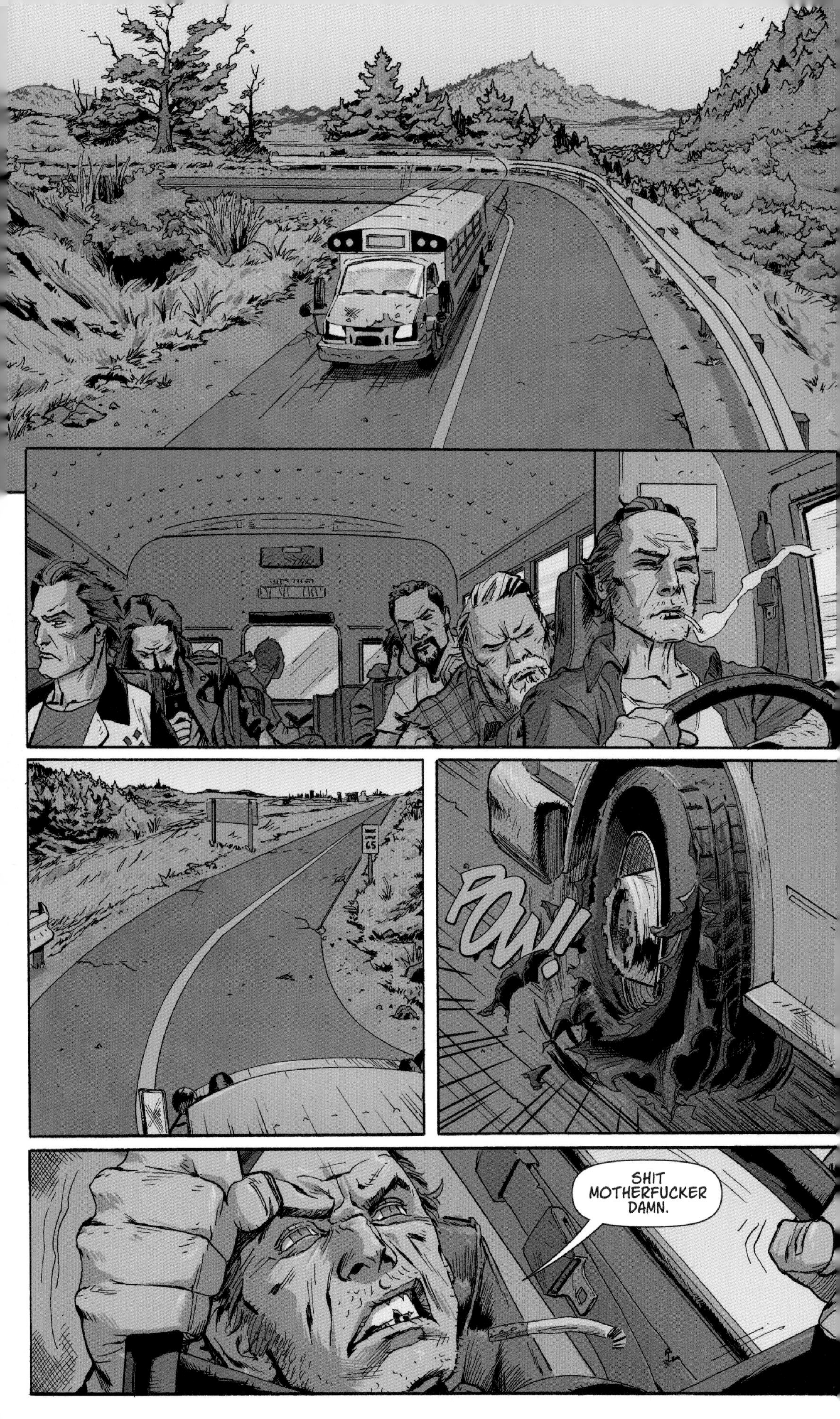
POW!
SHIT MOTHERFUCKER DAMN.

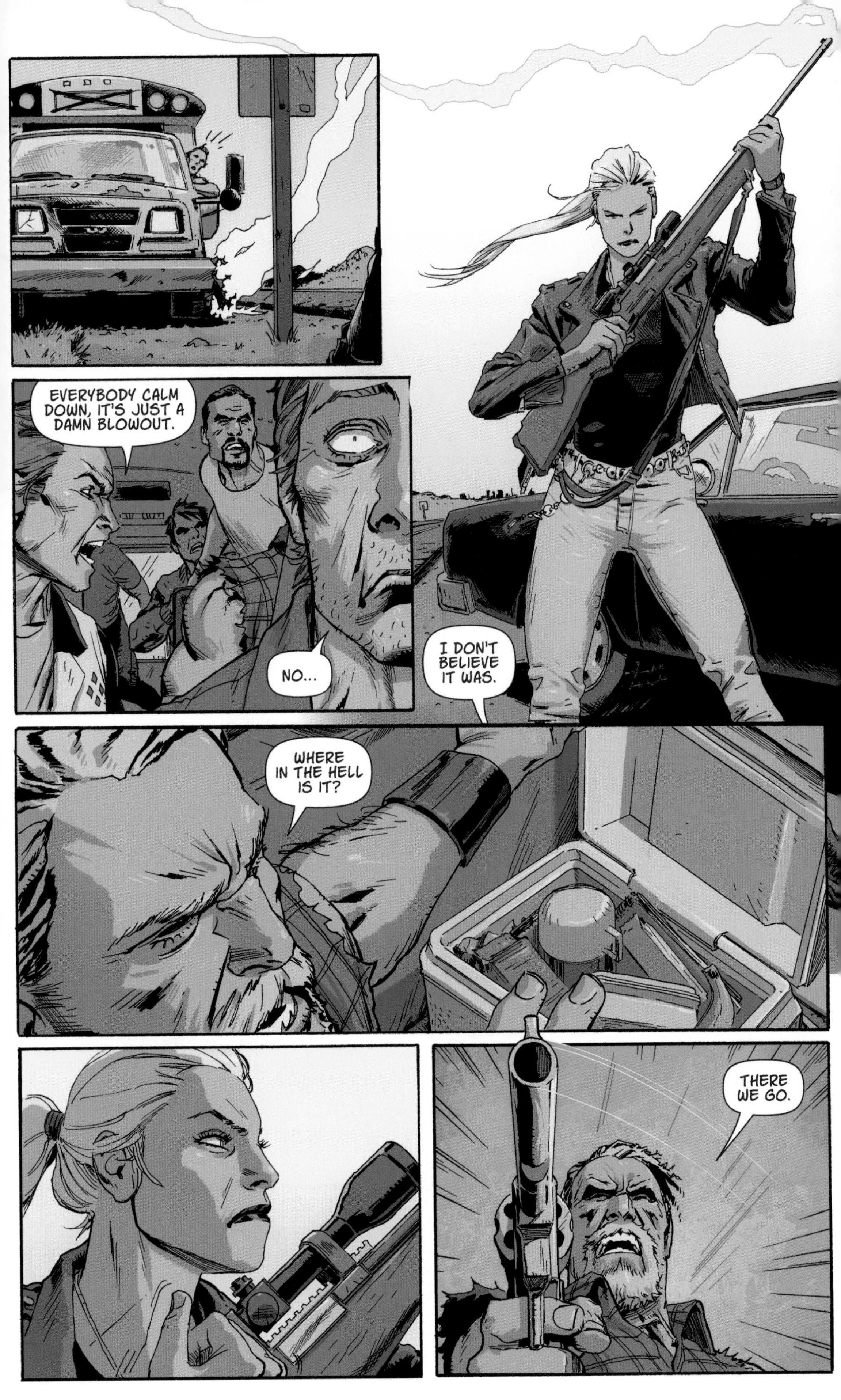
EVERYBODY CALM DOWN, IT'S JUST A DAMN BLOWOUT.
NO...
I DON'T BELIEVE IT WAS.
WHERE IN THE HELL IS IT?
THERE WE GO.

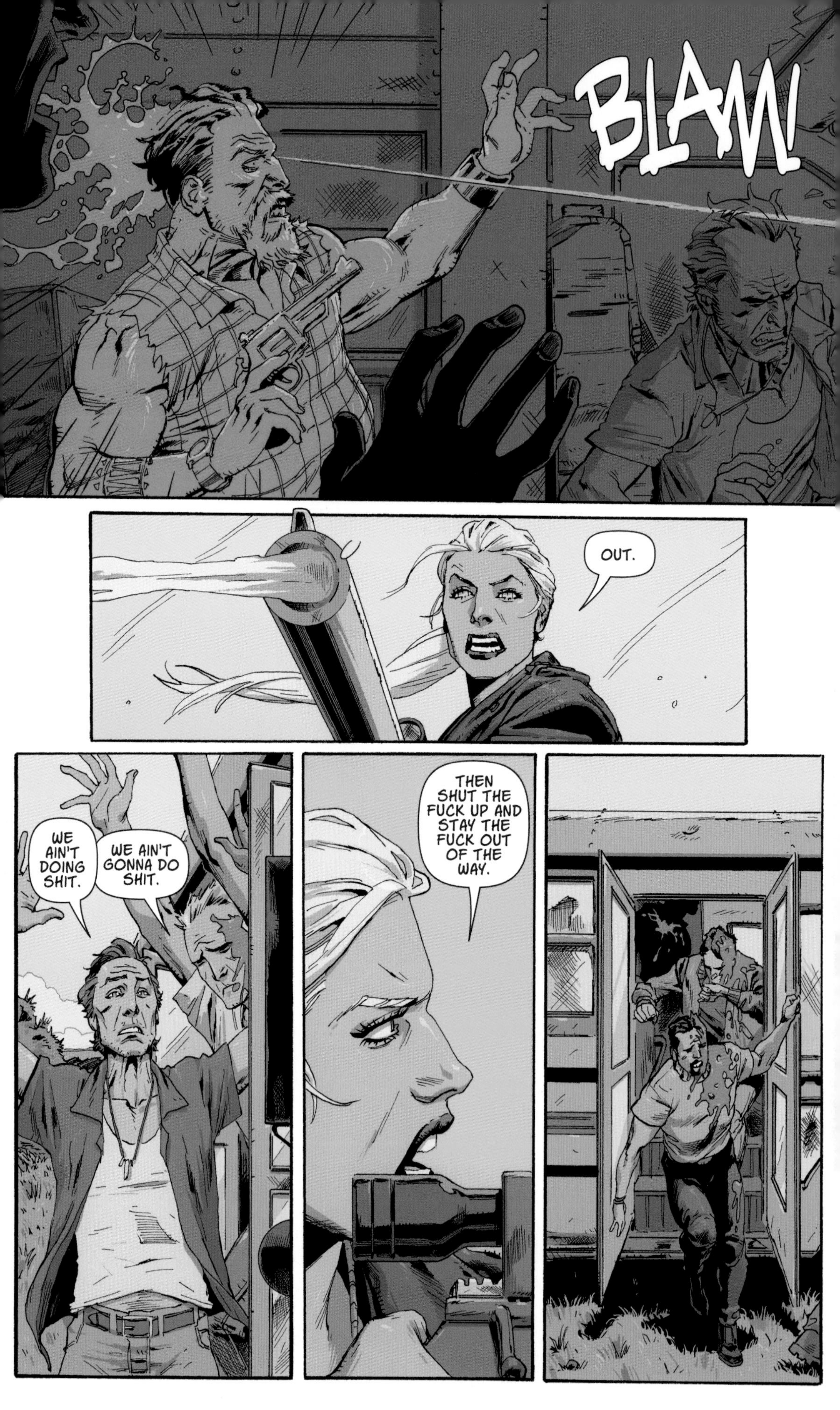
BLAM!
OUT.
WE AIN'T DOING SHIT.
WE AIN'T GONNA DO SHIT.
THEN SHUT THE FUCK UP AND STAY THE FUCK OUT OF THE WAY.

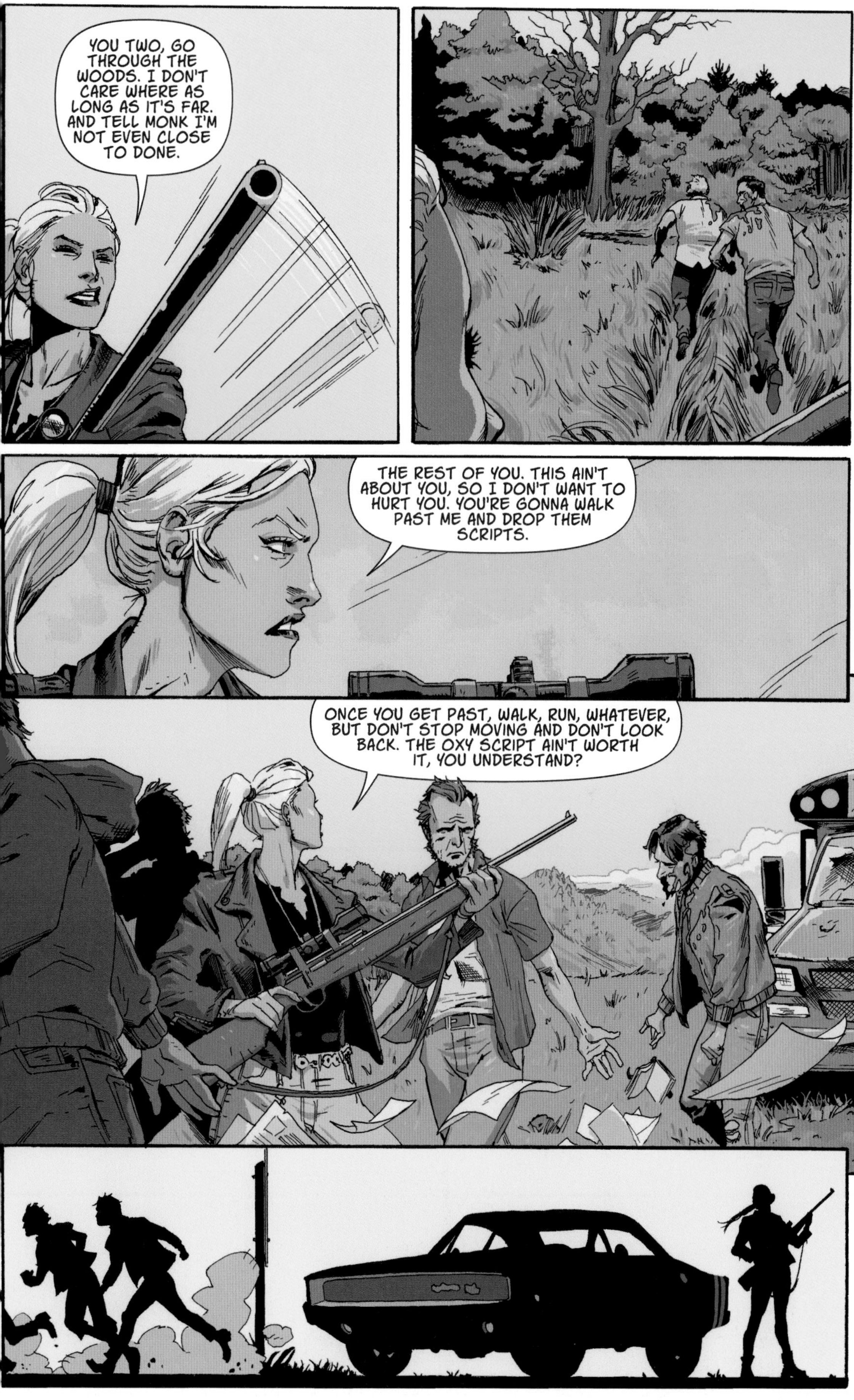
YOU TWO, GO THROUGH THE WOODS. I DON'T CARE WHERE AS LONG AS IT'S FAR. AND TELL MONK I'M NOT EVEN CLOSE TO DONE.
THE REST OF YOU. THIS AIN'T ABOUT YOU, SO I DON'T WANT TO HURT YOU. YOU'RE GONNA WALK PAST ME AND DROP THEM SCRIPTS.
ONCE YOU GET PAST, WALK, RUN, WHATEVER, BUT DON'T STOP MOVING AND DON'T LOOK BACK. THE OXY SCRIPT AIN'T WORTH IT, YOU UNDERSTAND?

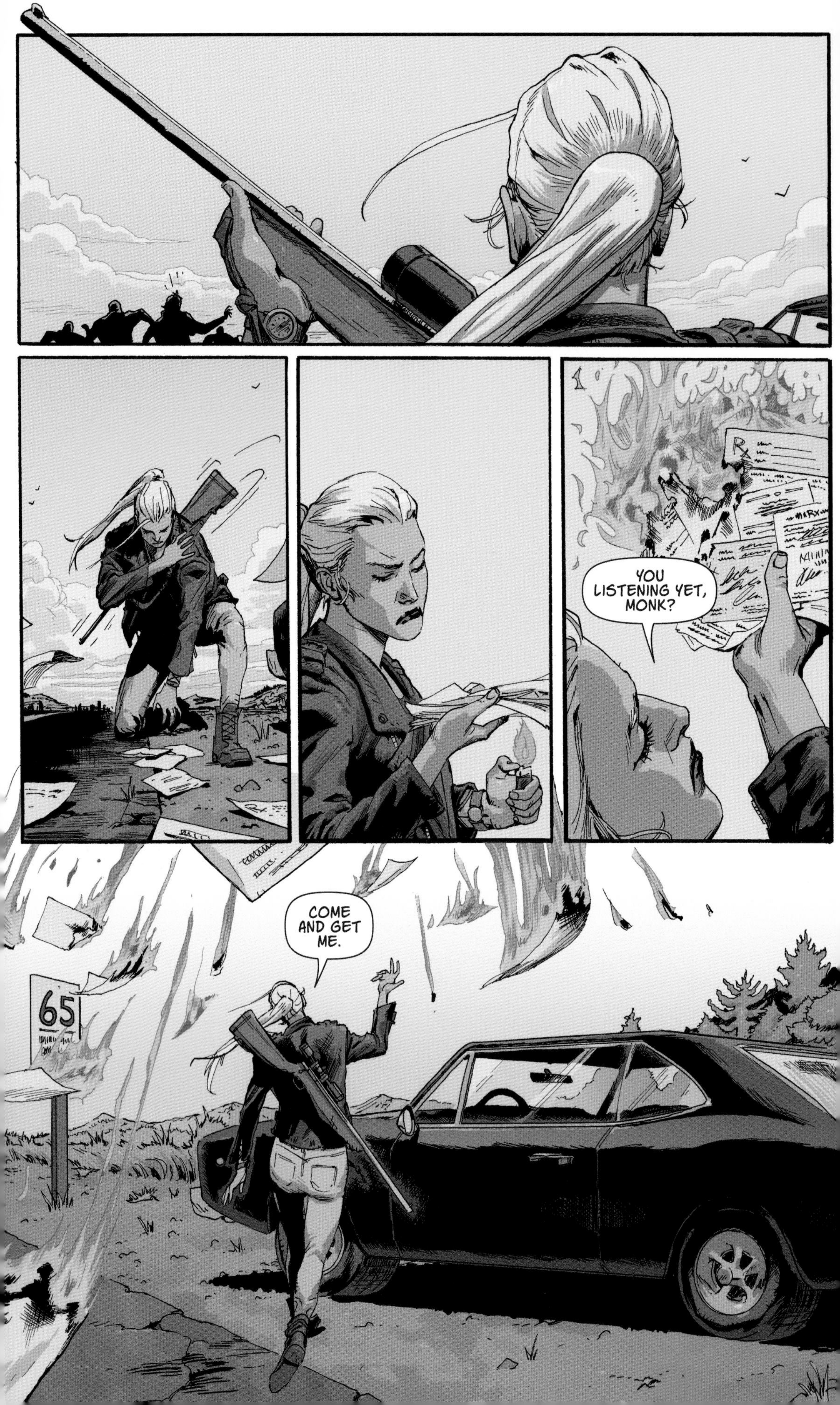
YOU LISTENING YET, MONK?
COME AND GET ME.
65

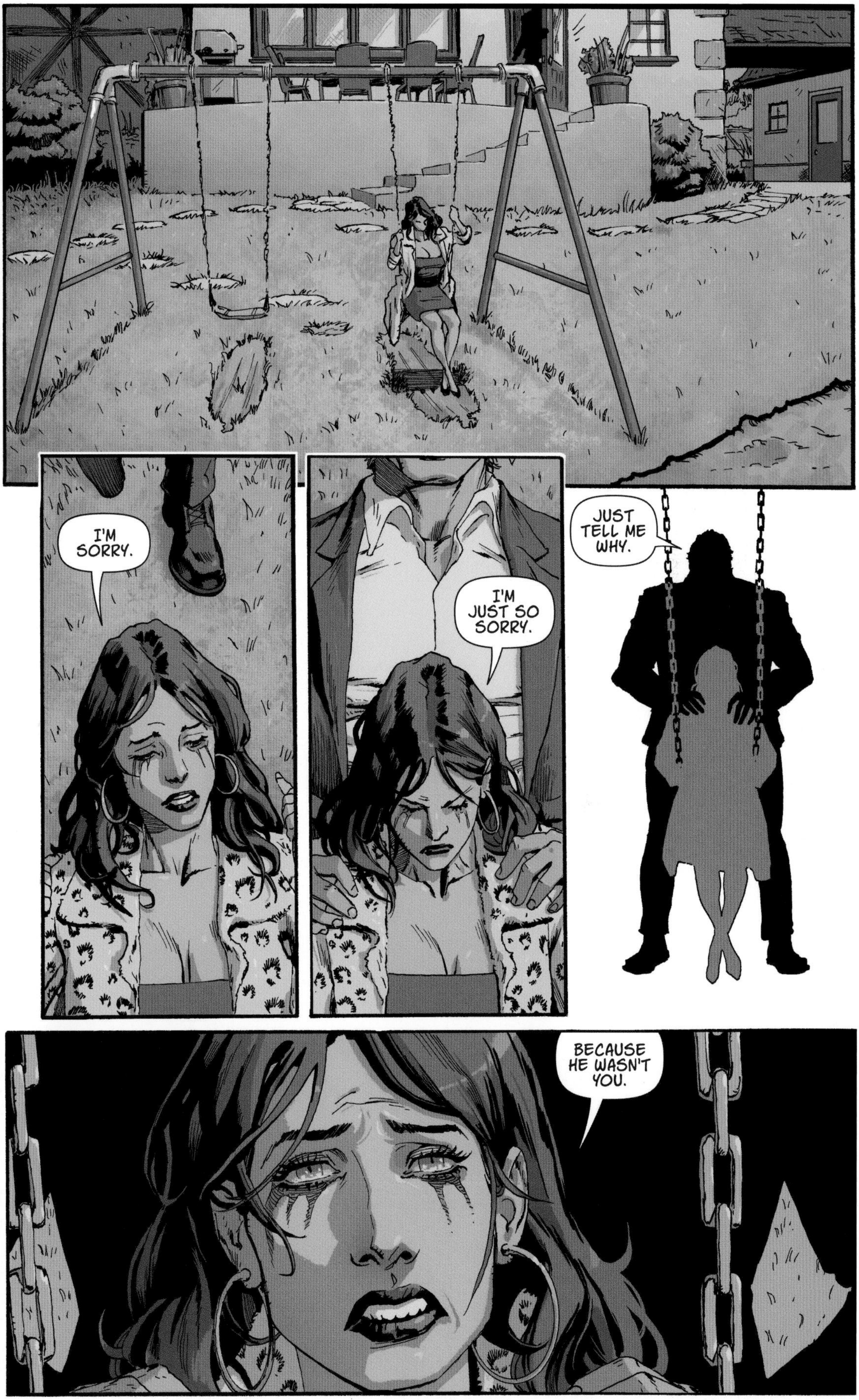
I'M SORRY.
I'M JUST SO SORRY.
JUST TELL ME WHY.
BECAUSE HE WASN'T YOU.

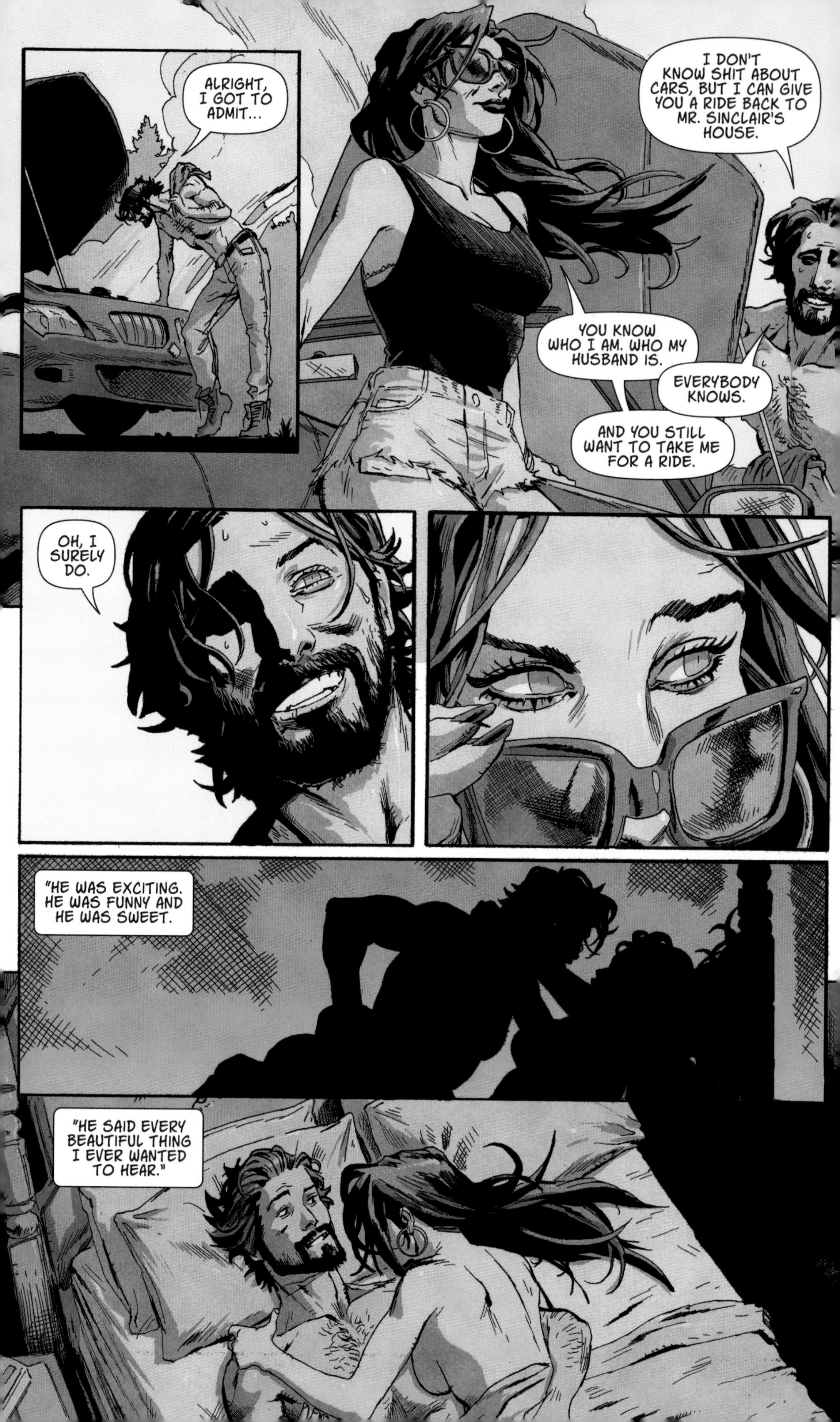
ALRIGHT, I GOT TO ADMIT...
I DON'T KNOW SHIT ABOUT CARS, BUT I CAN GIVE YOU A RIDE BACK TO MR. SINCLAIR'S HOUSE.
YOU KNOW WHO I AM. WHO MY HUSBAND IS.
EVERYBODY KNOWS.
AND YOU STILL WANT TO TAKE ME FOR A RIDE.
OH, I SURELY DO.
"HE WAS EXCITING. HE WAS FUNNY AND HE WAS SWEET.
"HE SAID EVERY BEAUTIFUL THING I EVER WANTED TO HEAR."

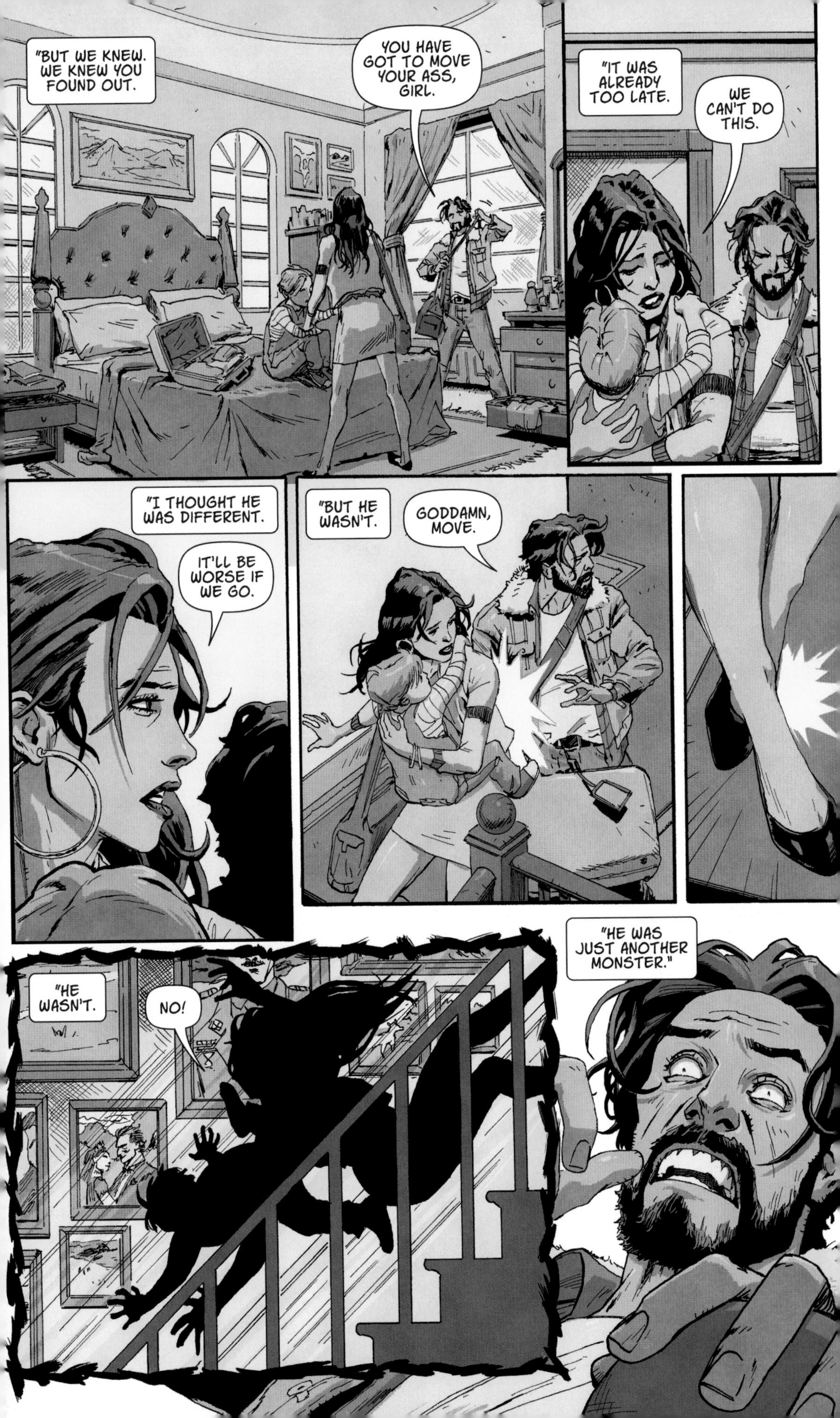
"BUT WE KNEW. WE KNEW YOU FOUND OUT.
YOU HAVE GOT TO MOVE YOUR ASS, GIRL.
"IT WAS ALREADY TOO LATE.
WE CAN'T DO THIS.
"I THOUGHT HE WAS DIFFERENT.
IT'LL BE WORSE IF WE GO.
"BUT HE WASN'T.
GODDAMN, MOVE.
"HE WASN'T.
NO!
"HE WAS JUST ANOTHER MONSTER."

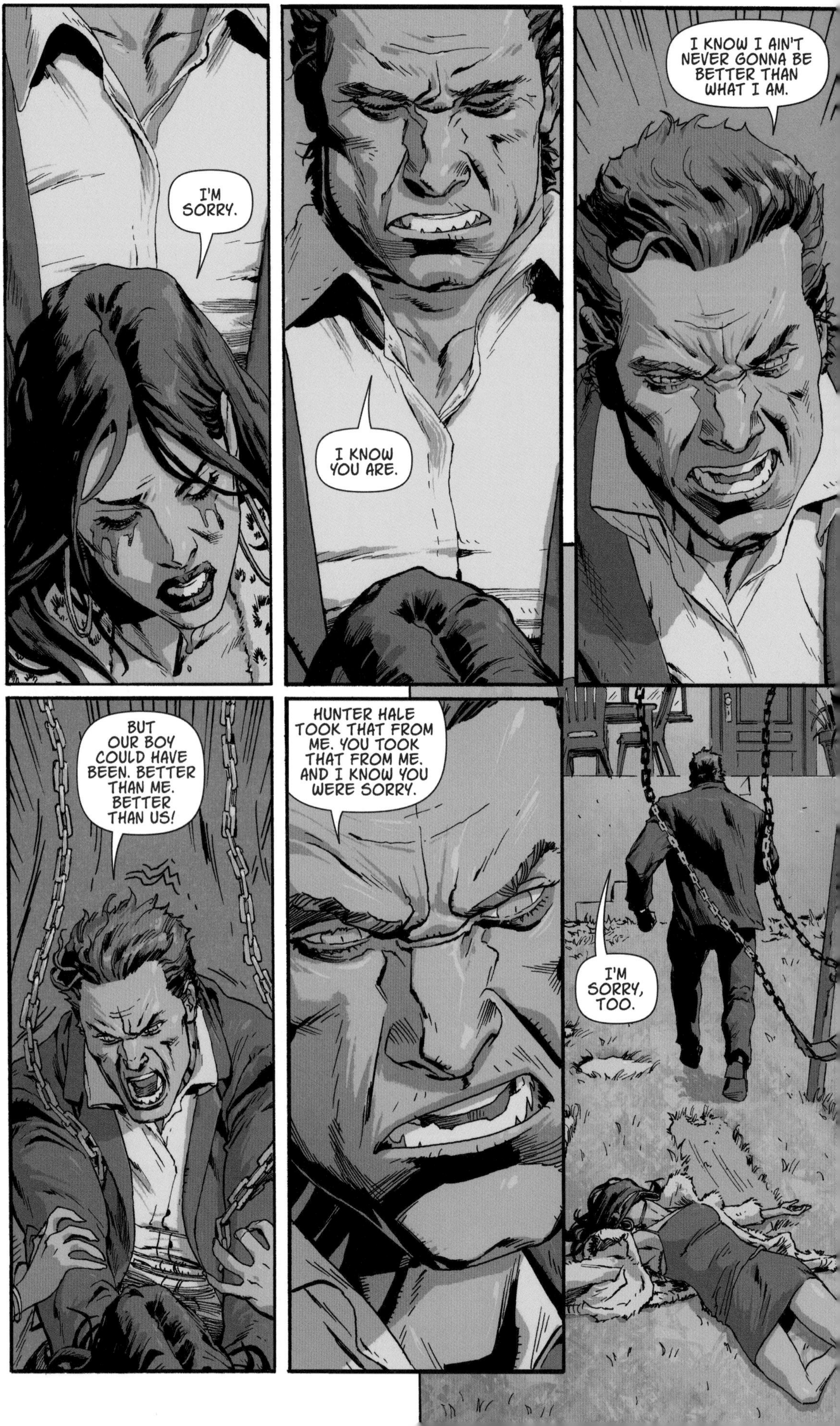
I'M SORRY.
I KNOW YOU ARE.
I KNOW I AIN'T NEVER GONNA BE BETTER THAN WHAT I AM.
BUT OUR BOY COULD HAVE BEEN. BETTER THAN ME. BETTER THAN US!
HUNTER HALE TOOK THAT FROM ME. YOU TOOK THAT FROM ME. AND I KNOW YOU WERE SORRY.
I'M SORRY, TOO.

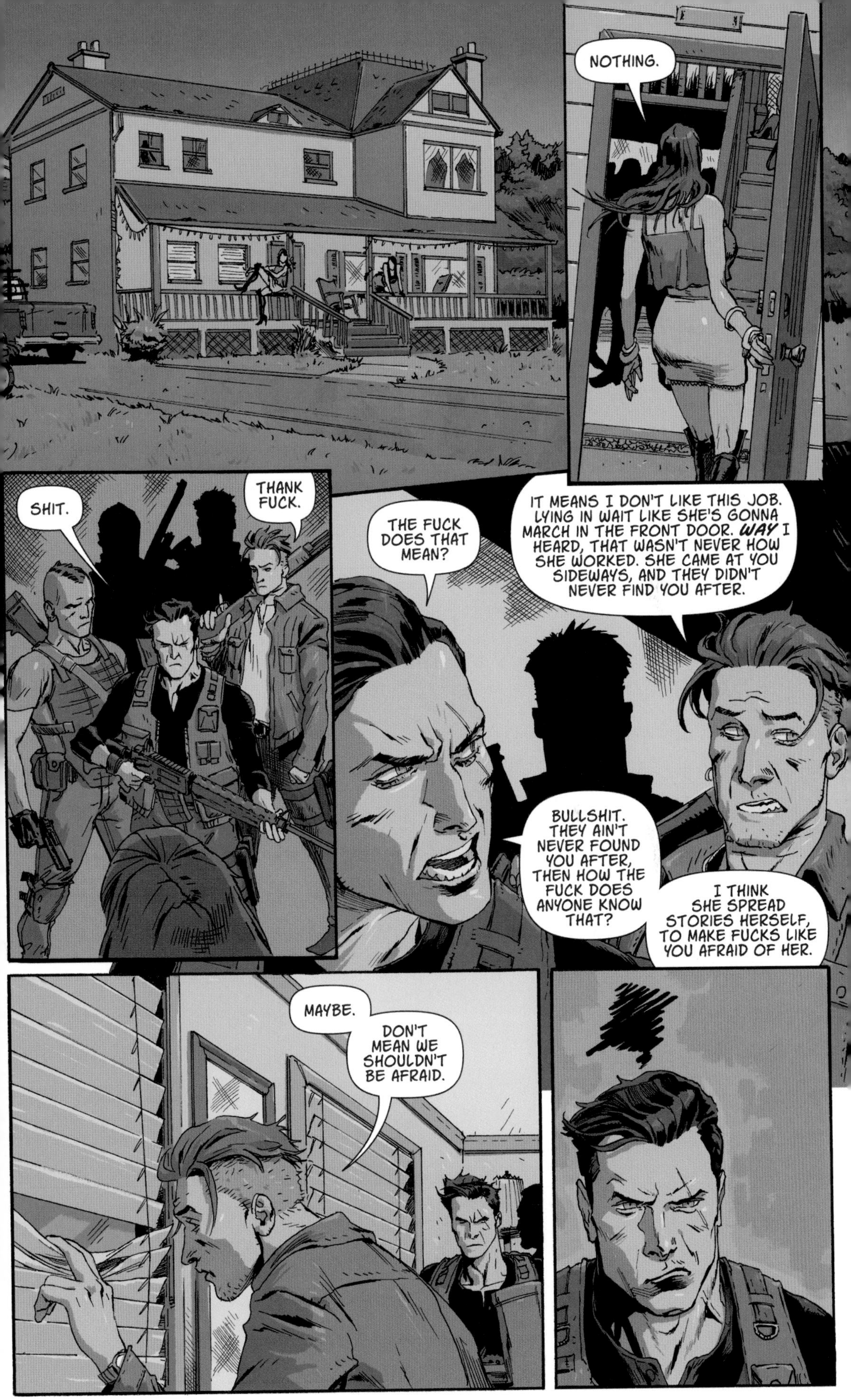
NOTHING.
SHIT.
THANK FUCK.
THE FUCK DOES THAT MEAN?
IT MEANS I DON'T LIKE THIS JOB. LYING IN WAIT LIKE SHE'S GONNA MARCH IN THE FRONT DOOR. WAY I HEARD, THAT WASN'T NEVER HOW SHE WORKED. SHE CAME AT YOU SIDEWAYS, AND THEY DIDN'T NEVER FIND YOU AFTER.
BULLSHIT. THEY AIN'T NEVER FOUND YOU AFTER, THEN HOW THE FUCK DOES ANYONE KNOW THAT?
I THINK SHE SPREAD STORIES HERSELF, TO MAKE FUCKS LIKE YOU AFRAID OF HER.
MAYBE.
DON'T MEAN WE SHOULDN'T BE AFRAID.

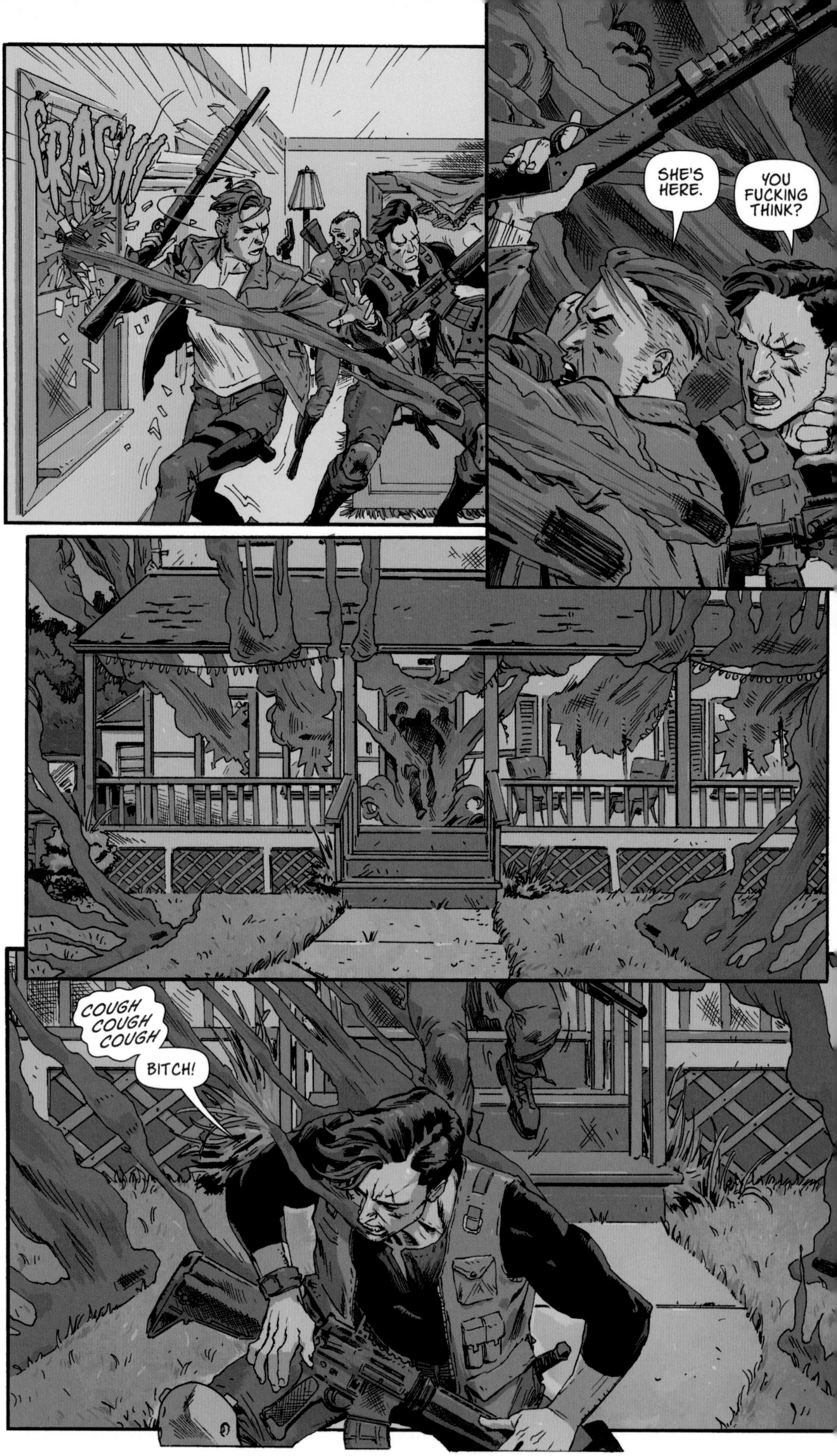
CRASH!
SHE'S HERE.
YOU FUCKING THINK?
COUGH COUGH COUGH
BITCH!

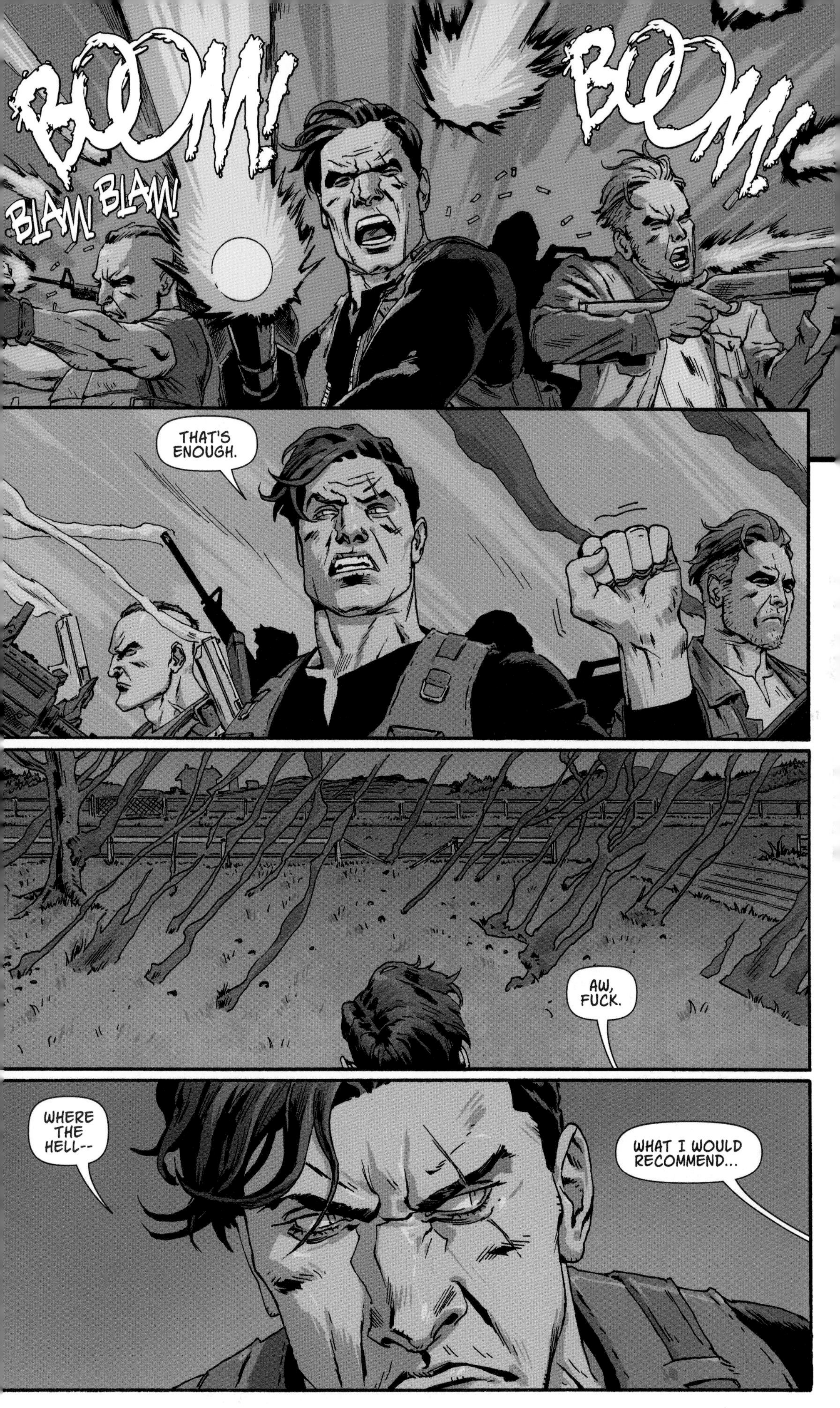
BOOM!
BLAM! BLAM!
BOOM!
THAT'S ENOUGH.
AW, FUCK.
WHERE THE HELL--
WHAT I WOULD RECOMMEND...

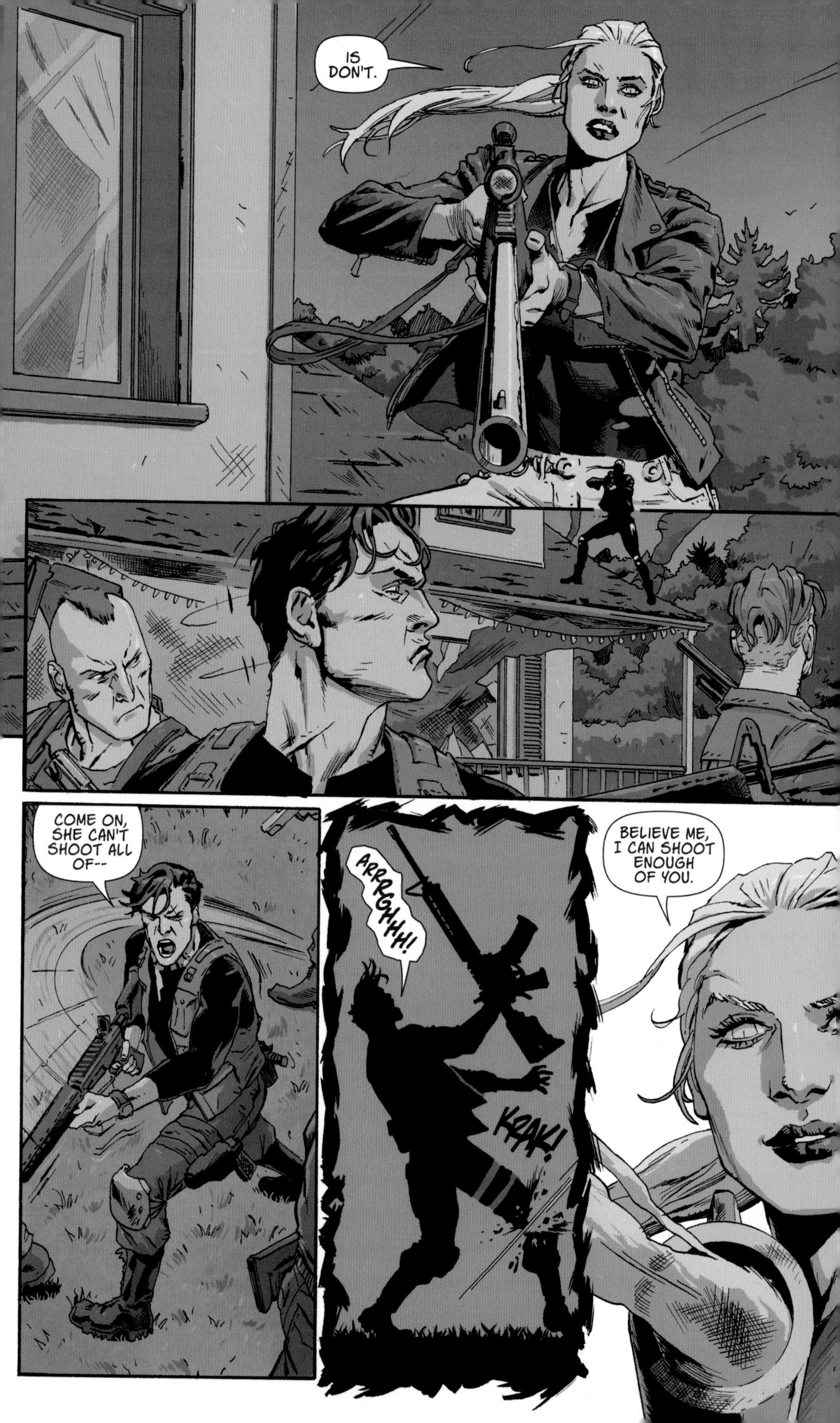
IS DON'T.
COME ON, SHE CAN'T SHOOT ALL OF--
ARRRGHHH!
KRAK!
BELIEVE ME, I CAN SHOOT ENOUGH OF YOU.

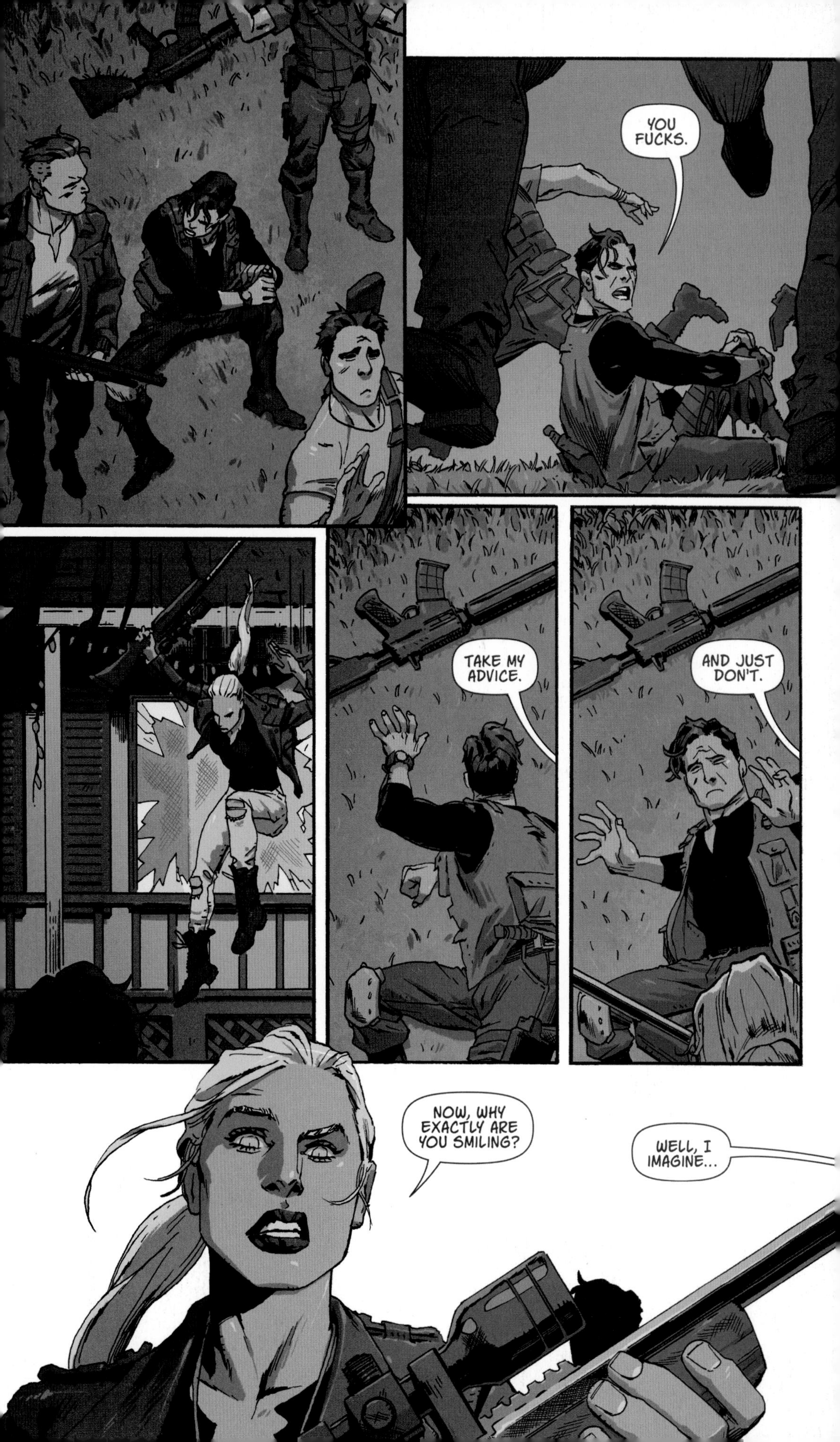
YOU FUCKS.
TAKE MY ADVICE.
AND JUST DON'T.
NOW, WHY EXACTLY ARE YOU SMILING?
WELL, I IMAGINE...

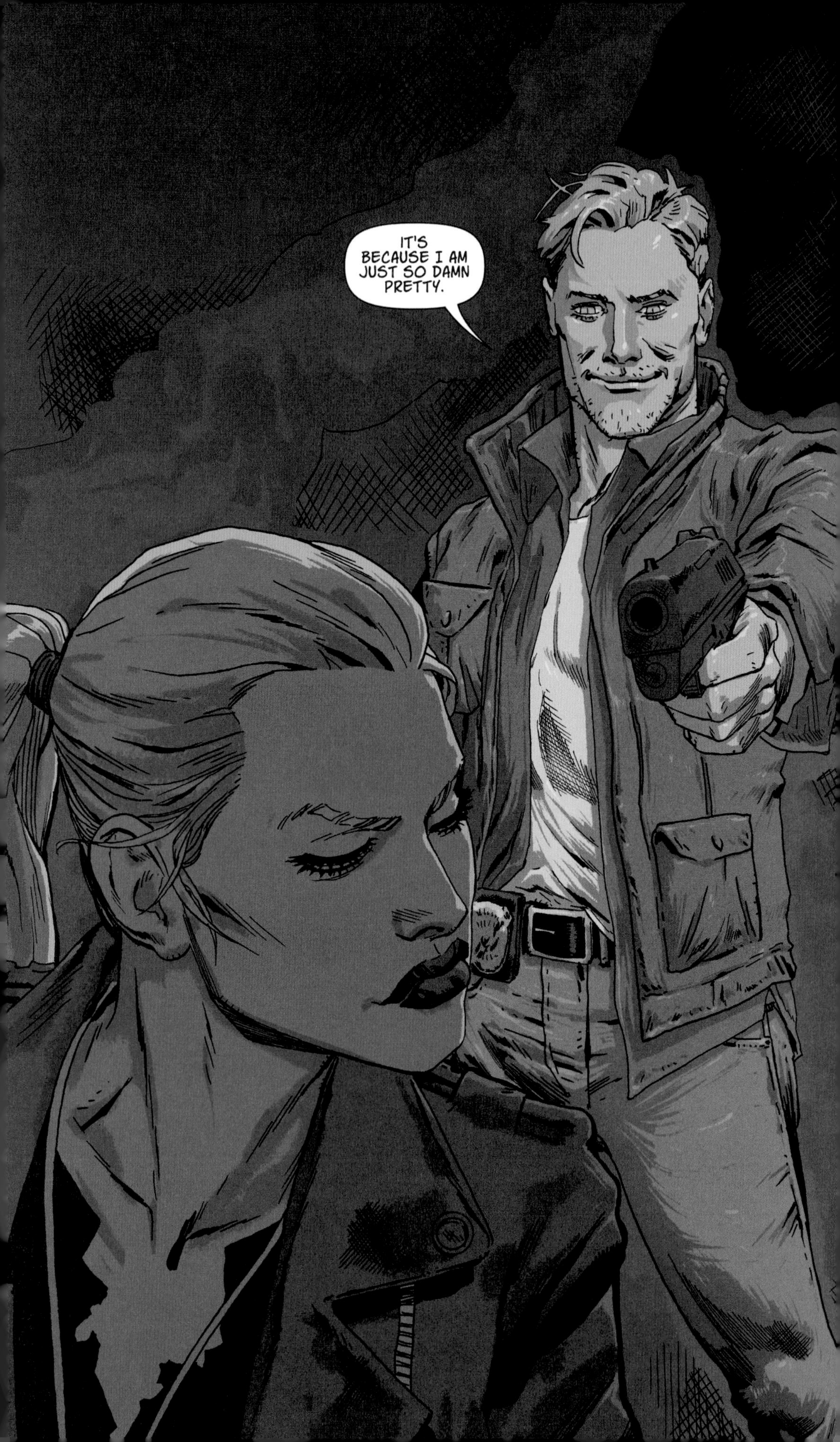
IT'S BECAUSE I AM JUST SO DAMN PRETTY.

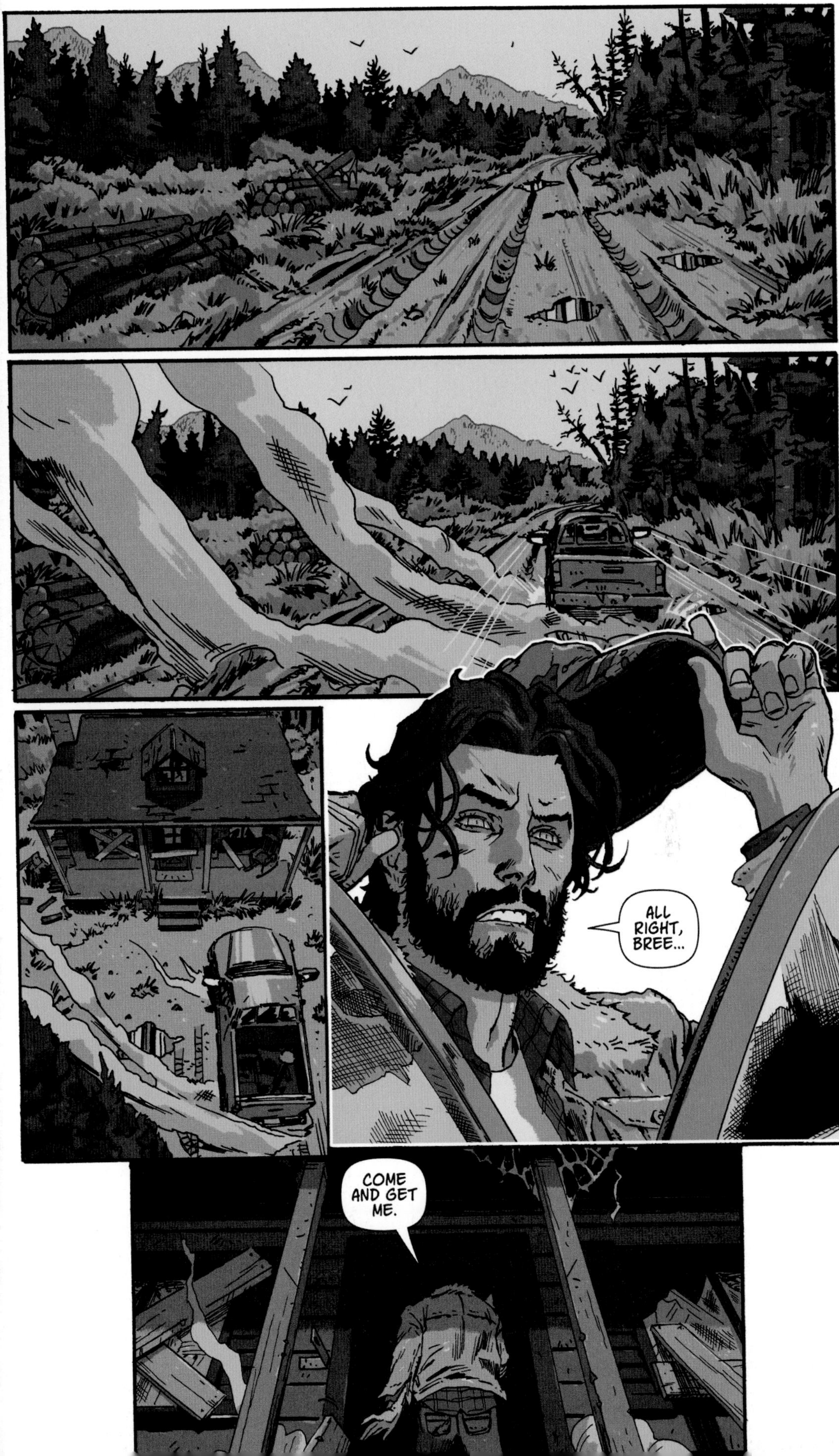
ALL RIGHT, BREE...
COME AND GET ME.

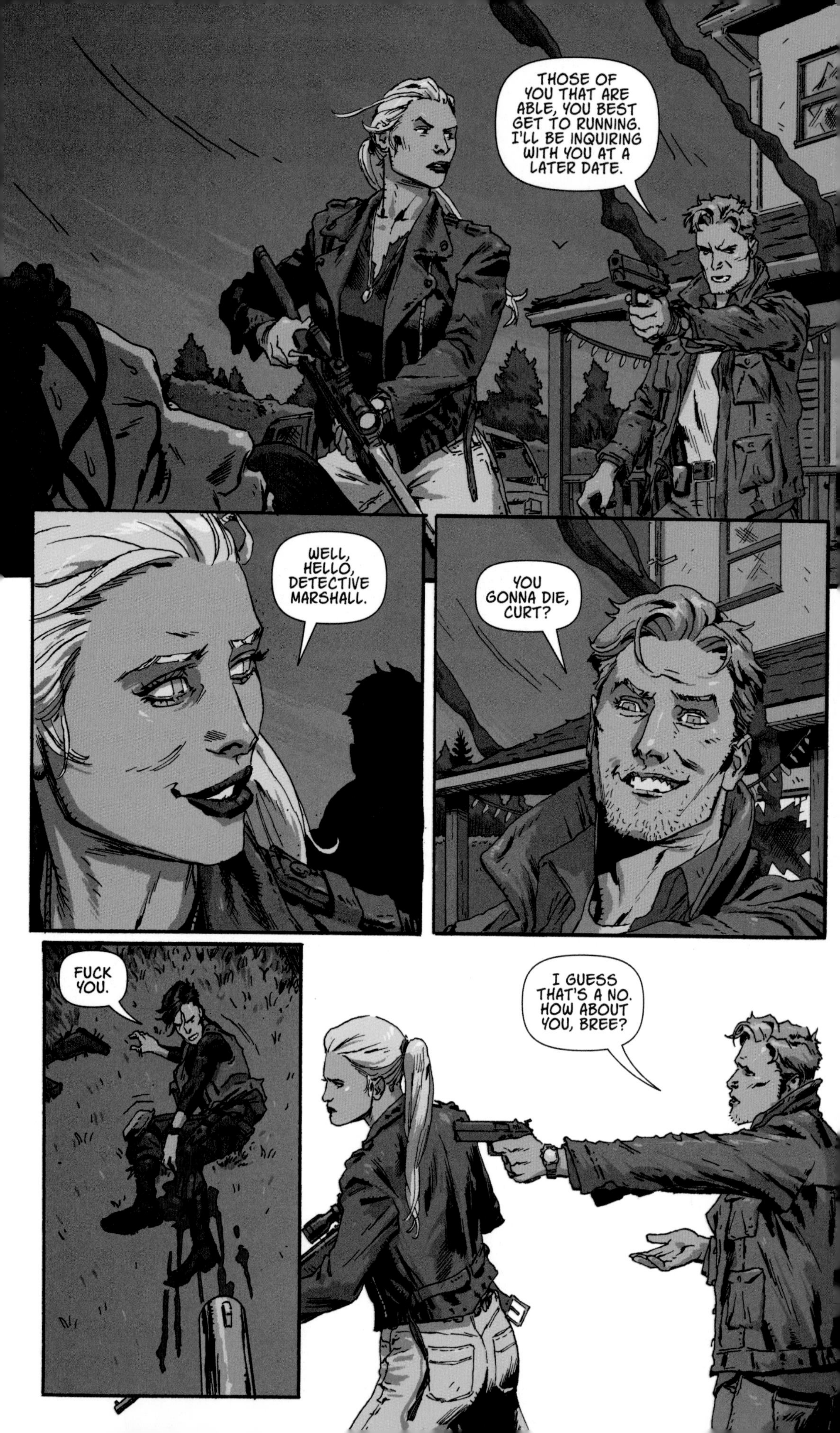
THOSE OF YOU THAT ARE ABLE, YOU BEST GET TO RUNNING. I'LL BE INQUIRING WITH YOU AT A LATER DATE.
WELL, HELLO, DETECTIVE MARSHALL.
YOU GONNA DIE, CURT?
FUCK YOU.
I GUESS THAT'S A NO. HOW ABOUT YOU, BREE?

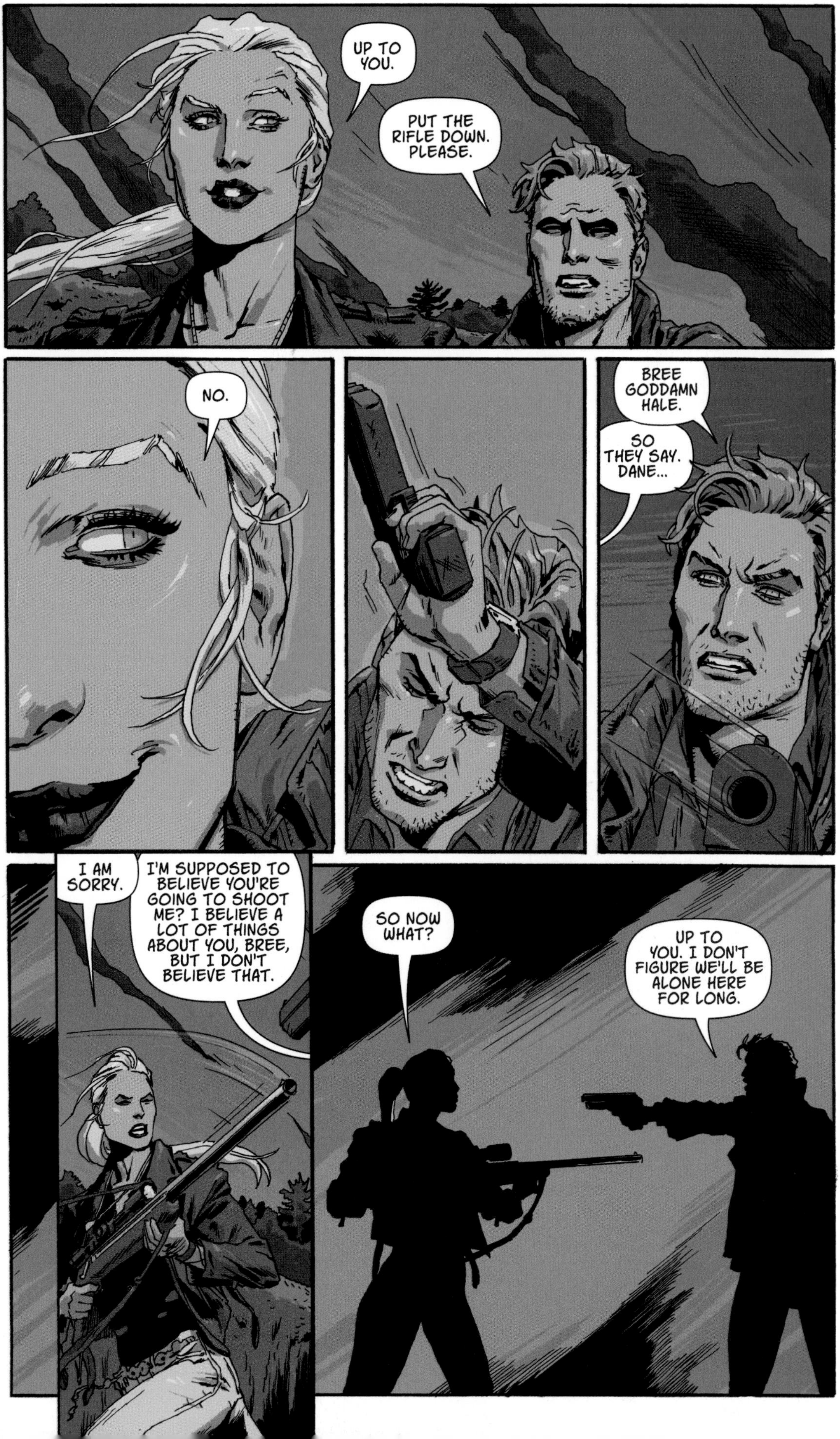
UP TO YOU.
PUT THE RIFLE DOWN. PLEASE.
NO.
BREE GODDAMN HALE.
SO THEY SAY. DANE...
I AM SORRY.
I'M SUPPOSED TO BELIEVE YOU'RE GOING TO SHOOT ME? I BELIEVE A LOT OF THINGS ABOUT YOU, BREE, BUT I DON'T BELIEVE THAT.
SO NOW WHAT?
UP TO YOU. I DON'T FIGURE WE'LL BE ALONE HERE FOR LONG.

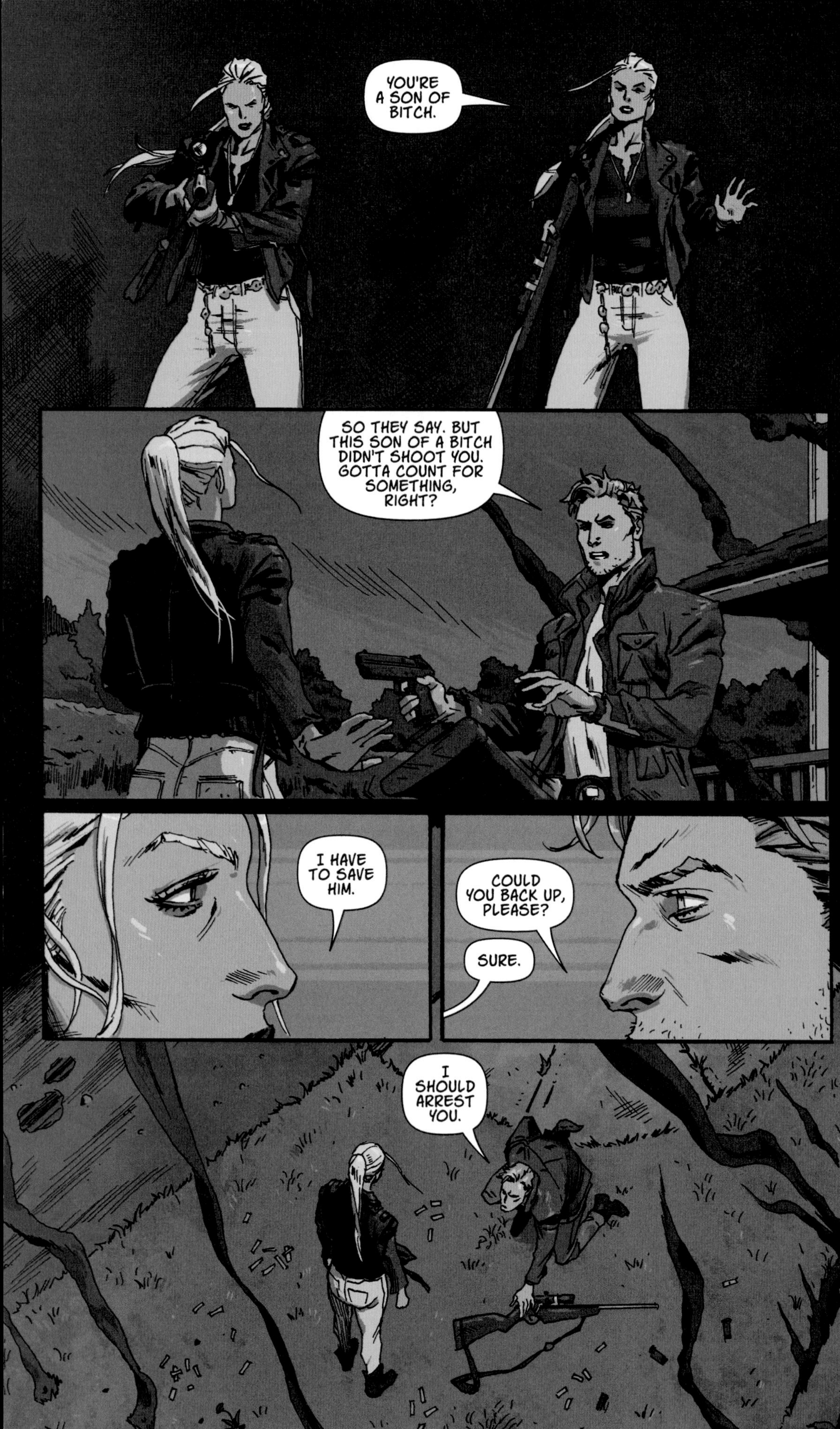
YOU'RE A SON OF BITCH.
SO THEY SAY. BUT THIS SON OF A BITCH DIDN'T SHOOT YOU. GOTTA COUNT FOR SOMETHING, RIGHT?
I HAVE TO SAVE HIM.
COULD YOU BACK UP, PLEASE?
SURE.
I SHOULD ARREST YOU.

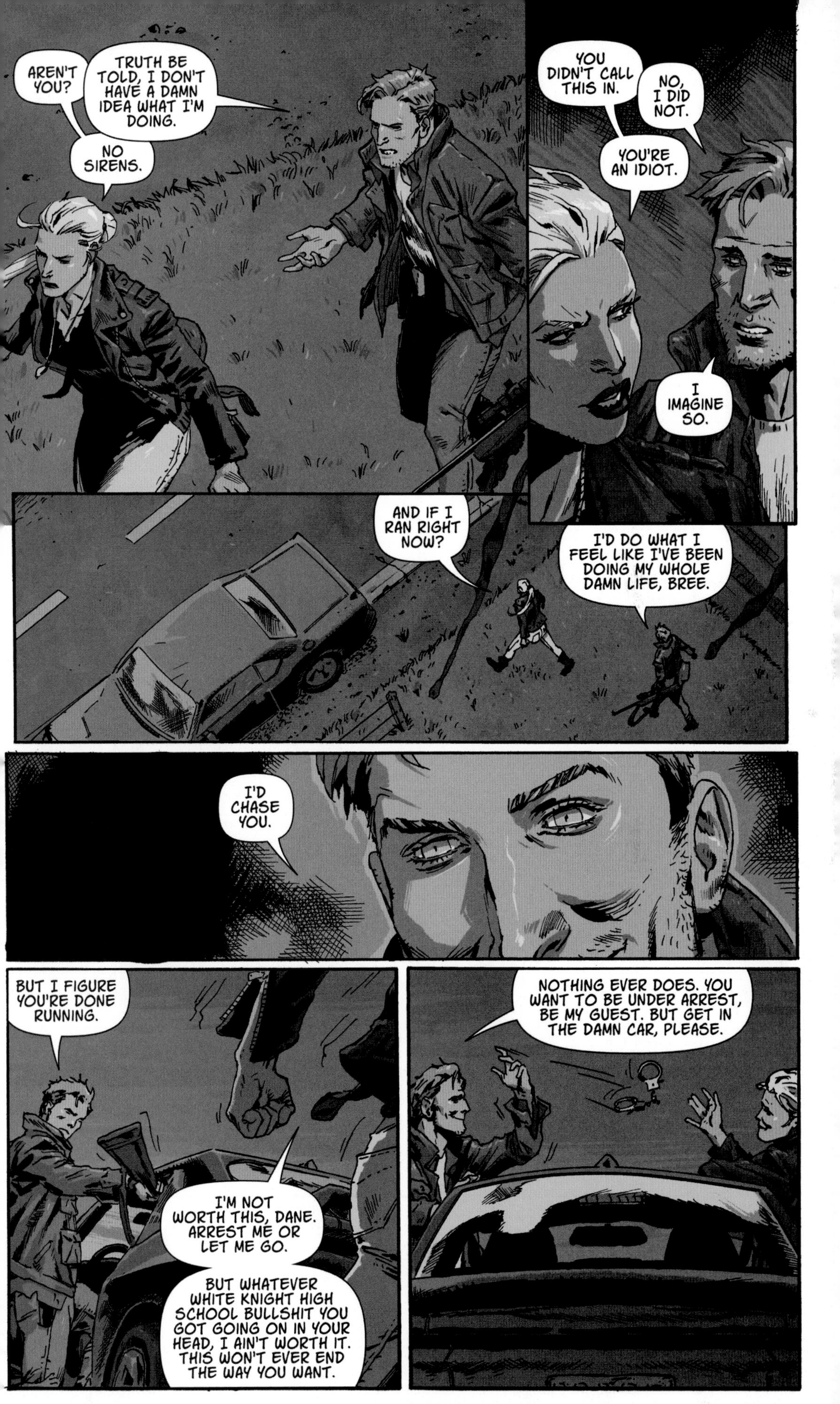
AREN'T YOU?
TRUTH BE TOLD, I DON'T HAVE A DAMN IDEA WHAT I'M DOING.
NO SIRENS.
YOU DIDN'T CALL THIS IN.
NO, I DID NOT.
YOU'RE AN IDIOT.
I IMAGINE SO.
AND IF I RAN RIGHT NOW?
I'D DO WHAT I FEEL LIKE I'VE BEEN DOING MY WHOLE DAMN LIFE, BREE.
I'D CHASE YOU.
BUT I FIGURE YOU'RE DONE RUNNING.
I'M NOT WORTH THIS, DANE. ARREST ME OR LET ME GO.
BUT WHATEVER WHITE KNIGHT HIGH SCHOOL BULLSHIT YOU GOT GOING ON IN YOUR HEAD, I AIN'T WORTH IT. THIS WON'T EVER END THE WAY YOU WANT.
NOTHING EVER DOES. YOU WANT TO BE UNDER ARREST, BE MY GUEST. BUT GET IN THE DAMN CAR, PLEASE.

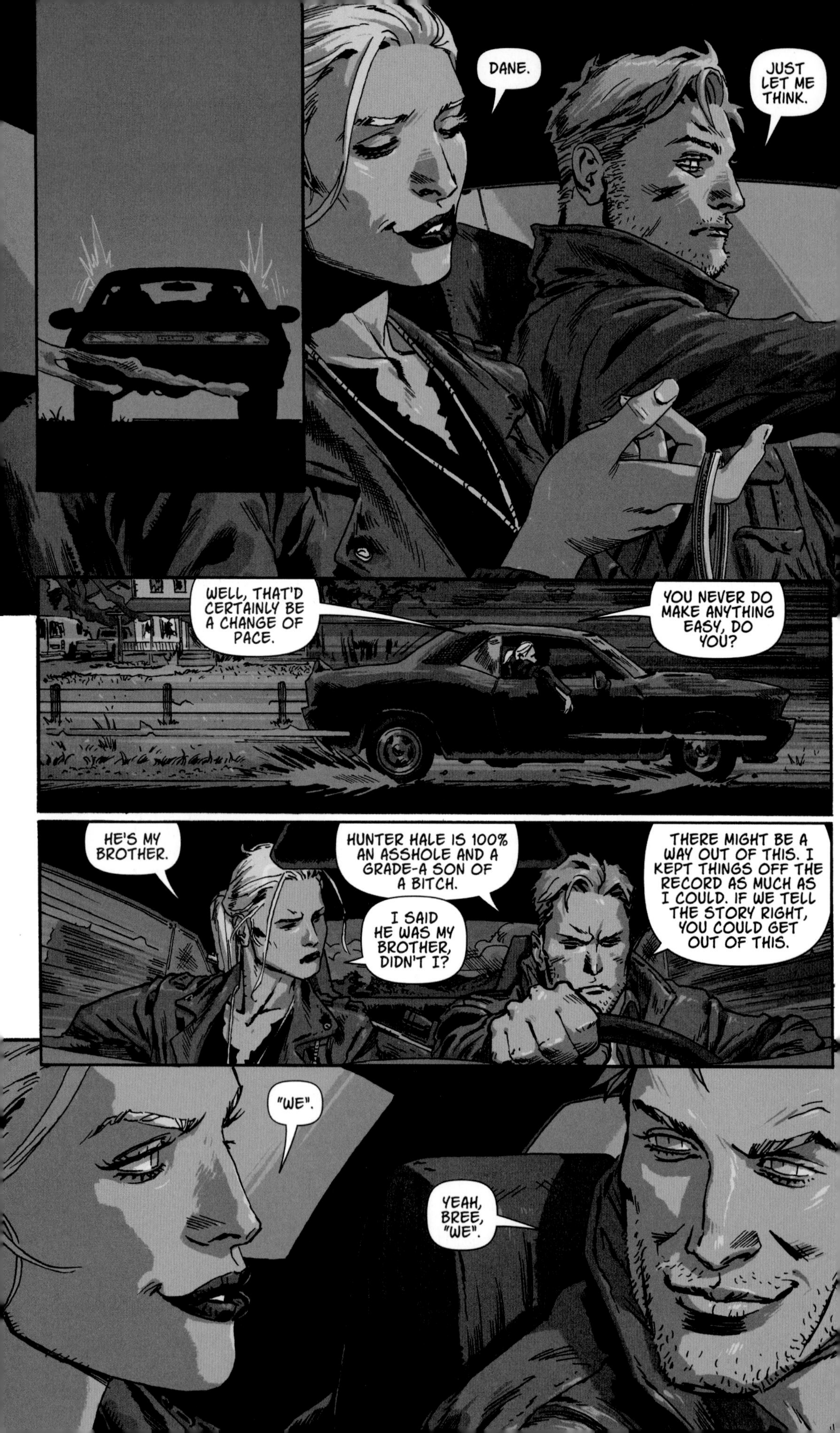
DANE.
JUST LET ME THINK.
WELL, THAT'D CERTAINLY BE A CHANGE OF PACE.
YOU NEVER DO MAKE ANYTHING EASY, DO YOU?
HE'S MY BROTHER.
HUNTER HALE IS 100% AN ASSHOLE AND A GRADE-A SON OF A BITCH.
I SAID HE WAS MY BROTHER, DIDN'T I?
THERE MIGHT BE A WAY OUT OF THIS. I KEPT THINGS OFF THE RECORD AS MUCH AS I COULD. IF WE TELL THE STORY RIGHT, YOU COULD GET OUT OF THIS.
"WE".
YEAH, BREE, "WE".

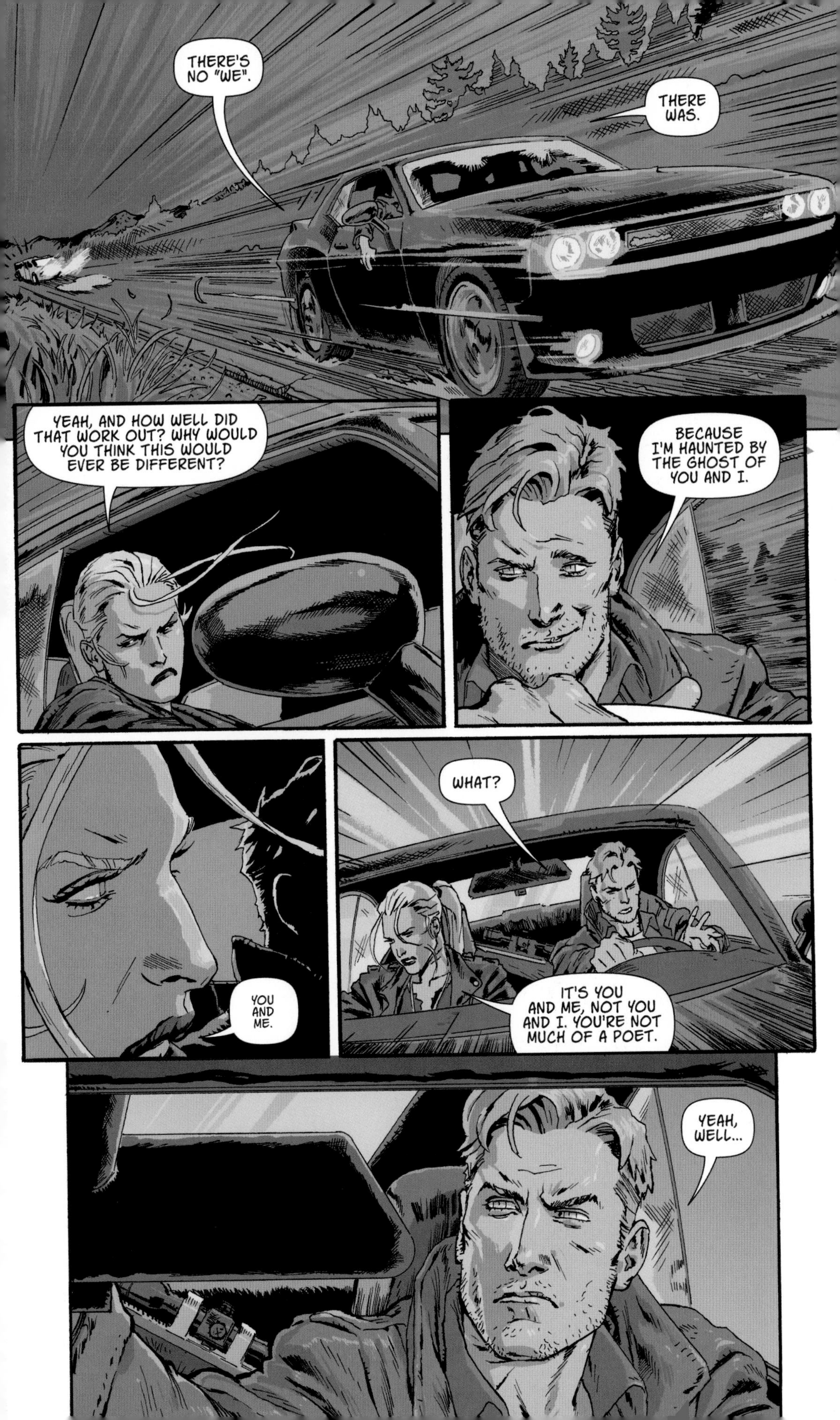
THERE'S NO "WE".
THERE WAS.
YEAH, AND HOW WELL DID THAT WORK OUT? WHY WOULD YOU THINK THIS WOULD EVER BE DIFFERENT?
BECAUSE I'M HAUNTED BY THE GHOST OF YOU AND I.
YOU AND ME.
WHAT?
IT'S YOU AND ME, NOT YOU AND I. YOU'RE NOT MUCH OF A POET.
YEAH, WELL...

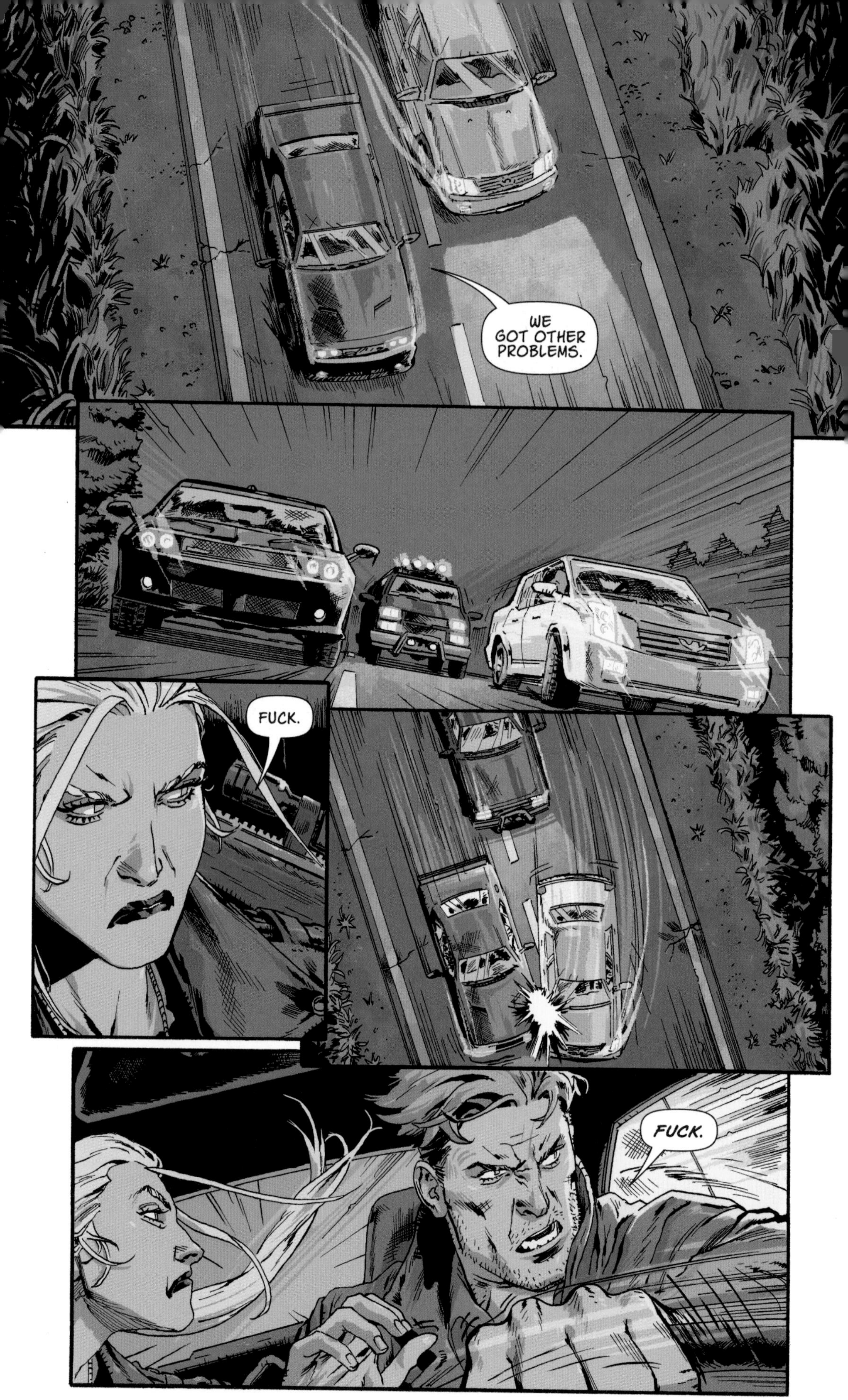
WE GOT OTHER PROBLEMS.
FUCK.
FUCK.

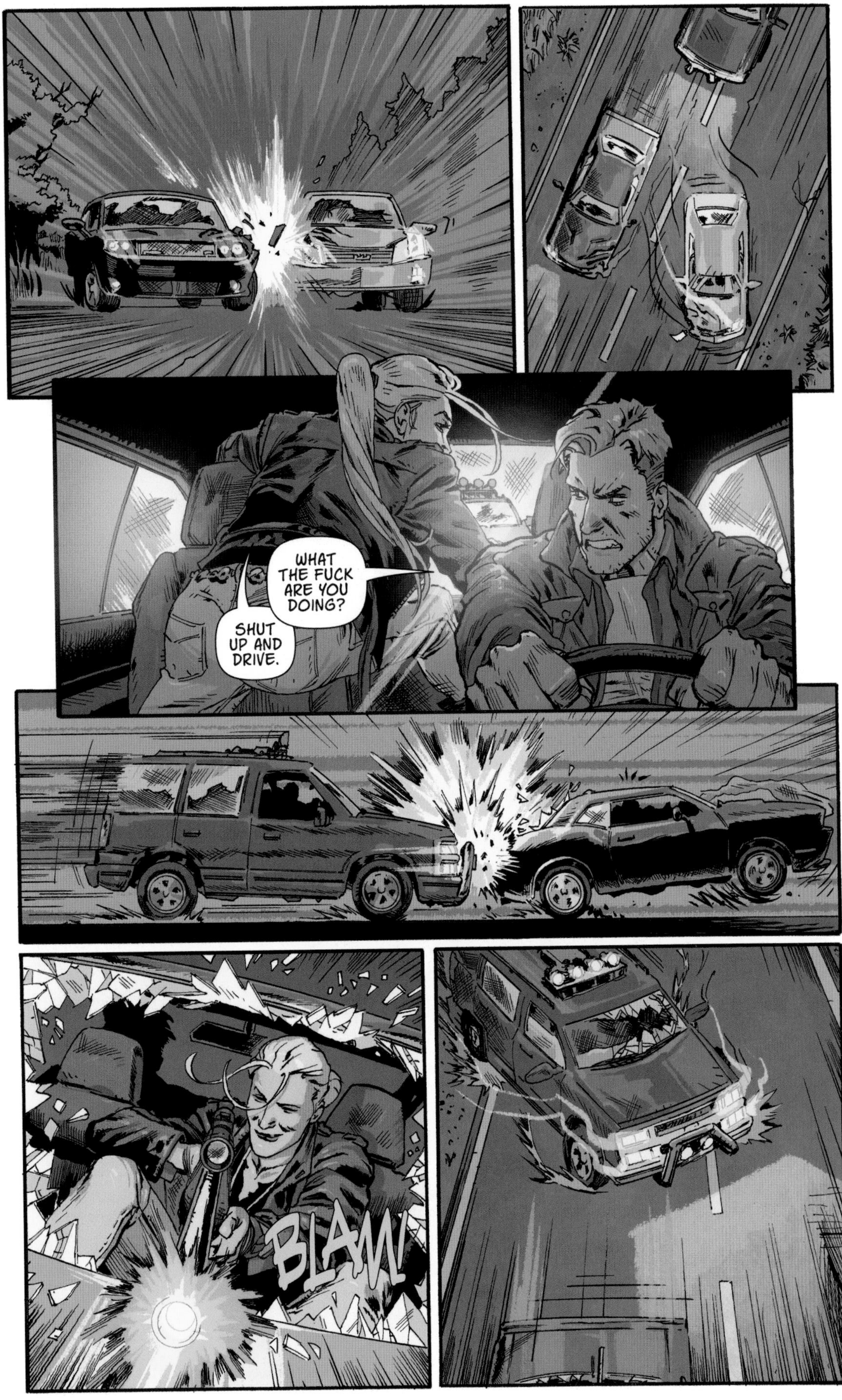
WHAT THE FUCK ARE YOU DOING?
SHUT UP AND DRIVE.
BLAM!

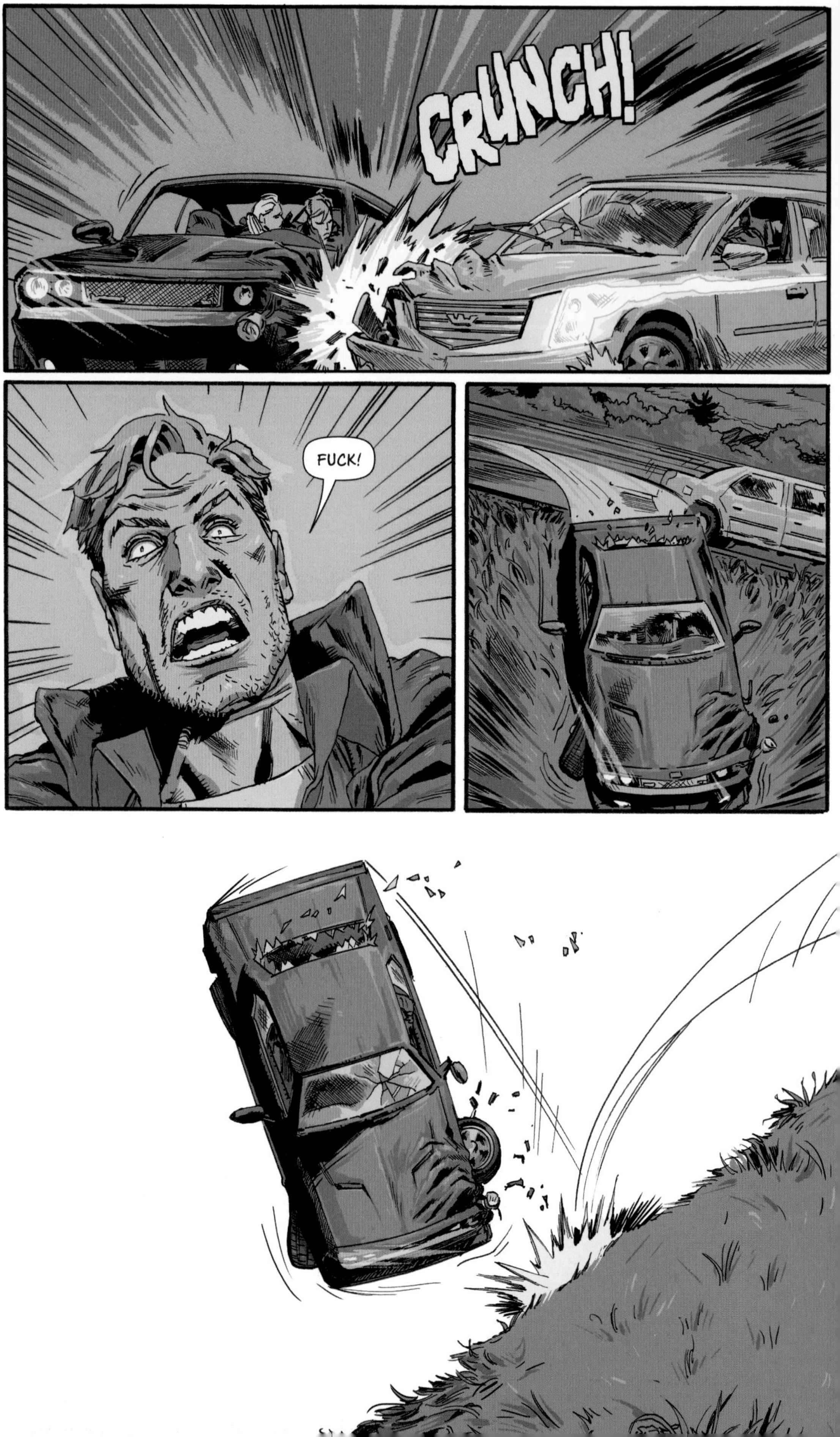
CRUNCH!
FUCK!

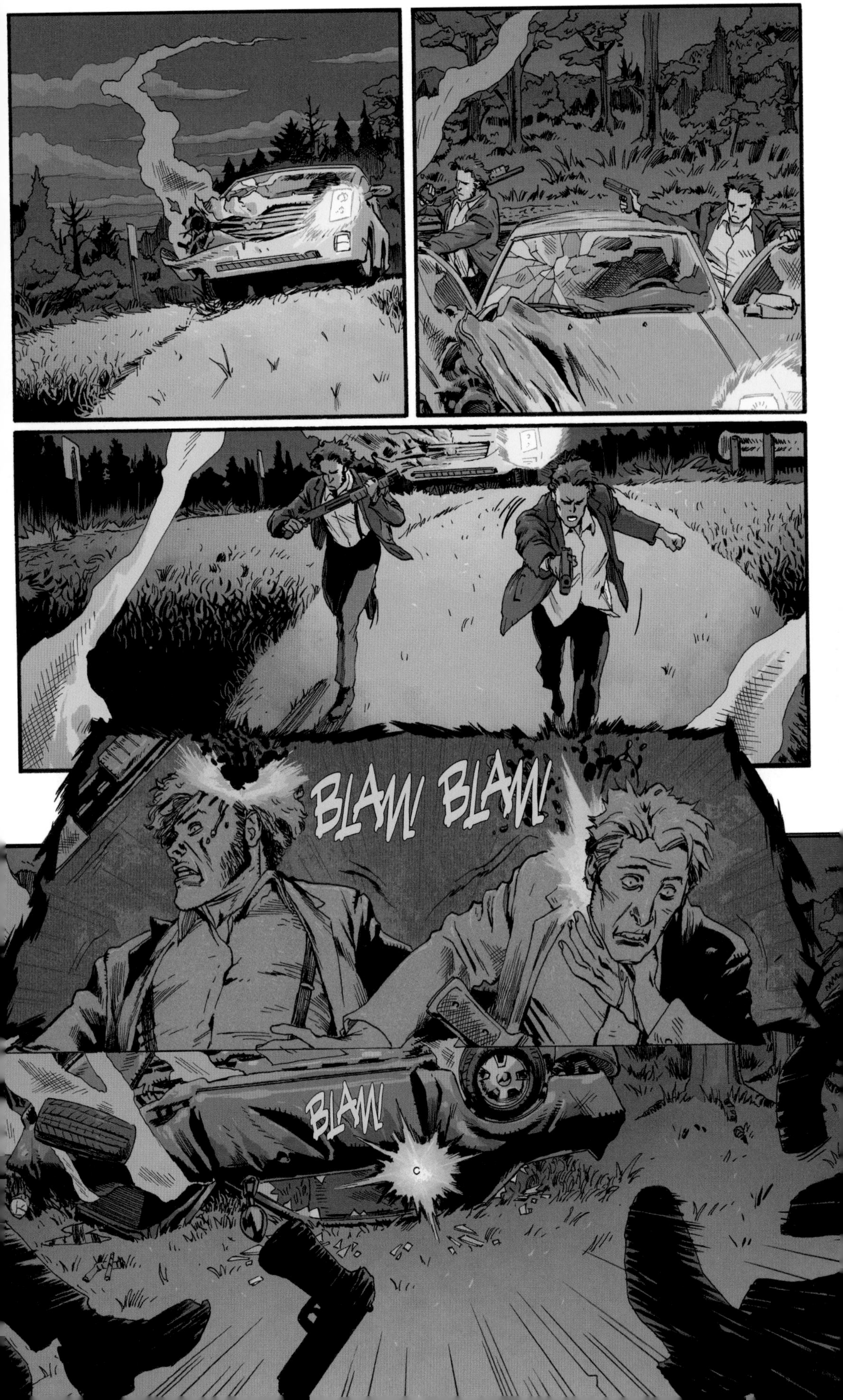
BLAM! BLAM!
BLAM!

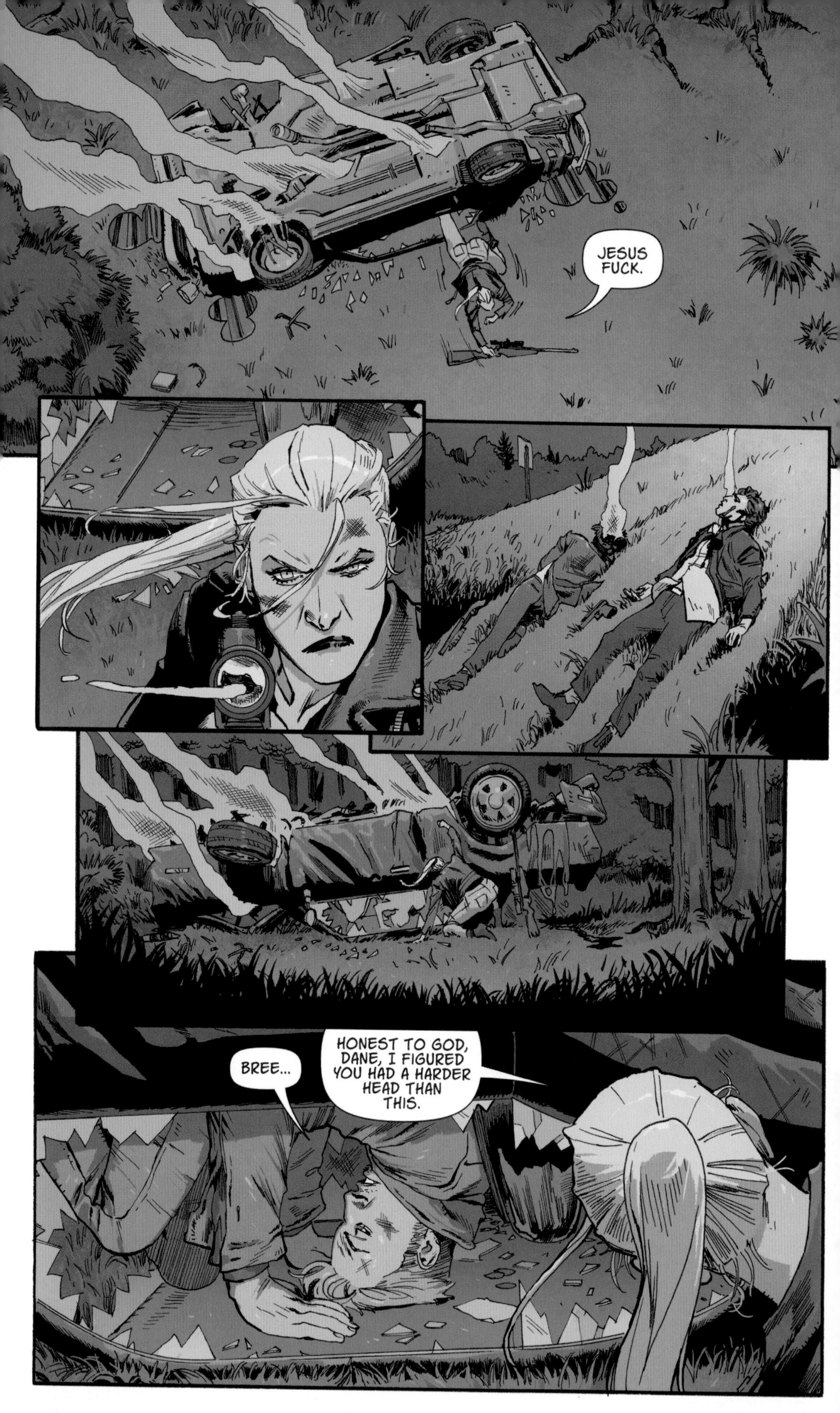
JESUS FUCK.
BREE...
HONEST TO GOD, DANE, I FIGURED YOU HAD A HARDER HEAD THAN THIS.

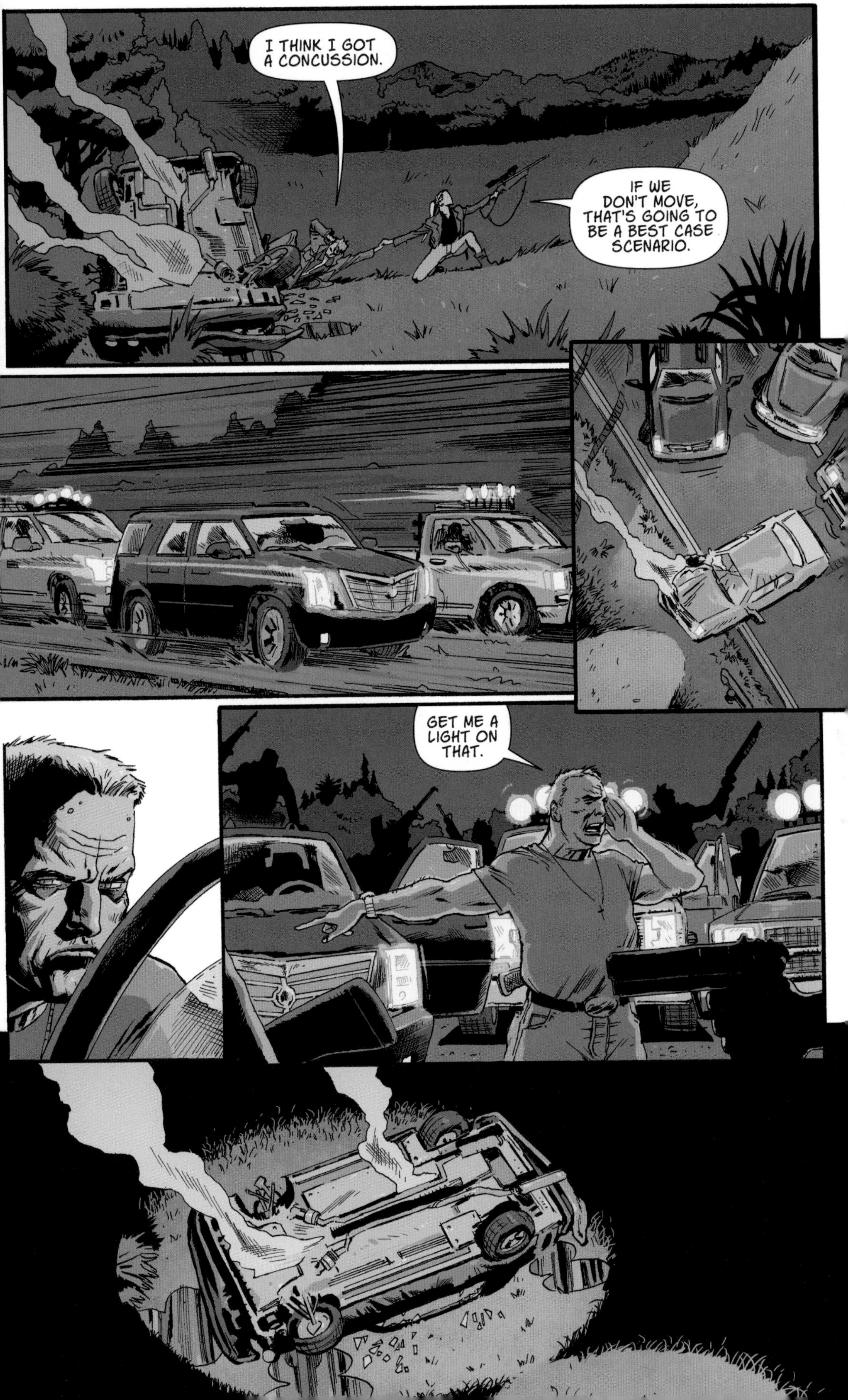
I THINK I GOT A CONCUSSION.
IF WE DON'T MOVE, THAT'S GOING TO BE A BEST CASE SCENARIO.
GET ME A LIGHT ON THAT.

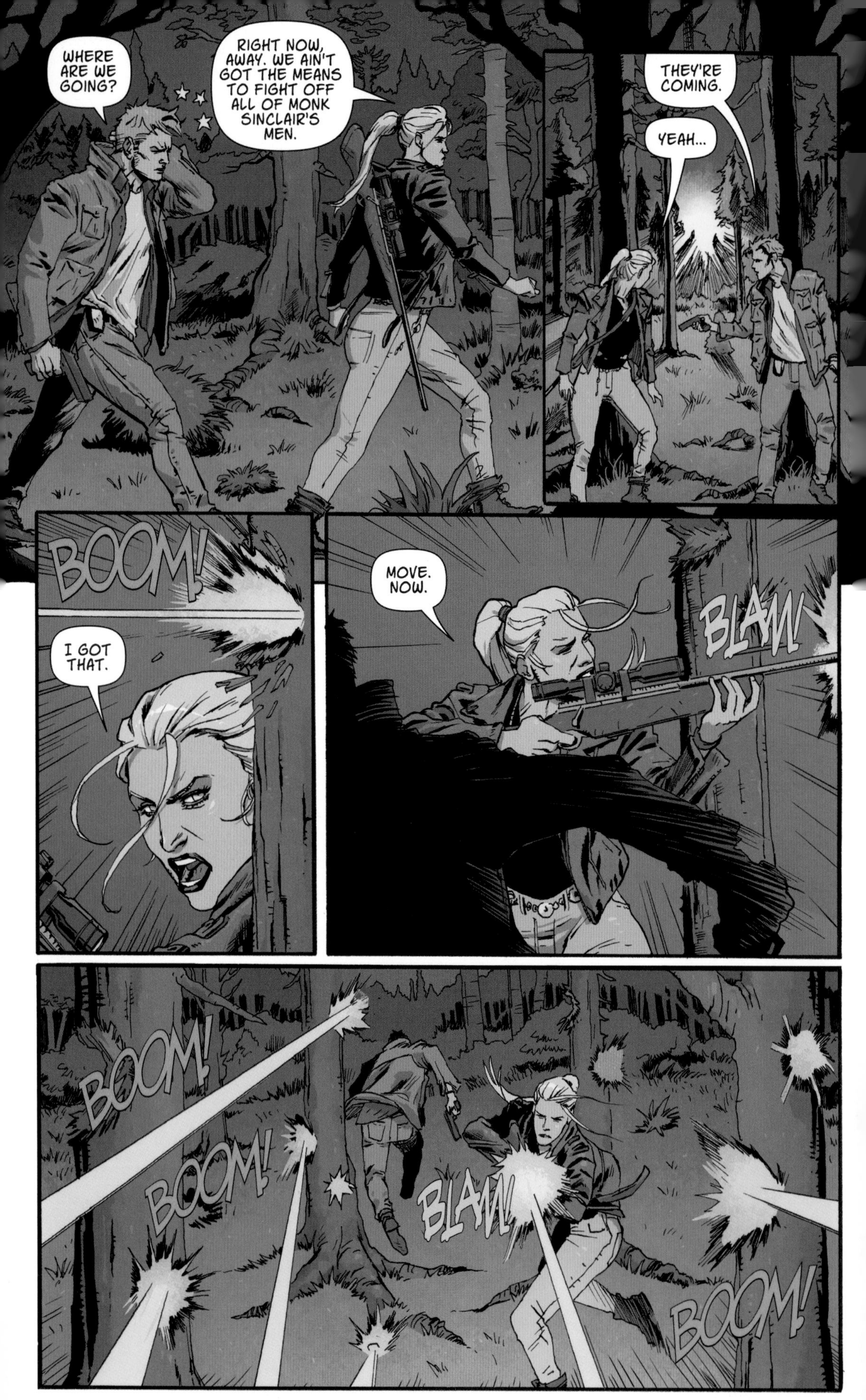

WHERE ARE WE GOING?
RIGHT NOW, AWAY. WE AIN'T GOT THE MEANS TO FIGHT OFF ALL OF MONK SINCLAIR'S MEN.
THEY'RE COMING.
YEAH...
BOOM!
I GOT THAT.
MOVE. NOW.
BLAM!
BOOM!
BOOM!
BLAM!
BOOM!

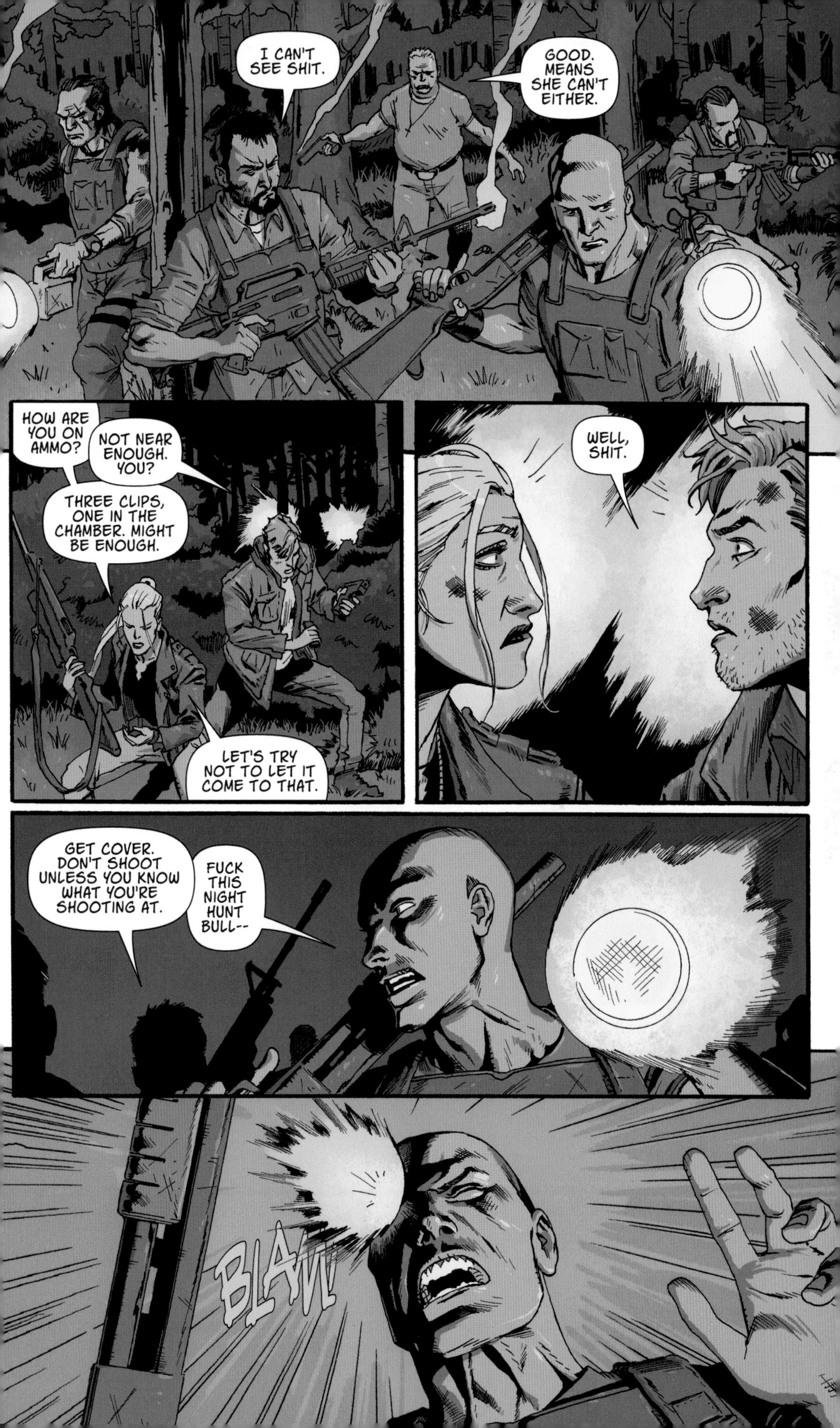
I CAN'T SEE SHIT.
GOOD. MEANS SHE CAN'T EITHER.
HOW ARE YOU ON AMMO?
NOT NEAR ENOUGH. YOU?
THREE CLIPS, ONE IN THE CHAMBER. MIGHT BE ENOUGH.
LET'S TRY NOT TO LET IT COME TO THAT.
WELL, SHIT.
GET COVER. DON'T SHOOT UNLESS YOU KNOW WHAT YOU'RE SHOOTING AT.
FUCK THIS NIGHT HUNT BULL--
BLAM

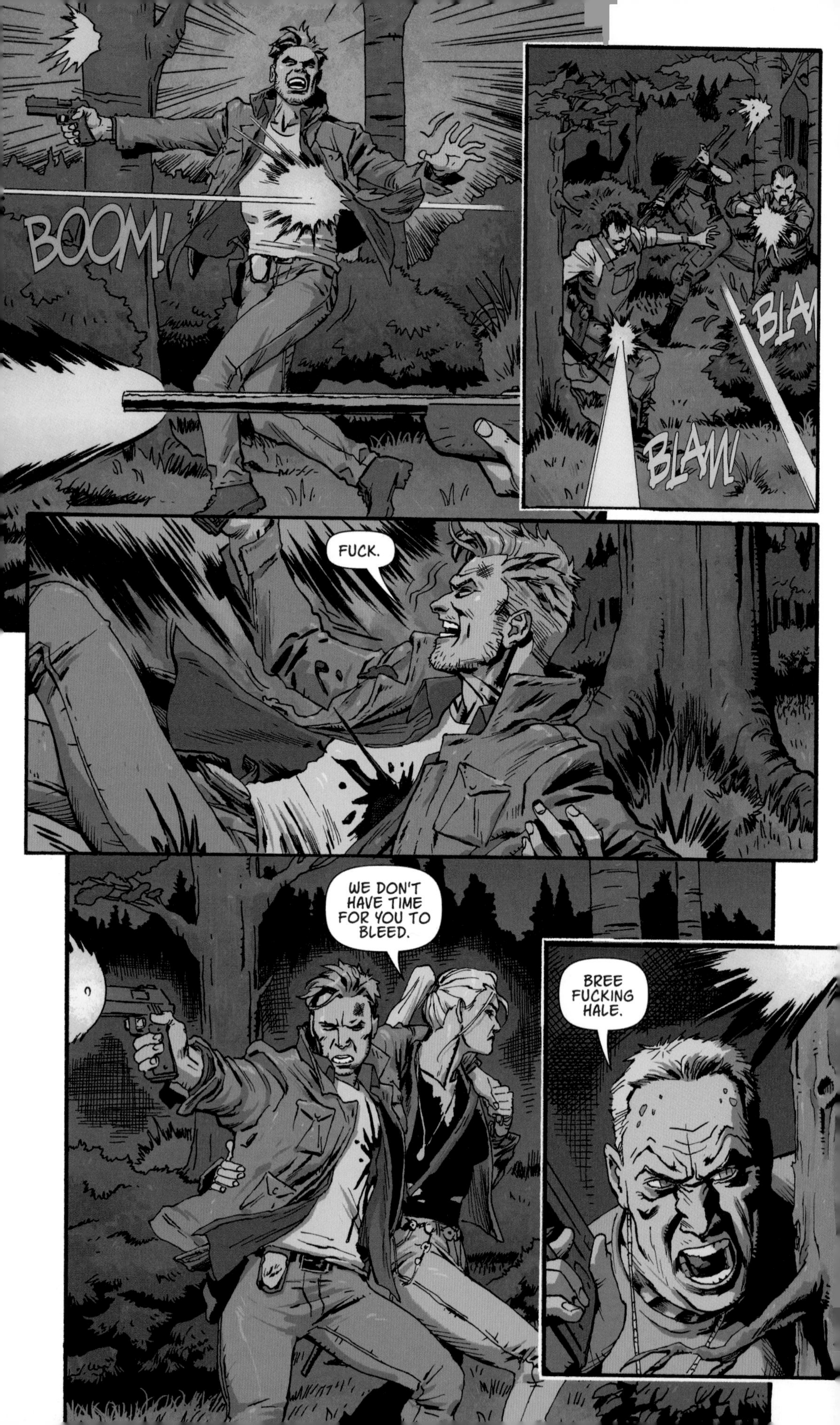
BOOM!
BLAM!
BLAM!
FUCK.
WE DON'T HAVE TIME FOR YOU TO BLEED.
BREE FUCKING HALE.

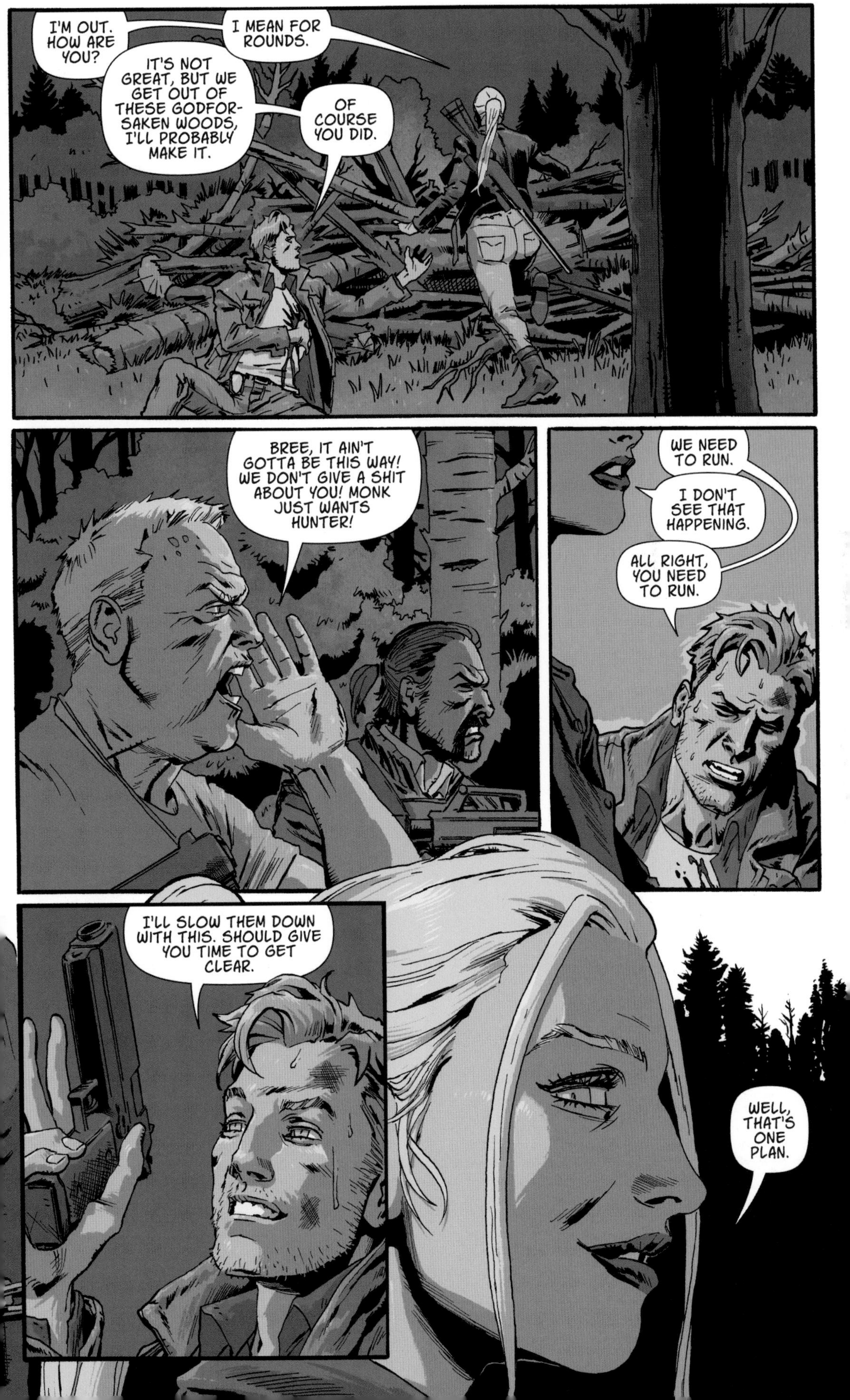
I'M OUT. HOW ARE YOU?
I MEAN FOR ROUNDS.
IT'S NOT GREAT, BUT WE GET OUT OF THESE GODFOR-SAKEN WOODS, I'LL PROBABLY MAKE IT.
OF COURSE YOU DID.
BREE, IT AIN'T GOTTA BE THIS WAY! WE DON'T GIVE A SHIT ABOUT YOU! MONK JUST WANTS HUNTER!
WE NEED TO RUN.
I DON'T SEE THAT HAPPENING.
ALL RIGHT, YOU NEED TO RUN.
I'LL SLOW THEM DOWN WITH THIS. SHOULD GIVE YOU TIME TO GET CLEAR.
WELL, THAT'S ONE PLAN.

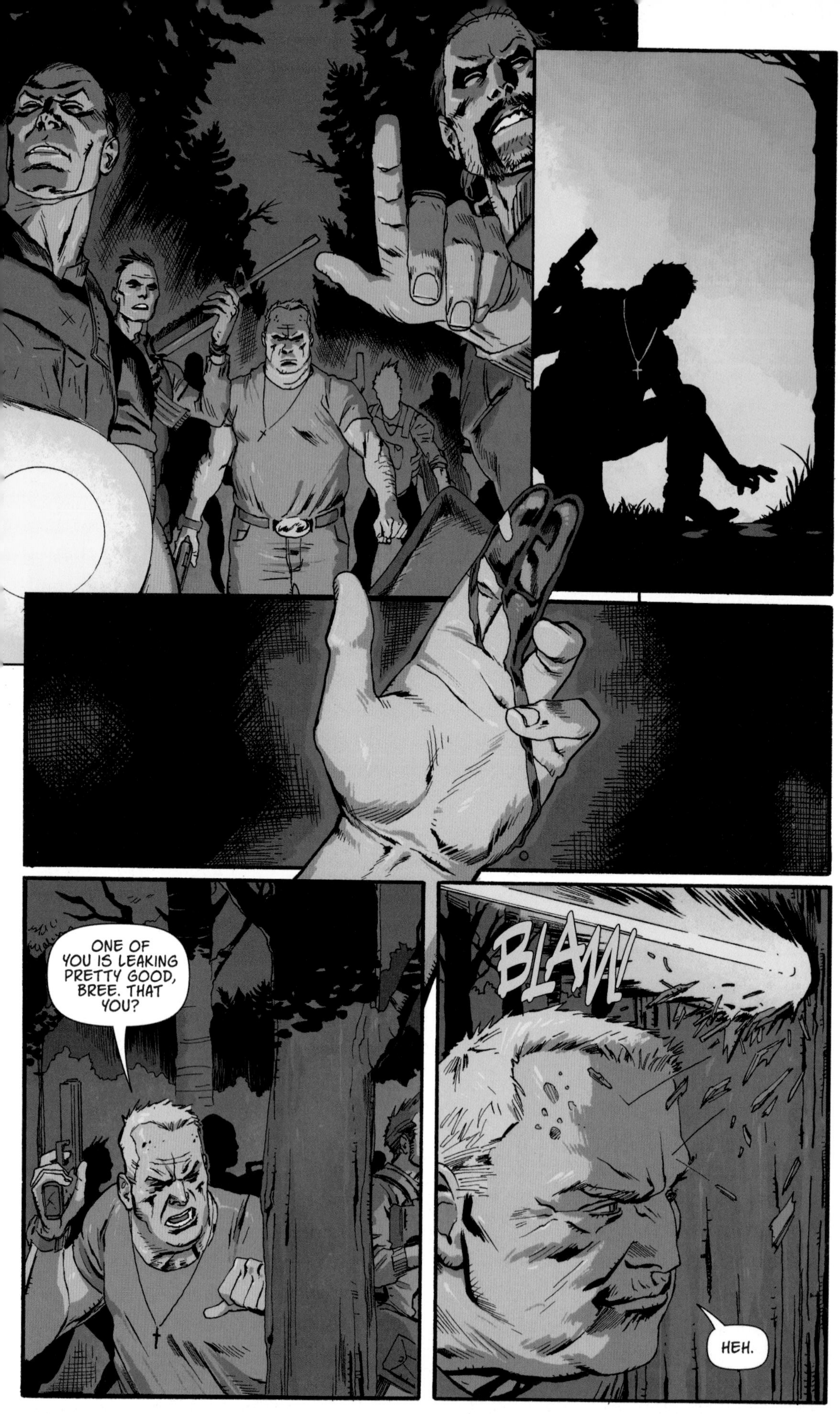
ONE OF YOU IS LEAKING PRETTY GOOD, BREE. THAT YOU?
BLAM!
HEH.

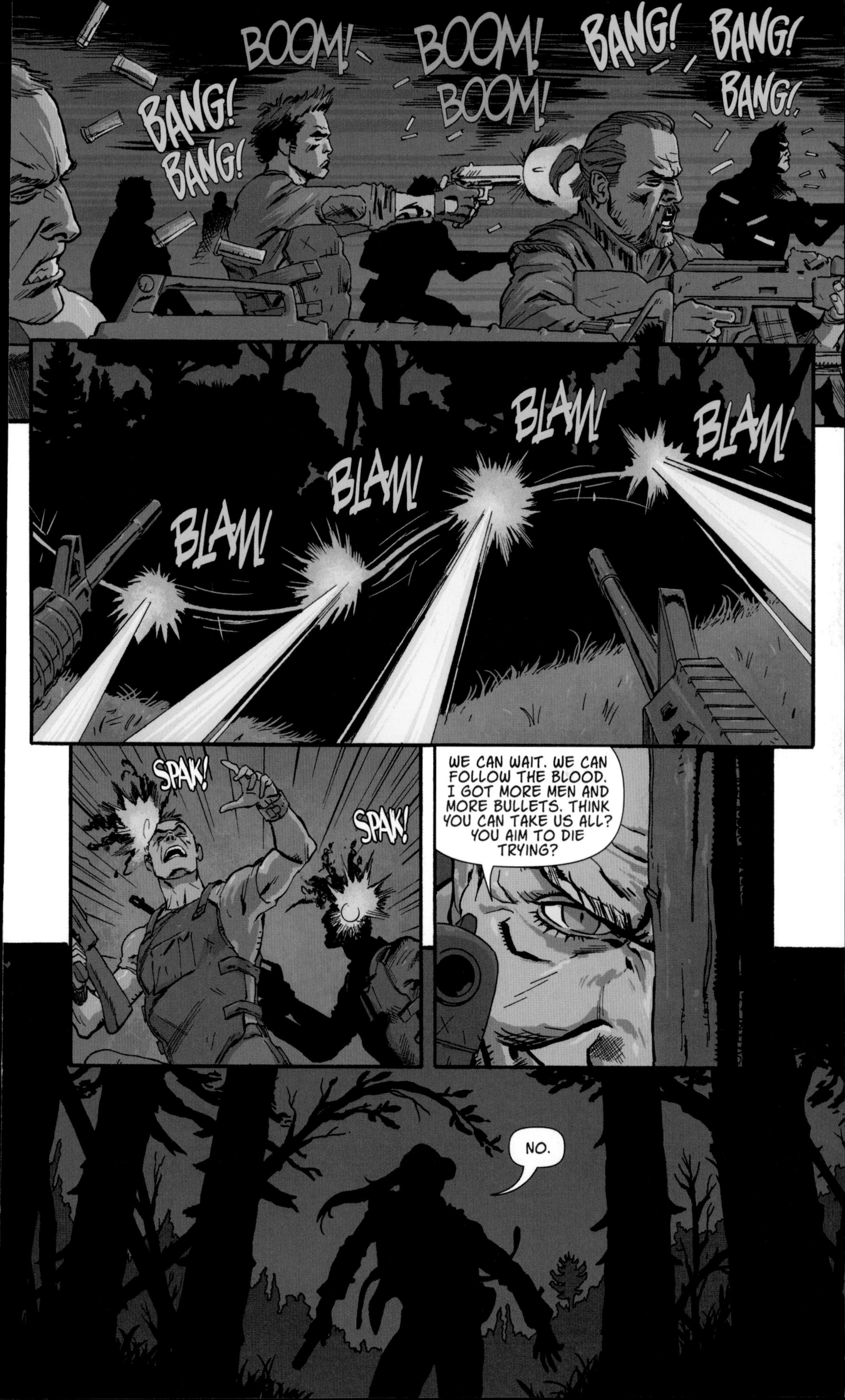
BANG!
BANG!
BOOM!
BOOM!
BOOM!
BANG!
BANG!
BANG!
BLAM!
BLAM!
BLAM!
BLAM!
SPAK!
SPAK!
WE CAN WAIT. WE CAN FOLLOW THE BLOOD. I GOT MORE MEN AND MORE BULLETS. THINK YOU CAN TAKE US ALL? YOU AIM TO DIE TRYING?
NO.

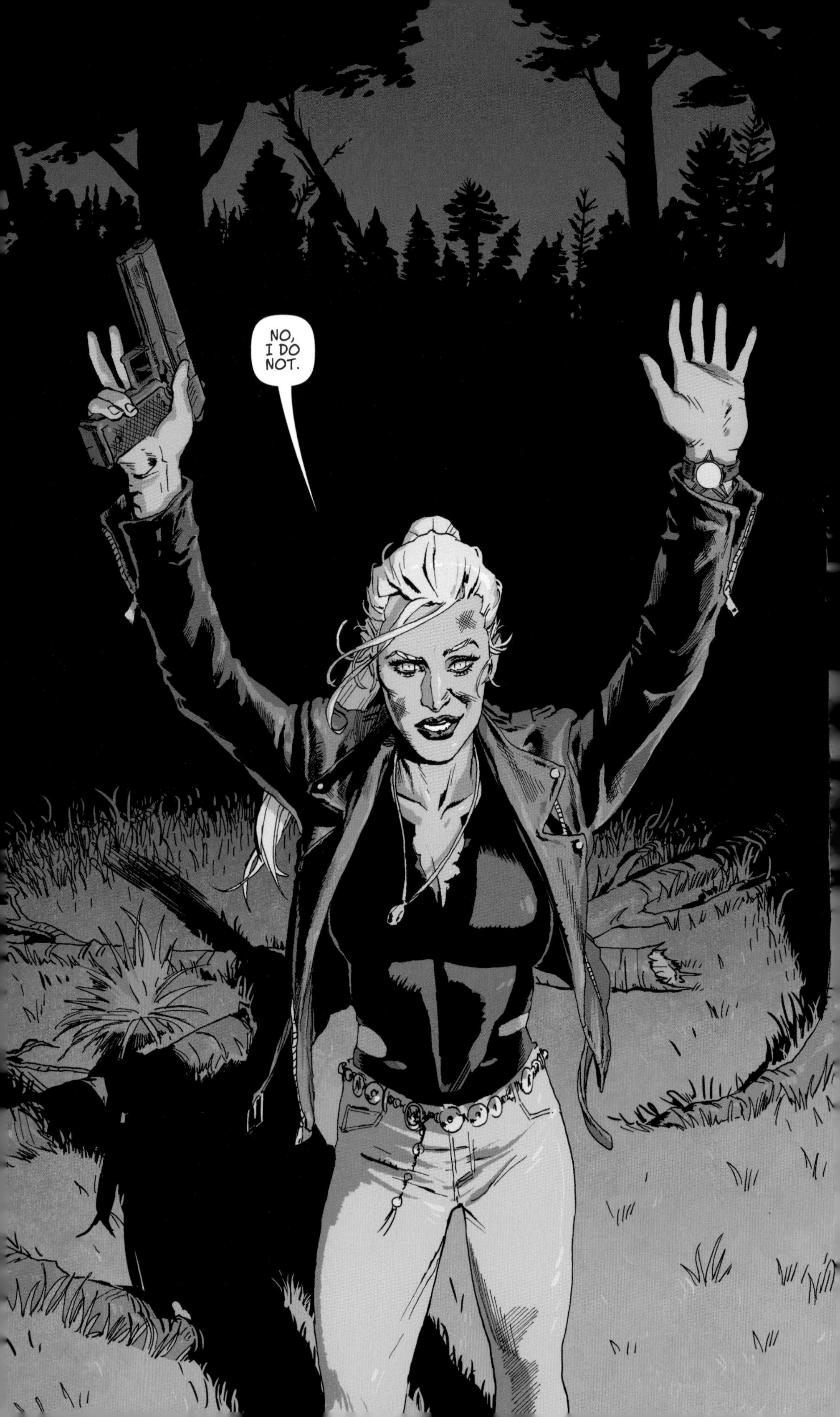
NO, I DO NOT.

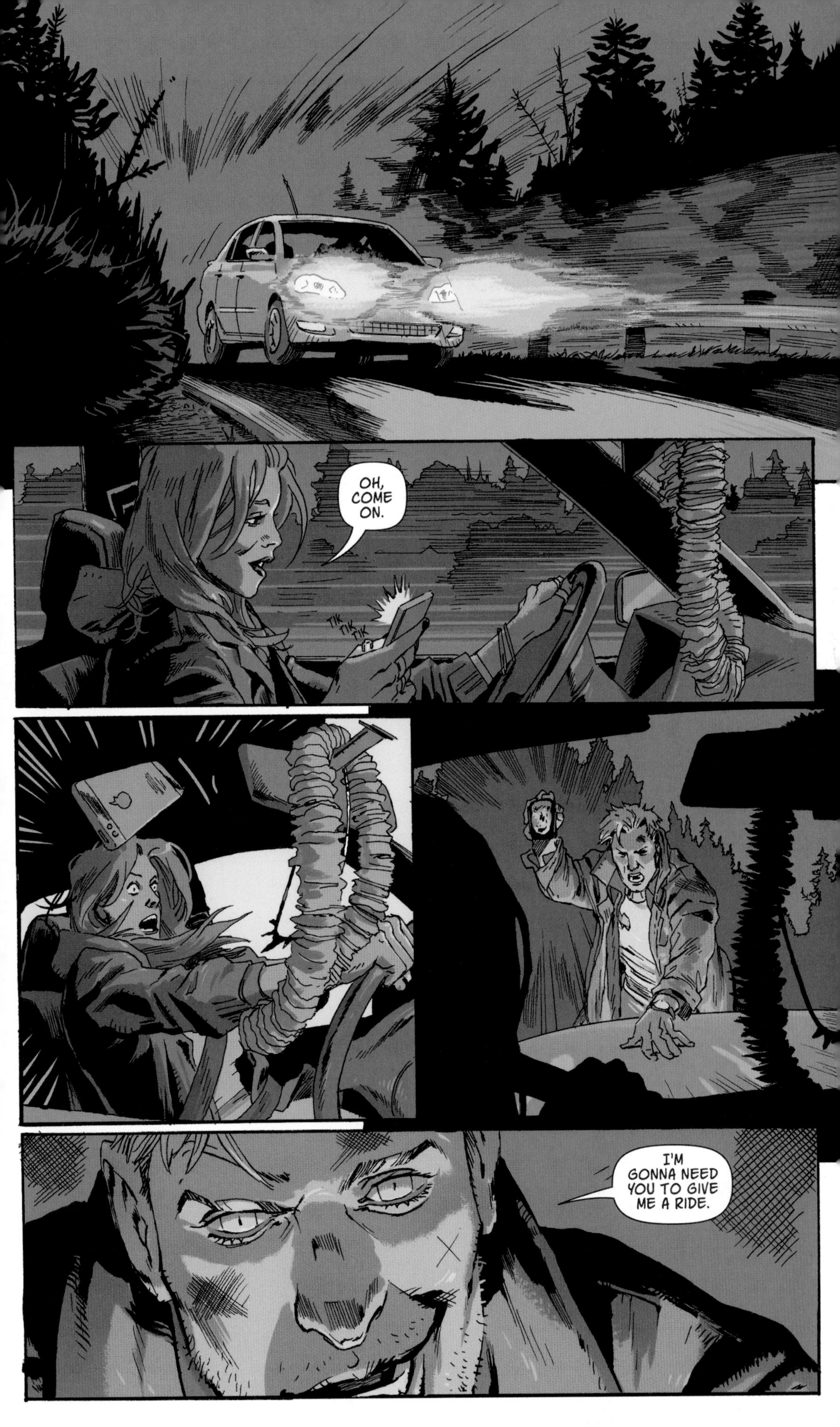

OH, COME ON.
TIK TIK TIK
I'M GONNA NEED YOU TO GIVE ME A RIDE.

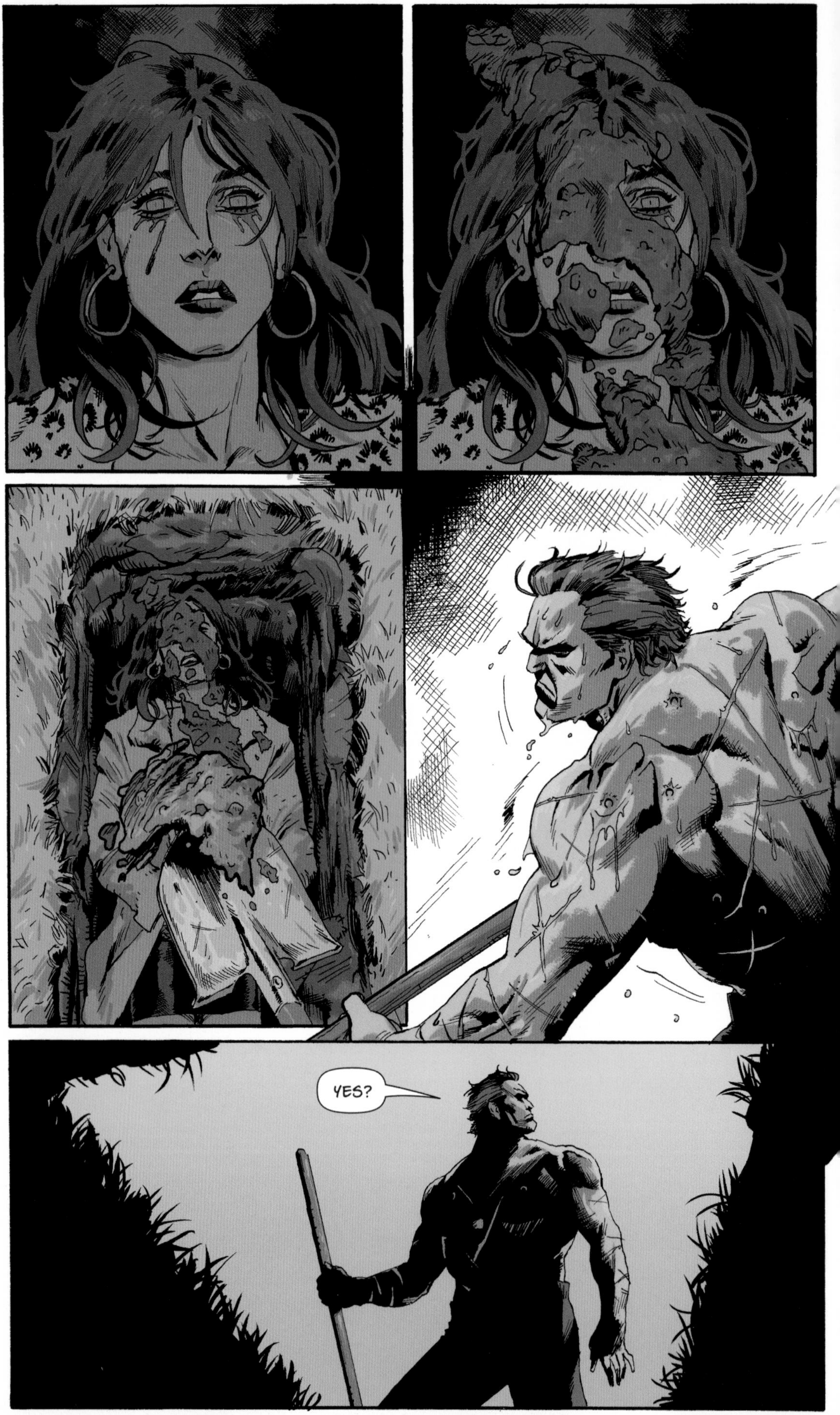
YES?

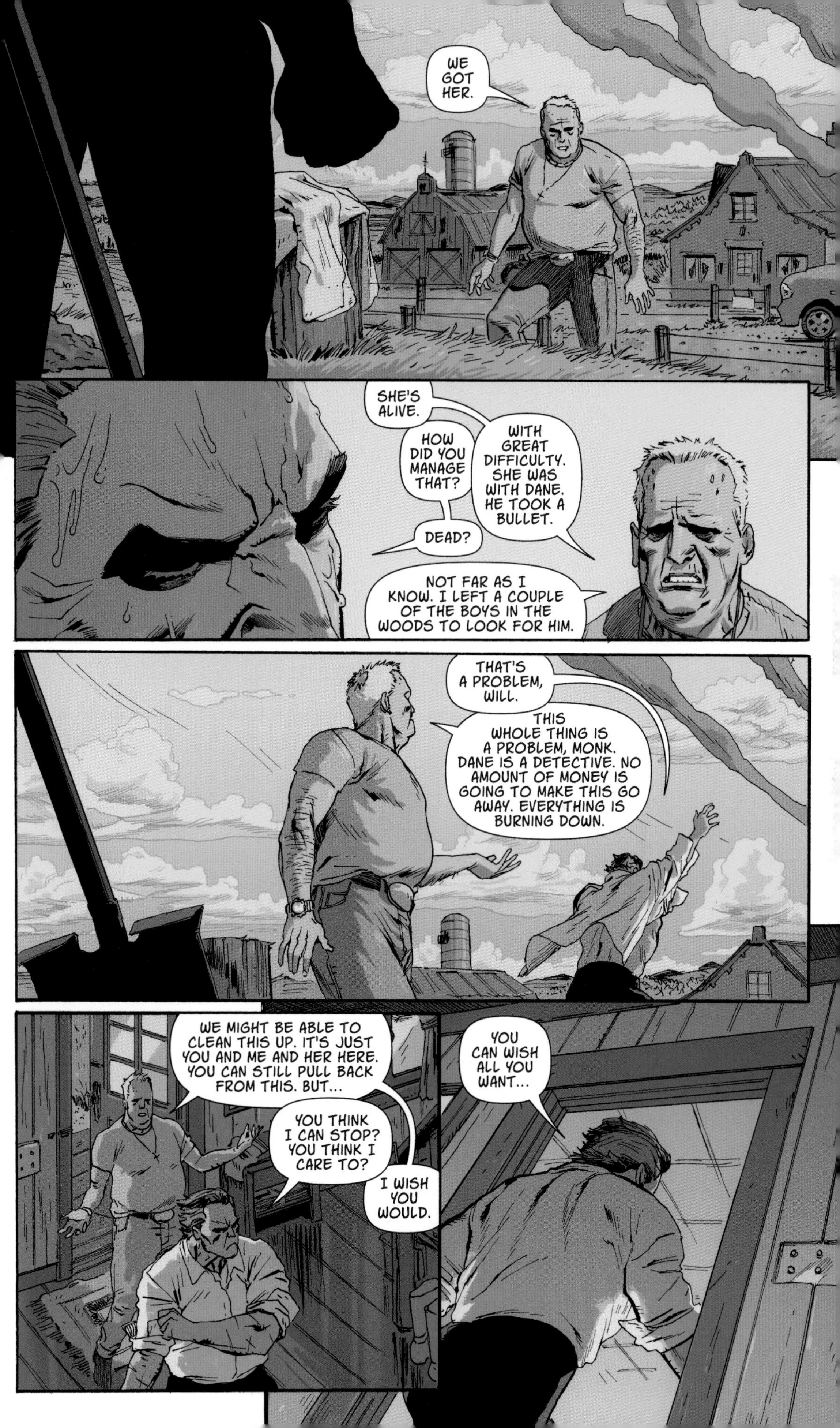
WE GOT HER.
SHE'S ALIVE.
HOW DID YOU MANAGE THAT?
WITH GREAT DIFFICULTY. SHE WAS WITH DANE. HE TOOK A BULLET.
DEAD?
NOT FAR AS I KNOW. I LEFT A COUPLE OF THE BOYS IN THE WOODS TO LOOK FOR HIM.
THAT'S A PROBLEM, WILL.
THIS WHOLE THING IS A PROBLEM, MONK. DANE IS A DETECTIVE. NO AMOUNT OF MONEY IS GOING TO MAKE THIS GO AWAY. EVERYTHING IS BURNING DOWN.
WE MIGHT BE ABLE TO CLEAN THIS UP. IT'S JUST YOU AND ME AND HER HERE. YOU CAN STILL PULL BACK FROM THIS. BUT...
YOU THINK I CAN STOP? YOU THINK I CARE TO?
I WISH YOU WOULD.
YOU CAN WISH ALL YOU WANT...

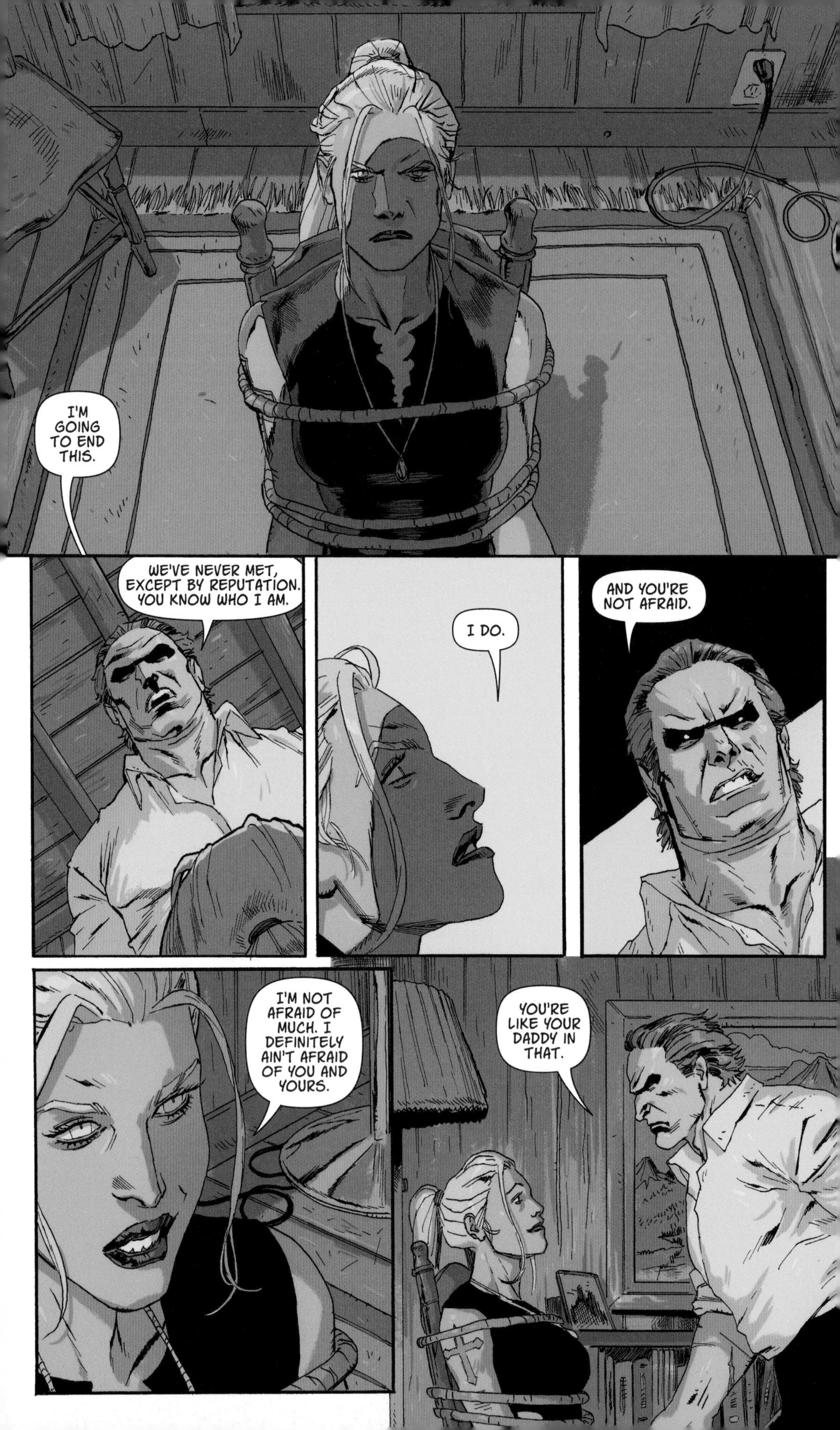
I'M GOING TO END THIS.
WE'VE NEVER MET, EXCEPT BY REPUTATION. YOU KNOW WHO I AM.
I DO.
AND YOU'RE NOT AFRAID.
I'M NOT AFRAID OF MUCH. I DEFINITELY AIN'T AFRAID OF YOU AND YOURS.
YOU'RE LIKE YOUR DADDY IN THAT.

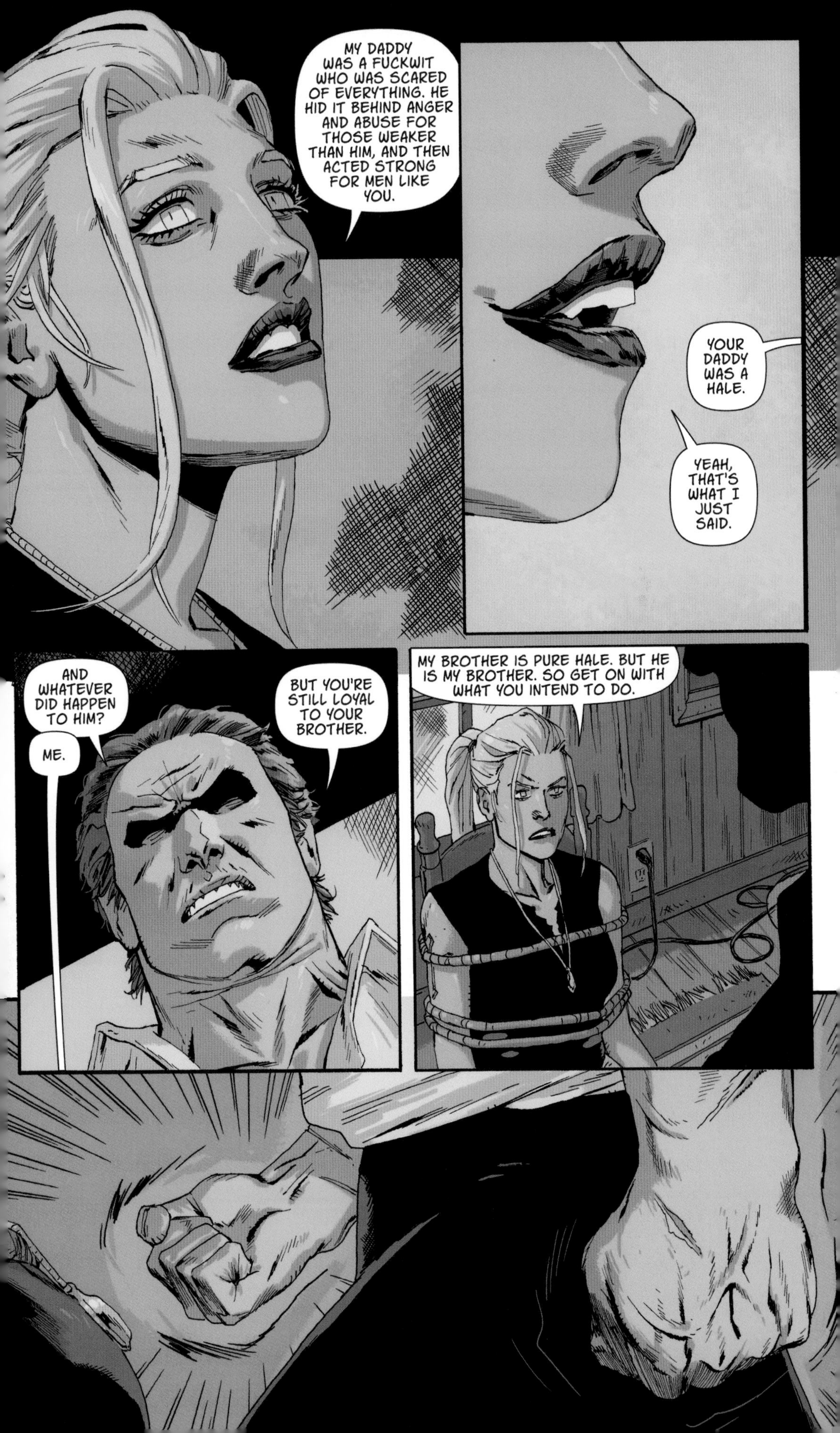
MY DADDY WAS A FUCKWIT WHO WAS SCARED OF EVERYTHING. HE HID IT BEHIND ANGER AND ABUSE FOR THOSE WEAKER THAN HIM, AND THEN ACTED STRONG FOR MEN LIKE YOU.
YOUR DADDY WAS A HALE.
YEAH, THAT'S WHAT I JUST SAID.
AND WHATEVER DID HAPPEN TO HIM?
ME.
BUT YOU'RE STILL LOYAL TO YOUR BROTHER.
MY BROTHER IS PURE HALE. BUT HE IS MY BROTHER. SO GET ON WITH WHAT YOU INTEND TO DO.

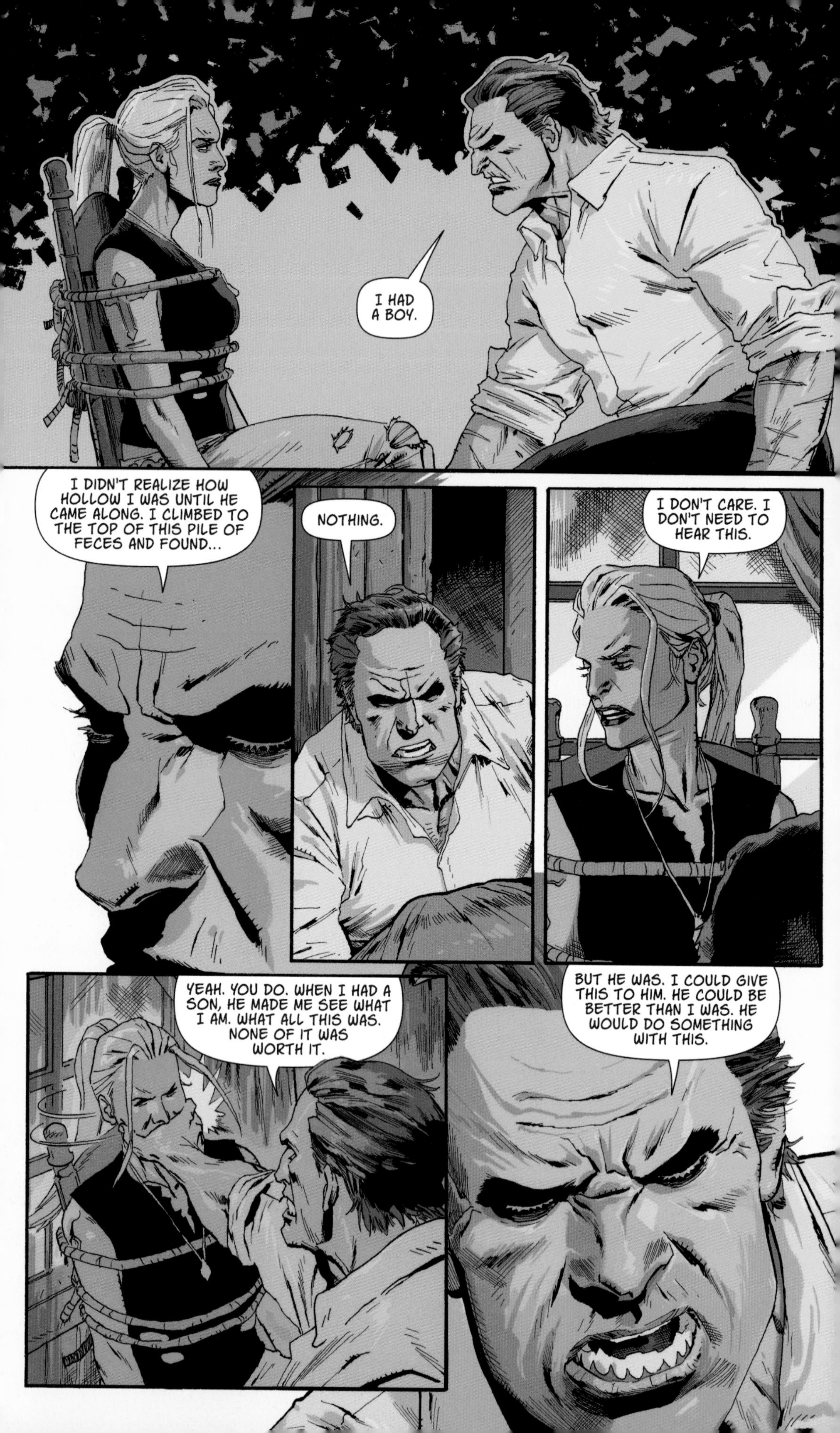
I HAD A BOY.
I DIDN'T REALIZE HOW HOLLOW I WAS UNTIL HE CAME ALONG. I CLIMBED TO THE TOP OF THIS PILE OF FECES AND FOUND...
NOTHING.
I DON'T CARE. I DON'T NEED TO HEAR THIS.
YEAH. YOU DO. WHEN I HAD A SON, HE MADE ME SEE WHAT I AM. WHAT ALL THIS WAS. NONE OF IT WAS WORTH IT.
BUT HE WAS. I COULD GIVE THIS TO HIM. HE COULD BE BETTER THAN I WAS. HE WOULD DO SOMETHING WITH THIS.

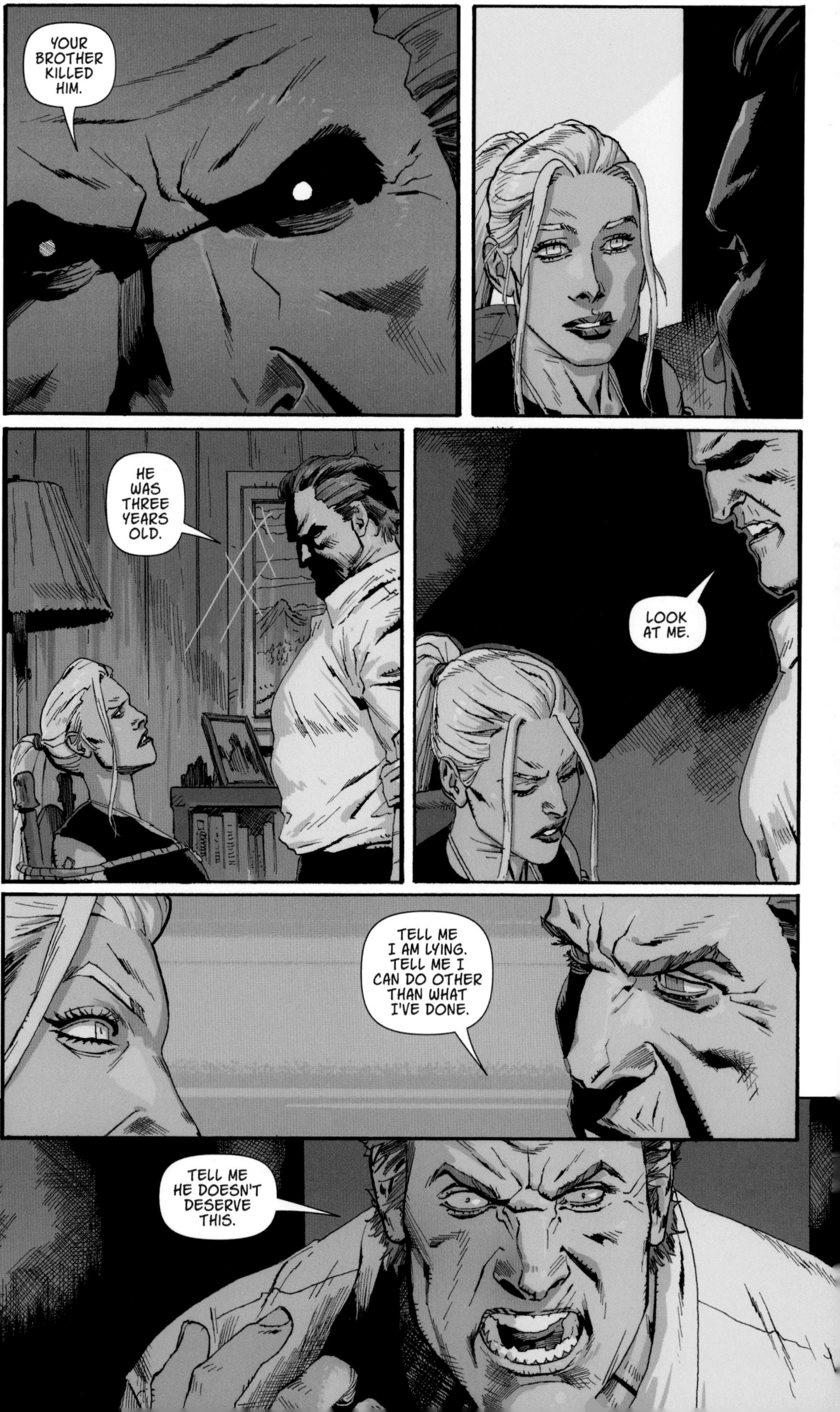
YOUR BROTHER KILLED HIM.
HE WAS THREE YEARS OLD.
LOOK AT ME.
TELL ME I AM LYING. TELL ME I CAN DO OTHER THAN WHAT I'VE DONE.
TELL ME HE DOESN'T DESERVE THIS.

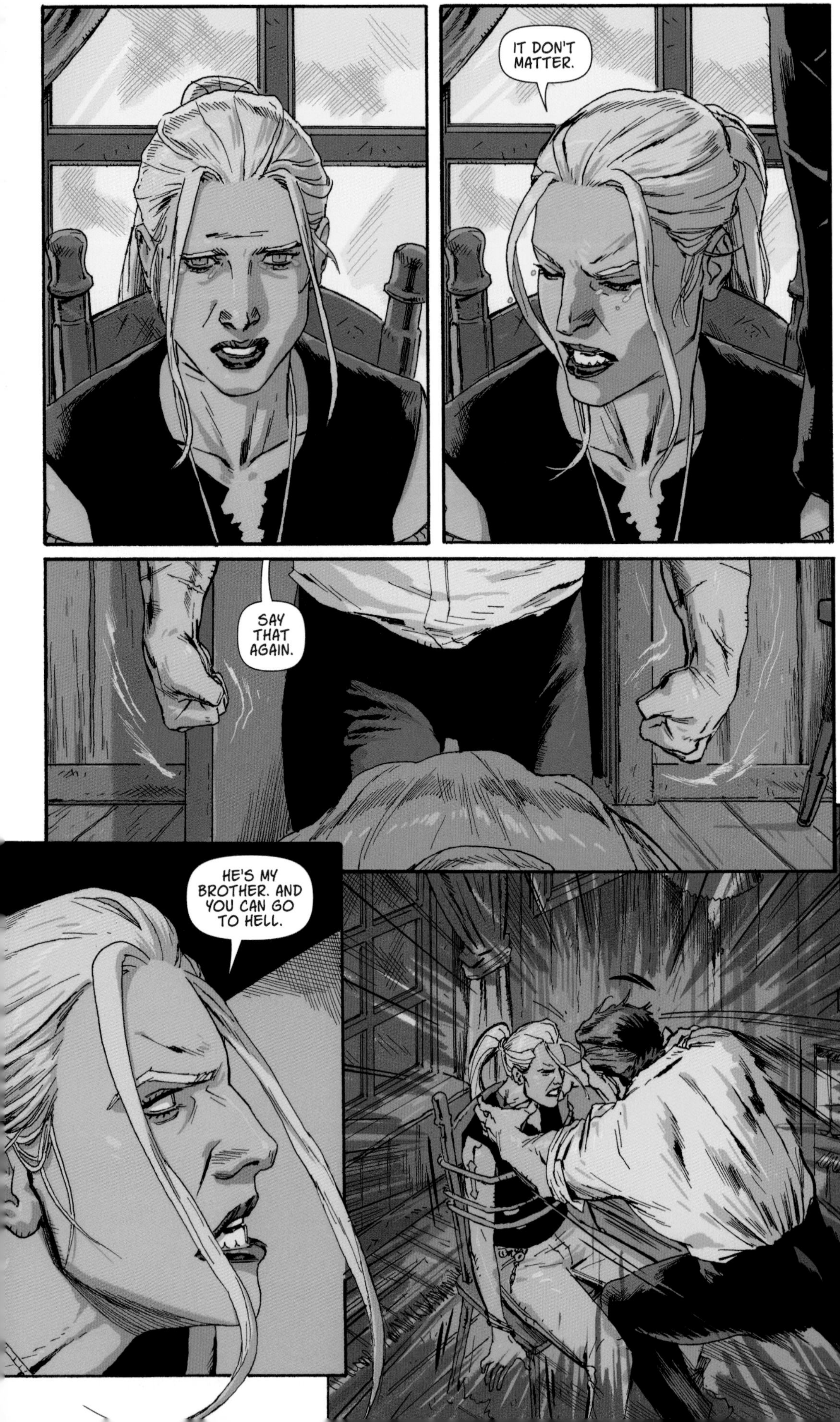
IT DON'T MATTER.
SAY THAT AGAIN.
HE'S MY BROTHER. AND YOU CAN GO TO HELL.

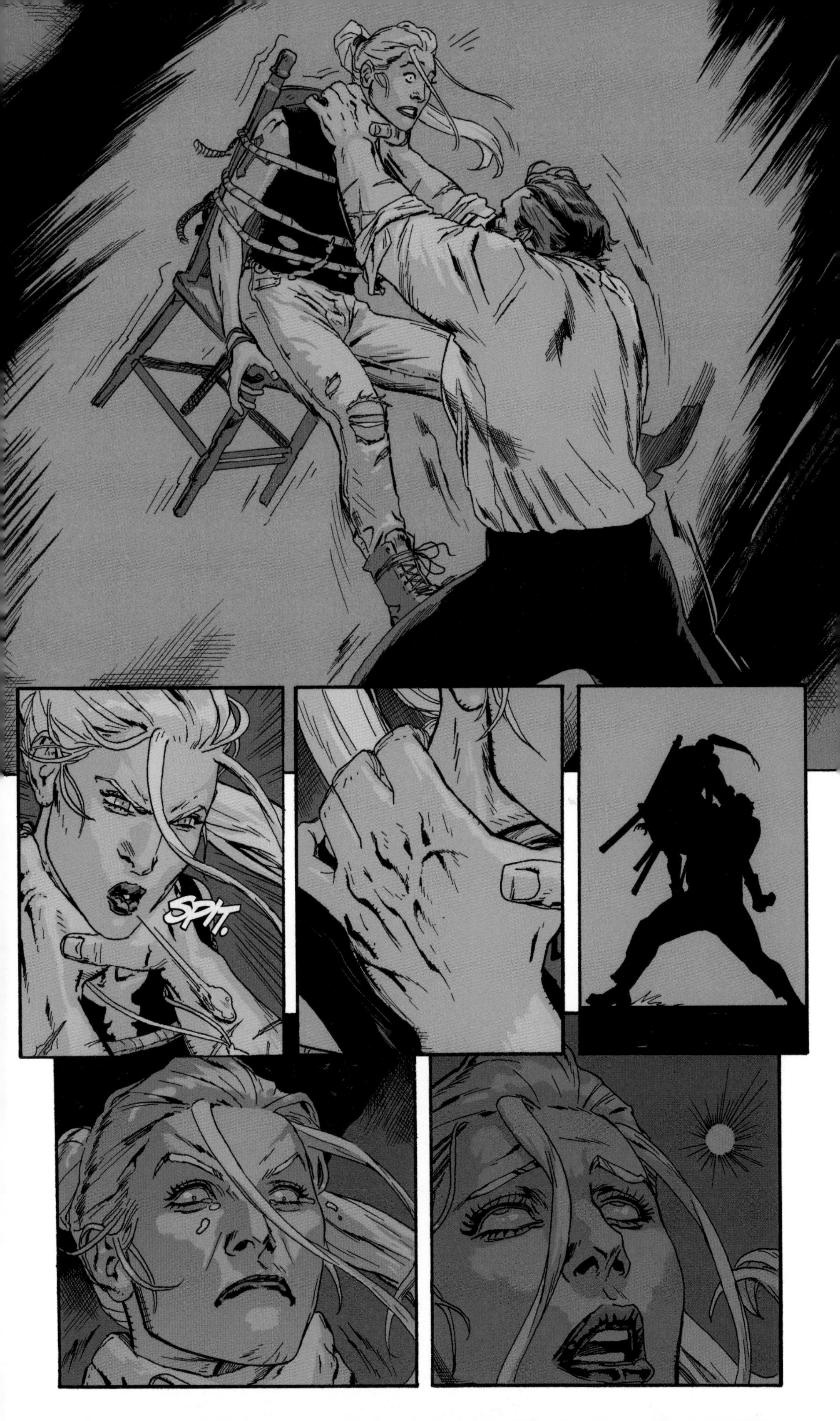
SPIT.

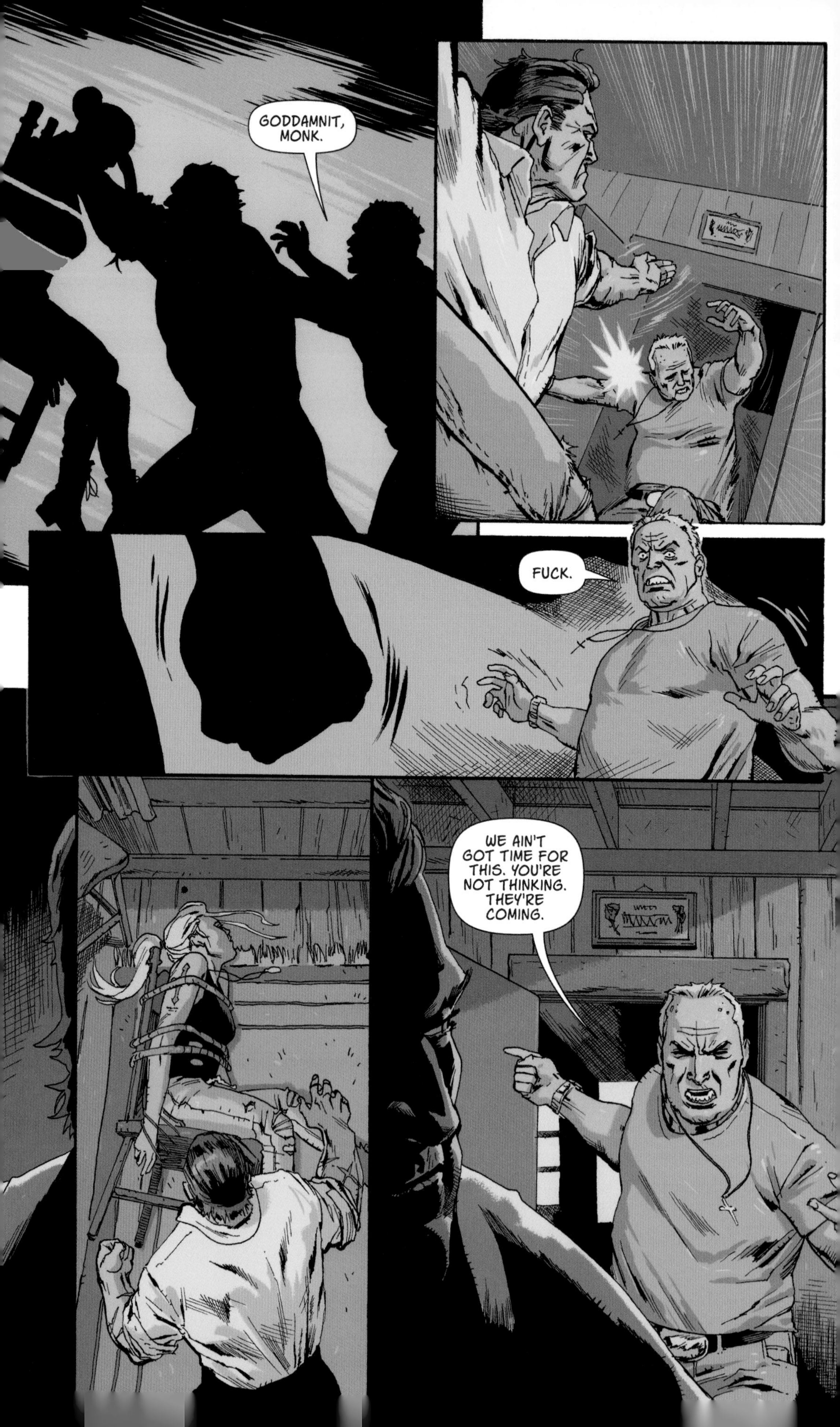
GODDAMNIT, MONK.
FUCK.
WE AIN'T GOT TIME FOR THIS. YOU'RE NOT THINKING. THEY'RE COMING.

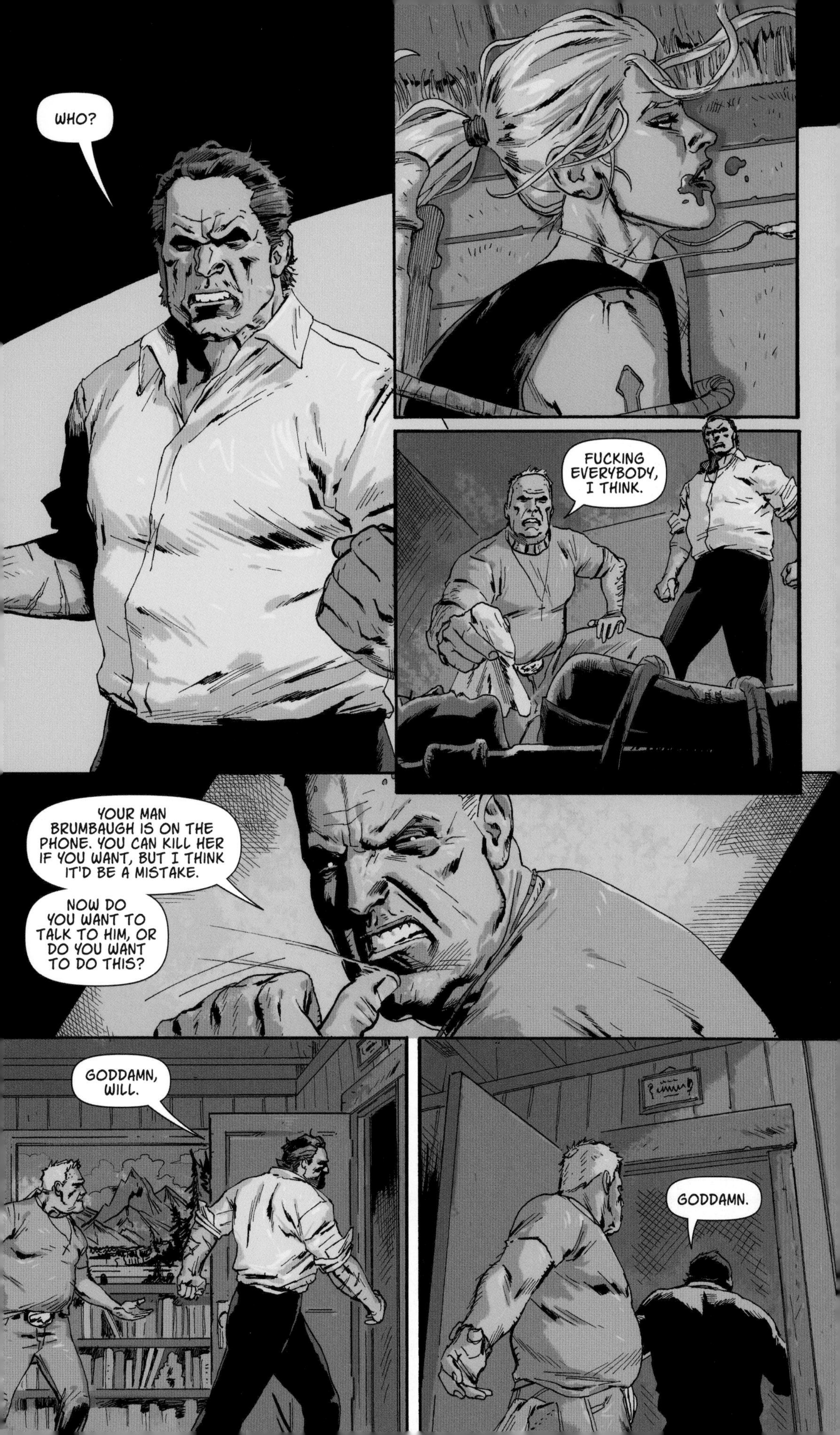
WHO?
FUCKING EVERYBODY, I THINK.
YOUR MAN BRUMBAUGH IS ON THE PHONE. YOU CAN KILL HER IF YOU WANT, BUT I THINK IT'D BE A MISTAKE.
NOW DO YOU WANT TO TALK TO HIM, OR DO YOU WANT TO DO THIS?
GODDAMN, WILL.
GODDAMN.

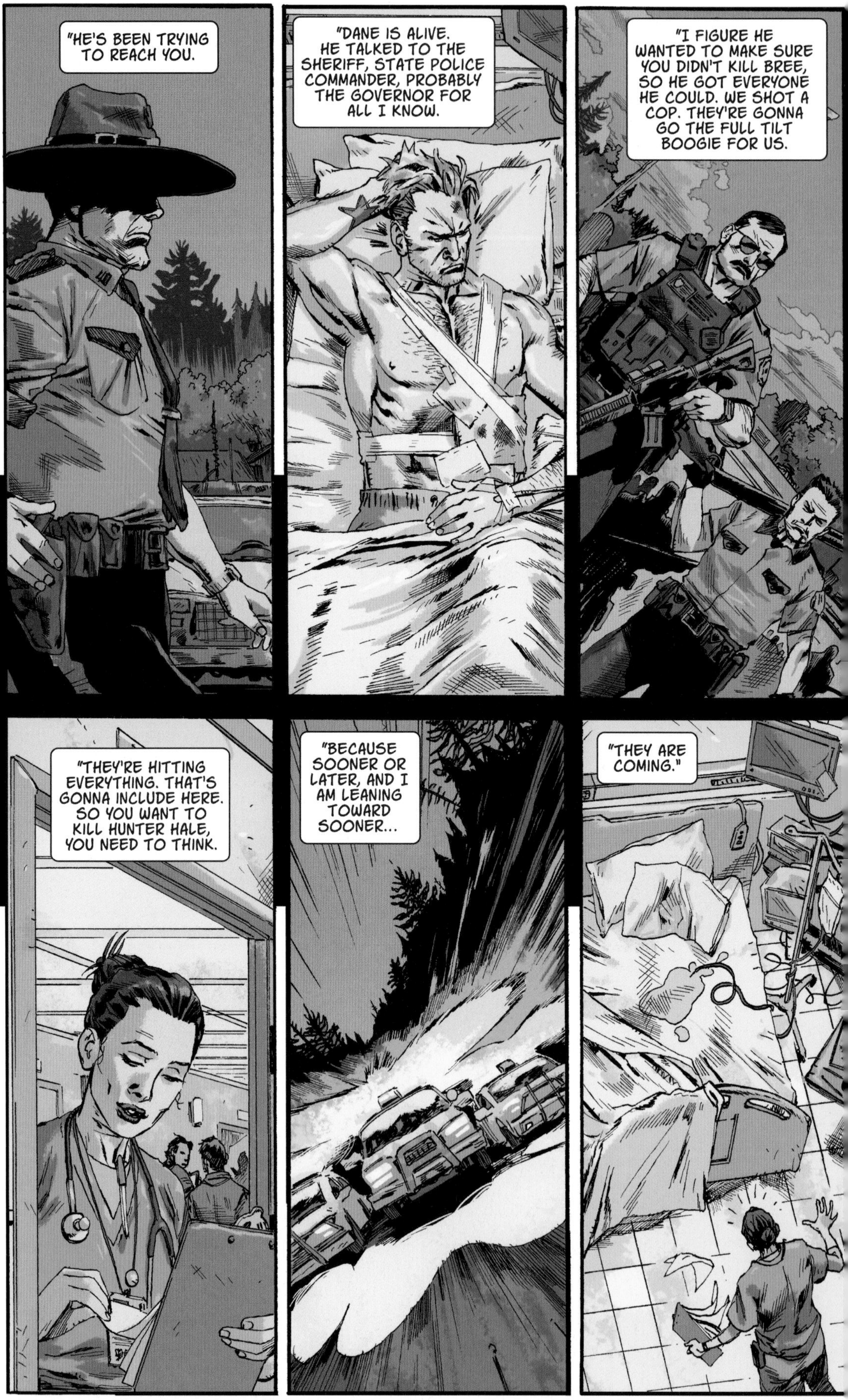
"HE'S BEEN TRYING TO REACH YOU.
"DANE IS ALIVE. HE TALKED TO THE SHERIFF, STATE POLICE COMMANDER, PROBABLY THE GOVERNOR FOR ALL I KNOW.
"I FIGURE HE WANTED TO MAKE SURE YOU DIDN'T KILL BREE, SO HE GOT EVERYONE HE COULD. WE SHOT A COP. THEY'RE GONNA GO THE FULL TILT BOOGIE FOR US.
"THEY'RE HITTING EVERYTHING. THAT'S GONNA INCLUDE HERE. SO YOU WANT TO KILL HUNTER HALE, YOU NEED TO THINK.
"BECAUSE SOONER OR LATER, AND I AM LEANING TOWARD SOONER...
"THEY ARE COMING."

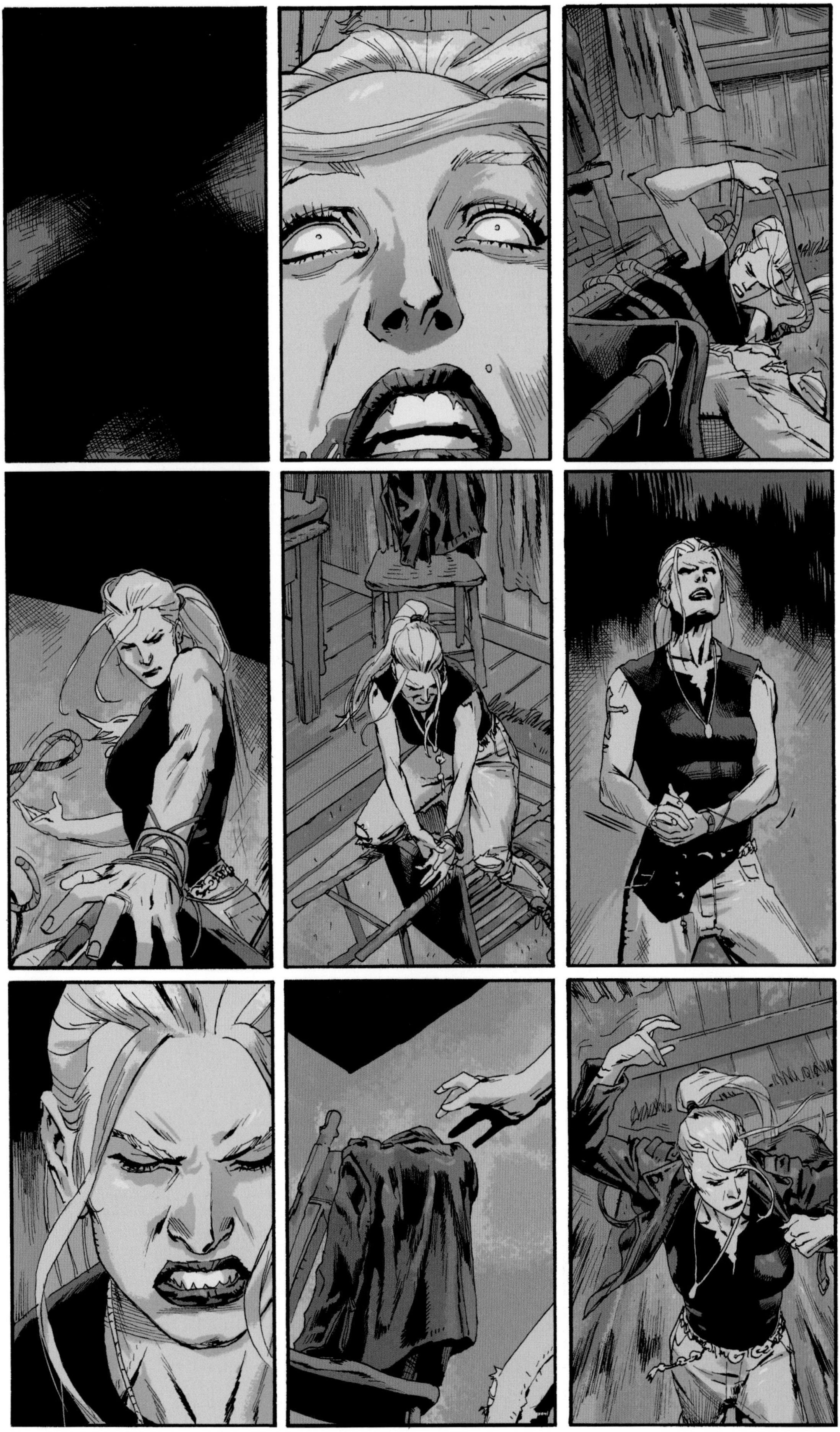

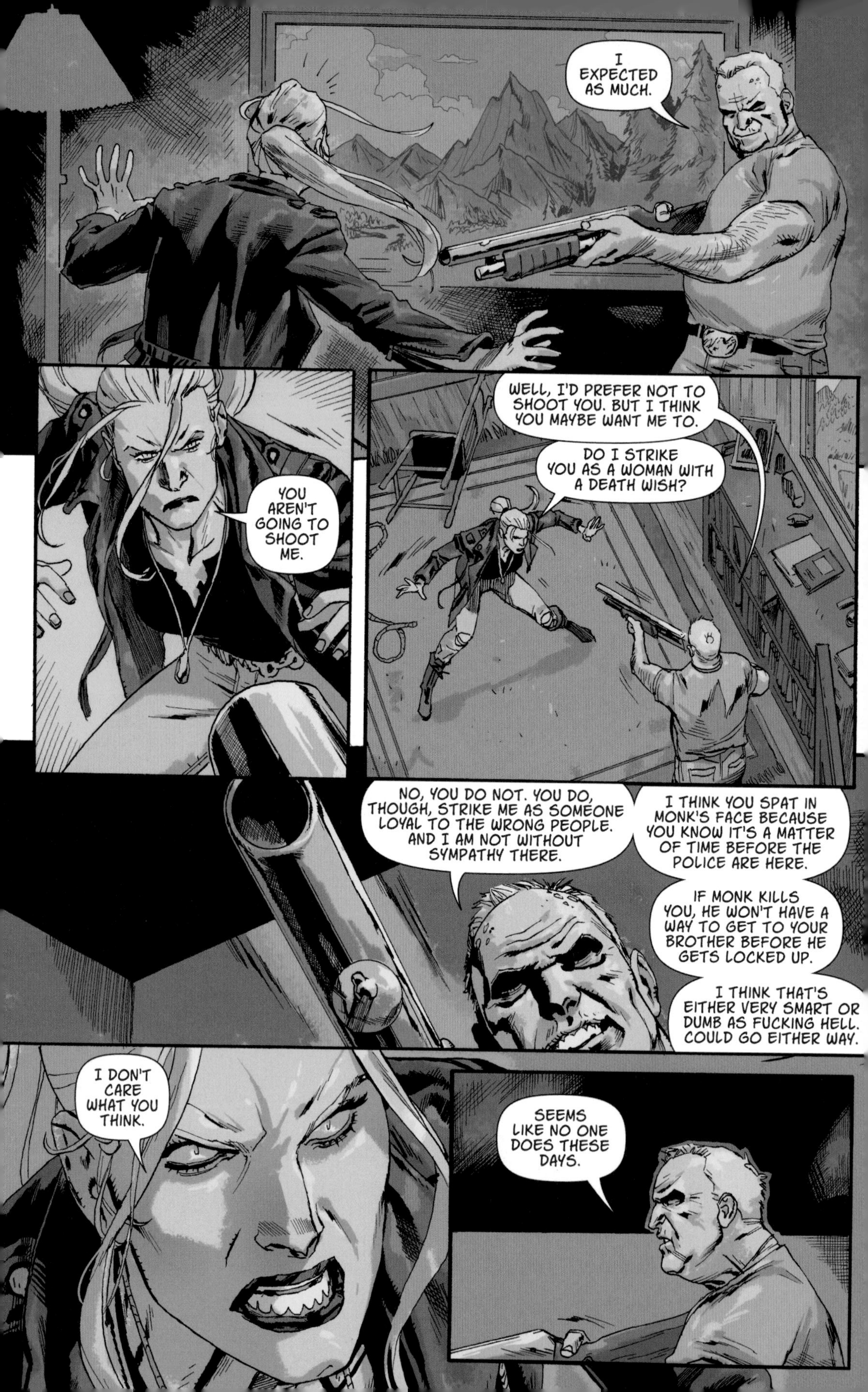
I EXPECTED AS MUCH.
YOU AREN'T GOING TO SHOOT ME.
WELL, I'D PREFER NOT TO SHOOT YOU. BUT I THINK YOU MAYBE WANT ME TO.
DO I STRIKE YOU AS A WOMAN WITH A DEATH WISH?
NO, YOU DO NOT. YOU DO, THOUGH, STRIKE ME AS SOMEONE LOYAL TO THE WRONG PEOPLE. AND I AM NOT WITHOUT SYMPATHY THERE.
I THINK YOU SPAT IN MONK'S FACE BECAUSE YOU KNOW IT'S A MATTER OF TIME BEFORE THE POLICE ARE HERE.
IF MONK KILLS YOU, HE WON'T HAVE A WAY TO GET TO YOUR BROTHER BEFORE HE GETS LOCKED UP.
I THINK THAT'S EITHER VERY SMART OR DUMB AS FUCKING HELL. COULD GO EITHER WAY.
I DON'T CARE WHAT YOU THINK.
SEEMS LIKE NO ONE DOES THESE DAYS.

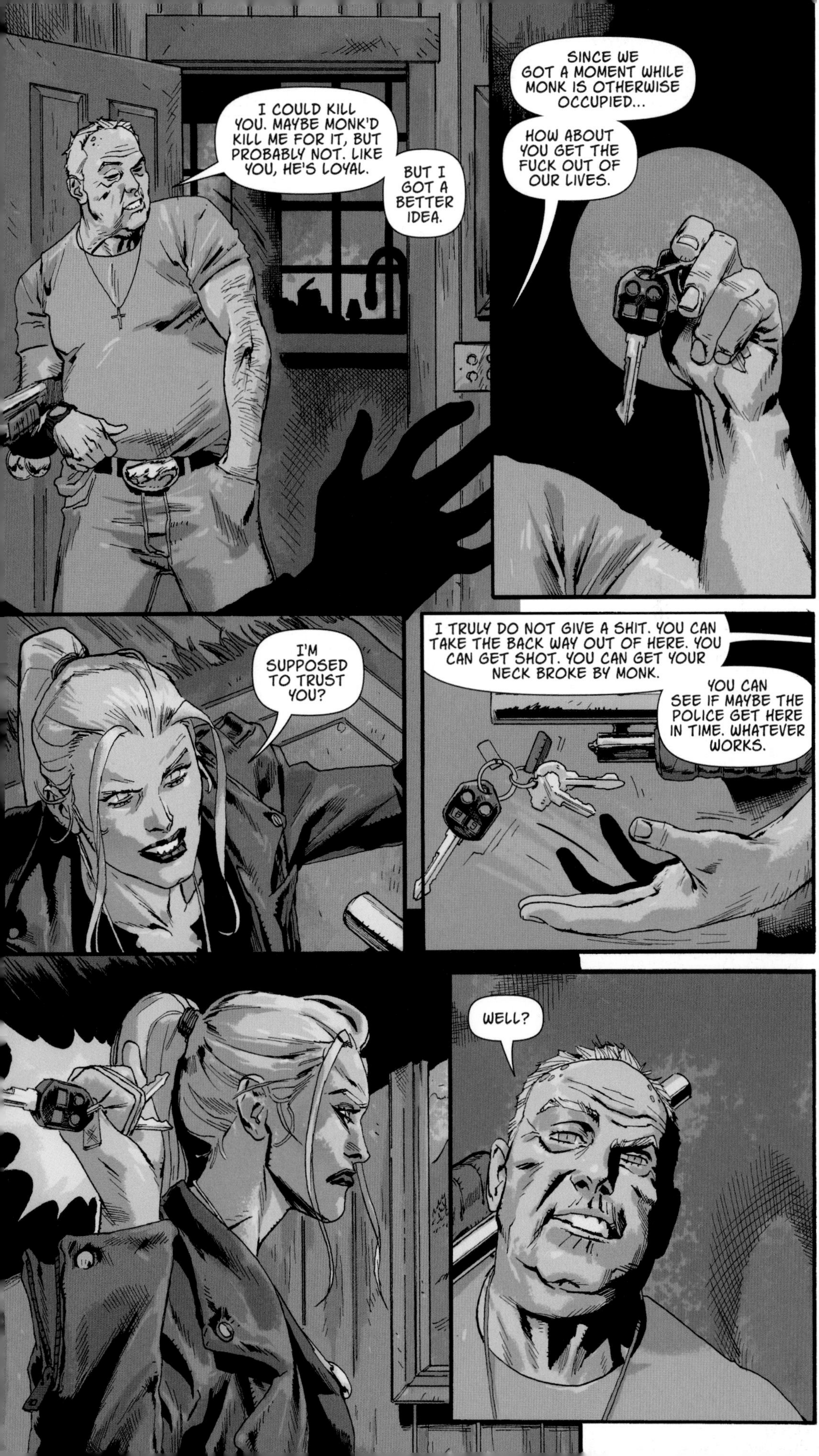
I COULD KILL YOU. MAYBE MONK'D KILL ME FOR IT, BUT PROBABLY NOT. LIKE YOU, HE'S LOYAL.
BUT I GOT A BETTER IDEA.
SINCE WE GOT A MOMENT WHILE MONK IS OTHERWISE OCCUPIED...
HOW ABOUT YOU GET THE FUCK OUT OF OUR LIVES.
I'M SUPPOSED TO TRUST YOU?
I TRULY DO NOT GIVE A SHIT. YOU CAN TAKE THE BACK WAY OUT OF HERE. YOU CAN GET SHOT. YOU CAN GET YOUR NECK BROKE BY MONK.
YOU CAN SEE IF MAYBE THE POLICE GET HERE IN TIME. WHATEVER WORKS.
WELL?

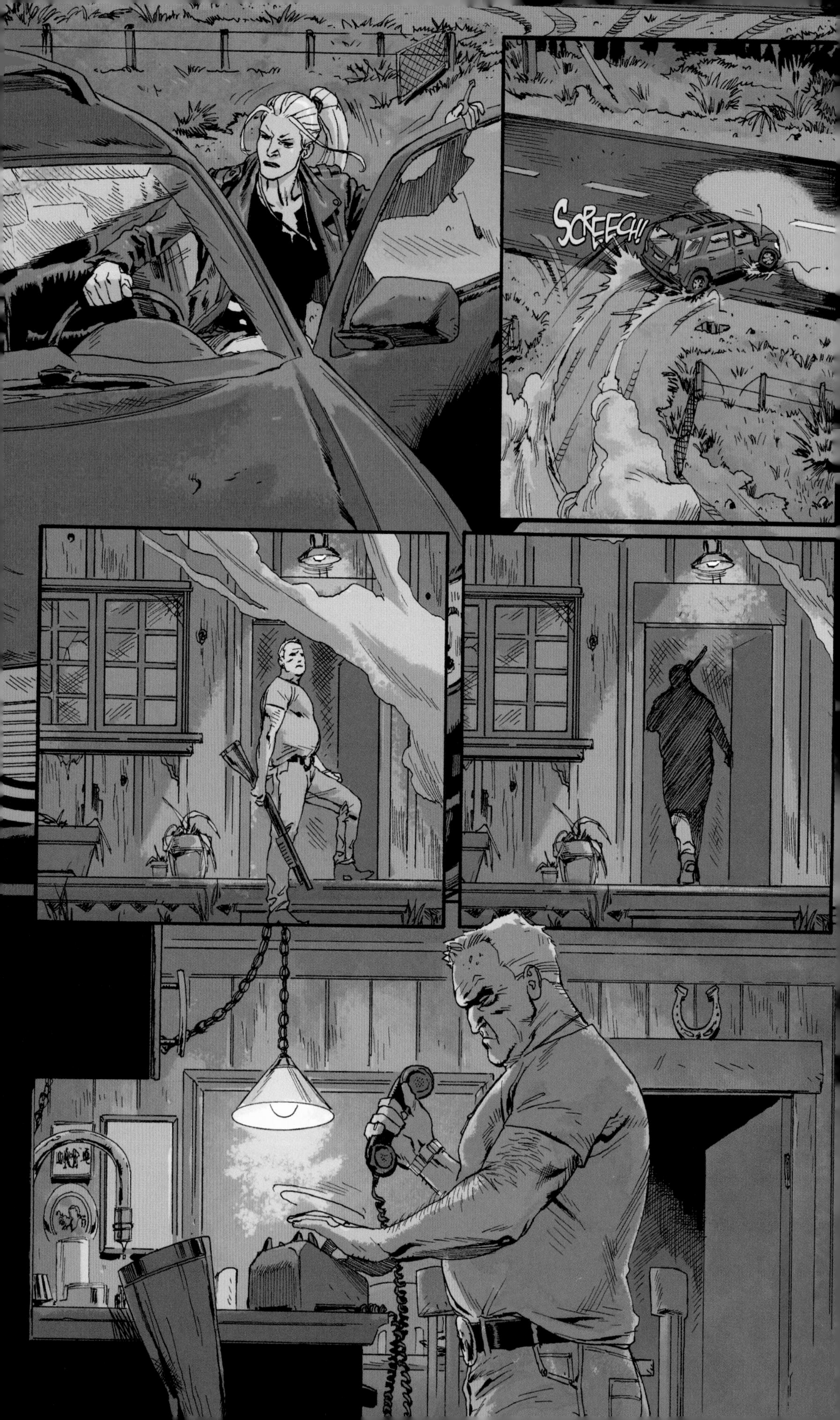
SCREECH!!

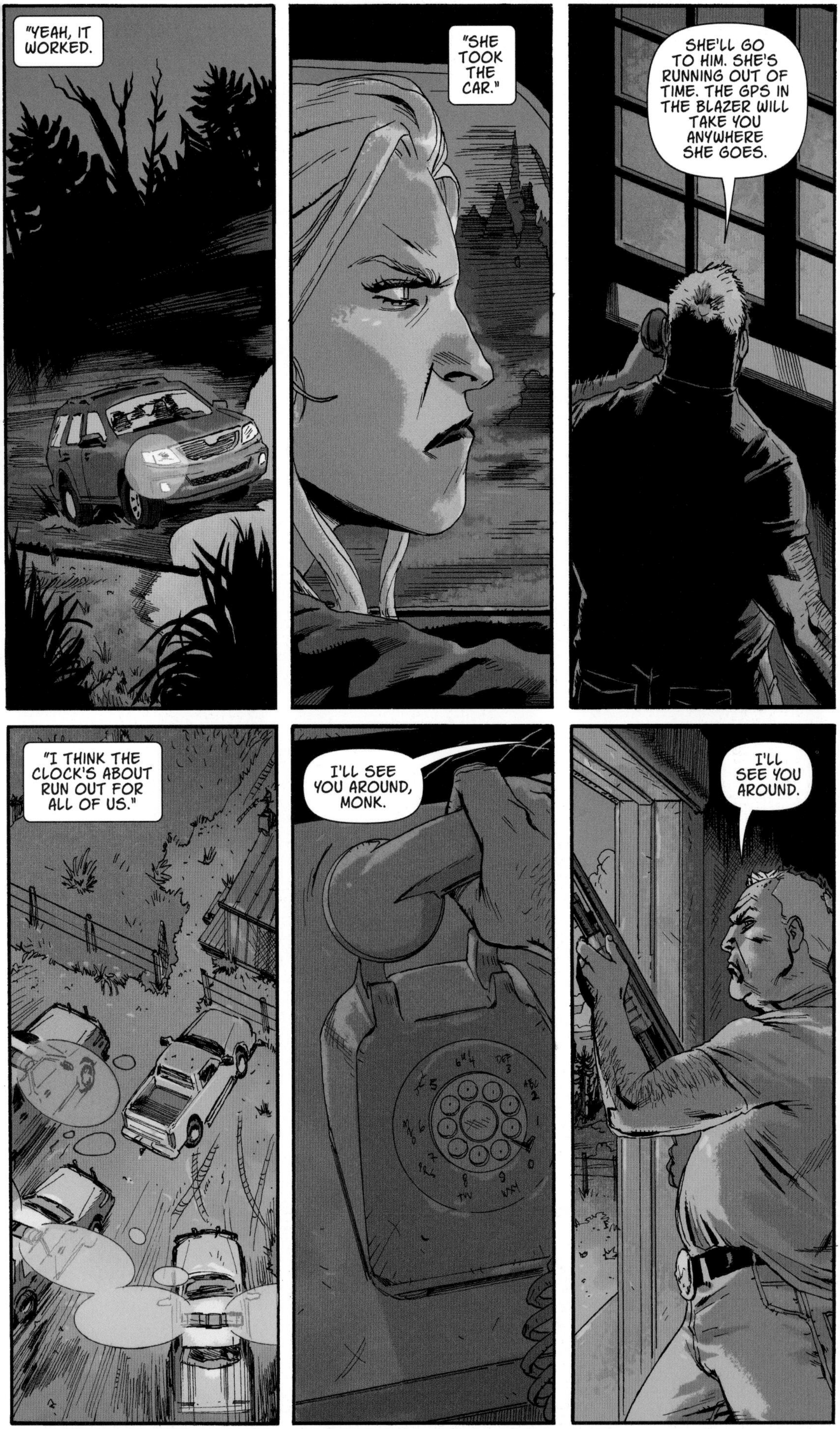
"YEAH, IT WORKED.
"SHE TOOK THE CAR."
SHE'LL GO TO HIM. SHE'S RUNNING OUT OF TIME. THE GPS IN THE BLAZER WILL TAKE YOU ANYWHERE SHE GOES.
"I THINK THE CLOCK'S ABOUT RUN OUT FOR ALL OF US."
I'LL SEE YOU AROUND, MONK.
I'LL SEE YOU AROUND.

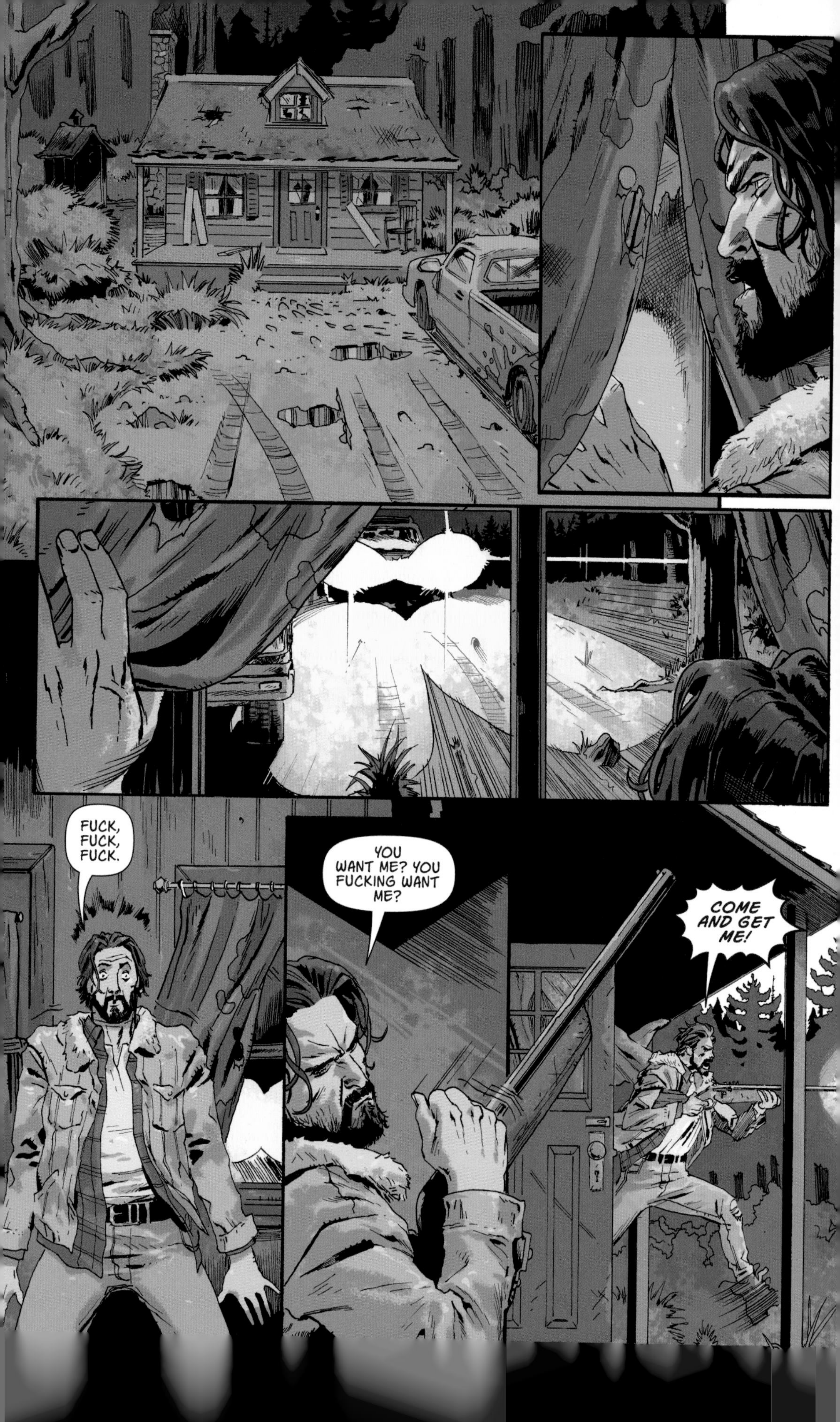
FUCK, FUCK, FUCK.
YOU WANT ME? YOU FUCKING WANT ME?
COME AND GET ME!

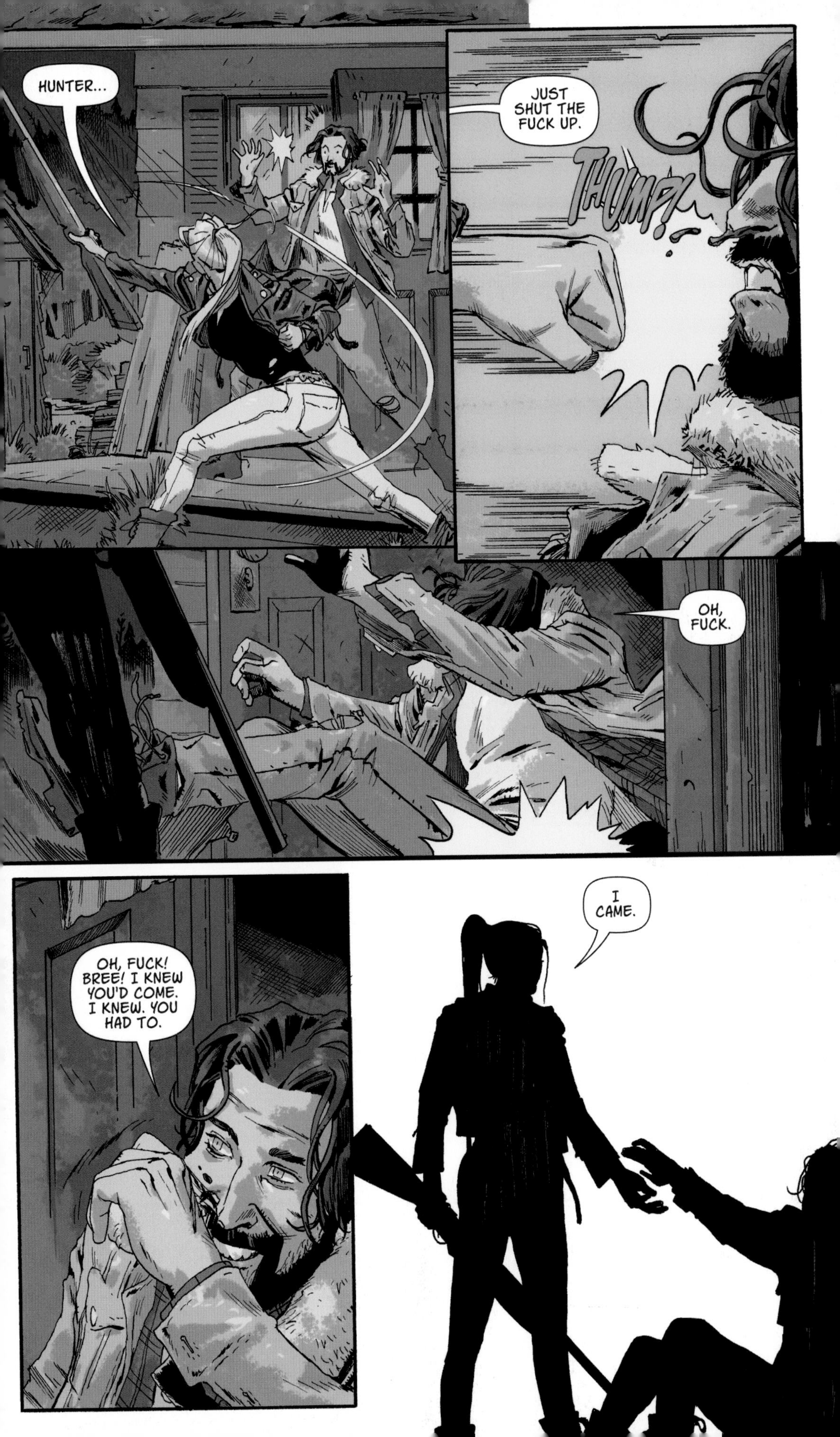
HUNTER...
JUST SHUT THE FUCK UP.
THUMP!
OH, FUCK.
OH, FUCK! BREE! I KNEW YOU'D COME. I KNEW. YOU HAD TO.
I CAME.

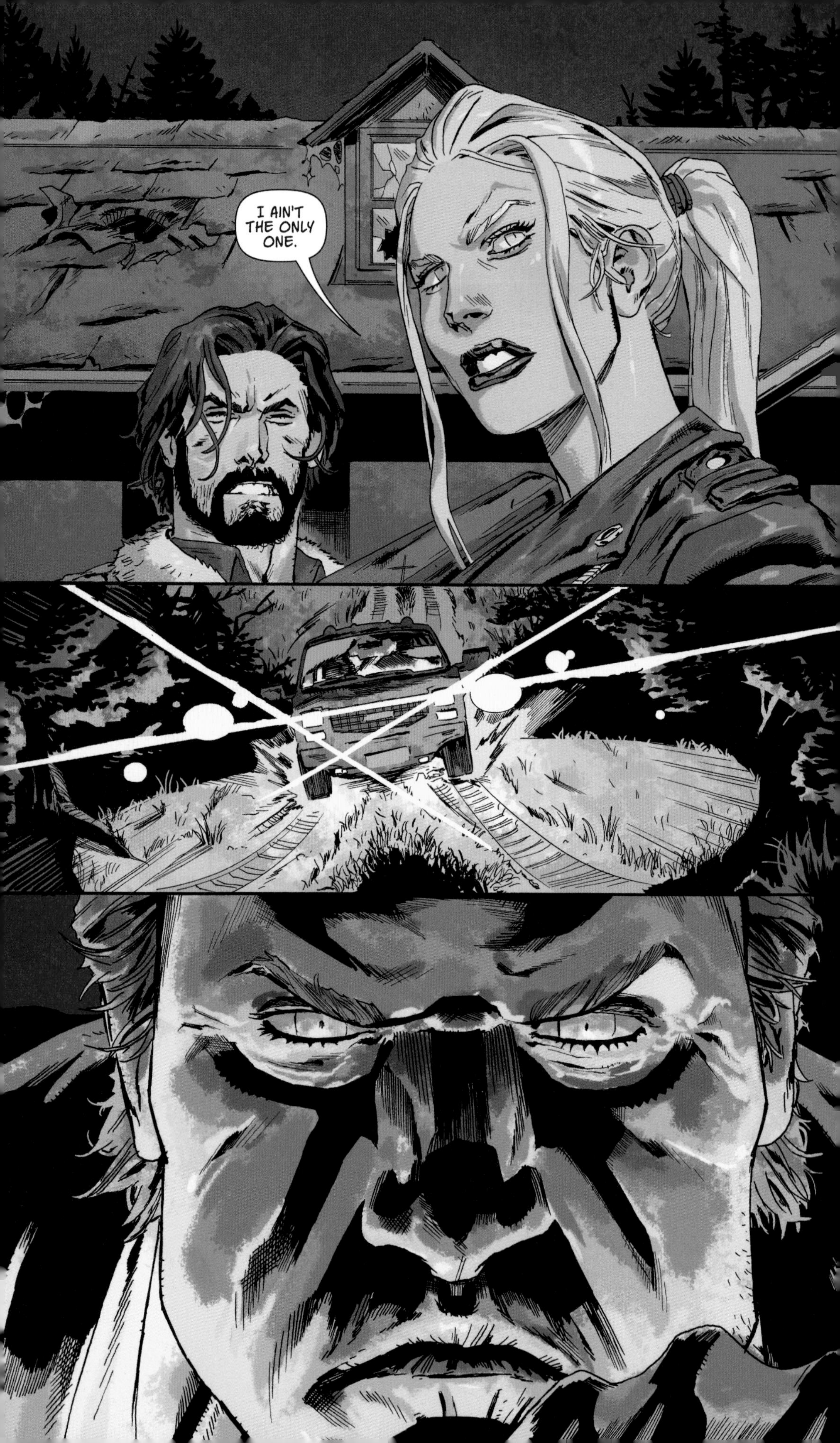
I AIN'T THE ONLY ONE.

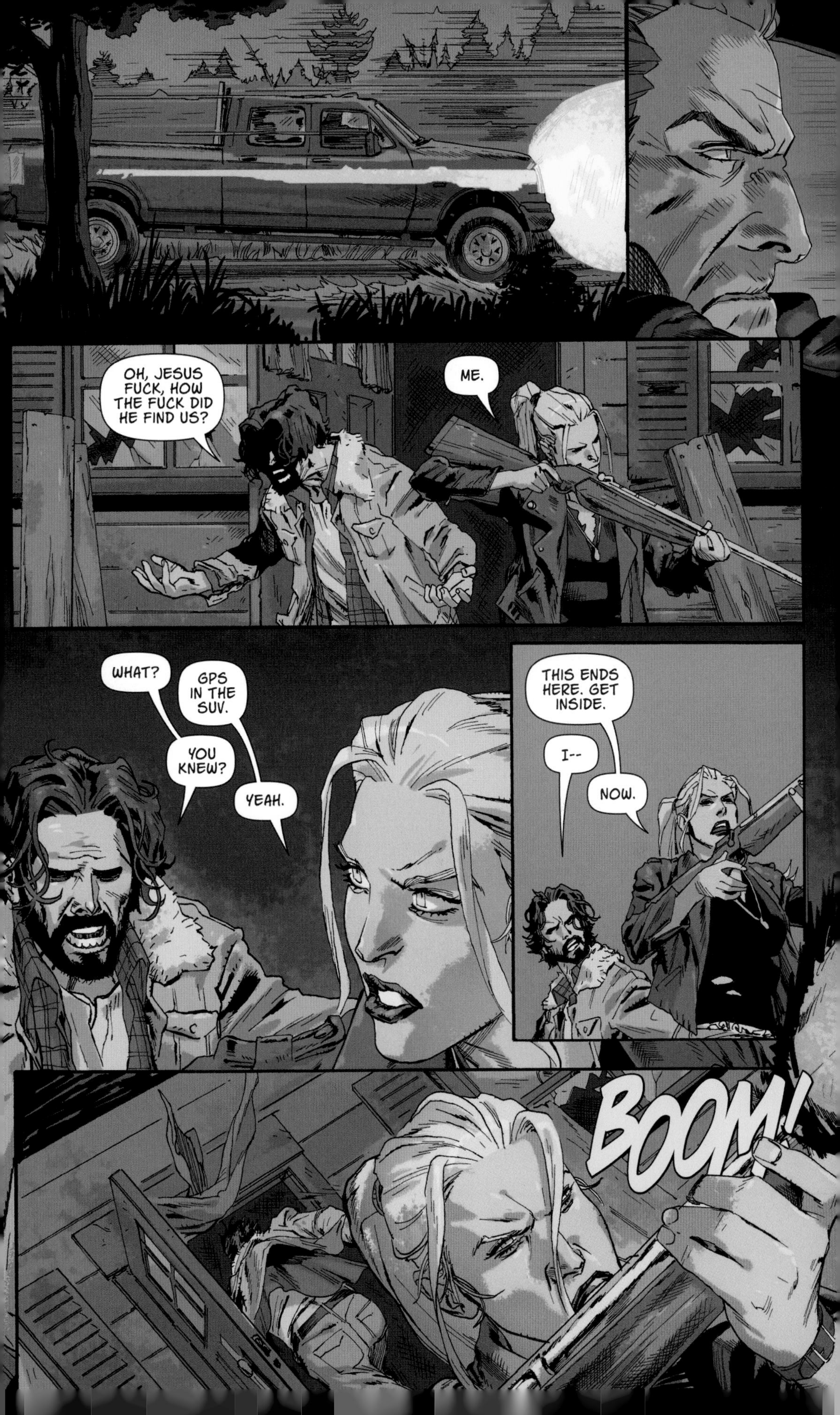
OH, JESUS FUCK, HOW THE FUCK DID HE FIND US?
ME.
WHAT?
GPS IN THE SUV.
YOU KNEW?
YEAH.
THIS ENDS HERE. GET INSIDE.
I--
NOW.
BOOM!

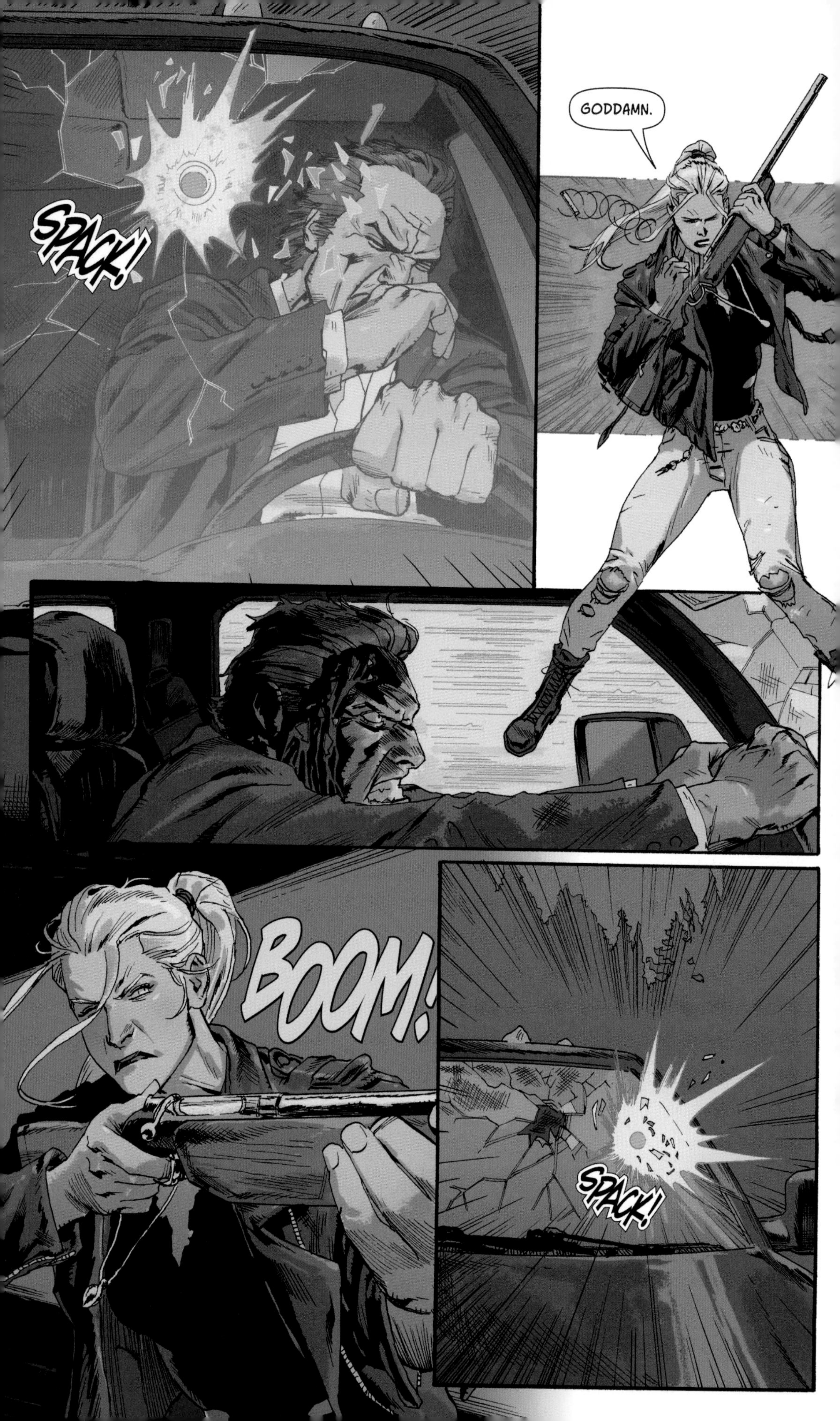
SPACK!
GODDAMN.
BOOM!
SPACK!

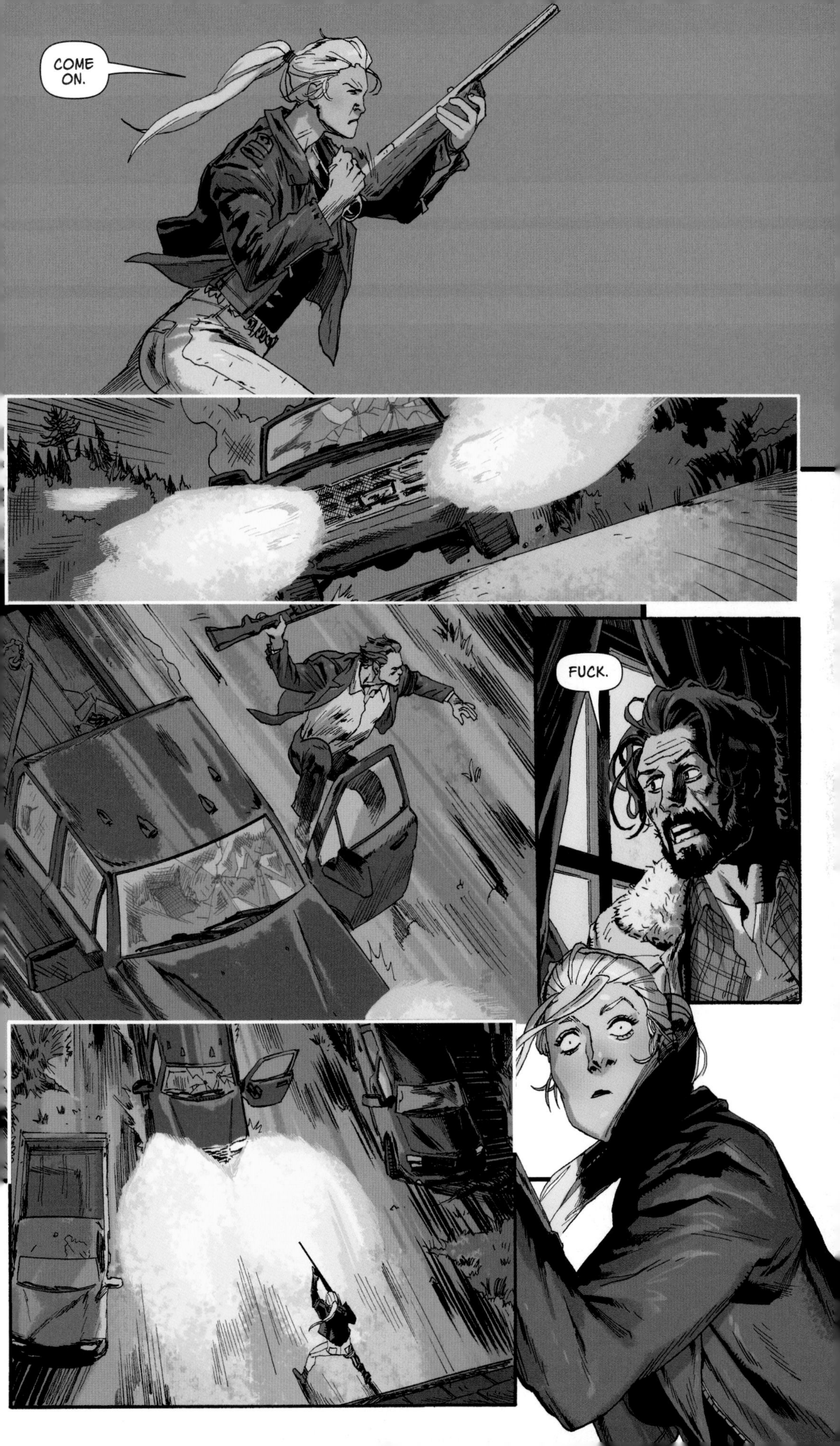
COME ON.
FUCK.

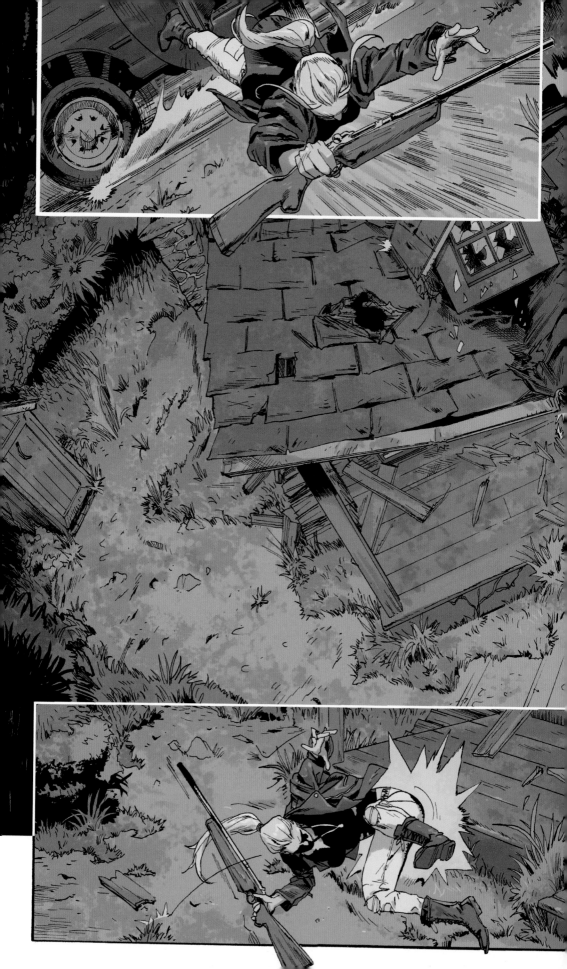

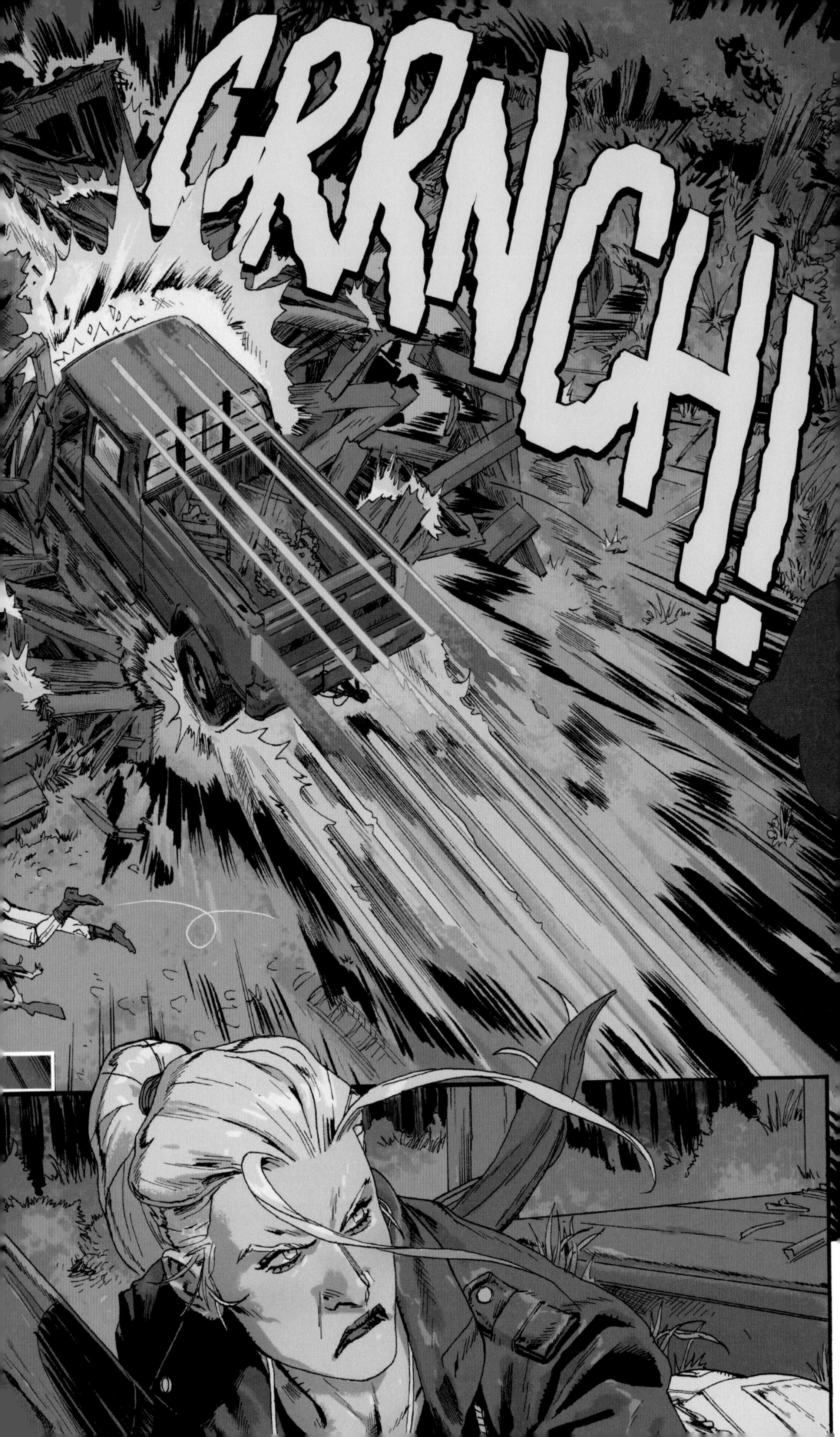
CRRNCH!!

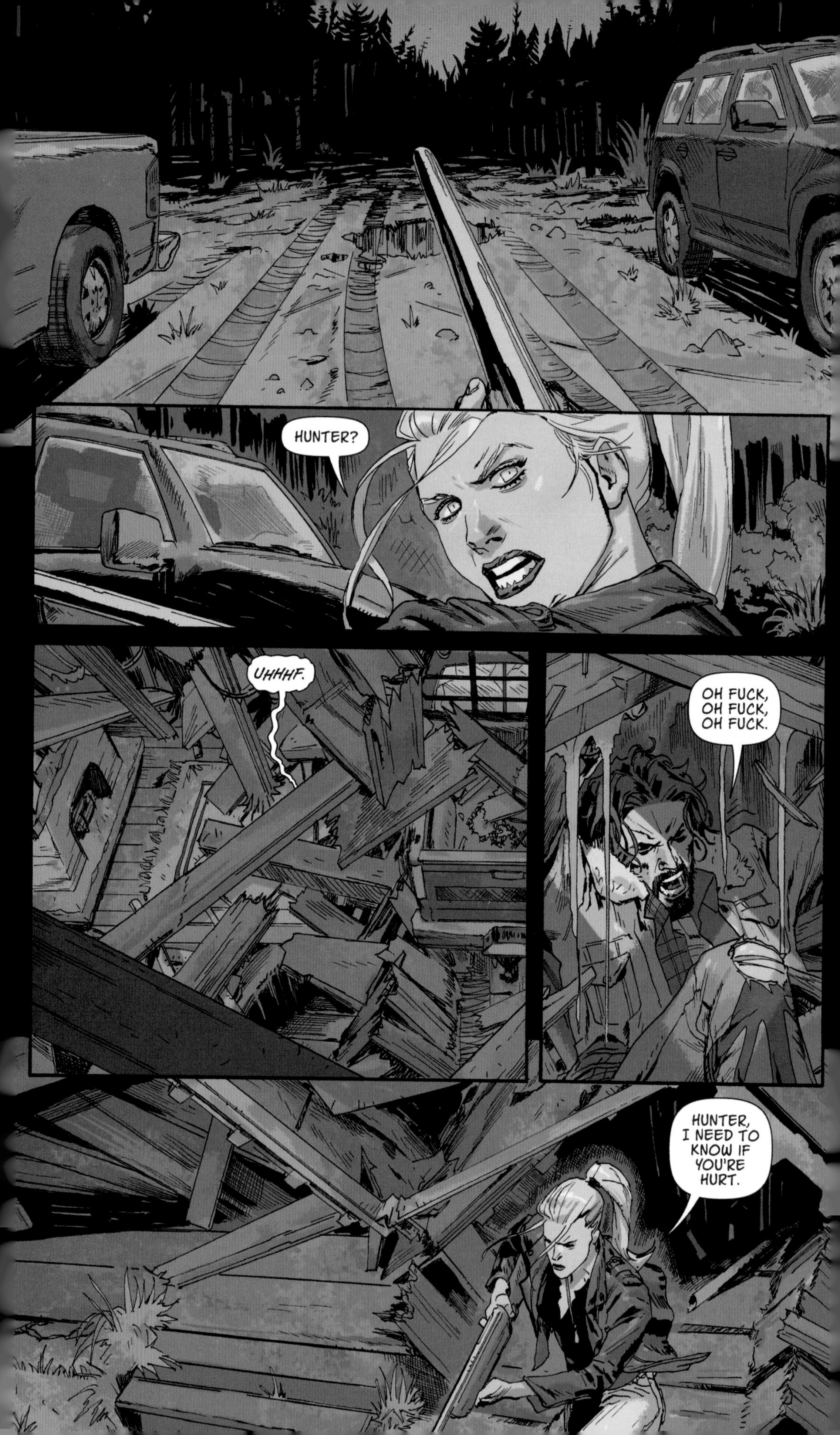
HUNTER?
UHHHF.
OH FUCK, OH FUCK, OH FUCK.
HUNTER, I NEED TO KNOW IF YOU'RE HURT.

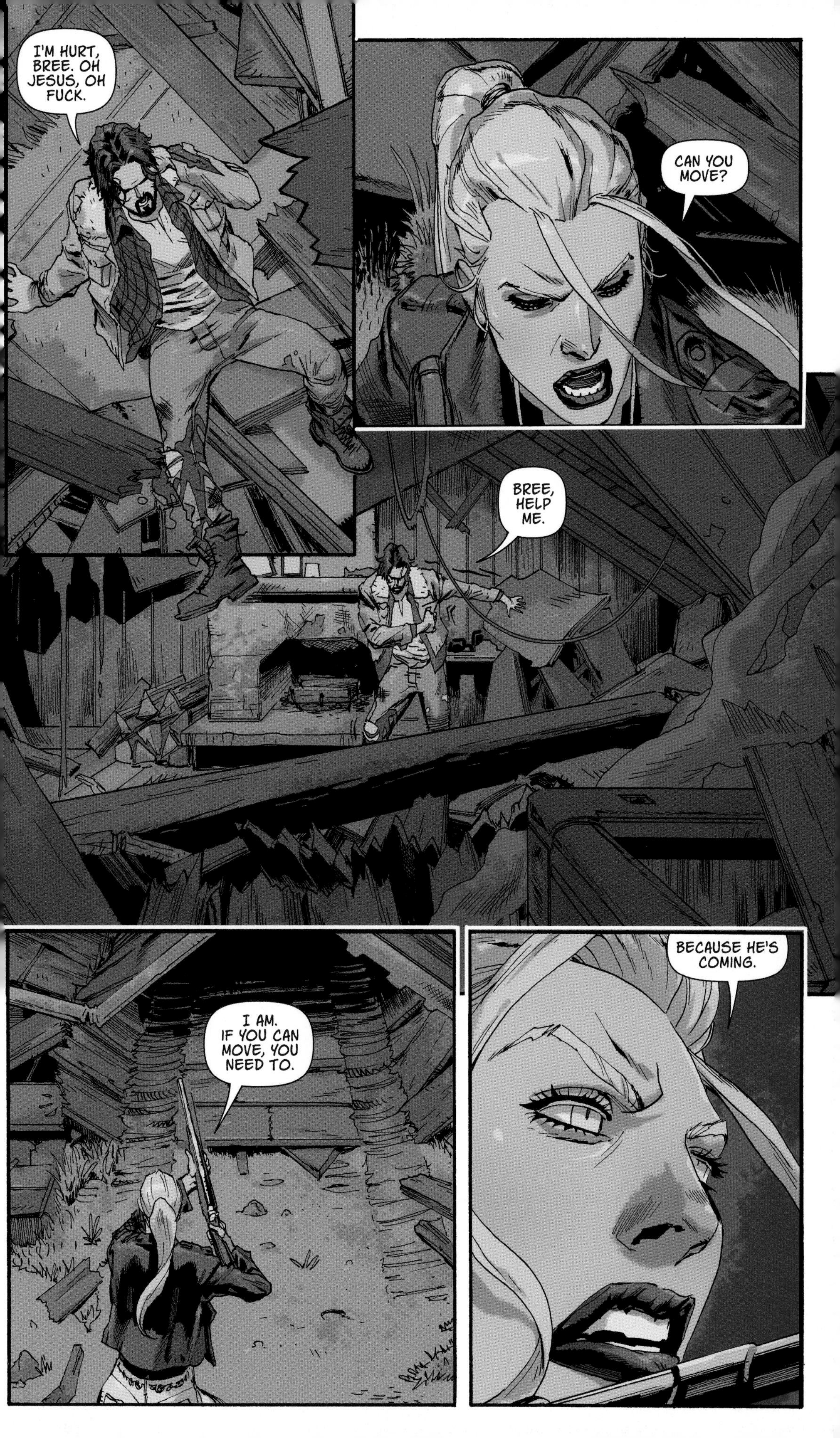
I'M HURT, BREE. OH JESUS, OH FUCK.
CAN YOU MOVE?
BREE, HELP ME.
I AM. IF YOU CAN MOVE, YOU NEED TO.
BECAUSE HE'S COMING.

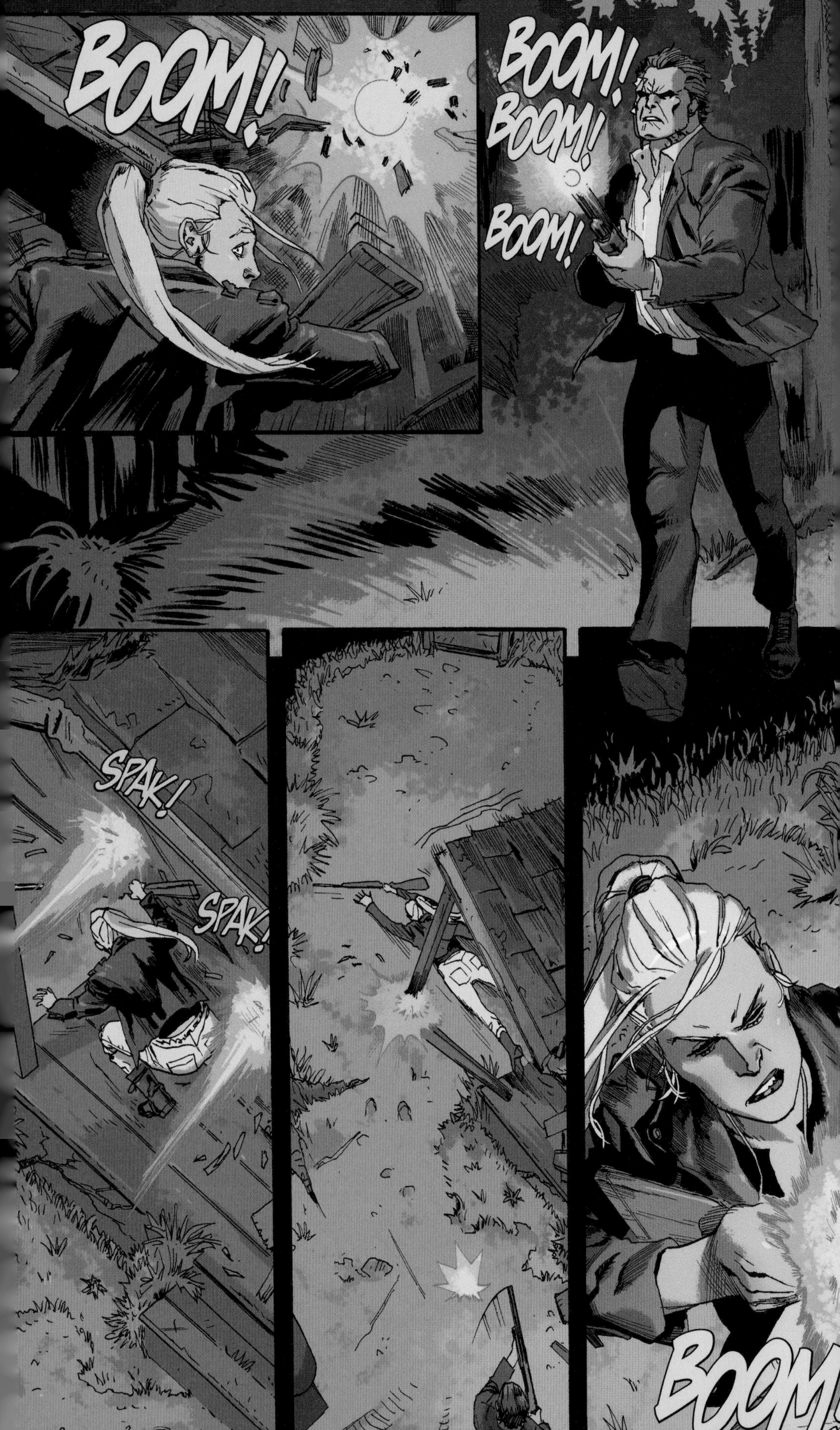
BOOM!
BOOM!
BOOM!
BOOM!
SPAK!
SPAK!
BOOM!

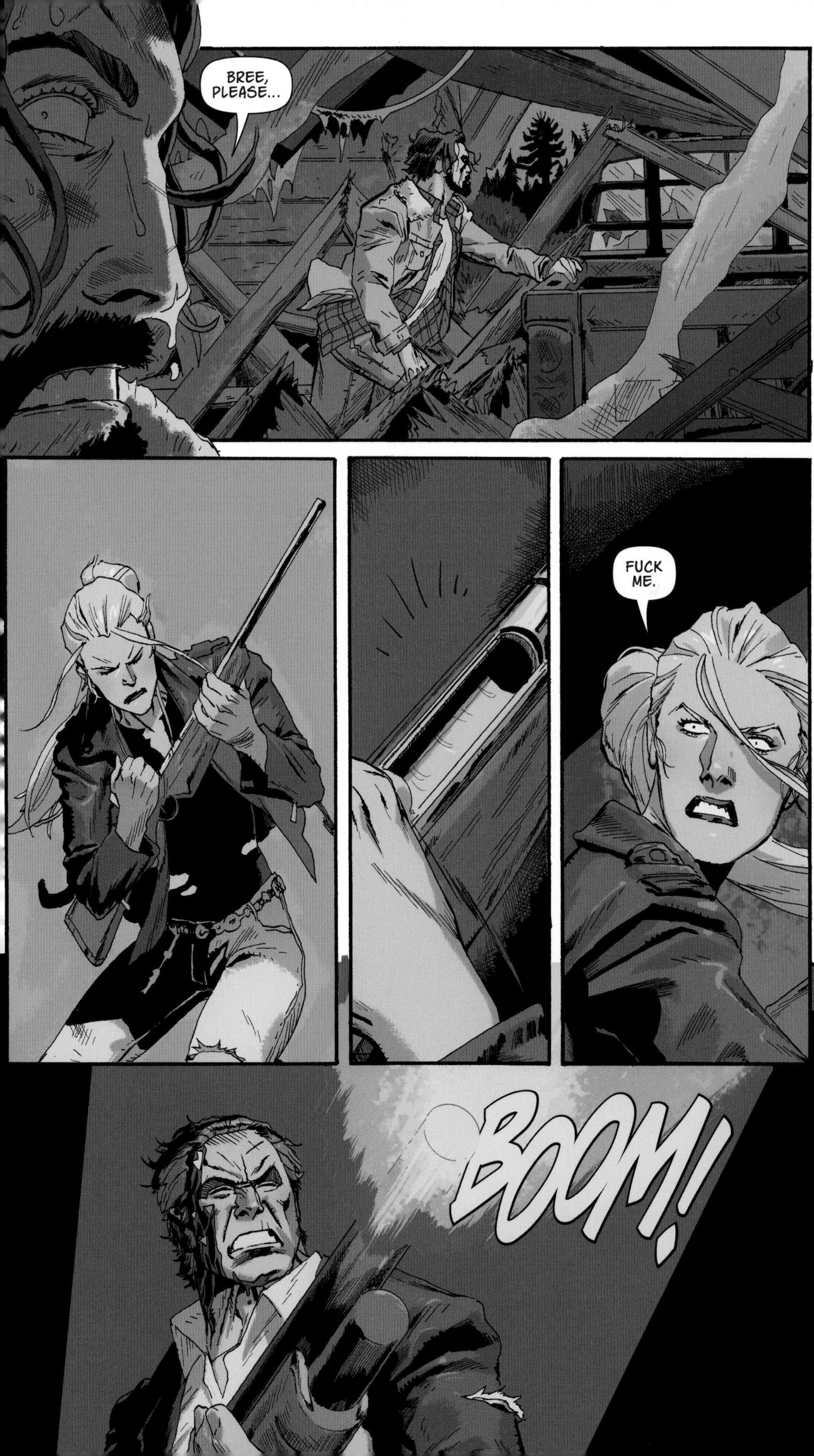
BREE, PLEASE...
FUCK ME.
BOOM!

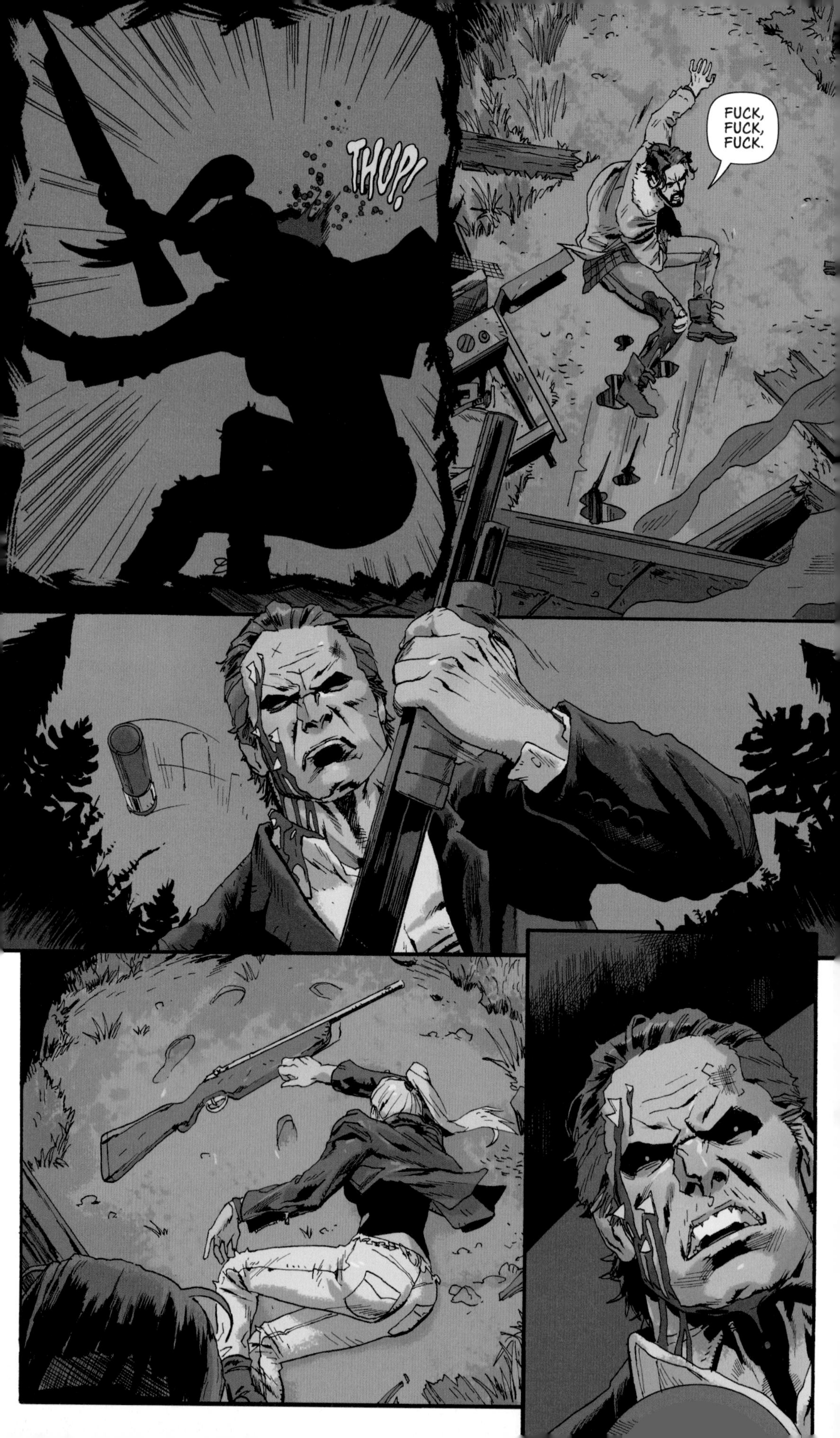
THUP!
FUCK, FUCK, FUCK.

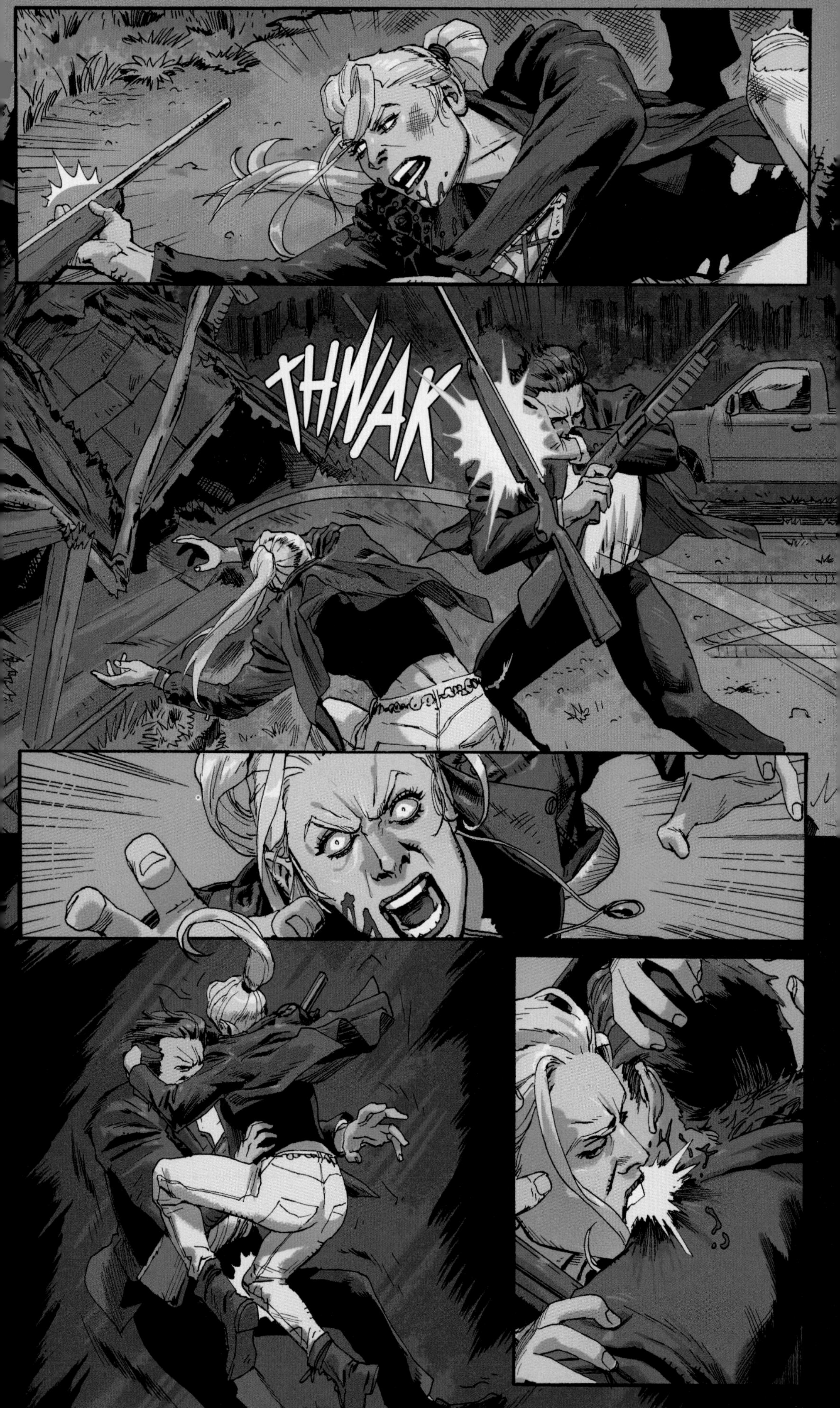
THWAK

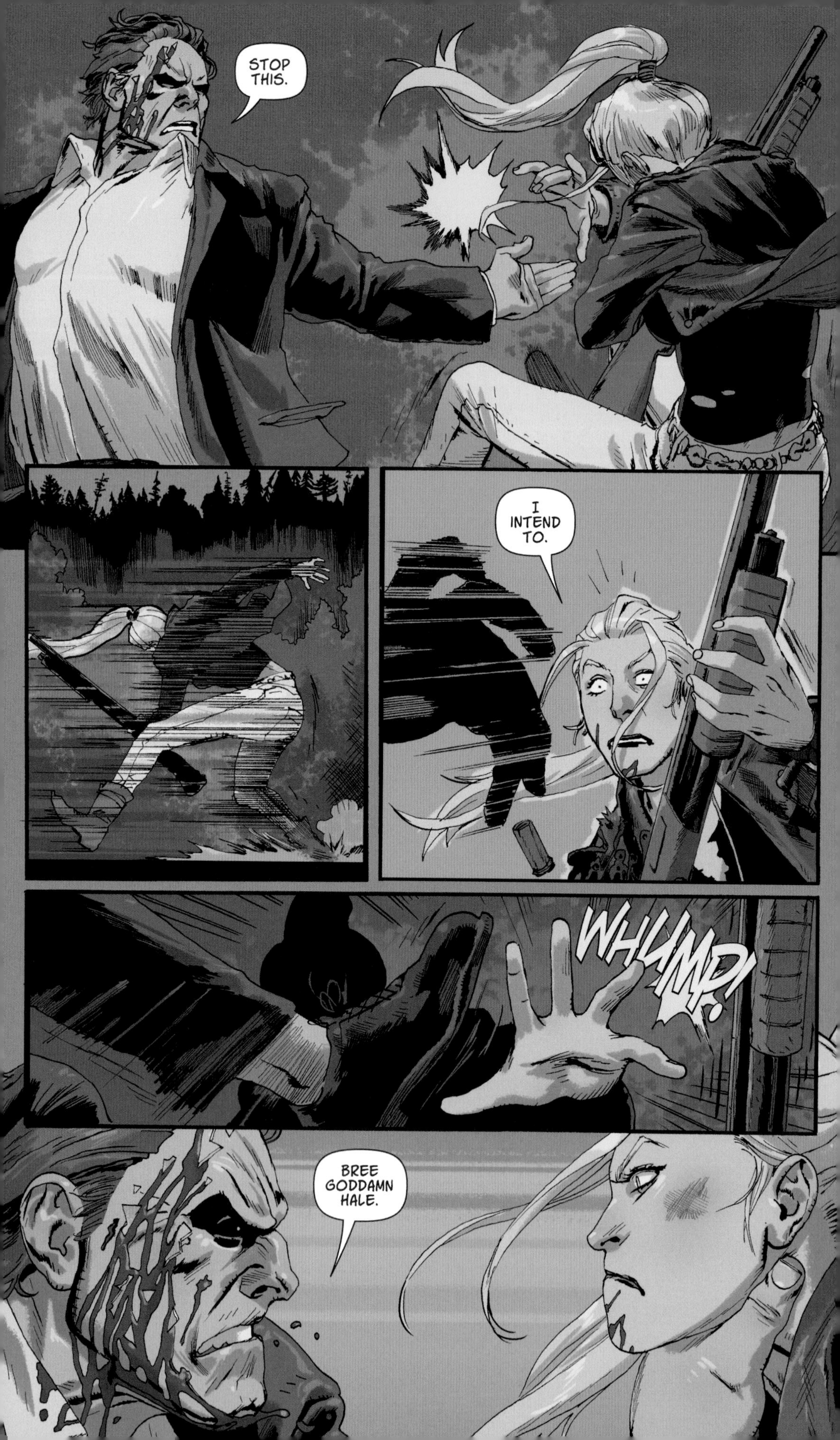
STOP THIS.
I INTEND TO.
WHUMP!
BREE GODDAMN HALE.

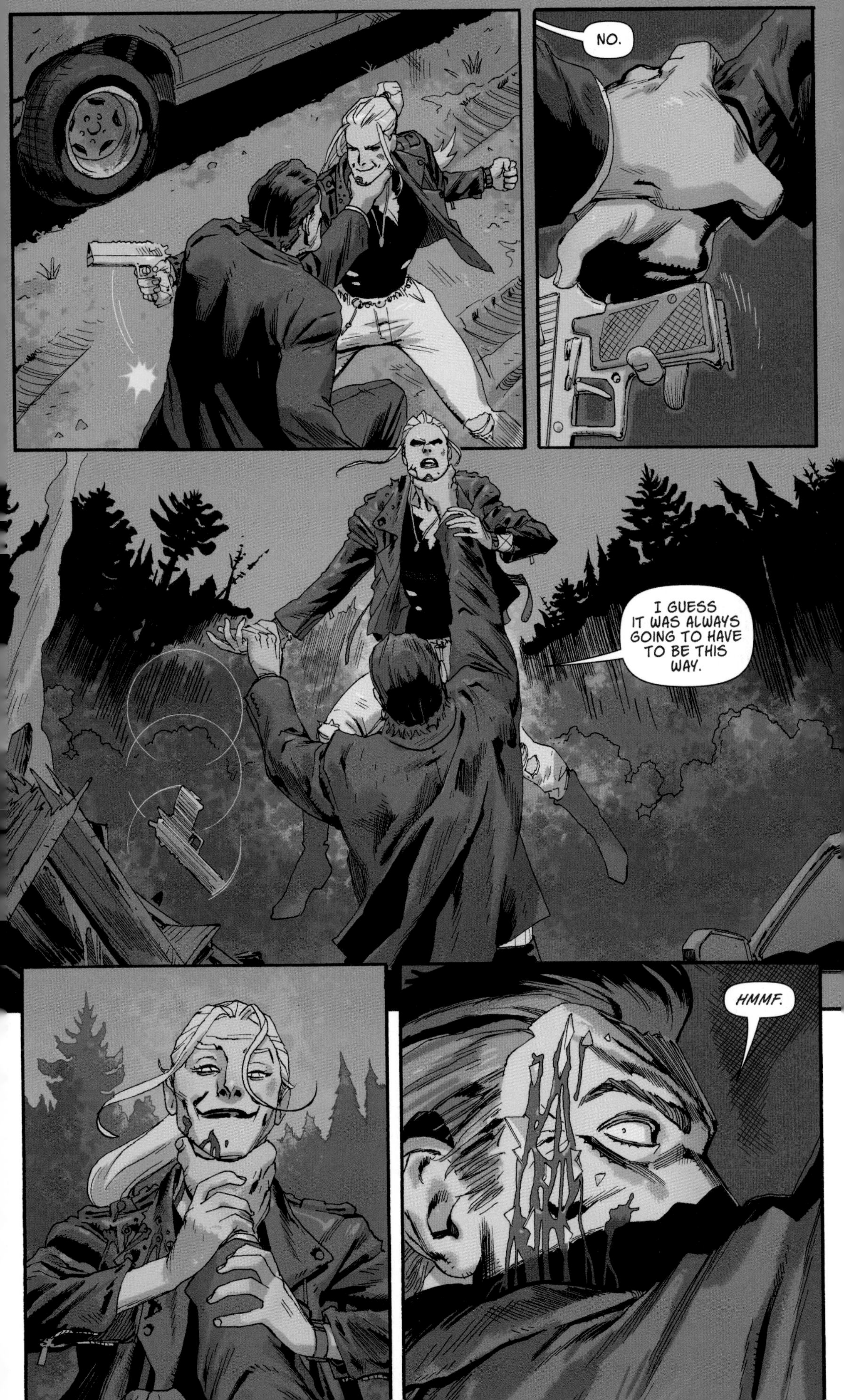
NO.
I GUESS IT WAS ALWAYS GOING TO HAVE TO BE THIS WAY.
HMMF.

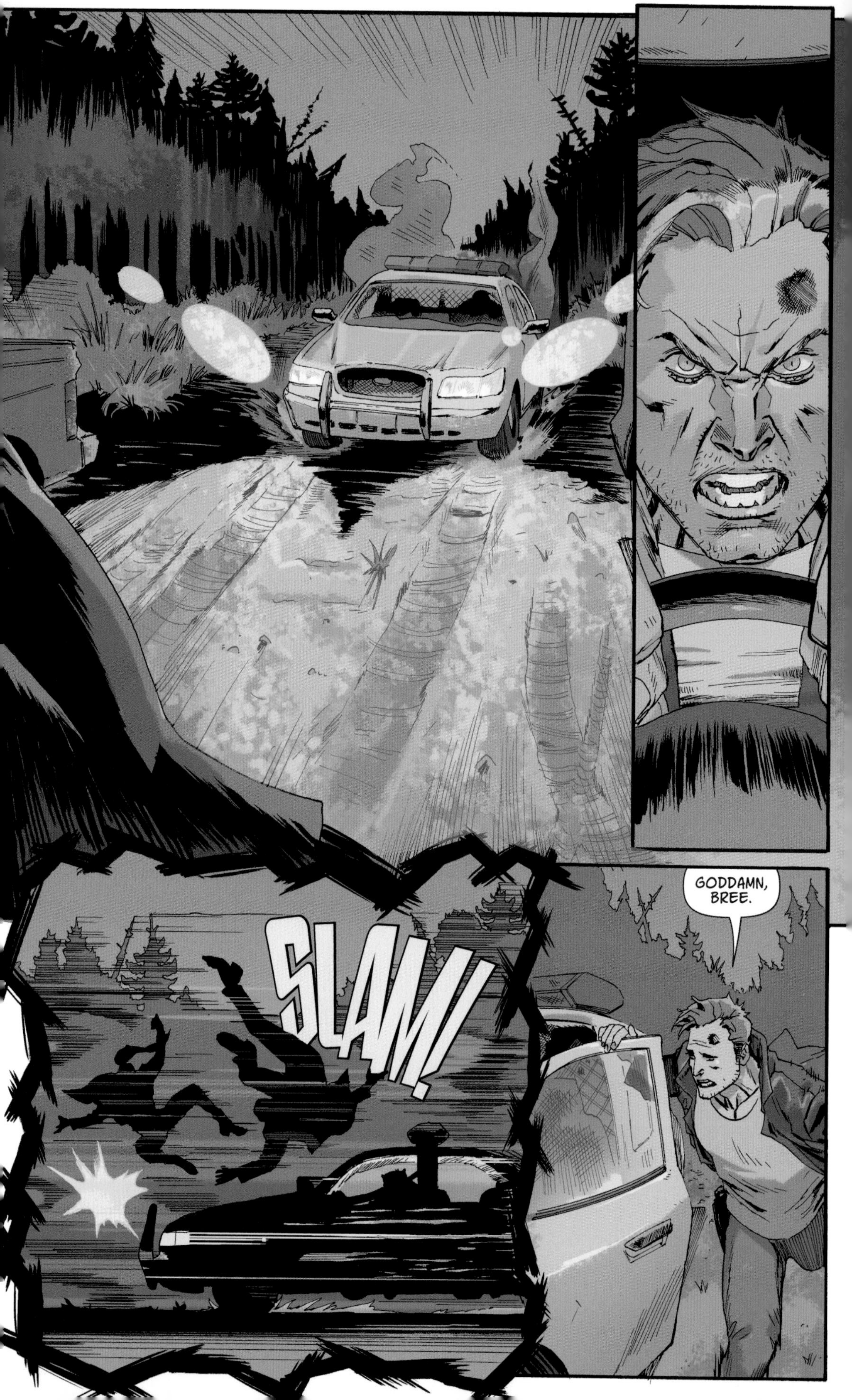
SLAM!
GODDAMN, BREE.

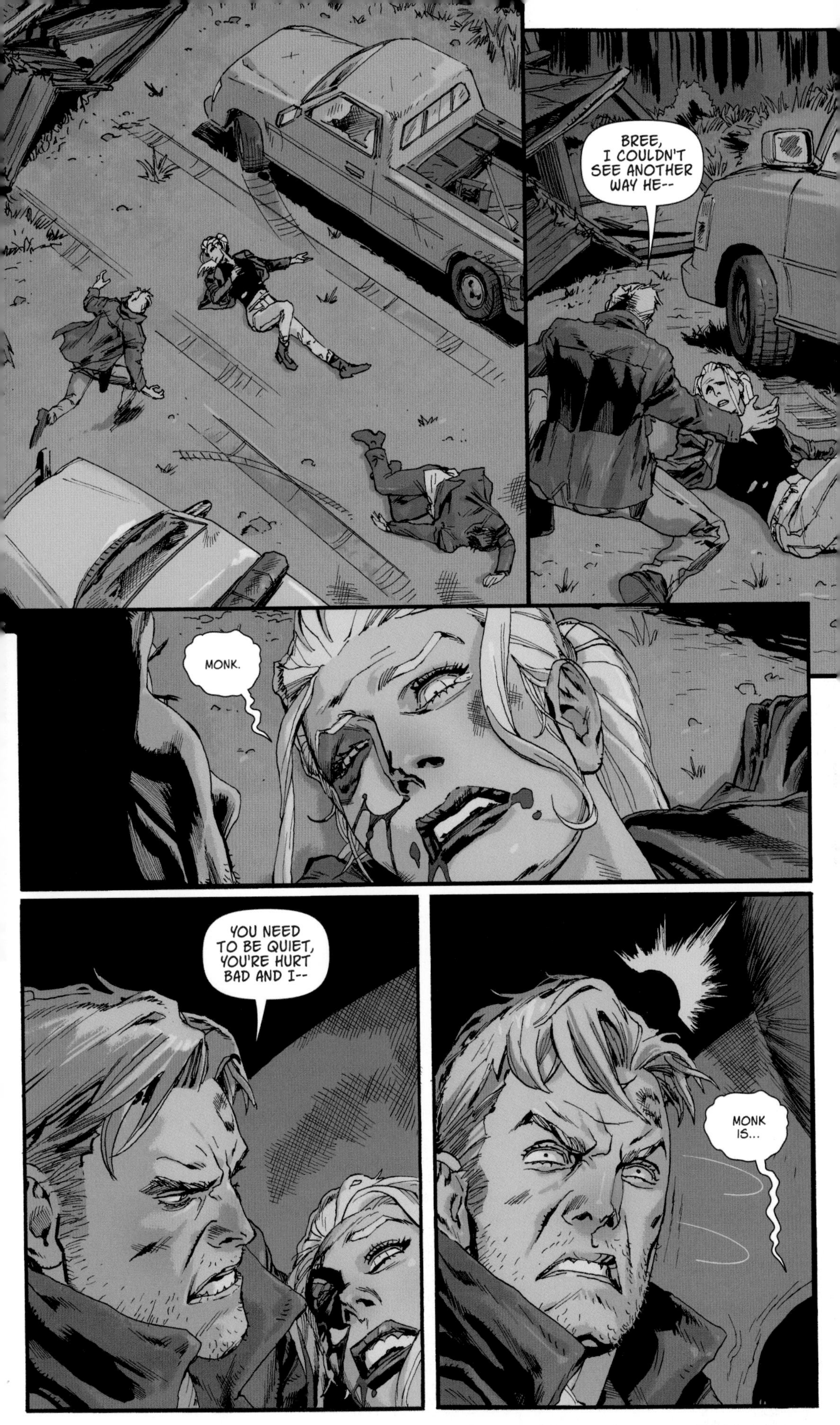
BREE, I COULDN'T SEE ANOTHER WAY HE--
MONK.
YOU NEED TO BE QUIET, YOU'RE HURT BAD AND I--
MONK IS...

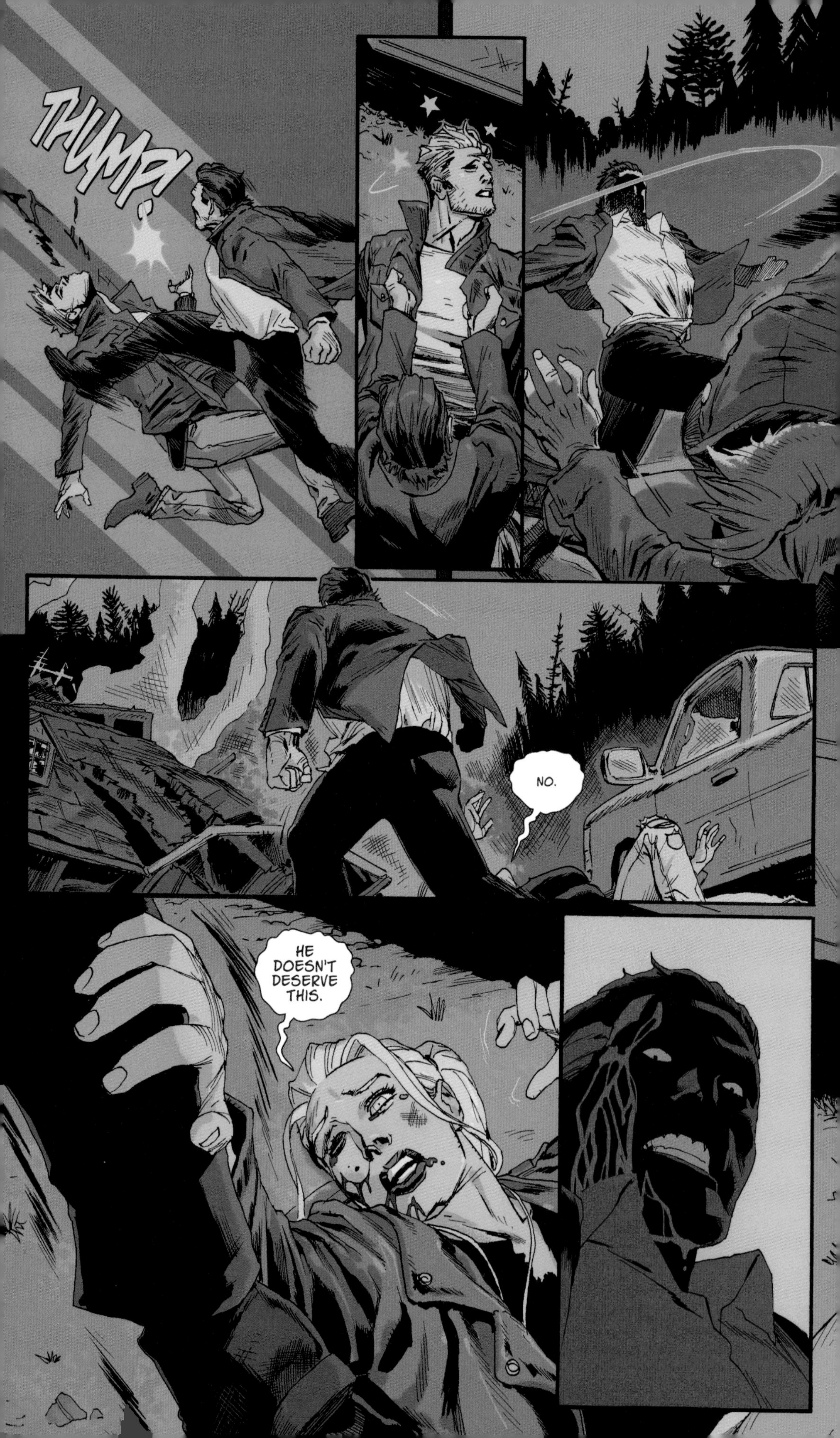
THUMP!
NO.
HE DOESN'T DESERVE THIS.

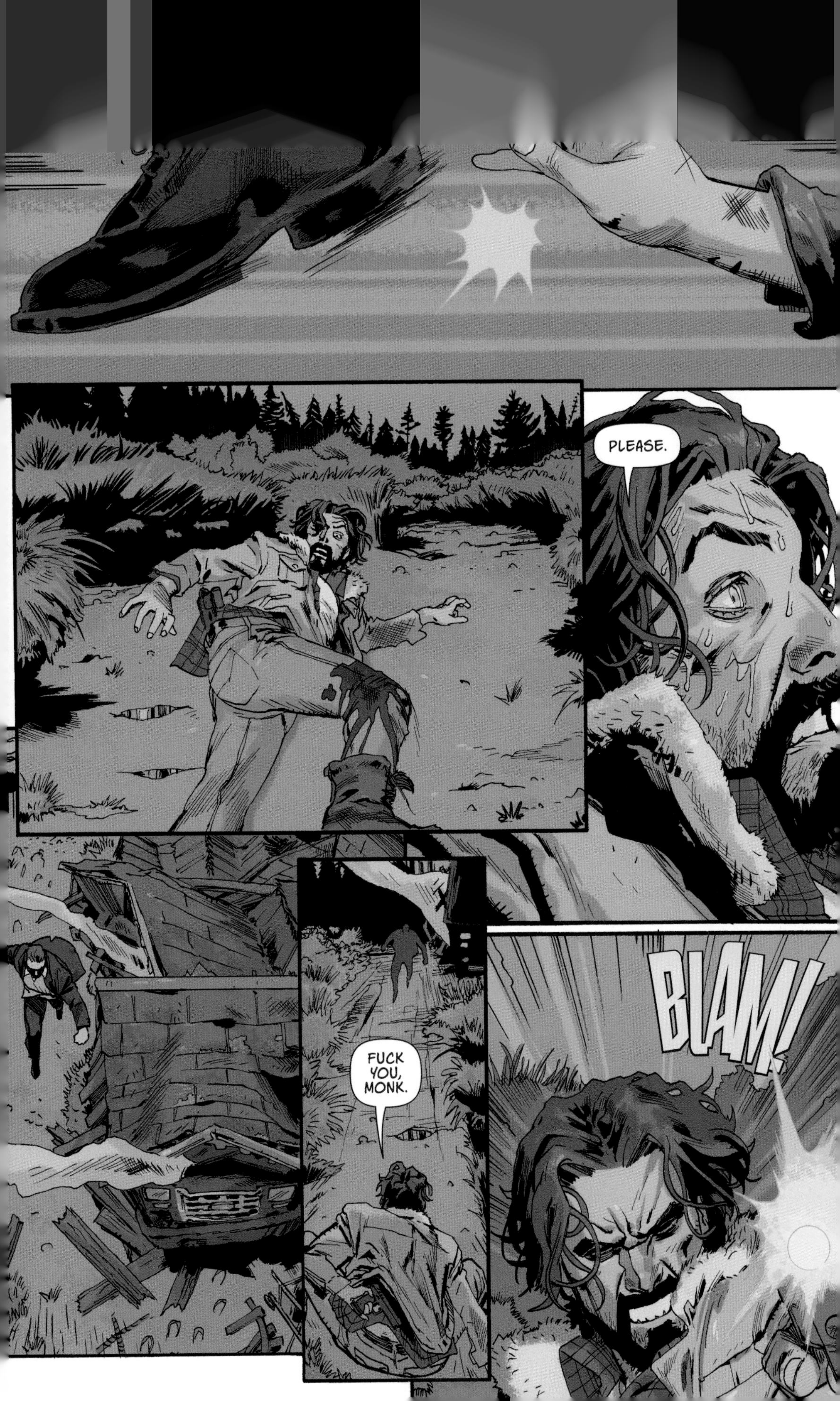
PLEASE.
FUCK YOU, MONK.
BLAM!

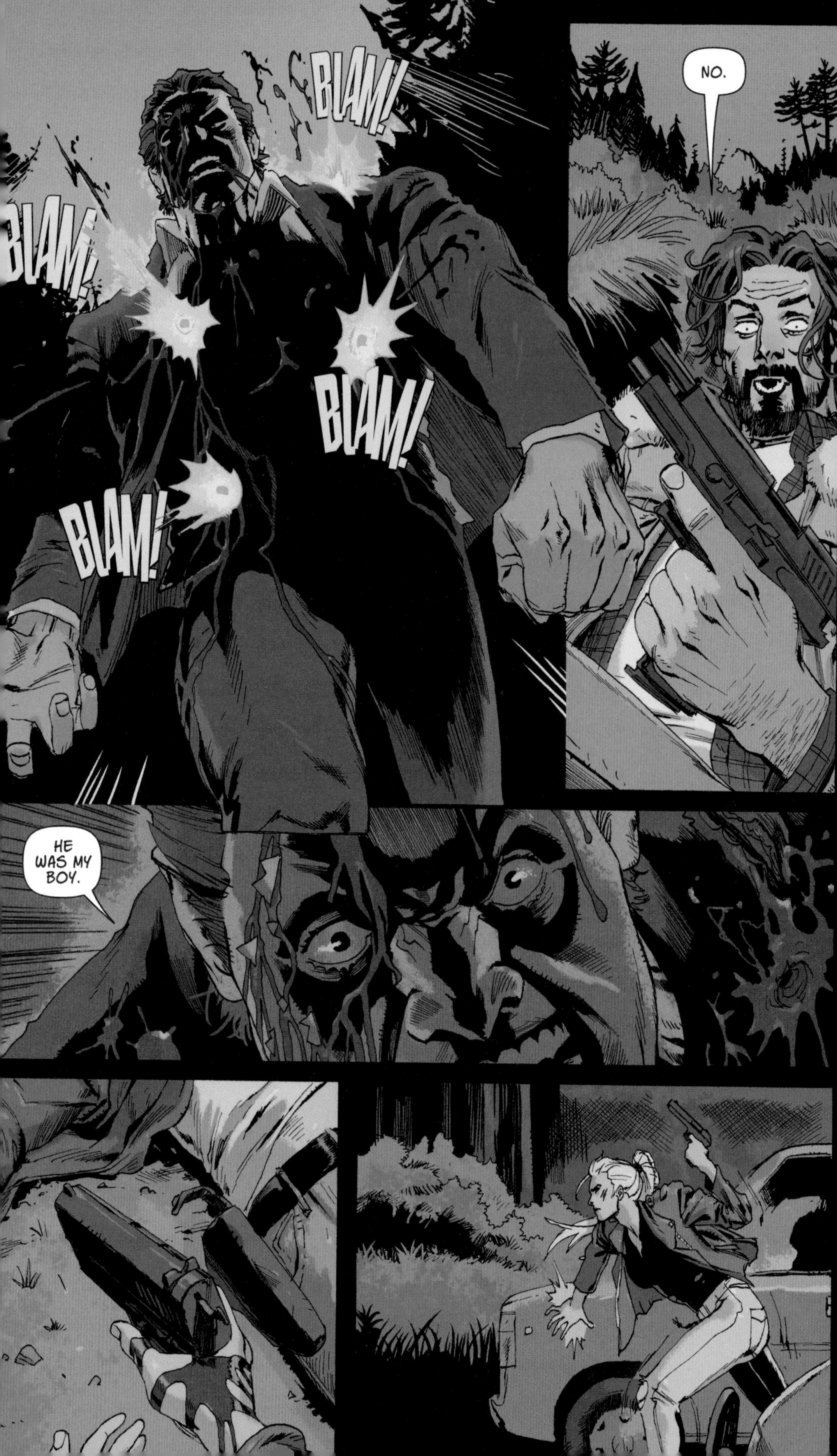
BLAM!
BLAM!
BLAM!
BLAM!
NO.
HE WAS MY BOY.

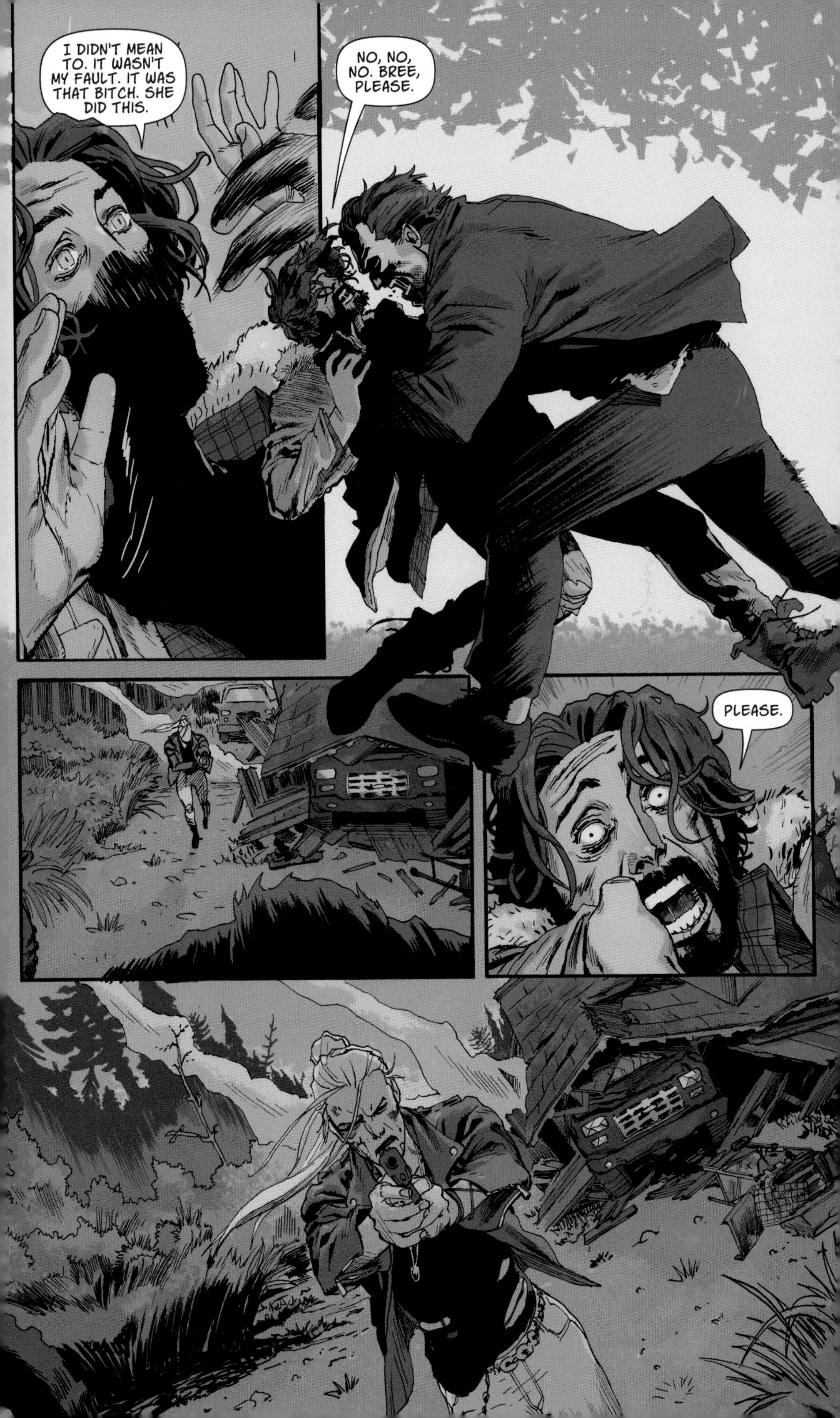
I DIDN'T MEAN TO. IT WASN'T MY FAULT. IT WAS THAT BITCH. SHE DID THIS.
NO, NO, NO. BREE, PLEASE.
PLEASE.

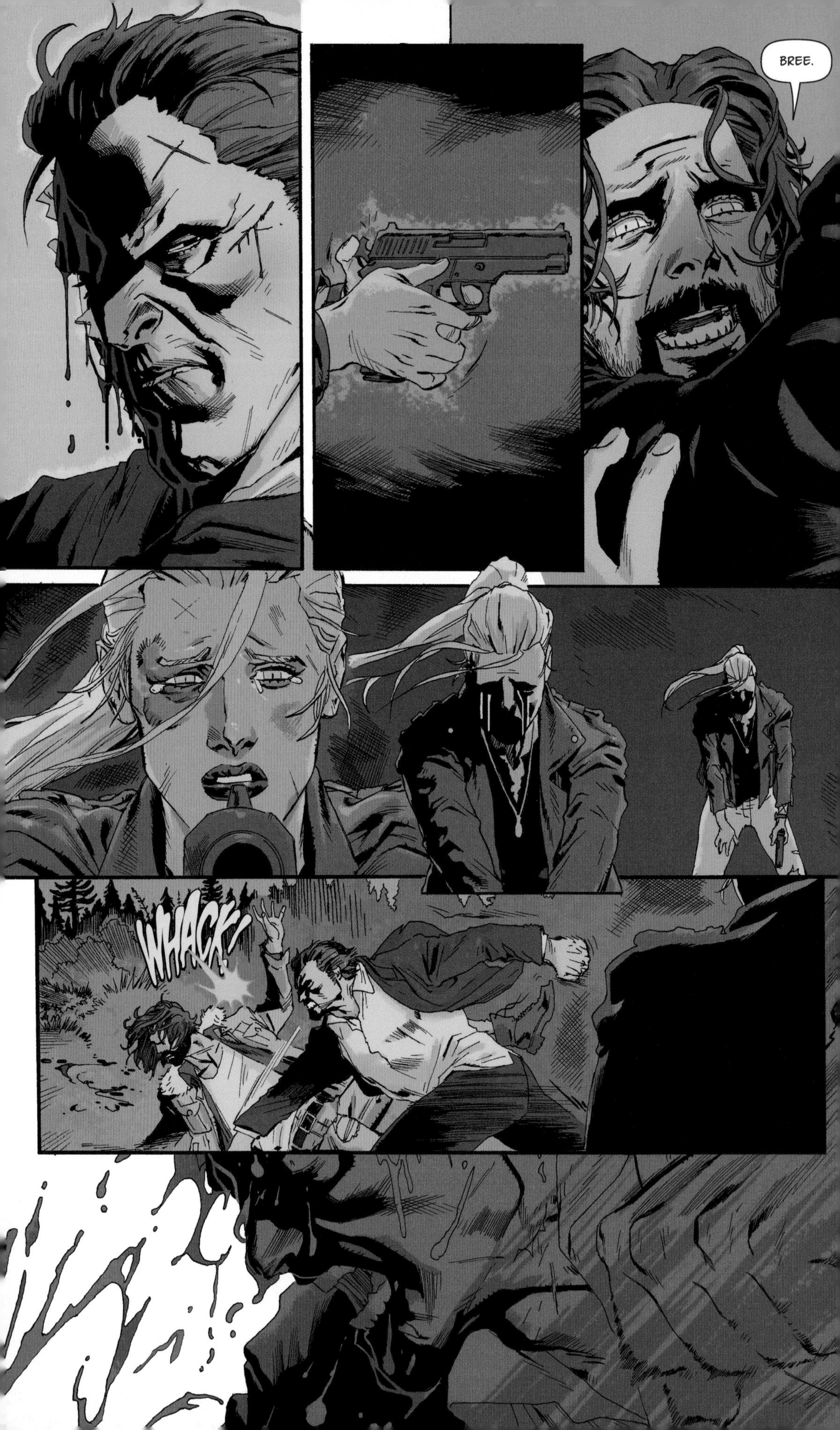
BREE.
WHACK!

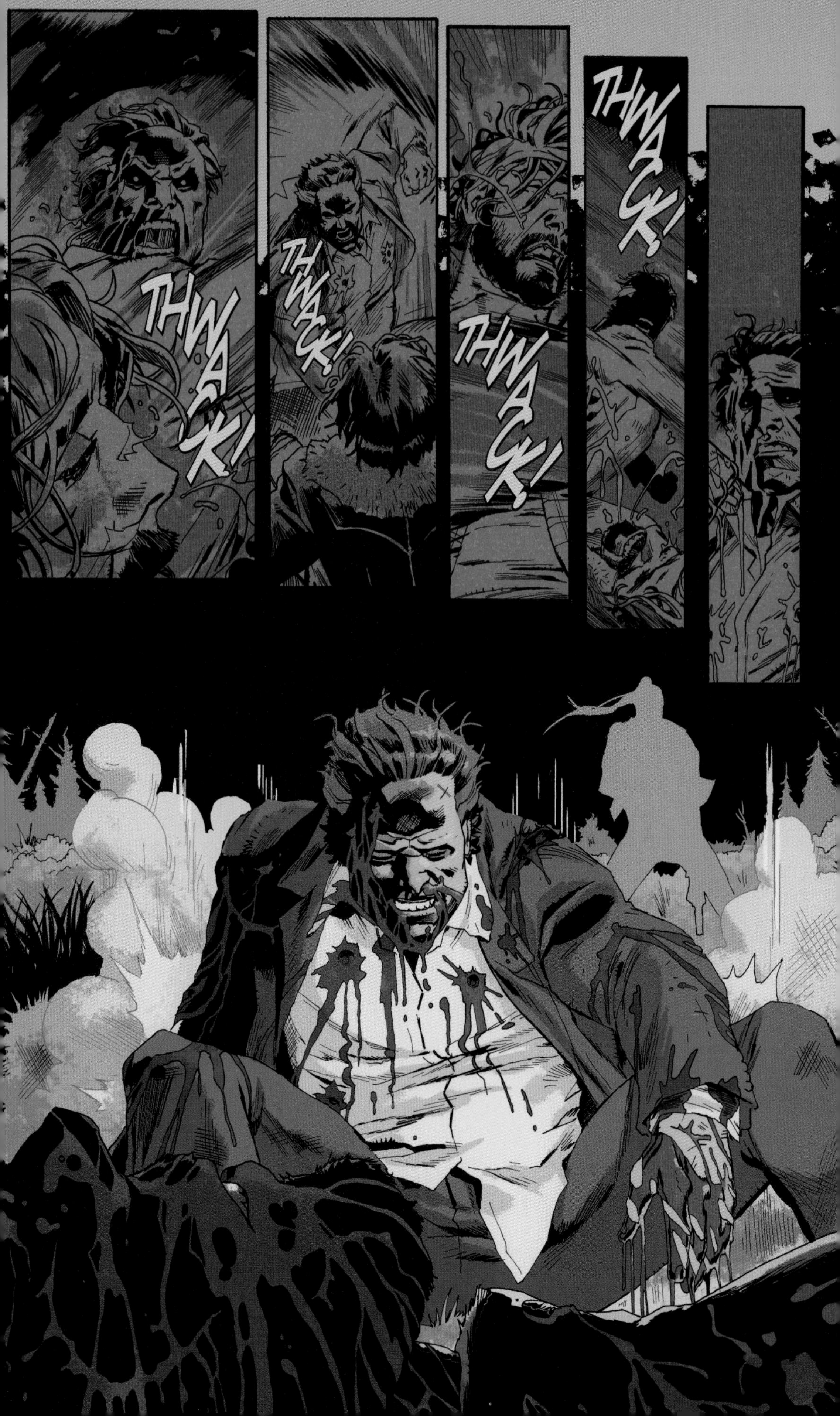
THWACK!
THWACK!
THWACK!
THWACK!

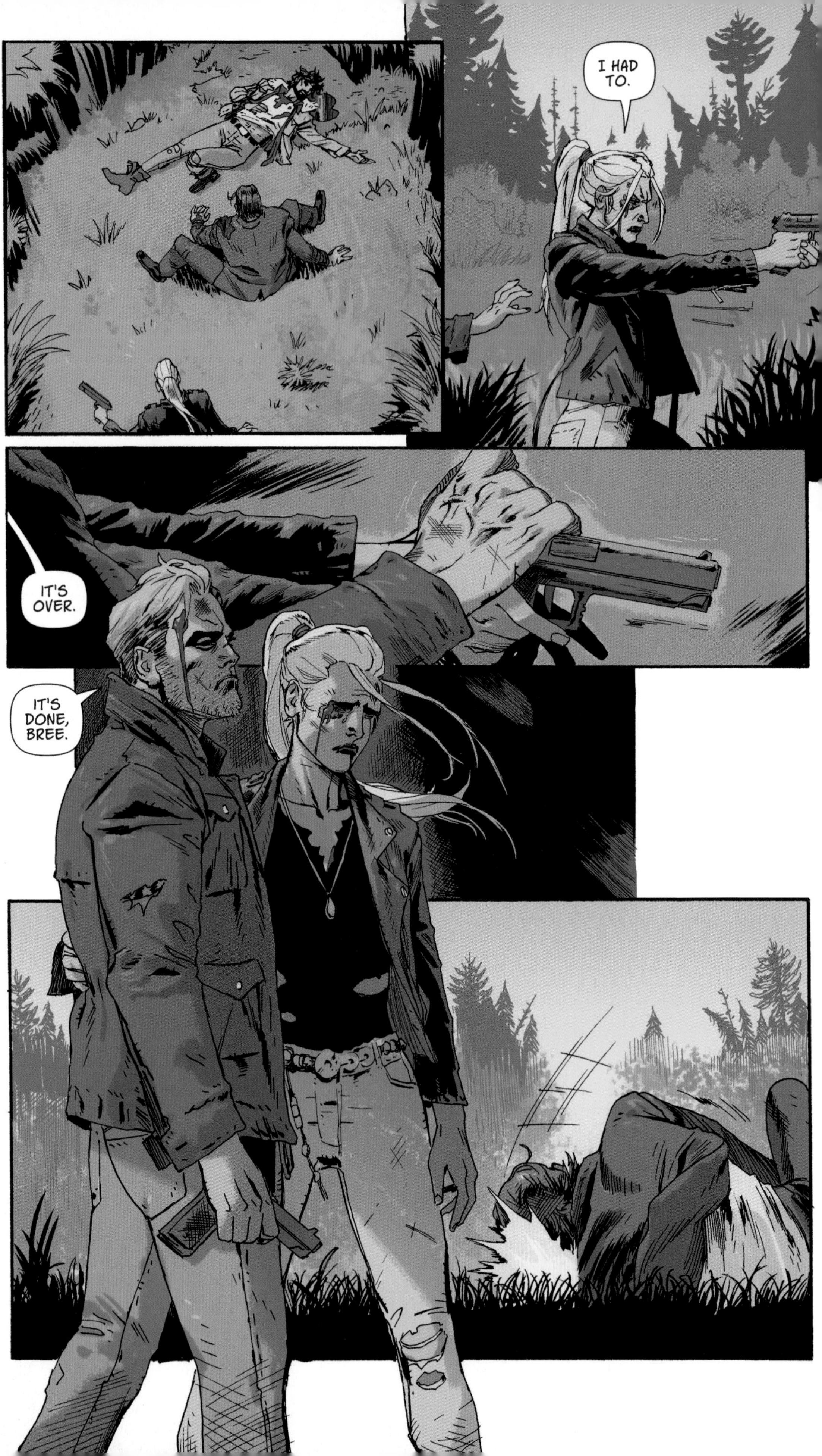
I HAD TO.
IT'S OVER.
IT'S DONE, BREE.

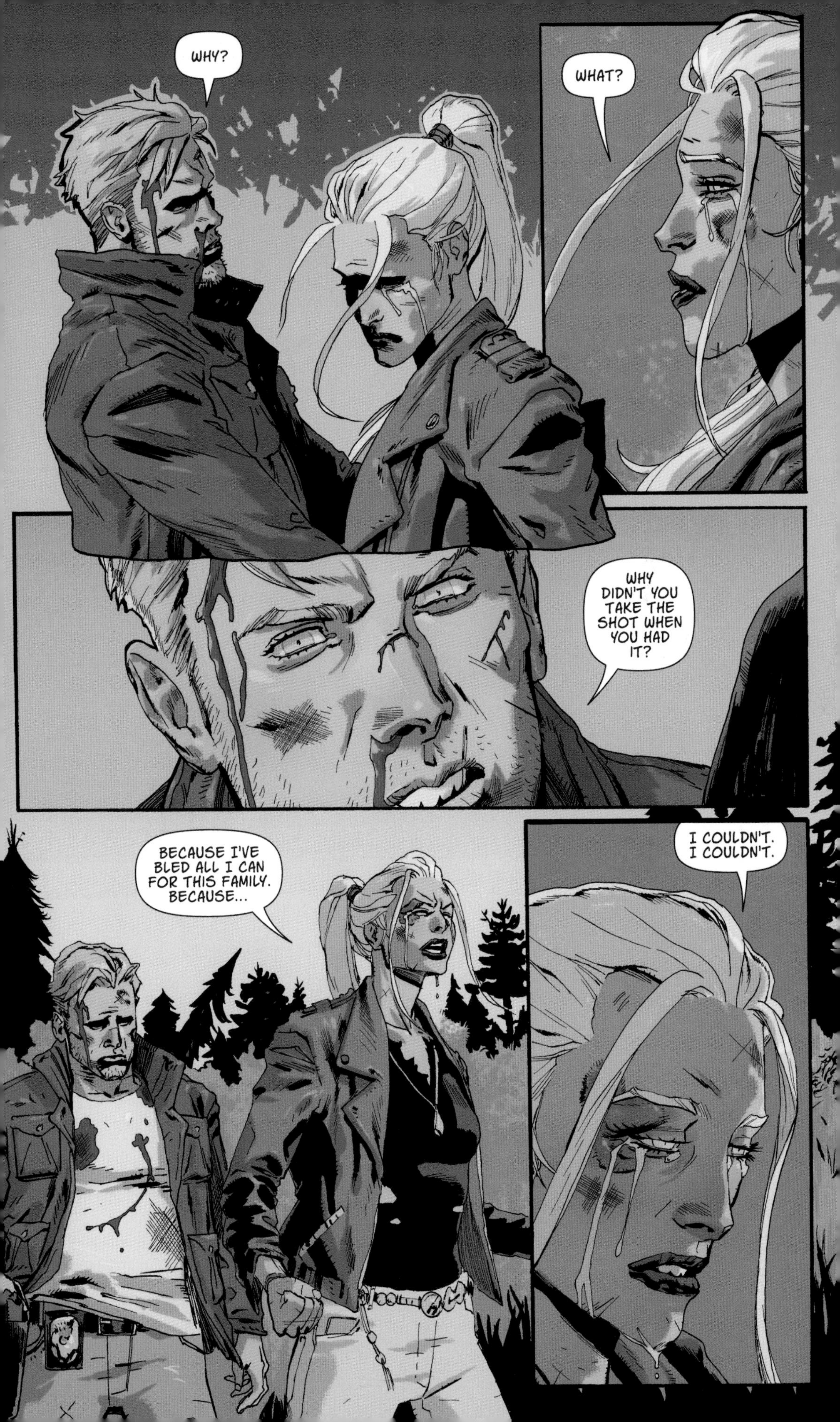
WHY?
WHAT?
WHY DIDN'T YOU TAKE THE SHOT WHEN YOU HAD IT?
BECAUSE I'VE BLED ALL I CAN FOR THIS FAMILY. BECAUSE...
I COULDN'T. I COULDN'T.

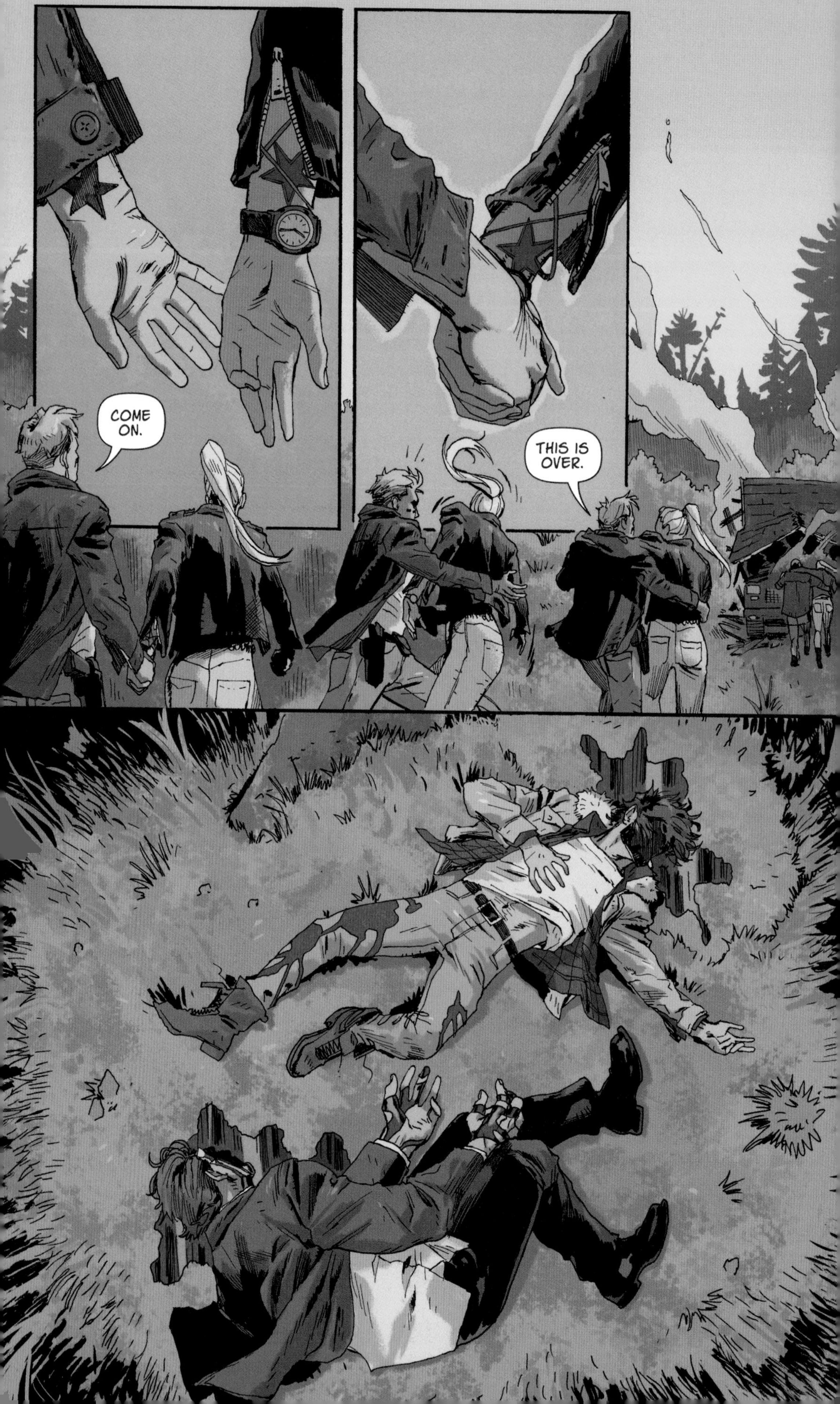
COME ON.
THIS IS OVER.

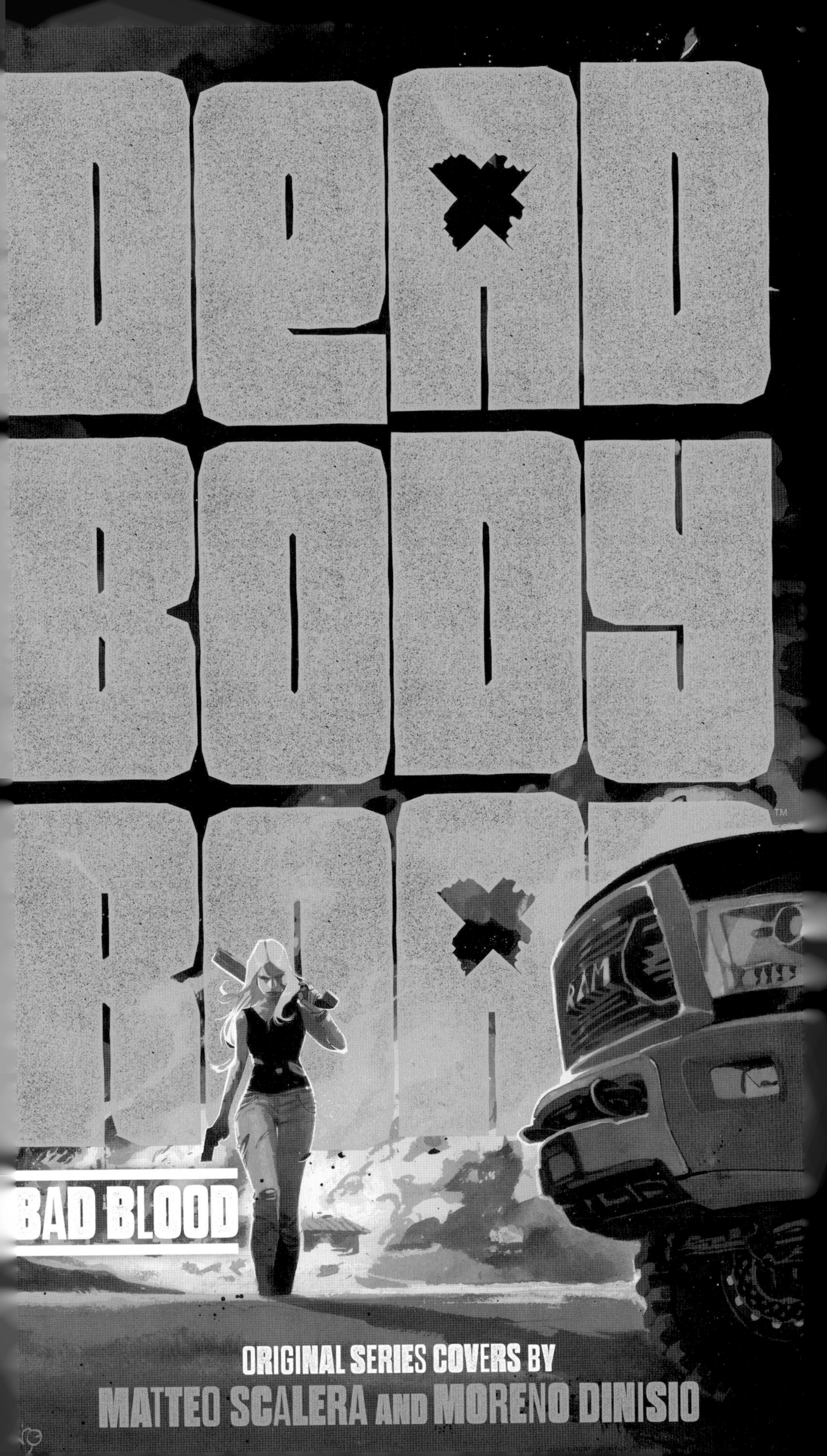
DEAD
BODY
BAD BLOOD
RAM
ORIGINAL SERIES COVERS BY
MATTEO SCALERA AND MORENO DINISIO

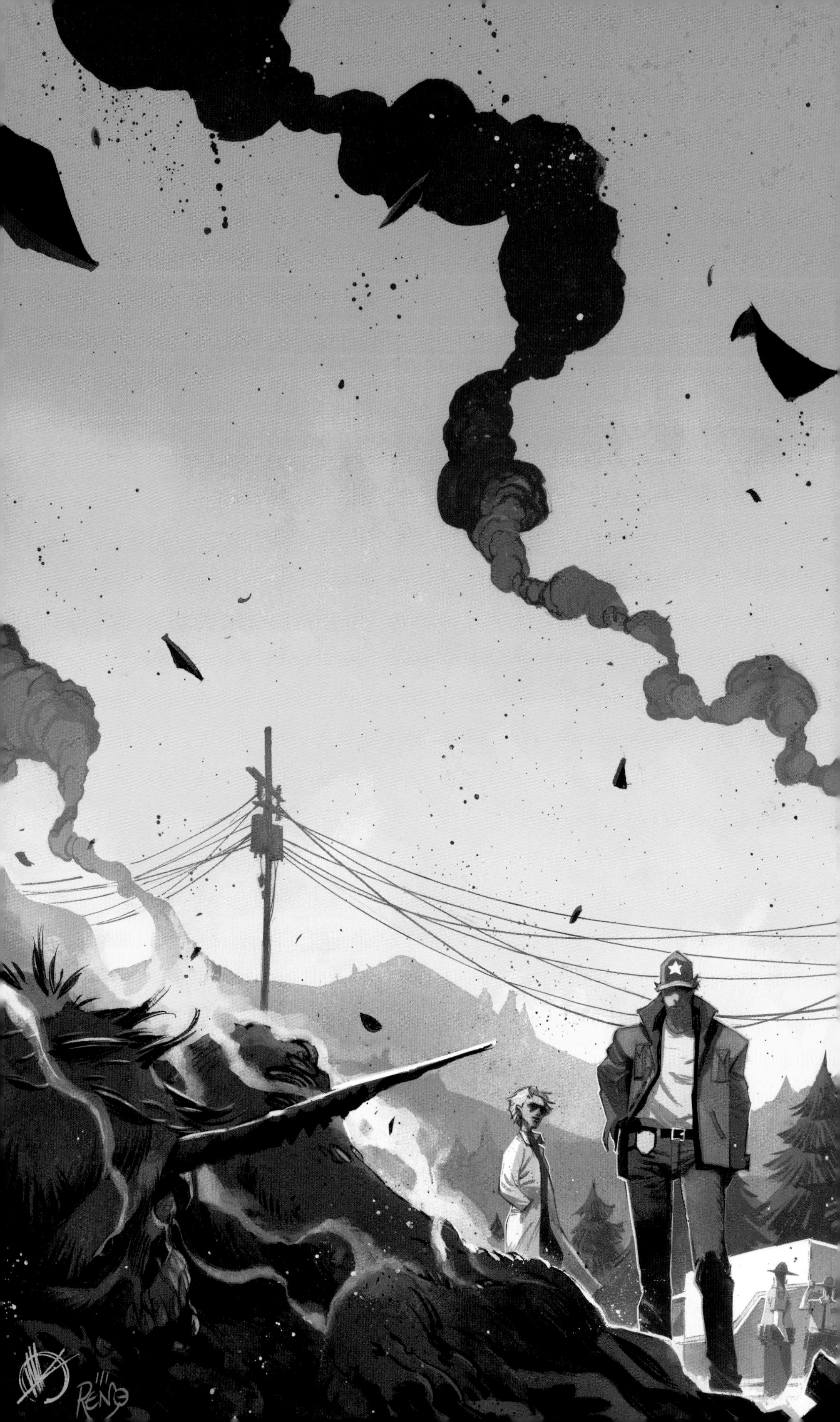

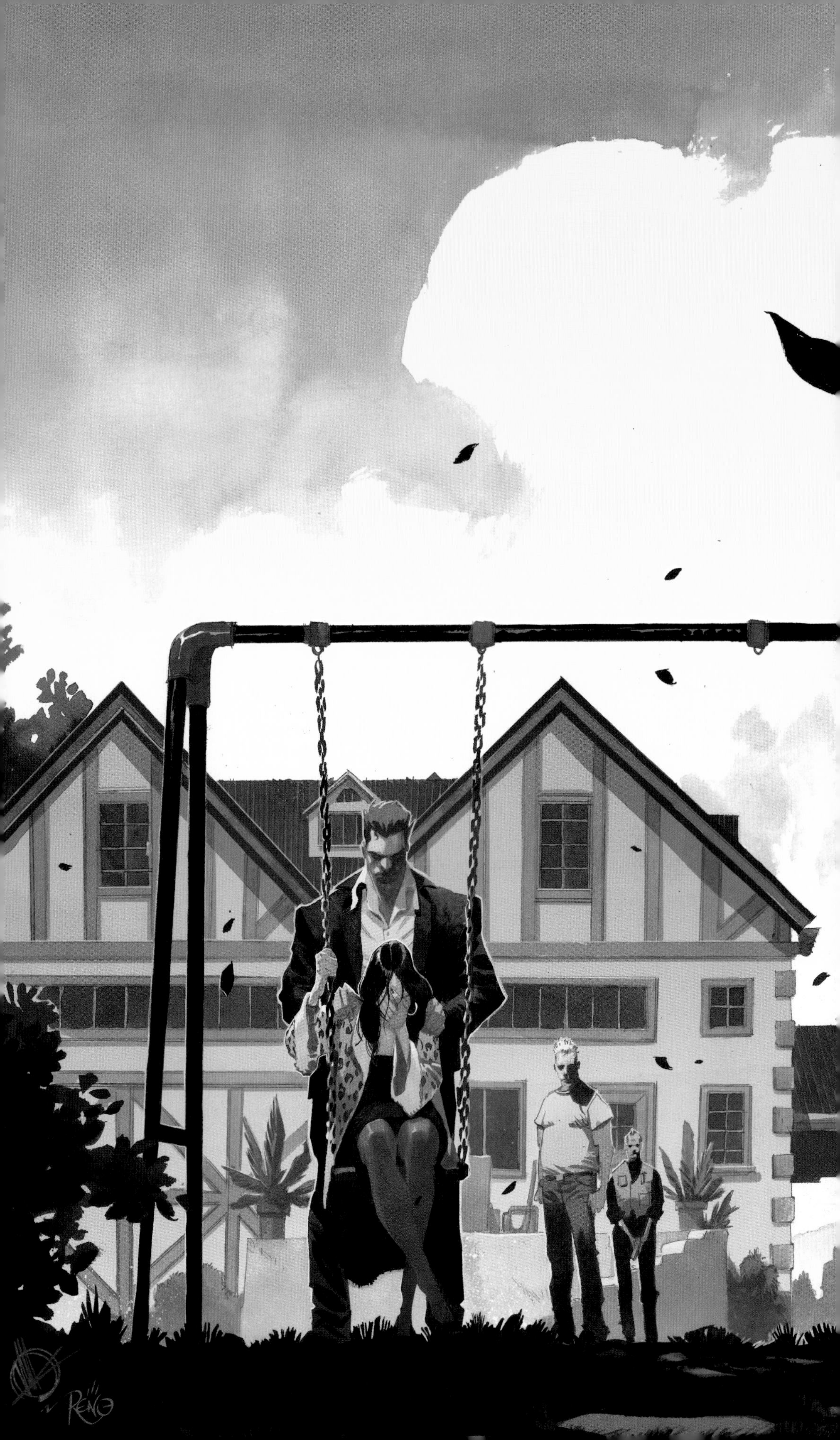

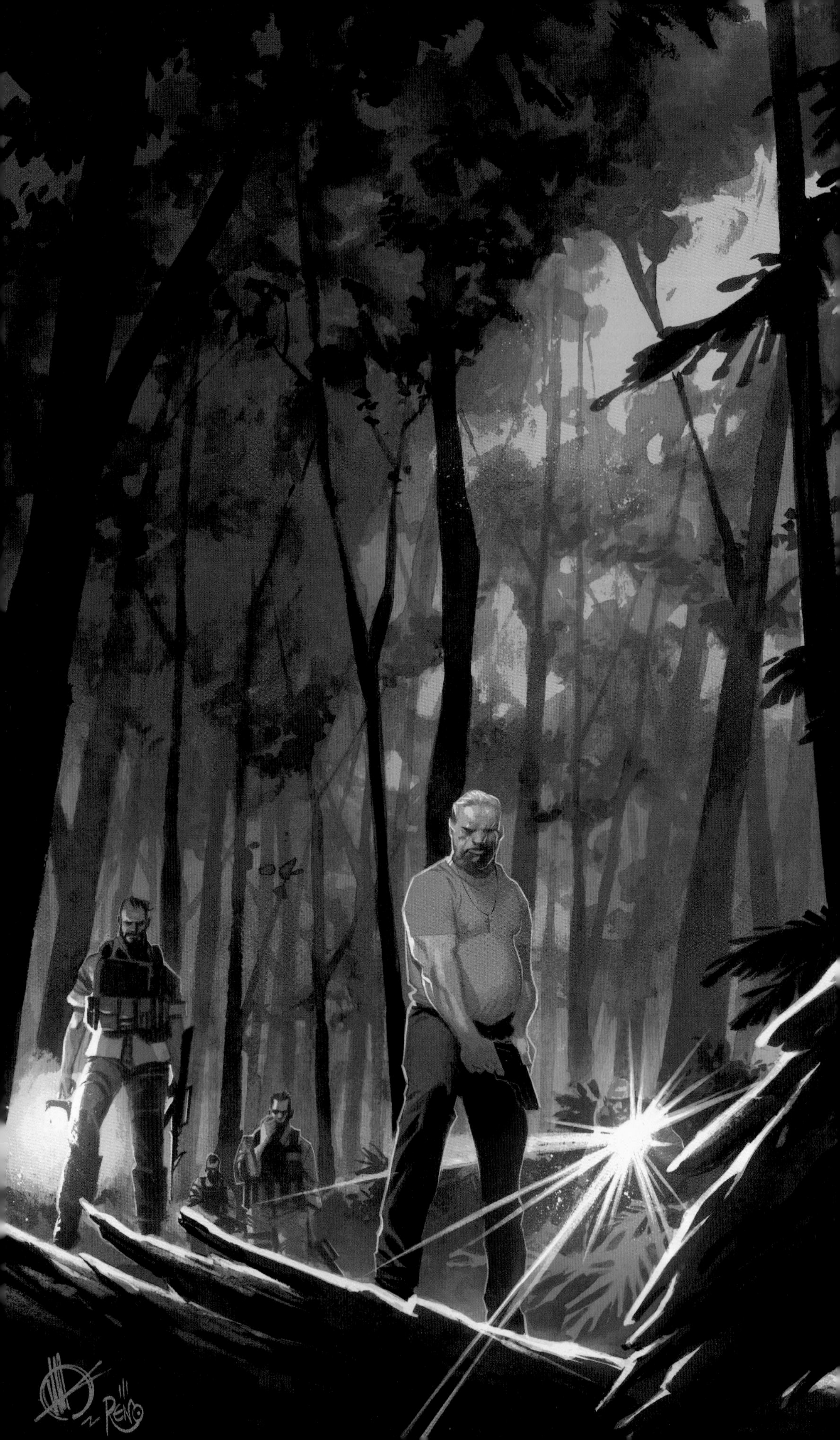

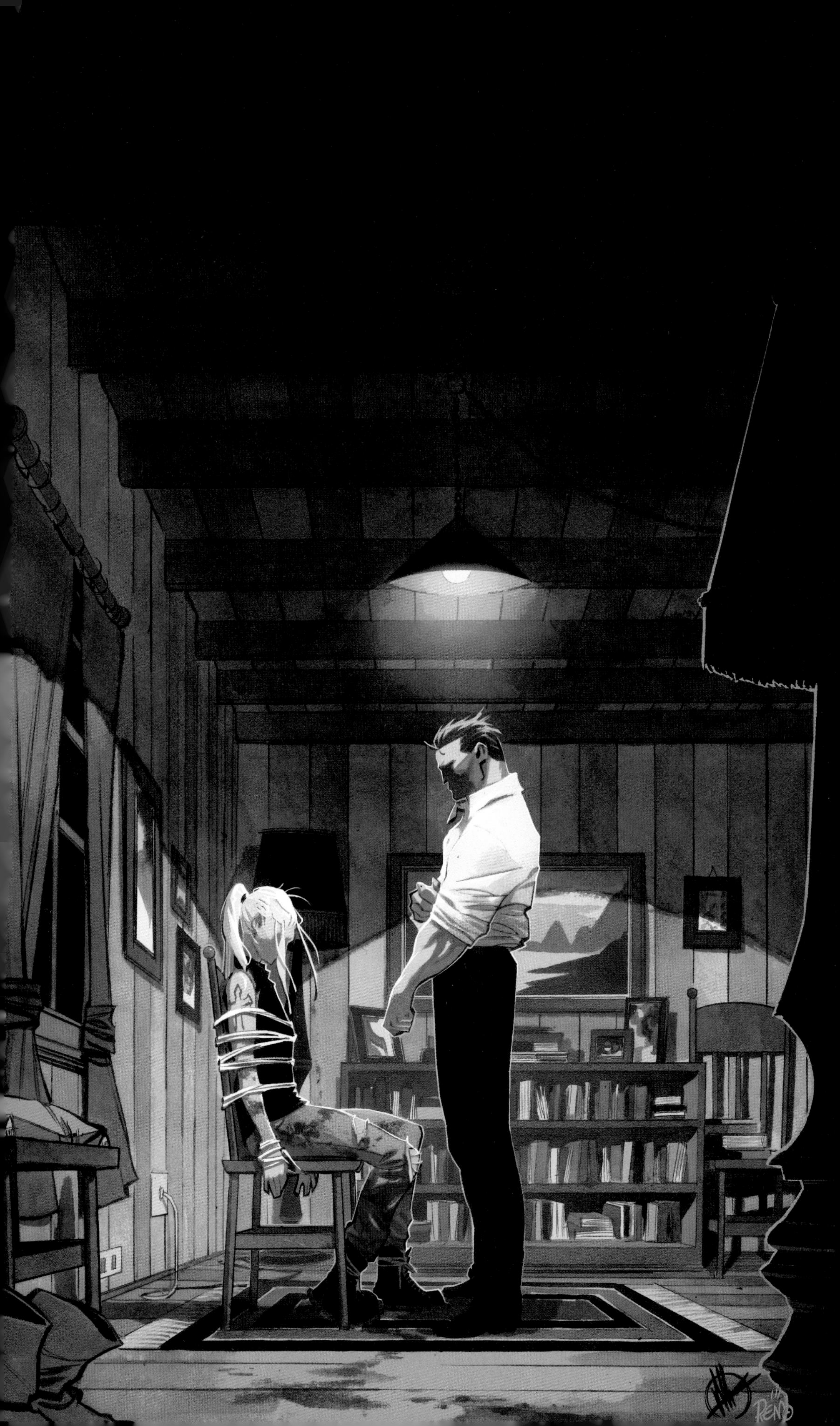

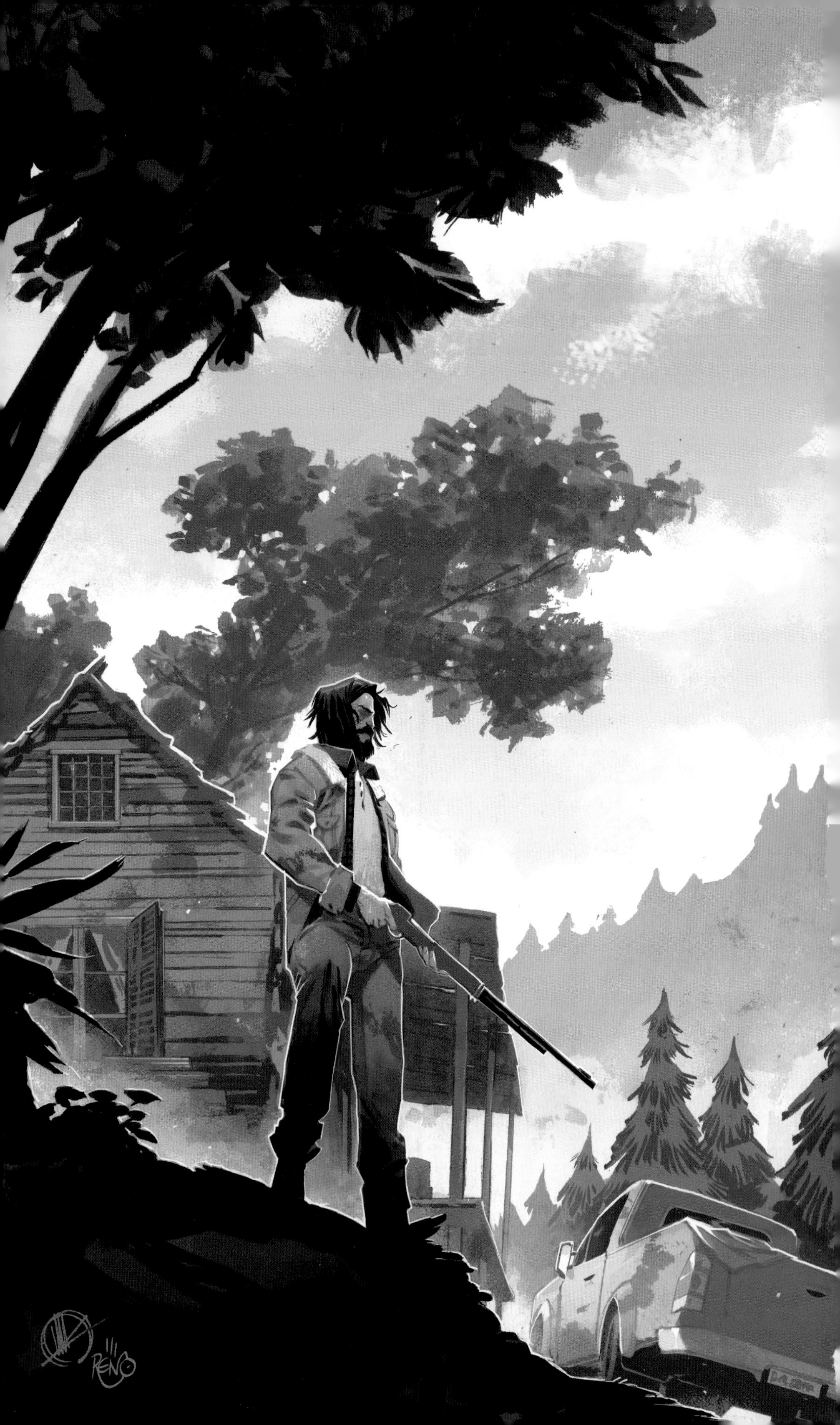